Seduced by Sabine

Seduced by Sabine

Regina Watts

PAINTED BLIND
PUBLISHING
LITERARY ALCHEMY

Seduced By Sabine: Season One of The Witch's Wicked Shorts
© 2021 Regina Watts

ISBN: 978-1-7363009-6-1

Text: Regina Watts
Book Design: M. F. Sullivan

http://www.hrhdegenetrix.com
http://www.paintedblindpublishing.com
publicity@paintedblindpublishing.com

ALMA MET THE WITCH while retrieving a lost drone for her brother, which seemed to be a modern update on the way this sort of thing happened. As it went in these stories, the neighborhood knew the woman was a witch—and as it went in these stories, Alma didn't believe a word of it.

Who'd ever heard of a real witch, anyway? This was just some cat lady. Some old woman who lived alone and probably knitted, and who did in fact answer the door wearing a black shawl of some kind, but who proved very quickly that she was not old…but that she did sort of look like a witch.

Alma's mental image of a witch, anyway. Most people probably did picture old ladies. You know: the sorts with warts on their noses and broomsticks between their legs. Alma, for whatever reason, had always pictured a goth chick somewhere between her twenties and forties. There she was, black hair piled atop of her head, a few strands flying this way and that like disarrayed raven feathers. The woman's strange acid green eyes narrowed against the sudden inundation of sunlight, struggled to adjust enough to focus on Alma, and eventually had to be shielded by her pale right hand for the first few seconds of their conversation.

"Can I help you?" Her voice was smooth as the motion of her arm, as soft as surely was the surface of her skin. Alma cleared her throat and tried to smile.

"Uh, hey! Hi! Uh—excuse me, I live down the street? My name's Alma. My brother—I'm really sorry, he just got this drone for Christmas last year, and, uh, it seems like he lost it in your back yard?"

"I shot it down," answered the woman flatly.

Alma's eyes batted. "Excuse me?"

The woman looked back into the dim halls of her renovated Victorian, lowering her arm in a jingle of metallic bracelets and glittering bangles. "Yeah. I finally decided it was time—so it's your brother who's been spying on me for months, huh?"

"What! Spying on you?"

"Oh, yeah. Doesn't anybody check what their kids—or their brothers, anyway—are doing with the nifty gadgets they get for Christmas and birthdays?"

Somebody was getting the fucking *chancla* when Alma got home! That little— "I'm so sorry—I had no idea, when, where—what—"

"You'll have to ask him that. I can only account for the times I've noticed, of course…"

"Ugh, of course. I'm so sorry, miss, uh—"

"Malbrook. Sabine Malbrook." The remote woman didn't offer her hand. She simply stepped aside, widening the berth of the door to permit Alma's entry. "Well, come on. You'd might as well pick up the pieces."

Flustered as her impromptu hostess shut the door behind her, Alma slid out of her running shoes at the door and tried—tried so hard!—not to stare at Sabine. What an appropriate name for such a bleak woman! The suitability and hefty connotations behind it lit a spark of strange fear in Alma's mind—or maybe that was the antique prosthetic hand mounted to the wall in lieu of a coat rack, some unlucky automaton's forearm waiting for a jacket or a wealthy visitor's fur.

"This is some house," said Alma with a nervous laugh, eye raking across carefully framed and dusted naturalist illustrations that lined the walls. Herbs; foxes; human jaws, bisected to permit insight onto the functions of the wagging mortal tongue. With a deep breath that she tried to make a pleasant sigh on the exhalation, Alma crossed her arms and spread her legs a bit as if she were at a softball game and waiting for something to happen. Waiting to hear the next crack of the bat before she took off running. "Somebody said you got a sweet deal on it after that dude up and left. I can't believe anybody would abandon a house like this!"

As Alma studied the high arch of the foyer ceiling, Sabine passed through the open doorway to the left of that long entry hall and led her guest into a drawing room filled with red velvet furniture. Ugh! Alma hated the feeling of velvet. How could anybody want to sit in a velvet chair?

"Most of this furniture came with the house," Sabine said. "I just gave it all some character." After glancing around quickly, Sabine plucked something unseen from an end table and slipped it somewhere upon her person. A tile or building block of some kind?

"Do you have any kids?" Alma was not the kind of woman to ask such a question, but in that moment she would have talked about theoretical physics if that was what it took to fill the air. This woman was so pensive—and the way she looked at Alma! Sabine made her so uncomfortable. It wasn't, like, a racial thing, or even a lesbian thing—because, let's face it, long hair and soft features or no, everything from Alma's posture to her style of dress screamed "I love pussy," as intended—but something else entirely. What, Alma wasn't sure. She hovered in the other doorway of the drawing room, one that led to another short hall and an outdated kitchen.

"No, I don't have any children. I don't like children. Every Halloween I turn off all my lights and eat discount candy in the dark."

This got Alma laughing, relaxing, her hands slinging into the pockets of her hoodie. "No wonder my brother thinks you're a witch!"

"Oh, well, he thinks I'm a witch because I am one."

With a suck of her tooth and a subsequent curl of her lip, Alma laughed and said, "Okay."

"You don't believe me!"

"Lady—Sabine—no offense, but I don't really, uh, go in for that shit, you know."

"What a dirty mouth you have! I'll have to wash it out with soap…or just seal it up."

Blushing, sputtering, Alma laughed after the delay of a second. Was that some kind of bondage joke? Like, ballgags? Maybe. Alma was in a casual relationship with a girl she knew from back in her roller derby days, (before the softball, after the stint in mixed martial arts), but it had been sort of fading out for awhile. Regardless, better to change the subject so as not to make Sabine uncomfortable if she'd misunderstood. "Well! Uh, so—where's that drone?"

"It's this way."

While following Sabine through that short hall and to the kitchen, Alma grew at once distracted: she walked into a rich wall of scent, chocolate and vanilla mostly, and gasped in pleasure at the aroma. "Oh, man! That smells amazing. Are you baking cookies?"

"I just happened to throw some in the oven…if you don't have anywhere to be for awhile, you can have some."

"Nah, I'm not doing anything." Reciprocate. Show interest.

Slide on in there, nice and smooth. Alma casually waved her hands, still within the pockets of her hooded sweatshirt. "Me and my girl, well—let's just say if I didn't call her tonight I don't think she'd be too worried about it."

Sabine's coy smile sent a hot little jolt through Alma's body. Oh yeah. Still got it, *chica*. "Well, then maybe you'll both be in luck. These will be just a few minutes more—why don't you wait in the drawing room? Make yourself comfortable."

Comfortable! Comfortable in a velvet chair…blech. Hands still in her pockets, Alma instead wandered past the empty fireplace and studied the ornaments atop it. A pair of cat-shaped, kitschy wine bottles being used as vases for flowers; a big ornamental clock that looked like it was bolted to the mantle; unexpectedly, some kind of floppy stuffed rabbit. Alma smiled at it, then meandered over to the bookshelf. That was how you figured a person out. She noted a lot of Roald Dahl and Shirley Jackson, then laughed to see, stacked in a little tower atop a large volume of Ionesco's plays, a collection of miniature books.

"Wow!" Unable to help herself, Alma picked up a tiny copy of *The King in Yellow*, turning it over and over in her hands with almost childish delight. The delicate volume was the size of her palm but contained every word of the original text, shrunken and even legible if she focused for a second. "This is so cool," enthused the athlete, turning to beam as her hostess emerged from the kitchen with a tea set arranged upon a polished silver tray. While Alma demonstrated the little book in her hand, Sabine's curious eyes flashed toward her, then lowered with the tray she set upon the doily-covered drawing room table. "Did you make this," Alma continued asking, oblivious to (or, at least, determined to plow through) her host's hot-and-cold demeanor.

"I did—I made each one." Sabine smoothed her shawl around her shoulders and, gliding up to Alma, produced from within the folds of her gown another tiny book, this one Bloch's *Psycho*. As she set the one third scale copy upon the tiny stack of its fellows, Sabine explained, "I used to be a bookbinder. When I took up dollmaking, the crossover was natural."

"Dollmaking! You make dolls?"

"I tried it once out of curiosity and I've never been able to stop."

"Better than smack," Alma said with a crass laugh, putting the tiny Robert William Chambers volume back into place. "Do you sell them, or what?"

"Oh, no. Sometimes I do make a doll for a friend who pays me, but mostly I keep them around for myself. I couldn't bear to let them go—I get so attached to them." With a more interested look than she had shown Alma since her arrival at the house's front door, Sabine cocked her head and asked, "Do you like dolls, Alma?"

"Well!" Laughing down at herself, at her sweatshirt and dirty jeans, Alma looked back up and admitted, "I guess it depends on the doll."

"Of course."

"Like—there's this Christmas morning picture of me. Early- to mid-nineties. For some reason they—my parents— they thought I'd like a Cabbage Patch Doll." While Sabine's pale nose wrinkled adorably, Alma waved her hand from the safety of her pocket. "Exactly. I was way more excited for the Power Rangers figures that year...it was just sad that they couldn't fit into my Batmobile!"

Yeah, yeah, still got it! Relaxing now, Sabine laughed in a free way and leaned her hip against the cherry wood of the bookshelf. "You're a tough girl, huh."

"Hah! I've never lost a fight, if that's what you're asking."

"Sounds like you're losing plenty with your girlfriend." While Alma blustered, Sabine smiled over her shoulder, off in the direction of the beeping oven timer. "One second...my atelier is across the hall, if you'd like to see my work."

Oddly enough, Alma did want to see the mysterious woman's work…and not necessarily just because she was trying to see what was under all those witchy clothes. Damn, forget the Yellow Brick Road! Wizard of Who? Get Alma any day, mamacita, she'd give you the little dog, too—etc. etc. Such were the wry thoughts of Alma away from the ticking clock and across the dim, wainscoted hall to the open room on the other side, but all those silly, flirty notions transformed to sheer astonishment the second she flipped on the light switch near the doorway.

Maybe it was the Christmas morning memory and all the Cabbage Patch associations with round, pudgy, obnoxious baby dolls. Staring, vapid eyes and creepy demeanors, ugh! Or it was a lifetime of struggle against heteronormative social standards. Dolls were considered "girlie." Ergo, in an effort to avoid being reduced to "a girl," Alma had spent most of her girlhood stringently rejecting the trappings of femininity. Girls were supposed to sit inside and be quiet and play with dolls; boys had the pleasure of running around, playing games, getting dirty. She had associated society's vision of femininity with a kind of submission that never sat right with her. By this point in her life, edging from her mid-twenties to her late twenties, Alma took her masculine aesthetic to be part of her personality. Attracted as she was to feminine women, she had come to view femininity as less the enslaving factor it once was…and sometimes she had to admit that she was a little jealous of women who could so freely prance around in sexy dresses, curling their hair, drawing all eyes. You know…dolling themselves up.

So, divorced as she was from the possible aesthetic pleasures of femininity, Alma had not been expecting to appreciate the aesthetic pleasures of Sabine's dolls. And divorced as she was from the aesthetic pleasures of dolls, she had never realized how beautiful a doll could be. In fact, the few finished one third scale simulacra lining shelves and standing on their own and trying out half-made beds and chairs were almost unearthly in their beauty. They were perhaps sixty to seventy inches high and strangely jointed, their faces realistic…yet somehow not. What a wishy-washy thing to say, but it was true! They were the faces of people from dreams—familiar faces, real faces once glimpsed in the crowd at a concert or a county fair. Faces perfected through the lens of the creative faculty, smoothed and elegant.

And the bodies! One body, headless and naked, was stretched upon a parchment paper-lined desk that was, like the paper shroud itself, covered in colorful chalk pastel dust. Alma felt as if she had come upon the site of some mummification ceremony, the preparation and embalming of a perfect resin corpse.

Emphasis perfect. To look at it closely felt an act of impropriety, as if Alma gazed on a gorgeous woman without her consent. The long figure and its perfect proportions bore absurdly sized pert breasts tipped with carefully painted pale nipples and even lightly dappled beneath, where they were darkly blushed as a real woman's bosom. And veins! By God, blue veins! A realistic network of them, painted as though gleaming through palely translucent skin.

There was no end to the detail. Little moles dotted its ribs and thighs, and Alma was, on close inspection, embarrassed to find the doll was anatomically correct in both its sculpture and its painting. And that wasn't all. Its queerly jointed knees, its similarly strange wrists and ankles, they were all fastidiously blushed and attended to with detailed blue veins as those trailing over the breasts.

What an eerie effect was had on Alma by the sight of this headless manikin! Just as she was gasping to see the tiny doll had even been given a matching French manicure and pedicure—that even the immobile knuckles of its delicate fingers had been illustrated by the careful application of some chalk pastel and perhaps a tiny pencil—Alma jolted to realize Sabine had materialized in the open doorway.

"Do you like me?"

Taken aback, then laughing at the question, Alma said, "Uh! Well, you seem—you know, pretty cool, actually—"

Though her red lips expanded in a smile, there was a slyness to it that implied so much. So much! Alma discreetly braced her hand against the edge of the workbench while her hostess swept to her side in a somber patchouli cloud. "No," said Sabine. "I mean, my self-portrait."

"Oh! Oh!" That vowel sound was all Alma could produce while looking in renewed shock upon the exquisite doll. "Oh," she repeated a third time, snapping herself out of her stupor with an incredulous laugh. "Is this you? Really? Get out of town."

"Uh-huh." Her eye gliding from Alma's face down to the doll's replica body, the witch—ugh, no, Sabine—smiled fondly. Alma caught herself holding her breath to watch a slender fingertip (manicure identical to that of the doll, Alma realized right then) glide over the doll's taut stomach and up over its breasts. As the strange woman shivered, she told her guest, "I like to play with all my dollies, you see—dress them up and give them lots of fun attention, instead of just letting them sit on a shelf all the time. But that means that after awhile you have to re-paint them…these joints, the color wears out."

"I see. What are they made of?"

"Resin," answered Sabine, "and, inside, elastic. Go on—touch it."

For some reason, this was perhaps the most scandalous invitation anyone had ever extended to Alma. Blushing, stuttering, she looked toward the doorway and said, "Well! I don't want to mess up your beautiful paint job."

"You think my body's beautiful? Thank you…I'm sure yours is, too, under all those shapeless clothes."

Alma was so busy scoffing that she wasn't expecting the woman to catch her hand and draw it to the cool surface of the doll's body. While she gasped to have her fingers drawn over the frigid, headless torso—textured in the manner of an eggshell but smoother to an almost unearthly extent—Sabine stared into her eyes, their faces at most a few inches apart.

"Don't worry," said Sabine. "The colors have been sealed… you can't smudge it without some pressure. Your hands are so much softer than I expected, Alma…you're awfully good at touching a woman's body, aren't you?"

Swallowing tensely amid the weird (somehow disturbing) flirting of this strange neighborhood reject, Alma cleared her throat, laughed a little, and gave up entirely when Sabine's head swooped upon hers for a long, audacious kiss. With a moan of surprise, Alma yielded in the instant, the silk-soft lips of this strange Malbrook woman almost as exciting as the flow of her bold tongue into Alma's mouth. As Sabine pushed Alma back against the workbench, the athletic young woman turned away her face to emit an appreciative moan.

"You think you like the way I touch *this* body! Wait until I touch your real one."

"That is my real one," whispered Sabine, exhaling as she guided Alma's fingers between the idol's cool resin thighs. "As real as this one…oh, Alma." While the doll-maker moaned to swoon against her visitor, Alma watched in bafflement and wondered about all the jokes she'd ever heard men make in front of her.

See, when you're a lesbian—especially the sort sometimes referred to as a "butch"—heterosexual men who are cool about it have a way of treating you like one of their own. As a result, you're exposed to a lot of male jokes. For instance, the tongue-in-cheek notion that the hotter a woman is, the crazier she is.

This was upheld by some men as a real rule and women were generally offended by it. Alma had, for her own part, actually sort of gotten it before—her (apparently, now ex-)girlfriend was pretty hot and also the type to, say, set your clothes on fire in the front yard—yet it had seemed a comedy cliché. Certainly not a real rule.

But damn. As fine as Sabine was, she was clearly just as much off her rocker. The tight body that pressed to Alma's through the fragrant layers of flowing fabric and her own hooded sweatshirt certainly felt as pert as that of the doll, and while Alma ran her fingers back and forth over the simulacrum's fastidiously-sculpted labia, that flesh-based body in Alma's other arm writhed as if truly stimulated. It was all undeniably bizarre, but there was something to be said about a chick so liberated she could, on the first fuck, introduce somebody to… uh…whatever this was. Yikes! Alma wasn't really sure what was going on but to be honest Sabine was so hot that she could have told Alma to do backflips through a flaming hoop and the athlete would have tried if it meant she had a chance.

Especially once the knitted shawl fell to the floor and Alma got to stare down into the black fabric of that swaying dress. The gown's overflowing bust, decorated with black and silver jewels, allowed a hint of bright pink nipple when the generous fabric fluttered away on a thin strap's sag. Alma pushed this strap away, bending to kiss the pale woman's fragrant neck. "I have to make sure you got all the details right."

"Go ahead," said Sabine, gasping as Alma's kisses descended to that hard pink nipple by following a highway of turquoise veins along the way. "Yes, yes, oh, make sure I haven't forgotten anything…just don't stop petting my pussy, Alma, go on, God! Oh, you're getting me so wet—"

Hey, babe, whatever it took. Safe, sane, and consensual, that was Alma's motto. As long as those three factors were met, hell! If Sabine's doll body was half as consenting as the human body she bared to Alma's greedy eyes, she supposed this was technically her first threesome. Two-and-a-halfsome, maybe.

Whatever it was, it was about to get her laid. Alma straightened up to admire the body Sabine revealed by pushing down the straps of her dress and shedding the fabric upon the floor. No underwear…no hair, either. Truly as creamy pale and exquisitely built as the doll. Alma moaned and lifted her right hand to touch the woman. That hand was stayed, led gently back to the doll. "Keep going," moaned Sabine, "don't stop, don't stop, fuck—oh, touch me faster, fuck, fuck, I love the way you touch me, Alma—"

Taking Alma's free left hand, Sabine guided this non-dominant one instead to the bare lips between her thighs. Alma groaned low on the contact. Dripping with desire and swollen with anticipation, Sabine's pussy was every bit as responsive and hot as the doll's was immobile and cool. Yet seeing this act unfold apparently had a significant effect on Sabine, because she was so slick that Alma felt her own wetness grow irresistibly. "You like that, don't you," she decided to say, gratified by the gasp this produced from Sabine's pouting mouth. "Yeah, you do, you dirty girl…you like it when I play with your little doll-pussy, don't you?"

"Oh! Ah, oh, Alma…" While the naked woman moaned, Alma eased a pair of fingers into Sabine's tight, yearning cunt. She moaned a little herself, fingering both bodies in time, the living one enthusing while touching its own breasts, "Oh, Alma, Alma, I wish you knew how good it feels to be touched in two bodies at once…mm—help me get your jeans off, Alma, here, let me—"

The dollmaker's dexterous hands made fast work of Alma's pants. Once she had stepped out of them, Sabine swiftly rearranged her doll body to permit its long legs to hang, thighs splayed, over the edge of the table. "Eat my pussy, Alma," said Sabine, laying on her back and sliding her head between

Alma's own spread legs. "Lick me all up while I get a nice taste of yours."

Damn! Crazy and hot, for sure. While Alma knelt, then lowered her drenched pussy over the strange woman's mouth to groan at the instant, fast-flickering contact of her wet tongue, she leaned forward and only briefly asked herself what she was doing. Was she really about to eat out a doll? Ugh. Apparently. It was pretty ridiculous, but the ridiculousness of it, the sheer perversity of it—the vague, unseemly coating of depravity with which the scenario was somehow glossed even though this was a simple figurine of resin and elastic— somehow inspired a new arousal of its own. Erotic humiliation had never really been Alma's thing, she thought, but, well… there was something to be said for how wet she became when she pondered the ridiculous nature of performing cunnilingus on a doll while that doll's maker and model returned the favor.

And, once gain…it was definitely worth it. Sabine's tongue and soft, sumptuous lips inspired moans and gasps that could only be rivaled by Sabine herself, who spread her legs, arched her hips and grew ever-more invigorated as if it was truly she who was the recipient of Alma's affections. While Sabine's tongue probed rapidly in and out of Alma's cunt, her face nuzzled up and left the athlete absolutely breathless. The alleged witch withdrew her tongue only to gasp against Alma's pussy, "Don't stop, oh Alma, oh Alma, Hail Satan, Hail Satan—"

Haha! Ah, goth chicks sure are crazy. Yeah, maybe it wasn't a hot chick thing at all. Maybe it was a goth chick thing. Or maybe it was just Sabine, who was so sensitive and so imaginative that she could get off just knowing Alma was licking a doll based on her. It was really something to be admired, in a way. No manual stimulation required. And either Sabine was very good at faking orgasms in a theatrical way, or the bucks and quivers of her legs were inspired with hardly any direct contact at all…but Alma didn't feel any reason to doubt the authenticity of this climax. As Sabine gripped her thighs and trembled beneath her, Alma paused her work to grin down.

"That feels good, doesn't it? Oh, mami, you're hot as fuck—doll body, human body, I love to look at you. Ah!" The strange woman's tongue had gone back to work and Alma moaned, grinding down against her lips and enthusing, "Yeah, yeah, keep going, don't stop, fuck, you're fucking crazy…I want to fuck you sometime, Sabine, I bet you like it rough."

"Mm…I bet you do, too."

"Oh, yeah, yeah I do." Lifting her hips at the patting indication of her hostess to let her upright, Alma tilted her head back and opened her mouth for Sabine's soaking kiss. Her lips were still wet with Alma's arousal and she moaned low to taste herself on the witch's supple lips, then more sharply as those manicured hands trailed up over her breasts. "I like a girl who can fuck me nice and hard," said Alma, turning back to run a fingertip over the miniscule valley between the doll's open legs. While Sabine shuddered, Alma focused on running her fingertip back and forth over about where the clit would be, then groaned as the dollmaker's hands located her nipples beneath her sports bra. Gently rolling them through her fingers, Sabine nuzzled Alma's ear.

"Oh, I'll be sure to fuck you nice and hard soon, Alma…but you have to be a very good girl for me if I'm going to do that. Yes…you have to do what I say." While Sabine's fingers slid into Alma's wet cunt, Alma moaned, leaned her head against the workbench, and looked up to focus on her effort between the doll's legs. "I'll make you a doll…and if I make you a doll, you'd better be good."

A doll, from an artist! Now that would be a cool gift. If nothing else, a cool conversation piece. Flattered, moaning as she approached a high peak of pleasure, Alma accepted a few more sharply stabbed kisses before leaning away to focus on kissing between the doll's legs. Sabine moaned sharply and continued, "Oh, what a good girl you are, yes, oh…will you still get so wet for me, so nice and dripping wet, when I've made you a dolly, Alma?"

While the crazy girl slid her fingers out of Alma's pussy to spank it a few sharp times, Alma moaned and looked down to watch her hand. "Oh, fuck, if you did something so nice for me, I'd let you do whatever you wanted."

"Yes you will," whispered Sabine, her fingers rapidly tickling Alma's achingly sensitive clit. While her guest dripped against the touch, Sabine continued, "Yes, you'll let me do whatever I want, because you're such a good girl, Alma…yes, oh, I'll teach you how to be good. Show you all the things I want from you. Then, when you're ready to be mine, I'll be very nice to you right back, and play with you whenever you need it. Oh, Alma! And you do need it, don't you."

"Fuck! Fuck, yeah, oh, Sabine, hurry, hurry, don't stop—"

"That's right, oh, that's right, get it all out of your system, pretty thing, go on—you'll have to be very quiet soon, so it's okay for you to be loud right now, just this time."

Okay, sister, whatever you said. Head swimming, Alma could no more formulate a response than she could remember her own name. There was only the urgent impulse to increase her pleasure—the desire to gather tension until that tension had no choice but to snap and leave her awash with the endorphins of their communion.

That was how it felt, this odd closeness that perhaps arose from her because of the intimate sharing of this strange affinity—whatever the reason, Alma gasped through the crashing sea of her orgasm and found herself gazing into the intense eyes of her occult neighbor.

Sabine's fingers slowed to ease Alma through her climax and by the time it had finished she had stopped the massage all together, reducing to a slow, sensual petting that was a pleasure all its own. As Alma moaned softly, Sabine smiled.

"That's right…good girl."

"Sorry my brother's been spying on you," groaned Alma with a weak smile of her own. "But to be honest, I almost get why he would."

"You should come back in a few days," Sabine told her in response, leaning in to kiss the corner of her mouth. "I meant what I said. Come back in three days, on Saturday night, and I'll make you a doll."

"You don't have to do that."

"But I want to."

Well—the offer *was* very flattering. Alma hadn't really known that many artists in her life, let alone somebody who created three-dimensional art of such detail and scale. "All right," said Alma while Sabine's smile widened. The so-called witch's eyes crinkled and she gazed once more down at Alma's mouth. After another, longer kiss, the athletic woman sighed and said with a soft laugh, "Your tea's probably cold by now."

"No, just perfect…will you stay and have some with me?"

"Ah, I don't know if I should." Coming back to her senses, Alma looked around, laughed, then reclaimed her jeans and panties. "I'd love to hang out longer, but my brother's probably wondering where I am by now."

"I understand…I don't know if that drone of his is functional anymore, but you'd might as well take it with you. And make him delete the footage in front of you."

"I swear, I will. What a twerp! Sorry again…but, uh, thanks." Grinning bashfully down at herself, Alma buttoned her jeans and said, "I've never done anything like that before."

"You could do so much more, if you wanted. My coven is coming over in a few days. You should watch us."

"Ah…I don't know, I don't really go in much for…uh, religious stuff."

"Witchcraft isn't religious in the way you mean it, but I understand if you're afraid. After all. There are dollies, and there are doll-makers. Not everybody's equipped to be the latter."

Weird metaphor! Weird lady. Hot as could be, though. And a good baker! Between the witchy aesthetic and the big old house, Sabine would make a first-rate abuelita someday. She sent Alma home with a package of chocolate chip cookies, a broken drone and a fuzzy feeling. That very night the athlete called up her girlfriend and said, "It's not working."

No point in stringing the poor girl along. Alma wasn't exactly expecting this…uh, whatever this was…with Sabine to be a long-term thing, but however it was going to end, it wasn't fair to her monogamous girlfriend for Alma to fool around with even the hottest hot side piece. This had been a long time coming and, to her credit, said girlfriend took it better than expected—but then again, what was she going to do about it?

After, alone in the dark of her room, Alma investigated the remains of the crashed drone. What a shot! This doll-maker was a scary lady. Didn't want to piss her off, for sure. Finding the internal hard drive undamaged, Alma removed this small hard drive from the ruins of the machine and hooked it up to her computer.

And she intended to delete the contents of the footage. Really! But, uh…she just wanted to check to see if the footage was even worth deleting in the first place. Like, what if Sabine was wrong about Alma's brother spying on her? Then Alma would just be deleting perfectly innocuous nature footage, sight unseen! It might even have been something her brother was proud of.

Better check it then—just to be absolutely sure there was something inappropriate to delete. Hm, hm…nature footage, park trees, yikes, cutting it kind of close to that branch…uh-oh, the neighborhood, yes, well, that was sketchy…

Ugh. Okay, now they were in Sabine's back yard. Alma recognized the house with a cringe. Yes, a cringe. Even as she failed to look away while the drone footage swooped in to hover before one of the upstairs windows, Alma cringed at her brother's behavior.

Of course, Alma was just looking at something that was already there. Just doing her sisterly duty! Protecting him from his own bad decisions…like the decision to surreptitiously film Sabine rising from her bath tub and wrapping her shapely lily body in a soft towel. Or, in another clip, zooming in on her ass from a distance as she bent over the flowers in the garden.

Or, worst of all, recording Sabine alone with some other woman.

Alma really, really wanted to close that clip, and she almost did. But—there was something so strange about it. She wasn't sure what it was at first, but soon she realized it must have been the room they were in. Yes, contrary to the stern décor of the rest of the gloomy old house, this bedroom was a cheerful pink, and either its windows were curtained with lace, or its bed was.

Hard to tell on the monitor, and hard to tell when she couldn't take her eyes from the sight of Sabine helping the naked blonde woman into a satin slip. Her hands glided up a splendid tan waist and over perfect breasts while the fair woman moaned, then leaned back in Sabine's embrace. Sabine caressed her in the guise of sliding the straps of the slip up her golden shoulders and Alma shuddered, goosebumps rising along her arms as though it were she who had been touched at that very second. Like a voodoo doll in video form.

When they were in place, the witch planted a few sensual

kisses along the ridge of the blonde woman's ear, then disappeared for a few seconds. When she returned it was with more strange, frilly undergarments, and Alma tried to understand what she was seeing. Most lovers undressed each other, after all, but here was Sabine, piece by piece assisting this gorgeous blonde into fluffy knickers and sheer stockings she carefully drew up one perfect leg, then the next. A wide, lacy petticoat soon obscured the stockings' termination. Once she had buttoned this, Sabine stepped back to admire her work, then again left the frame.

When she returned it was with such a mass of pink silk and white chiffon that, in another context, Alma might have struggled to recognize the object as a dress. Sabine's mouth moved and the obedient blonde lifted her arms above her head, smiling pleasantly as her hostess fit these long limbs into the fabric and maneuvered them through to the arm holes. It was an old-fashioned dress, Alma soon realized, like something from the cover of her auntie's cheap regency romance novels: the lace around the edges of the sleeves hung from the elbows in great fans, and a ruffle at the bosom was subsequently fluffed. Improved by Sabine's discerning fingertips.

The doll-maker smiled with pleasure when her work was finished and bent to kiss the blonde, who tilted her head back in flush-faced reception.

How long ago was this? Alma checked the data on the strange recording: two weeks ago. Very strange. Sabine hadn't seemed like someone coming out of a relationship. Maybe this was some casual thing…but that didn't seem right, either.

It was hard to tell what happened next because the women left the room, and that was about the peak weirdness of the recordings. You know, other than the existence of the recordings in the first place. What a lame person her brother was! Alma was going to give him a piece of her mind once she finished copying these videos to a DVD.

What? Don't judge her until you've seen Sabine in-person, man. That was all Alma would say. And be careful—judge too hard, and you might very well meet Sabine in person. Alma would never be really sure how powerful the woman's strange woman's magic was, which was saying something, considering the crass athlete's fate.

However, even then, Alma had to admit it. She hated to admit it, but she had to. There was kind of a magic to Sabine—a feeling that was hard to explain. On a cultural level, realistic American before she was a Latin American, Alma was aware of the notion of brujas though her family consisted of a bunch of down-to-earth, hard-working businesspeople. Her mother and father were both extremely level-headed and sensible, Midwest suburbia-influenced immigrants, and therefore secretly superstitious in some very intense ways. Paranormal events were not even to be spoken of in the house lest discussion somehow magnetize the atmosphere and draw bizarre entities to the family. So although Alma, a generation removed from even that level of belief, had never had any particular sense of the divine or of magic, she couldn't help but wonder after meeting Sabine if there wasn't something to her parents' concerns. There had been an atmosphere to that house, and while it may have been the strange old building itself, Alma had the feeling that the atmosphere was more related to the woman who lived there.

Did Sabine live alone, though? The question occurred to Alma only later the next day when she asked herself why she was still thinking about her spontaneous rendezvous with the strange neighborhood recluse. She wasn't really going to go back there, was she? Like, damn. The lady's work was cool and all, but what a nut. Making Alma eat out a doll! Acting like she could feel it…it sure was a convincing demonstration of pleasure, though.

Ugh. Weird thoughts to have. Weird thoughts inspired by a

weird woman. Alma kept thinking about that clip and trying to suss it out: she watched two nights in a row, pondering over it as if obsessive study might bring on new evidence. Instead it only indicated to her the sordid details—the intensity of pleasure portrayed in the blonde's dreamy eyes and the desirous droop of her lips. She was beautiful, sure, but more beautiful than that was Sabine, whose hands ran with such sensual appreciation over every inch of this blonde stranger's body. Contemplating the scene too long made Alma hot with a desire of her own—a desire to be touched like that. To be admired in the way Sabine admired this girl.

What a stupid dress, though! How weird to want to be admired in anything so cumbersome when it was so much easier to throw everything off and make love with wild abandon. Yeah, it was all weird…but…

But Alma still kept thinking about Sabine. Kept thinking about Sabine's offer, specifically. *I'll make you a doll.*

English! It was so ambiguous. Was that sentence an offer? Now, in retrospect, it was such a loaded sentiment. Maybe not an offer so much as a warning—a declaration of intent. Shuddering, Alma turned over in the bed of the childhood home to which she'd retreated a few years before on what was supposed to be a temporary basis. It must have been some kind of bruja thing, some witch thing that only made sense in her magical head…like, she wanted to put part of Alma's essence in a doll, or something. Who knew? It took a certain kind of mind to guess such things, and Alma was even more realistic than her parents.

So she liked to tell herself, anyway. Because the truth was that, by the end of the second day, Alma was fidgeting: but by the morning of day three, she was downright nervous. It was a Saturday and people wanted her to come and hang out. For whatever reason, she turned them all down. It wasn't like going out with her other friends would keep her from seeing

Sabine, but Alma just couldn't focus. She spent all day asking herself if she was really going to go over there to see what that strange woman in that strange house had to offer her. What she had really meant with her abstractly worded statement.

Deep down inside, of course, Alma knew—she knew, and she burned with such fierce curiosity that she simply couldn't resist. She couldn't help but to leave her house in the twilight hours of that evening and slip quietly down the street, shivering within the over-sized fabric of her sweatshirt against the evening chill.

Sabine answered the door so soon that Alma was sure the witch had been waiting for her. "I'm so happy you made it," said Sabine, her expression and manner all infinitely warmer than they had been last time—her somehow spindly little hand, as it extended to squeeze Alma's, just as cold. Just as soft.

"Come in! I've been thinking about you non-stop since you came over the other day."

"Me, too." While Sabine shut the door, Alma noted the workroom's door was closed. She could not explain the unnerving effect it had on her consciousness. "I took my brother's footage off of his drone."

"Did you watch it?"

After a rapid blink or two, Alma decided it was better to tell the truth.

She confessed, "Yeah, I did."

Sabine's eyes twinkled in the low light of the foyer, a crooked grin expanding over her rosy lips. "Did you like it?"

"I'm not even sure what I saw, to be honest."

"You should always be honest…take your hands out of your pockets, you naughty girl"—she landed a brisk swat on Alma's ass and the athletic woman leapt in surprise—"you won't get anywhere in life slouching around like that."

"Has that been my problem all this time? Maybe that's why I'm living at home again!"

Though Alma laughed, Sabine stared coldly into her until her laughter faded to a weak shadow of itself. "Uh…sorry."

"'I'm sorry, Madame.'"

"Hah—uh—" This time, for as tight and hard as Sabine's pale face became, Alma could not even formulate a full laugh and in fact fell back a nervous step. "I'm sorry, Madame."

"That's a good girl…we speak properly in this house, don't we, Alma?"

"I guess so…say, that reminds me"—Alma followed her strange hostess into the drawing room and found this time that the witch had already arranged tea and cookies in anticipation of her coming—"do you really live all alone here?"

"Of course not. My dolls keep me company…and, like I said the other day, my coven visits me. Usually once a month, but sometimes slightly more often."

"Sure." Not knowing what else to say and this time not having any alternative but to sit in the velvet sofa indicated, Alma poised upon the edge of one cushion and accepted, with a pleasant smile, a cup and saucer. "Thank you—so…all right, when people call you 'a witch,' I mean… You really think you're a witch, huh?"

"'Thinking' doesn't factor into it. It would be like saying you really think you live on Earth."

Alma was starting to wonder. With a sniff of her strangely colored tea and a careful sip of the hot, somewhat substance she forced down just to be polite, the athlete went on, "Yeah, but I mean, people believe all kinds of things when it comes to religion."

"I told you last time. Religion isn't an issue, either. Witchcraft is practical spiritual application. Religion is just the framework in which it operates."

Uh-huh. Sure was good tea! Sure was a good thing Sabine was so hot, otherwise Alma would have booked it out of there a minute or two into their first conversation. Still, crazy gave such good head! It was really dangerously easy to overlook all the questionable aspects of this allegedly magical woman and her hobbies when she was such a goddess draped in the frame of her overstuffed velvet armchair, the gray fabric of her dress rippling around her ankles and its bodice accenting the perfect globes of her breasts beyond compare.

"If you're a witch, can you show me some magic?"

"I hate it when people ask met that! That's just not how it works. Anyway…I've already shown you some magic, remember?"

"Oh yeah?"

"Uh-huh. My other body."

"Oh!" Laughing, blushing just to remember the sordid prior visitation and a bizarre multi-partner session like she'd never imagined, Alma said, "Well, I guess that's a kind of magic trick…more like performance art."

"You don't think doll bodies are real bodies?"

"Not bodies that have feeling, anyway."

"I wouldn't be so sure of that. Goodness, why, you can feel your dolly…why can't your dolly feel you?"

"Uh—lots of reasons. Dolls don't have brains, or nerves, or—"

"My dollies are very detailed," said Sabine, extending a languid arm for her teacup, taking a single sip, then rising with it as she said, "I suppose I'd ought to just show you…you're a visual person, aren't you, Alma. You learn from experience and doing."

"*Verdad*, I'm a woman of few words."

Sabine's smile flashed unnervingly at that, but she turned away without elaborating her thoughts. "This way, come on. I'll show you my finished doll."

This time, in that long and dim-lit hall, Sabine led Alma up the imposing staircase. Alma paused at the bottom of the incline and took a deep breath. Just a house! Why, she'd even seen pictures of upstairs rooms thanks to her brother's drone. She knew the house.

Nothing to be spooked about.

And it was the house that was spooking her, she told herself. The house, the house, and not Sabine, who moved without even glancing at the teacup in her hand—as if she had commanded it not to spill and had the utmost confidence it feared her sufficiently to obey.

Yes, perhaps that was why the house seemed so unnerving! It was as though the entire structure held its breath, waiting for some outburst of temper from its mistress.

Or 'Madame.' What a kinky bitch! Alma was just grinning to herself when she realized her hands were in her pockets. She drew them out despite her usual impulse to do the opposite of whatever others told her to do. There was something kind of fun about letting Sabine push her around, she had to admit.

And the rewards were significant. "This is my doll room," said Sabine, turning the ornate brass knob of a door near the top of the stairs and turning on the light with the same free hand she used to wave Alma inside. "Where I put all their furniture and things. Where they spend their days when I'm not playing with them. Isn't it nice?"

'Nice' wasn't really the word Alma might have picked had she had a few minutes to think it through, but since her hostess had suggested it, she was forced to lamely nod and roll with it. Really, the doll room was—uncanny.

That was the word. It was 'uncanny' to see these, at one third scale, not quite so little people frozen mid-motion in their daily lives. A pretty girl with chestnut brown hair sat drawing, her delicate hand clutching a tiny colored pencil and her other hand, inappropriately curved for the gesture as if intended to grip a teacup or some other object, instead held down the leaves of her genuine paper sketchbook. A pair of pretty young ladies in causal jeans and t-shirts, one with long white hair, the other with curly red, both of them playing with a tiny resin cat in yellow and black.

A regency-style young woman, a blonde woman, perched upon the edge of a to-scale divan, one of Sabine's tiny books open in her lap, her smiling eyes turned up and full of bright, uncanny light.

Yes—seeing them arranged in their various scenes, in full regalia and wigs and make-up, the dolls' eyes shone with uncanny life. Each one seemed to stare with real focus into Alma's face, and the more she looked, the more disquieted she became until at last she noted the table—no, the altar—in the center of the room. There, another doll had been positioned— this one, an unmistakable replica of Sabine. The doll's long black hair was pinned messily up atop her head in identical haphazard fashion, strands of it pouring down her resin neck and over the low cut of her bustier. Her slender limbs were artfully arranged across a crimson throne lit as though for the stage, and the train of her gown flowed down the seat, over the altar, and with its length provided Alma mental images of dragons and snakes.

But most incredible of all was what she had not seen last time: the doll's head. Its face resembled its owner's so closely that to look on it was both a marvel and a fright. If anything, the doll was somehow even more perfect than its creatrix. Alma had wandered over to it in a trance and now bent toward it, marveling in hushed tones over its every detail from the circles under its eyes to the soft, subtle differences in hue across its cheeks and chin.

"This is just incredible. I've never met an artist like you in real life before! How long does it take you to do up these dolls' faces?"

"Oh, it's not too much work…it's more or less the same as putting theater make-up on somebody once you get really good at it."

"I wouldn't know anything about make-up, for the stage or anything else..to do something like this, I don't know, it'd take me months!"

At Alma's laugh, Sabine emitted a mocking gasp. "Oh, no? You never wear make-up?"

"Come on, look at me! Do you think I even know what a Sephora is?"

"You should let me glam you up before I make you a doll."

Face flushing, Alma said, "Ah, I really don't know…I'm just not a make-up person."

"Please? You would look so beautiful." Slinking close, leaning into Alma's arms whether she was prepared or not, Sabine lifted her free hand and drew her eerie fingers along Alma's cheekbone. "Not that you don't look beautiful already, but, why, it's a different kind of beauty altogether when we're talking about cosmetics. I love to see the way a woman changes before and after. Don't you?"

"It can be pretty amazing, but I think I'd rather watch the transformations than try them out on myself. Make-up just never looks right on me."

"Oh, now, I'll bet that's only because you haven't had me doing it. Come on, pretty Alma…let me play with you. You'll love being my dolly."

With a clear of her throat and a glance at the many dolls around her, Alma said, "Well—I guess it has been a few years since I last gave dressing up a shot." And, of course, deep down inside, she was plagued by envy for those girls who pulled it off so easily. She wouldn't dream of trying to gussy up for public, but…well, every once in a while she did lock the bathroom door and try a little something. A little eye shadow, a little lipstick. None of it seemed like her, though, no matter what she tried.

She had very low expectations when Sabine flipped on the master bedroom light and guided Alma to the vanity seat…

but lots of anticipation for the room itself. The theme of Victorian medical illustrations was continued here, its damask wall coverings interrupted only by the occasional neatly-framed study of muscular anatomy. But the bed was certainly sprawling, and the old furniture—more leftover stuff from the previous homeowner, Alma expected—was so unique even Alma took notice of it.

Whistling, she enthused, "Boy! This vanity, that bed…this stuff is beautiful. Must be antique!"

"My mother gave it all this to me." Setting down her teacup, Sabine assessed Alma, sat her down so she was sideways at the vanity, then urged her, "Turn around…no peeking before I'm done." She leaned away only to open a small case poised on the vanity's edge. From this, the witch withdrew a small brush. "Ah," said Alma as Sabine swept on a daub of flesh-toned fluid from the bottle in her hand. "That stuff is cold!"

"Sh…only the first time, you get used to it…we have to take care of all the details. Dollies don't have any flaws…just accents. Some concealer"—she leaned away, satisfied with the workings of this brush, and fetched a fatter one to move on to another bottle—"a few beads of foundation, and you'll look as smooth as resin."

With Sabine's face hovering so close to hers, Alma had an ideal view of the dreamy aspects of the doll-maker at work. Yes—if ball-jointed dolls could see, this must have been what they saw when they came to life. Their first vision: Sabine, beautiful Sabine, dreamy, unfocused, her lips parted in pensive concentration to tease the viewer with a glitter of tongue. Alma inhaled and was immediately remonstrated with a swift swat of the make-up brush's handle against her wrist. "Don't breathe too much, you'll mess up my work."

"Sorry, Madame."

"That's all right, pretty dolly…I'll forgive you just this once. Better make sure we're on good terms now! You won't be allowed to talk soon— There! Nice and smooth!" Leaning back, beaming not at Alma's face but its superficial layer, Sabine fetched another few pots of various paints and colors from the contents of her case. With fresh brushes, she set to careful work.

"Have you ever done make-up for, like, professional reasons, or something?"

"Oh, no," said Sabine, tongue poking occasionally into the corner of her mouth as she carefully applied white eyeshadow along the arch of Alma's brow. "I just learned so I could treat my dollies better. It's no fun being a dolly if you're not a pretty dolly, after all…I couldn't stand the thought of making them and letting them have bland faces—worse, ugly ones. So I practiced, and practiced. And I got very good at make-up!"

"My mom seemed like she was always spending hours doing make-up when I was a kid. I never saw the point!"

"It's ornamental, isn't it? It should be, anyway, in my opinion. Some women identify with it completely as part of the trappings of their womanhood…but womanhood is separate from femininity, as I'm sure I don't need to tell you. Womanhood is inherent to anyone who identifies as a woman: femininity is one end of the axis on a dimension of expression. Close your eyes, please."

She obeyed and Sabine went on while applying a few layers of various eye shadows. "What a good dolly you are…have you ever dressed up in a pretty dress, Alma? Curled your hair, worn high heels, hit the town?"

"No way! I don't even know how to."

"Wear high heels?"

"Or curl my hair, or shop for dresses."

"Well! I'll have to help you pick your dress, then. I want to see my Alma all fun and girlie. Won't that be a nice change of pace for you!"

Flushed beneath the foundation that, she had been surprised

to see from the corner of her eye, matched her complexion very closely, Alma said, "Uh—well, maybe."

"Sure it will be—you'll be so beautiful, oh, won't the rest of my coven be impressed?"

Alma felt herself pale while Sabine leaned back to admire her. "You've got friends coming over tonight?"

"I can't make a doll completely by my lonesome. It's hard work! I'll need my friends to assist me, and anyway, they'll want to play with you, too…if I get a new doll and they find out that I haven't shared her with them, they'll hex me as soon as look at me."

"When you say 'play,'" Alma began, but her hostess was already springing upright to disappear into an adjoining closet.

"Let's see…I don't think we'll go for anything too elaborate with you…some dollies look good in period pieces, and of course you would look good in anything, but I don't think we'll go too far back… Oh! I know, here, hold on."

Beaming, delighted with herself, Sabine pranced back out and displayed a pink A-line dress that, while short, made Alma think of, well—Barbie. But old-fashioned Barbie, or maybe not even that. Maybe the mother of a bland set of dolls, the type who were mere accessories of the dollhouses they inhabited. "Won't you look adorable in this," said the witch, brandishing the article that would have made any woman from the 1950s envy. "Yes, oh, we'll curl your hair and get you some cute, frilly underthings, or nothing, I can't decide yet…"

"I don't know—this isn't really my style—"

Ugh, but that pout though. "You don't want to be my dolly, Alma?"

"Well—I mean, I'll try whatever, I just—I guess I have to get used to the idea."

"Oh, come on…you mean you feel the least hesitation about being a good dolly for my friends? You don't want three beautiful women to come here and play with you with me?

Touch you all over, praise your hair? Dollies get kisses all the time, you know…all kinds of attention."

Damn! Well—well, hell, you know, some opportunities did only come once. Still eyeing the dress with some reluctance, at last Alma said, "What happens in the dollhouse stays in the dollhouse, right?"

Sabine threw back her head with a giggle far brighter than her name. "It sure does," she said. "Come on, stand up…take off that sweatshirt. Let's see if I picked the right size for you."

Face and body growing warm, Alma rose with one last uncertain glance at her reflection. Damn, what a fucking babe! The red lipstick made her lips so big and pouty, and something about the dark eyeshadow the witch had applied really did make Alma look and feel sexy. She held her breath and closed her eyes all the same, though, unwilling to see herself in the process of transformation until she was all done. If she kept looking, she would back out. Better to just let the witch do what she did and see what happened.

"What a body, Alma! Oh…hold on." Laying the dress down upon her bed, Sabine slithered up and admired her guest. With an audacious pair of hands, she reached around Alma's back and unclasped the bra. While she pulled the underwire away, she gazed in that uncompromising way at Alma's breasts, then down the athletic line of her stomach. With a soft smile for the gray cotton panties, Sabine knelt before Alma and slowly tugged the underwear down her powerful legs.

"You're such a pretty dolly," marveled Sabine, running one hand back up Alma's leg, her thumb brushing along the damp lip of her groin and beyond. Alma gasped, laying her hand upon the witch's head, her pussy throbbing instantly at the contact.

"Now, now, dolly…mustn't touch, or move. You have to get used to being very still and quiet. Here…let me lift your arms, let's put you in your slip."

Breathless, Alma wanted to ask about the rest of the underwear, but Sabine was already presenting a silk slip in soft pink that she slid over her new doll's head. Sabine guided Alma's arms through the fabric and trailed her hands over the athlete's body to smooth the fabric into place. A feeling of absolute relaxation began to settle over Alma. It was strange how powerful it was, but there really was something calming, something comforting, about being dressed by another person.

And something erotic. While Sabine again knelt, now to fastidiously smooth the slip over Alma's body, Alma stole another glance at her reflection and couldn't help but produce a noise of shocked pleasure. The tight slip was so short it was almost a joke: it clung to every generous curve, accentuating the generous breasts attempting to spill from it, and from its hem her hindquarters overflowed.

Cool air from the witch's house grazed Alma's cunt and revealed to her just how wet she'd become when Sabine took her by the hand and set her on the edge of the bed. "Now, dolly, we have to make sure you're ready for the Sabbath…let's spread your legs and see."

Though she gasped, Alma stopped herself from speaking and relaxed into Sabine's touch. The witch pushed wide Alma's legs, gasping. "What a perfect dolly I have," moaned Sabine, bending forward to plant a few kisses down Alma's stomach. "So quiet and still. You'll be a very good dolly when my friends are here, won't you? Nice and quiet, just like this. Nice and quiet and wet right here—right in this nice, pretty cunt."

Sabine bent down and placed a kiss between Alma's spread labia, directly upon her exposed clit. While Alma moaned, the witch flicked a glance up at her and commenced the rapid serpentine motions of her tongue. Alma struggled against the impulse to make further noises and looked up at the ceiling, keeping her fast breathing as soft as she possibly could. Sabine's expert tongue beat rapidly against the transfixing center of Alma's nerves, then trailed down to plunge a few obscene times just within the entrance of her aching cunt. All the while Alma's hands itched to touch her, to grip the blankets, but oh, she forced her body to relax—forced herself to be totally still beneath Sabine's caresses.

As a finger slid in to replace the tongue that lifted away, Sabine murmured, "Now, we don't want you to cum just yet, Alma…but we do want you nice and excited, oh, yes, we want our dolly dripping wet. And you look like you are, huh, cutie." Sliding her fingers briefly out again, Sabine landed a burst of sharp spanks against Alma's clit. The wet sting rushed to the top of Alma's head and back down to the pussy that spread farther with her legs. When she noticed the movement, Sabine stopped again, laughing cruelly, leaning away. "Stay still, now, dolly. Let's give you something to make sure you keep feeling nice and excited."

Sabine leaned up and kissed her once lightly upon the ridge of the ear, then vanished from her sight to leave Alma confronted with her reflection in the mirror. The slip looked ready to give up any minute and its thin fabric revealed her nipples were hard little gems crowning her breasts. She ached to stimulate them, to touch herself everywhere she could, but she stayed still and good and quiet, astonished by her own compliance, her own thrill to comply. When Sabine returned with a short but still quite intimidating plug adorned with a blue gem and a small bottle of lubricant, Alma was shocked, but the hot flush of pleasure that rushed through her at the possibilities couldn't be denied.

Sabine made sure she saw it and, finding no protest, set the tools aside. "All right—turn over, dolly…"

At the gentle touch of the witch's hand, Alma did as she'd been bade. Her head swam as she was pushed over upon her stomach and the hem of the slip was lifted a few centimeters even higher than its already revealing position. The bottle popped open and Alma buried her face in the bedspread, humiliated as she was aroused, delighted to find the bed smelled like that same dense collaboration of patchouli and bitter herbs that accompanied the witch everywhere.

After setting the bottle back down, the witch placed one hand upon Alma's rear and spread her ass, then teased the tight hole that was unused to stimulation, let alone exposure. Alma's lips parted in a silenced moan as Sabine's lubricated fingertip eased into her ass, working slowly in and out before being joined by a second. "Have to stretch you out, don't we… we don't want it to hurt, no, we don't."

Then the fingers were gone. Instead, the tip of the plug pushed firmly against her ass. Sabine laughed softly as she encountered resistance, saying, "Now, dolly, just relax…that's right, oh, that's right…doesn't that feel good."

Alma's breath hitched as her eyes widened but she somehow managed not to moan with pleasure. The toy filled her inch by inch and the feeling was so humiliating, so erotic in its filthiness, that her cunt grew all the wetter and her head burned flaming hot. While she buried her face more intensely against the sheets, the witch pushed the toy up to the flange and spoke with a voice brightened by a smile of satisfaction for the final effect.

"How nice you must feel…that's right, we want our dollies nice and excited all the time. Happy to be played with. All right, you just wait there…"

Again, the witch absented herself. Alma, heart pounding in her ears and cunt throbbing to be touched, had to wonder what she was doing. Why was she being so docile? Where was this pleasure coming from? She wished to touch herself but even found herself thinking that a doll wouldn't do such a thing…so she didn't. What a strange mindset! What a strange experience. She had to admit, though—at least, in the realms of her own head—that the plug's disgracefully exciting feeling was wonderful, and each slight shift of her body caused a tightening around it that she was shocked to so enjoy.

After a few moments Sabine returned with clean hands, a headband that matched the dress she'd already picked, tan hosiery and garters, and a pair of red heels very close to the shade of lipstick that decorated Alma's lips. "What a good dolly you are to be so still. Oh, I just love that slip on you! But it's time to put your hose on, and your dress. Here—"

With a hand under Alma's arm, Sabine sat her up and smiled into her face, rearranged some of her hair, then encouraged her to extend one long leg. Flushed to sit on her ass and the gem of that plug within it, humiliated to be looked in the face while wearing such a thing, Alma tried to stare into space as a doll would and Sabine chuckled at the effort.

After sliding the garters up Alma's legs, she then, one tan stocking at a time, slid the nylon up each limb. The witch's face was flushed by the time she cradled Alma's foot to help it into her left shoe, the tickling sensation against her arch, muted by the nylon, somehow causing another throb of pleasure.

"I think my friends will be here very soon," said Sabine, gazing with pleasure between her charge's legs before rising to pluck up the dress. With the fabric draped in her elbow, she bent to slide her hands beneath the dolly's arms and help it—her—upright. "How are you feeling, Alma?"

Alma couldn't respond and stared in a flushed daze off into space, aching for her mistress's touch.

"Good," said Sabine with pleasure, gently caressing Alma's cheek before navigating her arms into the dress and out through the sleeves. "Isn't that very, very good. What a nice dolly! The best I've had in years."

The fabric of the pink dress flowed down around her thighs. Alma's face and throat reddened at the thought of wearing this garment and the slip beneath without any underwear. If she bent over, the plug would be easily exposed. Nonetheless,

Sabine only eased her back down at the vanity and said, "Let's get your hair all pretty and curled. Then, by the time we're done, our friends will be here! Aren't you excited to show off?"

The doll didn't respond. The doll had to admit it was fascinating and a little disturbing how beneath its mistress's hand it had somehow seemed to lose its identity, its sense of self and drive to argue. In fact, now that it was liberated from its old personality by this freedom of being a doll, it had a new appreciation for its looks. Oh, it really was a stupendously beautiful dolly. Glamorous and busty, its mouth formed by its red lipstick into a sensual pout, it was the kind of dolly any man or woman would have loved to fuck. Especially as Sabine curled its dark hair and arranged the results around its lovely copper face.

"What a nice, beautiful little dolly you are…oh, my friends will just love you." Sabine had slid the headband into place just as the house resounded with a doorbell's ring. The dolly was surprised but didn't even jump, it was so dedicated to being still for its mistress. With a delighted look, Sabine cried, "They're here! Oh, good…come on, dolly." Hastily cleaning a few things up in the room and smoothing the bedspread, Sabine took the doll by the hand and helped it stand. "Let's go downstairs and greet our friends. You can help me serve them tea before the meeting starts."

Downstairs, Sabine threw open the front door and smiled wider than the dolly had ever yet seen her. She and her friends all cried in delight and the watching toy marveled at the beautiful trio of women that poured into the house, each more regal than the last. The first had beautiful bleach-blonde hair arranged in a bun that permitted the tumbling down of only a few curls, enough to frame her sharp-darting eyes and point the eye down to the tanned bosom that peered out of her lavender blouse; the second, a lovely dark woman with an elaborate set of braids and a sumptuous smile, paused to kiss

Sabine's cheek before stepping past her; the third, a redhead as glamorous as a countess and wearing rings enough for the role, admired not Sabine, but the doll who glowed with pride as this stranger enthused, "Why, what a nice, new toy!"

"Isn't it wonderful? I just love to look at it…go on, dolly, why don't you serve us that tea? I'm sure our friends are parched."

Flush-faced and nervous but eager to please, the doll hurried through the sitting room and into the kitchen overflowing with sweet scents and many strangely bitter ones besides. A silver tea service was already arranged with cups, and the kettle was hot; the dolly only needed to pour the water into the waiting tea pot, which it carried along with the rest of the tea set into the den all abuzz with activity.

Imagine its surprise when it walked back into the den to find the witches already removing their clothes while chattering away as gaily as birds. Were dollies allowed to be embarrassed? Its face burning along with the rest of it, the doll averted its eyes and slipped quietly into the center of the room. When it had set the tea service down upon the coffee table waiting there, it straightened up to discover all eyes upon it.

The redheaded witch had extended her body along the chaise longue and reclined with one hand draped casually over her hip. "Where did you find this one, Sabine?" She had ceased her stripping at her lingerie. It was an old-fashioned outfit with a scarlet garter belt and an ornately laced bra to match, but no underwear. The doll realized it was staring at the fiery thicket of beautiful orange curls between the woman's thick thighs when Sabine answered the question.

"I think I told you girls about that drone that was spying on me…"

As Sabine told the story, the dolly tried to avoid openly gawking at the other women, who had stripped down quite a bit further than the redhead and now, naked, curled together upon the sofa. The blonde stroked the arm of the couch and studied the doll while the braided woman listened carefully to Sabine's story, laughing all the while. Meanwhile, the redhead curled a finger.

"Come here, dolly...let me take a closer look at you. What beautiful skin you have, oh, it's perfect. I don't see a single blemish." When, waved forward after a tentative glance at its mistress, the dolly edged toward the redheaded witch, the object gasped to have its skirt lifted. Its face seemed to catch fire while the witch admired everything now exposed, but its face wasn't the only thing set to burst into flame. "It's almost too bad it's going to be a dolly! With skin like this, it would have made a very nice sofa...or a footstool. Wouldn't you like to be a footstool, dolly?"

The doll knew better than to respond and kept its eyes averted while the redhead inspected it, running her soft hand up its leg to lightly squeeze the flesh of its rear. Seeing the doll's shy gaze, Sabine commanded it, "Look at our guest, dolly. Don't dollies always look at the girls who play with them?"

Face burning, the doll lifted her eyes to the redhead who fondled it, now patting the cheek of its ass and flicking the gem of the plug Sabine installed. "I love a dolly I can sink my hands into...oh, she's got such strong limbs, but, why, her backside is so soft and fun to grab! How wonderful." While she demonstrated by grabbing the doll's flesh, the redhead grinned up into its face. "Come on, dolly. Come here—let me see if your tongue is as cute as your soft little ass."

At the tug of its hand, the doll knelt upon the floor between the redhead's spread legs. "I don't need any potion to be ready for a hard-working little doll," she assured the toy, glancing toward the sisters of her coven as they sipped on tea and watched, the two strangers murmuring and fondling one another while Sabine appreciated the scene from the overstuffed armchair beside the fire. Her eyes were gay with levity and her hands occupied by the teacup, but her posture was some how so sensual and splayed that it was enough to urge the doll right on.

"Especially not one so sexy," Sabine agreed as the doll went to work on the redhead, bowing down to spread the lips of the woman's cunt and finding her, as promised, already we with anticipation for the night. As the doll went to work, tongue thrashing, the beautiful woman above her gasped and widened her legs. "I don't think anyone here really needs a potion, of course...but it does make things a little more fun. And it stopped this one from complaining early on!"

"Complaining! Why, a doll, complaining..." The beads of the braided woman's hair rattled with her laughter, her dark head thrown back with glee. She had already finished the bitter-smelling potion that the blonde nursed somewhat more fretfully, having little taste for it and pouting her lips swollen by magic so that really they already possessed an almost permanently sullen, certainly kissable sense of malaise. While her nose wrinkled in displeasure, the dark witch with her arms about her nudged her with one broad thigh. "Come on, set an example...you're half a fuck-doll yourself, you'd ought to be more eager. Look how that one's warmed up!"

"I'm not a doll," protested the blonde, scowling, forcing herself to endure another sip of the concoction while, in the background of it all, Sabine sighed in exasperation and set her empty teacup upon her saucer. The blonde went on, "But I have to admit, you're right...of all the dollies you've let us share, Sabine, this one might be the giddiest to please us!"

Who knew if that was true or just some witches' teasing, but a secret voyeur hidden in a coat closet or—say, in the form of an overstuffed armchair from which Sabine pushed herself—would have been forced to admit that the doll did go to fast and eager work on its mistress' first friend. By this time in the conversation it had really thrown its proverbial back into proceedings. As the redhead moaned and thrashed in the embrace of the longue where she lay, the doll's rapid tongue was soon joined by a teasing finger in the joyful art of tormenting that fiery and, soon, soaking cunt. This redheaded witch panted in ecstasy, back arching and the high heels in which her stockinged feet remained clacking on the carpeted floor like the cloven hooves of a demonic beast.

Sabine had by now advanced upon the other two. With barely more than a glance at her braided friend, the paler of the two dark-haired witches snatched the teacup from the blonde's unready hand. The bimbo gasped in unaffected terror, but her eyelids nonetheless fluttered with heady bedroom desire. Sabine descended upon this youngest witch, clearly the whipping-girl of the coven, for a fast and furious kiss. Then she told the braided woman, "Hold her down," and grinned at the sound of a husky Haitian laugh that accompanied the tightening of those strong, dark arms around the limber limbs of the blonde.

"Oh, no, please, that stuff is just awful—"

"Open your mouth, little bitch, we want you nice and horny tonight—" With one hand, Sabine forced open the delicate jaw of the hot little blonde. With the other she poured the remainder of the tea, steaming and bitter, into the bimbo's gaping mouth, then let the teacup shatter on the floor while she kept the blonde's hair yanked back. "Swallow, you slut! Swallow for our Dark Lord's pleasure. Satan will be coming tonight, yes, the King of Hell! Please Him, please our wicked father. Swallow the brew like you'll swallow His cum." At this suggestion, the blonde, who had already begun to swallow as commanded, moaned through the fluid and coughed a little. A few drops of the potion, light grey as the lightest cinders, dribbled down her jaw and over the pale pink nipples of her bosom. Nonetheless, Sabine stroked her face, saying, "Good girl, good girl…won't the god of this world be pleased by your obedience!"

Terror surged through the doll at all of this, but how soon that terror fled! Could dolls feel fear, after all? What knew a doll of fear? It pleased its mistress's friends as it had been commanded and knew nothing of fear, or of its own arousal or even its own craving to be touched. As the redhead responded to its fast, hard work, the doll answered in kind. Soon, mere seconds after a subsequent increase in the depths to which its fingers plunged, the redheaded witch's body had tightened sharply around the source of their stimulation. The tight grip devolved into a series of fast flutters and soon the witch panted, gripping the back of the doll's brunette head and keeping its quick working tongue pressed against her clit until her orgasm had reduced to a mere shimmer of internal muscle structure. At last, she pushed the doll away, gasping.

"By fuck, what a sweet mouth this one's got!" The redheaded which fell back upon the longue with a low moan, writhing and running her hands over her breasts once she removed her scarlet bra. "I'd play with it all day if it were mine. Who's next? Take it away from me before I keep it to myself all night."

"Oh, me," whined the blonde, whose legs had splayed since swallowing the potion and who, in addition to the caresses of Sabine and the braided witch, now fondled her own breasts and tried desperately to touch herself between the legs. Sabine caught her hand on several instances, each time uttering a cruel little chuckle and sometimes delivering a kiss. "Me, me, oh please, I hate that potion, oh! It always turns me into such a whore—"

"That's why I insist you must always drink it..." Laughing, Sabine bent over her doll and, with a look of pleasure, tipped its head up for a kiss. "What a fine doll you are! It took you a little while, but you're doing just as we say, aren't you?"

The doll could find nothing to say, because of course it wasn't a talking doll. It was a sex doll, and, like the hot little sex doll it was, it went as docilely as a lamb to the blonde before whom its mistress dragged it. While the eager wench nearly screamed with the first contact, her waxed cunt visibly dripping with delight, Sabine sat beside them to stroke the doll's brown curls. "Yes, what a hot little doll…it's too bad. This dolly doesn't seem very open to the idea of letting our Lord fuck her!"

The braided woman laughed while, slowly running her fingertips over her glistening pussy, the redhead encouraged, "Oh, get over his gender…his cock is the best!"

"It's true," said Sabine, "but I think, since it's lucky little Gina's turn tonight"—the blonde gasped and the doll realized this must have been her—"we'd might as well do the doll's fucking, ourselves. It's been awhile since we've taken out the cock, hasn't it?"

"Oh! Yes!" The redhead's voluminous curls surged around her shoulders as she sat upright, her hands extending away from her pussy and down her creamy thighs. "Yes, let's play with it tonight. Why don't you wear it, Sabine? I love the way you fuck me."

"I'll have to wear it to deal with the dolly," said Sabine, smiling tenderly down at the doll who was already on the verge of extricating an orgasm from the sensitive blonde bimbo. While Sabine plucked hairpins from the white-blonde bun and let Gina's tresses fall around her trembling shoulders, the doll's fingers slid deeper to curl within the heart of pleasure. Oh, Gina was soaked! By now the doll was, too, but its little toy heart drummed in its breast to think of its mistress fucking it…especially in front of all these other girls, and yes, maybe even in front of a man. Just a man, surely. Surely not really the Lord of the Flies.

"Let me go get the cock," enthused the redhead, springing up, her heels clicking up the stairs. "I get first dibs on using it…get ready, Bernice."

The braided witch laughed, her teeth flashing in an eager

smile. "I've been waiting for months now, Hazel! Why don't we take that thing out more often?"

"Because," gasped Gina, head tilted back and eyes unseeing toward the ceiling. "Because, because…because taking it off is so awful!"

"It's nothing one doesn't get used to." Giggling somewhat, herself, Sabine delivered one last pat to the head of the doll and then reclined in the arms of the same chair she'd favored before. With one leg draped over the side and the other flat upon the floor to display herself to the room at large, Sabine drew her hands over her legs and to the apex of her pale thighs.

There Sabine slowly stroked her pussy, watching the unfolding scene and, while she pushed her fingers into herself, sometimes sliding them back out and brushing her glistening knuckles against the velvet fabric of the chair where she masturbated. All the while she moaned, her moan the most exciting thing the doll had heard all night. Its pace increased and, with an abrupt spell of thrashing, Gina reached a point of hard orgasm. Her pussy clenched around the doll's copper fingers and even though it was a doll and not permitted to feel things, it could not help but marvel at the tension of the girl's tight cunt.

"Oh, what a good job you do, dolly! Didn't I tell you, Bernice? It's a very good little doll, isn't it."

"It sure seems to be…I won't know until I try, though, will I? Come here, pretty doll." While the braided woman spread her legs to reveal the valleys of her beautiful dark pussy, this flesh even blacker than the rest of her, her limber arms extended and she offered the doll a generous kiss. "Ah," she said with pleasure, leaning back and pushing it down to work, "you taste like my sisters…add me to the mix, go on—ah! By Pan, it's quick!"

Her limber back arching with the working of the doll's tongue, Bernice moaned and curled her long fingers into the doll's by now quite wild hair. She pushed its head down hard against her clit and the doll responded eagerly, sometimes even scraping its teeth for the added bit of daring stimulation. Meanwhile Sabine writhed upon the chair, grinding her pussy against the velvet and toying with her nipples as she moaned. Her bare foot braced against the furniture's arm, rubbing back and forth as she said, "Yes, oh, it's the worthiest of slaves...oh, fuck, is the touch of velvet on the skin not so pleasing to the senses? What say you, Gina?"

"Oh..." Moaning, the blonde recovered her senses just enough to lift her head from where she had collapsed beside Bernice. Seeing what unfurled beside her semi-conscious body, Gina bit her lip and leaned over to caress the limbs and heaving bosom of her darker sister. "Velvet, leather, silk, all the things we can make of humans with our magic please me to lie upon."

"Of humans, and whatsoever else it pleases us to make into furniture...ah!" Sabine's head lifted with her laugh of delight as the trotting of the redhead's heels reached her ears. She sat up, legs splayed and cunt oozing upon the chair as she cried with delight to her friend, "It looks so fetching on you, Hazel!"

"I always have wanted one of these...not because I want to be a man, but just because I love to do the fucking. What do you think, doll? Aren't you excited for your mistress to take her turn with this big thing?"

At the redhead's invitation, the doll lifted its head from its work, albeit only reluctantly...then, with far more enthusiasm and sense of mystery. The beautiful witch now bore, not a strap-on as expected, but a bona fide cock she stroked with pleasure. The tense organ throbbed in her grip, bobbing into an upright point when she released it to trail her fingertips to the base with a shudder. "It's so sensitive...I must put it to the task of fucking one of you trollops this very minute. Shoo, doll, get out of the way, let Bernice and I resolve an old matter."

As the blonde slut also hurried up from the couch, Hazel pushed past the doll and bent her head over the braided witch who moaned and at once yielded her kissable lips. As their tongues intertwined and glistened between opening mouths, the braided witch leaned back into the couch and gasped. Hazel wasted no time making use of the wet cavern the doll's hard work had encouraged: she pushed the magical dick deep into her dark friend, who moaned and thrashed to be penetrated before the others of her coven.

"Oh, it's hard tonight! Sister, sister, how do I feel?"

"Positively delicious…what a useful dolly you are. How you've made Bernice drip! Fuck, ah—yes, what a wet slut you are tonight." Gasping, tossing back her head and pushing her hair from her face, Hazel thrust her new cock deep into Bernice's splayed cunt and produced wails of pleasure from them both. As the two women played with the enchanted toy, Sabine gestured for the doll to crawl over. It did, eyes low, then looked up only when its mistress was able to grab its jaw and incline its head.

"You don't need to be so shy, dolly…here, oh, use that pretty tongue on me. Bacchus, but I'm drenched! See how desperate your mistress is? Oh, it's unbecoming…"

Sabine spread her legs wide and used her fingers to part her labia. With a gasp of delight, the doll went to the task for which it had been most eager, and as the blonde held Hazel's fiery locks back to help her kiss Bernice, Sabine thrashed against her new toy's mouth.

"Oh, fuck! Yes, yes, oh, what a good dolly I have…yes, fuck, ah, I'll play with you so much more often than my other dollies, oh, you'll be my new favorite, my most loved of all… won't you be happy when I take you down and let you please me like this? And won't you be wet, yourself…oh, I didn't even show our friends—go on, dolly! Pull up your pretty dress a little and show the room your nice jewelry."

Though the doll gasped, its face burning, it could not help but obey. Letting its tongue do all the work, the doll reached back and drew the hem of its dress up high over its ass. The slip left the plug exposed and the other witches cooed and jeered over the glittering gem.

"Oh, how cute," enthused the blonde.

Bernice, who had titled her braided mane back to laugh, ran her hands over her own breasts and moaned. "Isn't it a pleasure to be so full?"

"You could have two cocks in you tonight if you'd only let yourself," chided Hazel, gripping Bernice's thigh to pound deeper by the thrust. "But, I suppose it's important to have boundaries…and that's what anal plugs are for, isn't it."

The doll couldn't stop the moan from trailing past its lips even as it kissed and lapped at Sabine's oozing nectar. Above it, its mistress gasped with glee and thrashed in the arms of the chair, gripping its back behind her head while screaming, "Yes, yes, oh, yes!"

Though it had not yet had that many interactions with its mistress in the grand scheme of things, the doll was already acquainted enough with her body to recognize an orgasm reaching its natural development.

Now the doll slowed down her lapping, hoping to extend the witch's orgasm. As Sabine moaned in frustration, the sisters of her coven laughed. Hazel twisted to deliver a lascivious kiss to Gina's mouth before diving back down to give Bernice's tongue a thrashing.

All the while her hips worked the cock in and out and Bernice keened wildly, her pleasure reaching greater heights by the second until, at the same time as Sabine despite the doll's best efforts to extend its mistress's pleasure, the two witches being made the current center of attention came together with a high cry, a shared moan, a glance at once another as though each in assessment of the other's pleasure.

"Oh, yes," gasped Sabine, legs splaying lazily wide while her fingers curled through the doll's hair. "Yes, I've found a very good dolly…isn't that right, Father."

The lamps in the living room sputtered their light as if fluttering in an orgasm of their own. While the doll fell back from its mistress, all those lights cut out completely. As they reestablished to the sound of the poor doll's gasp, the armchair was proven a mere container for the man within. Dark haired, fit with glittering blue eyes only a few shades lighter than his suit, and wearing a wicked smile the doll swore might have been decorated with a hint of fang, he held Sabine in his hands and slid his embrace along her body while she moaned.

"That's right," said the Devil, kissing the column of his unholy daughter's throat. "You have such a good eye, Sabine… all my girls do. How pleased you make me!"

The doll reddened from the tips of her ears to the clavicle at the base of her throat while the witches gasped in delight. Blonde Gina was the first to scramble up and the other two followed once dissevering themselves, all three of them leaning over the armchair to caress and lay their kisses upon the demon prince who manifested from the furniture of the home.

"Tell your toy it doesn't need to be embarrassed," the Devil told Sabine, his hands roving over her breasts before one lifted away to cradle Bernice's jaw and deliver a kiss to her dark, almost perpetually scowling mouth. "I have no time or interest in objects like you girls do…I only take such pleasure in the making of a doll because it pleases you four fine succubae."

"Would we were blessed with such infernal blood," Hazel crooned, her hands trailing down the Devil's chest and already setting about in the removal of his tie. "Hail, Satan!"

"Hail, Satan," answered the other three in frightful unison, at once engaged in the Devil's undressing while he laughed.

"Wait now, my girls, it never does to be over-hasty…let's deal with your doll first, before we enjoy our chthonic rite.

Hazel, I saw you had the cock, didn't you? You'd ought to give it to Sabine now, let's help her make her doll."

"But I love wearing this thing," the redhead protested, a slightly anxious look crossing her face. "And anyway—why, it's so hard to take off—"

"Then permit me," said the Devil, reaching back with a great hand and tugging on Hazel's throbbing erection. She gasped—pleasurably, at first—but soon her gasp increased to a high scream that made Gina cover her ears in fear. Sabine and Bernice both watched with absolute glee, moaning in stereo as, while the doll watched and found itself too shocked or too far gone to scream, the Devil tore the fleshy prick right from the screaming redhead's groin.

As she fell away with a sob and a torrent of blood that splattered down her pale thighs, Satan smiled at what remained in his hand. Detached from a user, the magical prick shrank down and revealed it was little more than the mummified member of some dead man. While the doll openly stared, incredulous at it was afraid and still more horrified than either one of those emotions, the Devil lowered the withered dildo down between Sabine's legs and trailed its head along her spread, wet cunt.

"Here we are, my favorite daughter…ah, light of my fallen soul, by Yahweh's hateful eye but you have gotten wet." The severed penis slid easily into Sabine's dripping pussy and she moaned to receive it, her back arching and her hands reaching back to grip the shoulders of the demon prince as once she gripped the back of the chair.

"Oh, Master"—she trembled with her desperate moaning, her quaking legs bending at the knees to allow her bare feet to gain purchase upon the edge of the chair—"Master, oh, my Dark Father, oh, Hail Satan!"

"Hail Satan," answered the others in time, even Satan himself.

The doll, of course, would not have answered that if it could, being as it was too full of fear to embrace the true god of this hideous world. The cock, once slid into its mistress's body, seemed to grow in size. Sabine's mouth fell open and her brow furrowed as if in pain, but her eyes stayed locked to the prick that her female companions at once took to stroking. While the organ grew in size and liveliness, taking on the form, for all the world, of a great, throbbing, living penis—with blood from Sabine's body, no doubt—Sabine moaned and tilted back her head to receive the kisses of the suited devil. Satan ran his hands over Sabine's bosom and even helped bring the cock to life with a few strokes of his own, and when he was satisfied in his fondling, he released her from his kiss to admire the sight of the well-endowed girl in his lap.

"Very fine," said Satan, "very fine, indeed. Go on, my girl. Play with your dolly."

Sabine's eyes fell on the doll as if only just remembering it, and the doll in that second seemed to feel as though it were just then remembering itself. With the predatory motions of a panther Sabine flowed from the Devil's lap and descended upon the gasping doll to take its face in her hands. Seeing only lust in the depth of her new toy's face when all the fear was pushed away, Sabine lowered her head and plunged her tongue deep into the doll's gasping mouth.

"Don't be shy, dolly," said Sabine. "I want to see how well you take a nice, throbbing cock…woman's or man's, it doesn't matter to me at all."

Meanwhile, just as panting Hazel recovered enough to dizzily sit up, the other two witches had fallen into the Dark Lord's lap and took their turns receiving the passion of his hungry mouth. Back and forth he turned, lifting his head to greet Hazel with quite a furious spell of affection as she draped herself around him. "You greedy girls are so bad at taking turns," he remonstrated, reaching up to lightly pat the redhead's cheek, his pat gradually increasing to a small slap.

"Only with the cock, Father." In the center of the room, Sabine drew the doll upright to be pushed into the chaise longue where it had eaten out Hazel. While its legs splayed with the manner of its fall and revealed everything left bare beneath the dress, the witch that had laid claim to it made that claim full well-known. "With dolls, we're much more generous…pull up your dress like a good fucktoy, doll."

Struggling to avoid so much as biting its lip, the doll drew the hem of its dress high up its hips and offered itself more completely to the witch who stroked her cock before it. This throbbing member soon pushed up against the doll's soaking pussy and both it and its mistress moaned, the latter running the head of her cock along the quivering cunt-lips of the former. "Why, what an excited dolly you are! So pleased to serve your mistress that not even our Father could put you off. He might have chosen to appear as a woman, you know, but he loves to make people suffer…perhaps if you hadn't been so obstinate you might have been rewarded by the sight of how beautiful he is when he chooses the feminine form."

Yes, that was almost regretful, but dollies didn't have room for regret—not when a hot witch was plunging her throbbing dick deep into the pussy that ached to be filled like its well-attended asshole. The doll realized as its cunt was filled to the hilt that it had never experienced penetration in both holes at once before, and it thrashed and throbbed and struggled not to scream before at last remembering that to be a good doll it ought to stay still. It struggled to, forcing itself to relax and this relaxation subsequently increasing its pleasure as it was totally, mercilessly used.

"Sweet Mephistopheles," gasped Sabine, her eyes fluttering shut as her hips eased into rhythm between the new toy's legs. "Oh, lesbians! What tight cunts they have…former lesbians, anyway. Not as if dollies have proper genders, do they…oh, oh, ah, Hazel, you should have tried her out before Father took the cock from you! If you ask me nicely I'll be sure to let you try this dolly next Sabbath, oh, fuck—"

How difficult it was to be still! Almost totally impossible. The doll's body craved to buck its hips and arch and moan, to beg Sabine to fuck it harder, to touch it elsewhere—oh, to extol aloud the sublime pleasure of being filled both fore and aft! But dollies couldn't speak…nor could they desire. The doll tried to console itself with this notion, staring into its mistress's beautiful face, and instead focused on the joy it felt to think it was good use to its mistress. Yes, to think it was so very pleasing to its mistress, who panted and moaned and leaned to plant a lurid kiss upon the dolly's gasping mouth.

"Isn't it lovely to see your sister playing with her new toy… why don't you three join her?" The Devil smiled fondly up at Hazel and patted Gina on the ass to produce a high-pitched giggle, a bawdy little shriek. At his urging, the three witches hurried to surround the chaise longue…oh, and if it was difficult for the dolly to stay still before, why, it was almost impossible now. While Bernice lowered her finely cut ebony face over the dolly's gasping golden one, Gina ducked her head to apply her tongue to the task of whipping an orgasm from the new toy's aching clitoris. Sabine, meanwhile, fucked away; Hazel nuzzled the doll's ear while fondling its breasts, sliding a hand into its innocent pink dress to roll a nipple between her fingers.

And all the while, all the praise the foursome had for the doll was repeated in a kind of chant, fond words gasped by Sabine, whispered by Bernice, moaned by Hazel. The only thing keeping Gina from adding her own murmurs of, "Good dolly, what a nice, pretty dolly, oh, yes, doesn't it feel so good to be a sexy little fuck-doll for us, don't you love it when we use you," was the busy work of her tongue, but her eyes were curled into such a catlike smile that the expression seemed praise enough of its own. As the trio caressed the doll, Sabine filled it until it senseless, pushing its hips up higher and hammering her dick home while the Devil appeared behind her to caress her throat. He planted a few almost chaste-seeming kisses upon Sabine's high cheekbone, gazing only into her pretty profile while she pleased herself with the body of the doll.

"It does bring me joy to see you girls so happy…do you think your dolly is close, Sabine? Ah, seeing you nymphs play together always makes me eager to get a move on things."

"She's nearly there, Master…oh, yes." Her thighs slapping against the doll's ass, Sabine laughed while her new toy whimpered with the intensity of its pleasure. "Yes, I feel it… poor dolly, what's wrong? Want to moan, don't you? Want to thrash around and beg me to go faster? Well, you can't… you're just a cute, stupid little doll, a hot little toy made to take my cock and eat my cunt, and you love it, don't you? You can answer—the one word dollies are allowed to say is 'Yes.'"

"Yes," screamed the doll, "yes, yes, yes!"

"Uh-huh…that's what I thought." Chuckling, Sabine pounded harder, deeper into the quivering orifice that was more satisfactorily filled by this mummified cock than by any plastic device or rubber toy it had ever hosted. "Come on, you hot little bitch…yes, that's right, cum for Madame, cum for Satan—"

"Hail Satan," screamed the other witches while Sabine laughed in the embrace of her evil father.

"Hail Satan," Sabine intoned, burying herself deeper into the doll by the thrust. "Hail, Hail, Hail Satan—ah! Ah, haha—"

The other witches gasped while, at last, a high scream of abominable pleasure tore from the new doll's throat. As its cunt twitched around its owner's cock and its body thrashed unwillingly upon the longue, Bernice and Hazel held it down with a cruel pair of laughs. Only Gina admired the climax for its own sake, lifting her head to smile fondly up at the pretty dolly and the pleasure they'd brought it.

"What a nice doll," said Satan approvingly, stroking Sabine's hair from her face and bending her head back to kiss her. "You have good taste."

There was no focusing on anything but the internal sensations—not for that spoiled little dolly. The orgasm, once begun, seemed somehow not to stop. In fact, it seemed to spread out of its body and into the room at large, which quivered and spun as though the house were but a grand amusement park ride. While the ceiling tilted, ready at any second to collapse beneath the doll's blinding pleasure, it gasped in sudden pain. It seemed as though the cock within it, already large, grew only larger by the second. At its whine, Sabine jerked herself away and the doll realized the cock had not been growing. Rather, the doll was shrinking.

Its mouth opened to emit a scream but, lacking a windpipe as dolls do, no noise rose from its open mouth. The witches laughed and Satan, a dark twinkle in his eye, reached down to stroke Sabine's cock while delivering a kiss upon his favorite's open mouth. "What fun," he said, glancing down at the throbbing member wet from the sex doll's cum. "Why, your dolly seems almost scared, Sabine."

"I can't imagine why…it's what this one really wants, after all. Yes, to be a doll—to be used by us. Well, now it gets its wish…it gets to enjoy all the attention it can stand from me, forever and ever." While the edges of the doll's vision went black—a blackness that quickly spread to consume its entire view of the world—Sabine threw her head back in a cruel cackle. "Isn't it lucky!"

Alma's eyes opened and, as the saying went, she was at once sober as a judge. All traces of the strange aphrodisiacal effect had by the potion vanished in her unconscious state, and in that deep dreamless slumber she had lost all perception of everything. This was one of those sleeps where a person practically forgot their own name, let alone the contents of the day before.

The day before—what had happened the day before? Alma tried to remember going to bed but she couldn't. She couldn't remember anything for a very long, hard few seconds of being awake, until, distantly, she heard Sabine hum, "Let's see, what else, am I forgetting anything?"

"What sports do I play?"

A terrible chill swept through Alma's cheeks and her eyes widened toward the ceiling that she had once struggled to recognize but now, in a strange and distant way, placed as being part of that—witch's house. Yes, that witch. Alma didn't want to admit it but—but things had happened, strange things, and Alma hadn't been anywhere close to herself. What a depraved night that was! So depraved and out-of-character that, as she was at once awash in racy memories, there was some delay before Alma recognized the other speaker. Who could blame her for the length of time it took? It wasn't every day you heard your own voice coming from somebody else, clearer and livelier than any recording.

Alma's mouth opened in shock and she tried to speak. Not only did no sound come out but she realized that she simply wasn't breathing. Wasn't suffocating, either, but definitely wasn't breathing. And though she was sober, well—

She was very, very numb. So numb that she couldn't seem to feel anything below her neck. Her mouth opened again and she could almost hear herself screaming the word "Help!" but no sound came out.

Meanwhile, the conversation carried on, Sabine addressing this woman with Alma's voice. While the athlete futilely screamed on and on, or tried to, Sabine listed a few things she had deduced about Alma and then said, "You'll figure out the rest once you're living in her house…your kind always do. Oh! But keep an eye on that brother of hers. If he grows up to be an attractive young man, send him my way…I'm sure I'll still be a very attractive young woman by then."

With a gay laugh, Sabine led this stranger with Alma's voice out from whatever room they inhabited. Alma tried to turn her head but failed and her panic rose more by the second. What had happened? Had she been paralyzed somehow by whatever drug was in the tea the witches gave her? Had they done something to her while she was unconscious?

And what about that man?

The tapping of the witch's feet returned to the room, nearer all the time. When Sabine appeared over Alma's head, the athlete's face surged with terrible fear. Now Alma also remembered something else—remembered the feeling of shrinking, her dress and all, just before she blacked out.

"Oh, dolly! You're awake."

Delighted, Sabine lowered a huge hand to caress Alma's cheek. Alma's mouth parted as though to gasp and the witch went on. "I did a little work on you while you've been asleep. Would you like to see your new face? I think you'll like it, it's so pretty…I was just sending your replacement out. Don't worry. No one will ever know that you're gone."

Alma's brain burned in ever-deepening fear. Rather than picking her up around the waist, for some reason Sabine slid that huge hand around the back of Alma's head. Either she was well and truly mad or the witch's hand was large enough that her whole palm fit to the back of her skull.

Either way, Alma tried to whip her eyes up toward her hairline, because it almost felt as though she had no hair.

Hair wasn't the only thing she was missing. As the witch lifted her before the standing mirror in the corner of what Alma now recognized was the house's doll atelier, Alma understood at last why she could not move, nor scream, nor speak.

She was not just small. She was nothing but a severed head. A resin doll head around which Sabine's fingers curled like the legs of a terrible ivory spider.

"Don't you think I did a good job with your lips? Look at that hint of gloss…you look so lively even before you wake up! How cute you are." Smiling, Sabine turned Alma's face toward hers and admired her own handiwork, the hints of blush and dappling of light color making the texture of the smooth resin come alive as human skin. "I'd kiss you, but I'd hate to smudge your face…oh, well, maybe one kiss won't hurt—what else are dollies for?"

The witch's lips, of incredible size from Alma's small perspective, pursed in a pillowy pout and lowered for her right eye. For small Alma it was as if a seventeen-foot alien grizzly bear of some kind leaned down and kissed her on the brow: it was horrible, and terrifying, and although the kiss made the resin of her forehead tingle with the heated pleasure of contact, there was nothing comforting about it. The kiss was only another in a continuous litany of truly nightmarish realizations.

"Isn't this nice! You get to have the pleasure of being my dolly forever now. I'm so happy Father helped me make your replacement…that's what we need him for, why we save doll-making for our Sabbath rites. It's one thing to turn a human into a doll, after all, but making a fake human out of thin air is a little more complicated."

"Oh, I wouldn't say that."

With a gasp of delight, Sabine looked over her shoulder and cried, "Lord! You would come visit me now?"

"Sabine, beautiful Sabine, you know I need no occasion to visit you."

Alma couldn't move her doll eyes, but she didn't have to.

From her vantage cradled in Sabine's palm she recognized the devilish man who crossed the room and passed into her field of vision to kiss Sabine passionately upon the mouth, the witch sighing, moaning, offering herself with absolute abandon.

"Father! Let me put my dolly down…and put her wig on her! Poor thing, I'm sure you don't feel very delicate and feminine without your hair."

As she pulled the wig cap over the doll's head, she enthused, "Oh, Master! Thank you again for your help, I'm so happy with her."

"This is why I love to come visit you, Sabine…you're so grateful. Everyone else only ever calls on me because they want something…you're one of my few witches who call on me for the simple pleasure of my company."

"Of course, Father. I'd rather sit with you and hear a story or spend the evening in your embrace than ask for anything!"

"You're the only doll for me, Sabine. Is this its body?"

"Yes, I haven't even shown it! Look, dolly." Beaming with pride, Sabine turned the angle at which she held the head and permitted Alma to behold her own headless body, a work of ball-jointed resin art as much as anything else that had come through the witch's workshop.

Every detail was so exact that it was alarming. Just like the other doll she had seen mid-preparation, the soft shadows and shading differences of different parts of the skin served to bring the resin to a special kind of life. And, just like the last doll, it was even anatomically correct.

"I think I made you maybe just a little bustier than you were before, but I'm sure you won't complain, right? Look how perky!"

With another laugh, Sabine ran her fingertip around the doll body's left nipple. Alma would have gasped if she had lungs: instead her mouth opened wide and her bright resin eyes widened at the shock of disembodied pleasure. Oh! She felt everything, absolutely everything, though her head was severed completely from her form.

"See how nice? I love everything about your beautiful body, Alma…I couldn't alter most of it. It was just sexy from the start! I only made a few little adjustments…but these tight abs, oh, I love your stomach…" While the witch spoke she drew her fingertips down the cool curve of the body's stomach. Alma's eyelids fluttered and she incredibly felt herself getting wet even without being attached—and she absolutely felt the great witch's fingertip, so huge and dangerous but so soft and stimulating, as it slid between the body's legs and caressed its anatomically accurate slit.

"It's too bad that when you're like this you don't have any hole for me to fuck," the witch lamented, "but it's good for a dolly to go without for awhile, I think. You'll get to do lots of other fun things with me, instead! You'll love sleeping in my bed with me, and cuddling me…I'll kiss you and pet you every night, and brush your hair, and sing you songs, and maybe some night when I'm feeling generous and you've been a very, very good dolly, I'll make you big and let you cum a couple of times." Her fingertip circled upon the doll at the point where Alma's clit should have been and, had the resin eyes in the severed head been attached to the inside of the skull with anything more than putty, they would have rolled up into that artificial head.

"Girls are so cruel to their dolls," the man whose identity Alma didn't want to acknowledge said with a chuckle in his low voice. A spank rang out in the air and Sabine gasped in pleasure, saying, "Oh! Master," as the man went on. "Why not give your poor doll one last treat before you finish putting it together? It's been very good…and it's not as if we can ignore how much it's giving up to be your new favorite dolly."

"I guess that's true…here, I know! I love it when all my attention is in my doll and Father does this to me."

Beaming with pleasure Alma had yet to see on her—a pure, bright, honest sort of smile that was somehow the most terrifying thing of all in that moment—Sabine spread the doll's resin legs and, after a bit of careful adjustment of the ball joints of its knees, admired the headless cadaver arranged as though a ready recipient for one of several sexual acts. Then, planting a kiss on the top of Alma's cool resin forehead, Sabine placed that severed head down between the body's splayed legs so that its lips grazed a cunt so smooth it seemed somehow wet simply because of how perfect the material was. At the very least, her lips glided against the surface while she gasped, this spark of stimulation yielding another one of those trapped moans.

"There! Now, you just play with yourself while your mistress plays with her Lord…be sure you finish, though! If I come back before you're done, well, you might be out of luck for a little while."

"Sabine, Sabine, you wicked little bitch…come here—"

As the witch giggled with wild delight to be so called by her dark master, helpless Alma wished once more to scream for help. To scream for release. Anything! Anything at all. What she really wanted more than any of that was to go home—to confront the creature that was stealing her identity, at that very minute walking in through the front door and ingratiating itself with the family as if it had known them for years. For all of its life.

Beyond the resin thighs which barred even her immobile peripheral vision from taking in the context of the sounds Alma heard, the witch gasped amid kisses and the occasional sharp-sounding spank landed by the leader of her coven. With no escape and no choice, no way to turn her head, Alma found that she couldn't stop from stimulating herself. The lips of her mouth brushed the labia of her doll pussy whenever she so much as gasped—generally, as one might suppose, as a result of the sensations from teasing her own cunt without meaning to. Oh, it was torture! Her body throbbed even though she was detached from it and the yearning was no less immense for this separation. Far from it…if anything, her drive to have her craving satisfied was now more powerful than ever.

As the witch let out a particularly obscene, prolonged moan and a piece of furniture shifted beneath the weight of the woman thrown upon it, Alma gave up and parted her lips. At least her tongue was mobile! It slithered out and ran along the carefully carved slit between the doll body's legs, and the caress was so shocking, so powerful, that Alma had the urge to curl her toes.

How strange! All these phantom sensations came upon her as she repeated the motion, the synapses of her brain firing to try to shift a leg or even move an arm.

But the limbs of the body all the while remained immobile. On the other side of the room Sabine, unseen, begged, "Oh! Master, yes, yes, oh, my Dark Lord, please, give me your cock— oh, I can't wait, fuck, you make me so wet just by walking into the room—"

"Ah, Sabine…my unholy daughter. Only you could flatter the Devil, Himself. Here, feel—"

"Fuck! Oh, sire—master, oh, master, your prick is always so hot to the touch! It makes my hand feel like a doll's hand, it's so big, oh—fuck!"

At Sabine's pained scream, as much of agony as it was of sheer orgiastic delight, Alma's tongue moved into rapid work slightly motivated by sadistic pleasure at the thought of the Devil's monstrous cock jamming deep into the bitch's hateful cunt. Oh, but it was a hot cunt, and the thought of Sabine being fucked by some man moved Alma in more ways than sadistic ones.

She was envious, bitterly envious of both of them, and hated not being able to see past the resin of her own thigh.

Yes, all that was going on and she couldn't even look!

Her efforts at self-pleasure, then, were somehow largely motivated by spite. That should have been embarrassing, but once you were reduced to a severed head you tended to be well past the concept of dignity as a whole. It didn't matter. Nothing mattered.

There Alma was, the pleasure building between her thighs while she licked her own cool doll-pussy, the control and precision of pleasure this afforded her a unique experience like truly no other.

Why, if she had been left here to her own devices, or been able to remove her own head and put it down there, she never would have needed another human being again! It was incredible to tease herself, running the probe of her tongue just down to what should have been the dripping entrance of her cunt and instead meeting that hard resin crack that was impassible no matter how realistic the pleasure she felt, or dreamed she felt.

Furniture rattled off in another part of the room. Alma's pace increased even further while Sabine, sounding as though she almost sobbed, screamed amid the rhythmic rattling of the table upon which she sat.

"Master, Master! Oh, Hail Satan! Hail Satan! Fuck, fuck, fuck, yes, oh, Satan, my jackal—"

"About to cum already, Sabine? That's good, that's very good…let me have it, ah, I love the energy that peels off of you…"

As Sabine's voice rose up in a sharp cry, a shout of pleasure that surely echoed through the house, Alma's fast-working tongue focused around the area of her missing clit. The sensations were nonetheless as potent as they would have been if the nerves were still there and, pushed onward by her mistress's heartfelt cry, Alma's mouth opened wide in a shockingly powerful orgasm of her own.

While her lips trembled and her heavy-lidded eyes fluttered completely shut under the waves of pleasure, the demon prince's thrusting continued to rattle the table until, with a groan from him and another scream from Sabine, all the noises finally came to a stop.

"How pleasing you are to me," the man murmured to Sabine. "My very own favorite doll."

"Oh, Father!"

Their lips produced a series of low, lurid smacks; so did something else. A zipper went up and while, for her own part, Alma slowly recovered her senses, the man told Sabine, "I have to go for a little while, Sabine, just away on business…but I'll be back before you know it. Look for my signs."

"I will." Another kiss rang out in the air: noxious green light flashed in the room and stung Alma's eyes. By the time her vision cleared, Sabine was by her side again, smiling down at her and carefully cradling the head—that head that was, Alma was slowly appreciating, really and truly all she consisted of—between those giant hands. "Well! Did you have a good time? I hope you got to finish at least once…it might be awhile before I take off your head or make you big again. All right…"

Smiling, holding Alma in one hand, Sabine used the other to sit the body up. Though it stayed uncannily, it slumped forward without the head to produce the final amount of tension, the silver hook upon the stump of its neck inviting Alma's placement. As Sabine ran her fingertip into the groove beneath Alma's chin, the neck hole by means of which the hook was meant to be pulled through the head to keep it attached to the neck and promote the integrity of the doll, another, altogether more powerful kind of pleasure rushed through the witch's victim. Having Sabine's finger there was like having every part of her touched at once, somehow! Like Alma's internal organs were being caressed by God. Her mouth opened as if to beg for more and Sabine laughed at that.

"Like having your neck hole fucked, do you? Not many dollies do…well, maybe if you're good, that's how we'll play one of these times. For now, let's get you dressed and off to bed! Dollies can't be late for bedtime…don't worry, though. I'll be sure to hold you all through the night. Aren't you a lucky little dolly?"

The Witch's Dirty Laundry

SABINE STRODE into the laundry room wearing nothing but her underwear. This, you'll surely want to know, was as black as her hair; black as her soul; black as the pupils of those green-crowned eyes that landed upon her own nude reflection and smiled into the mirror.

"Isn't the male gaze interesting," she said as though aloud to a friend. While she spoke, she turned away from the mirror to let it see her ass as she bent to open the door of the washer. "First, that term! I hate it. "The male gaze." As if women are incapable of objectifying women! As if women learned how to be lesbians only by aping men. Haven't these philosophers ever heard of the concept of parallel thought before? The Zeitgeist? You know."

With a great huff, the witch straightened up and tossed a few armfuls of laundry into the bin open nearby. The cheeky black thong that was her poor excuse for underwear had ridden up the crack of her ass and, seeing the effect in the mirror, she decided against fixing it. Instead she propped a foot upon the washer to lean forward as she sorted out the clothes.

"I'm not saying that the male gaze isn't a concept in and of itself, but, well, the idea that artwork featuring beautiful women is just a manifestation of "the male gaze" has always rubbed me the wrong way. Can't women appreciate aesthetics? Can't women admire other women?"

Pushing a few strands of black hair over her shoulder to send them streaming down her back, Sabine peeled, from amid the throng of lacy black garments and flowing gowns, a man's dress shirt. She straightened it out, lashed it in the air, then frowned and slapped at a particularly egregious wrinkle with the back of her hand.

"For instance, I don't think Sappho was pandering to the male gaze. I think she was pandering to her own gaze. And what about when *men a*re objectified in artwork? Like all those hot boys in Caravaggio, or—I don't know, the young man that captivated Shakespeare? You knew that, right? That Shakespeare was bisexual. Read your sonnets with their scholarly context and you'll be very surprised…then all those plays about sexy women dressed up as men will make a lot more sense."

Laying the shirt over the edge of the drier, Sabine turned away for the ironing board that rested against the wall. As she snapped it open and its metal legs ground into place with a rusty whine, Sabine continued, "The truth is that it's not the male gaze…it's the sexual gaze. And the sexual gaze can alight on anything. A man, a woman, a plant. What the term "the male gaze" teaches us is that men are bad. That their mere gaze sexualizes a woman. My mother always told me, "Sabine, honey, you'd might as well wear whatever you want, because you could be the most modest girl in the world and the boys would still find a way to get off to your ankle." What about the women, Mommy? Goodness! I love a good ankle, myself."

With a laugh down at her own and an artful turn of her delicate foot, Sabine plucked up the shirt and arranged it on the ironing board. Now she was a bit tenderer with it, running her hand over the fabric, her fingertip caressing down the valley of a wrinkle along the breast. While her thumb and forefinger idly rubbed back and forth upon the fabric of the collar, she said, "By treating the concept we refer to as "the male gaze" instead as "the sexual gaze," artwork becomes different. What does it teach us now? The term "the sexual gaze" teaches us that anything, in the right context, can be sexualized. That sexuality is a matter of viewpoint…that beauty is natural any inequality between the sexes on the basis of aesthetic factors is a condition of social living."

Sabine turned away and leaned up to a nearby cabinet, huffing a little. Oh, she wasn't short—if anything she was quite tall—but for some reason this world was just built for men. "See what I mean?" She glanced over her shoulder to the mirror again and thumbed toward that too-high cabinet, her breasts lifting high with her renewed efforts to reach. Finally, annoyed, she climbed atop the washer to carefully balance on her knees. "This house is years old. Decades! Who's done the laundry for decades? Women. And how are these cabinets placed along the wall? At a height suiting men!

"That's the real problem. It's not the sexual gaze in artwork, or even in life. It's that men are only ever thinking about other men. Men are, or have been, anyway, the carpenters, the architects, the engineers. The scientists! Did you know most research studies exclude women because there are just too many variables involved with them? As if that means we don't count! Or how about the fact that the speculum was designed by a sadistic man who got off on torturing his slaves, which is how he designed the thing in the first place?"

After getting back down off the washer with the iron in her hand, she looked around for the outlet. "Where were we…yes, that's it." Plugging the device in and leaving it upright upon the edge of the ironing board to heat up, Sabine looked around for her cigarettes, remembered she hadn't brought them, and while leaving the room she said, "Sex is a transcendent experience, or it should be. Western religious connotations aside, the sacredness of sex is celebrated all over the world. Tantric sex is only the longest-standing form—most pre-Roman goddess religions embraced sacred prostitution of one kind or another, and transgender priestesses, too."

Taking the stairs from the basement two at a time, Sabine sprang through her kitchen, passed into the drawing room, and, as she bent over her pack of cigarettes, produced a triumphant, "Aha!"

First she pulled her hair up into a messy bun, lifting all those black strands high away from her shoulders to get it from her face. Exposed to the cold of the house, her nipples tightened and the flesh of her white breasts dimpled; she shuddered but nonetheless carried on while lighting a cigarette from the pack. "So, if sex is transcendent—and that's a debate in and of itself, but let's assume for the sake of argument that there must be something special about this act that the Catholic church begs us to keep to ourselves—then the sexual gaze is elevating. Sacred."

The witch took a long, sighing inhalation of her cigarette, eyes fluttering shut as the nicotine rushed through her blood. She stood, one hand on her hip, appreciating the flavor of the tobacco before she glanced at the clock, tutted, and strode back down to the basement with her cigarette trailing smoke behind her. "The sexual gaze, when applied to activities that are not inherently sexual, shows us that everything has the transcendent property of sex. Everything. There is aesthetic beauty everywhere—beauty itself is the context, the purpose of the world. Order is pleasing to us, beautiful. Disorder is displeasing to us, ugly."

Sniffing with displeasure at the pile of clothes, Sabine turned her attention instead to the man's shirt and the iron beside it. She removed the cigarette from her mouth only briefly, only to tap her pinkie against her tongue and thereafter press it to the sizzling surface of the iron. Pleased, Sabine placed her cigarette back in her mouth and merrily puffed while spraying the shirt with a few spritzes of steam. "You know, I've always liked old pin-up girls...the figures are nice to look at, but the scenarios are my real favorite part of those paintings by, oh, Glen Elvgren or Art Frahm. Especially Art Frahm—if you know anything about pin-ups, he was the guy who kept putting celery into all his paintings. Whenever his women were coming home from the store, they were always buying celery for some reason. Probably says something about his childhood, but I hate to speculate about things like that."

At last—at long last!—Sabine smoothed a long-fingered hand down the front of the shirt. Then, gazing tenderly upon it, petting it a few more times, she let this free hand pin the shirt to the board and ran the hot iron over its smooth, high-thread surface. "Oh! Look at that...I love ironing, it's so satisfying. Nice and smooth...isn't that nice, ah..."

The cigarette dropped a piece of ash upon her bosom from where it hung at the corner of her mouth, but Sabine paid it no mind. She was far too busy caressing the shirt with the iron, smoothing out its wrinkles and stroking her fingertips along it as tenderly as she might a lover's body. "The thing that's fun about pin-up scenarios is that they're sometimes so creative. Oh, you have the classics...women on beaches, sunbathing in the yards, waiting in skimpy lingerie for their lovers. Then you have other ones, way more fun. Girls bowling, or female firefighters, or just a hot housewife getting on a city bus at the second her skirt blows up. Pin-ups always look shocked, too. 'Oh no,' they seem to be asking, 'how could this happen *here?*'

"That's why I love pin-up girls. They teach us that beauty is absolutely, positively everywhere you look—even in shocking places, mundane places, places you'd never expect. 'You mean even now I'm beautiful? You mean even while I'm just doing the laundry, you're getting off to it!' It's flattering to some women and it's wretched to others, but it's not just men doing it. It's women, too. I'm a woman, and I look at pin-ups all the time. This is being written by a woman, too—oh, well, of course I know it's a book."

Laughing, Sabine lifted the shirt with a roll of her eyes and flipped it over upon the board to do its back. The soft hiss of the iron as she slid it along the fabric reminded her pleasantly of a man's pain, and she smiled while she said, "I'm a witch, after all…a very powerful one. You think dolls and human furniture all the only things I can do, can make? Oh, I can turn a man into anything, as long as I'm inspired to."

As she set down the iron, Sabine glowed with satisfaction. She paused only for an appreciative drag upon her cigarette, then caressed the front of the shirt again. The dark tips of her nails tickled over the surface of the fabric and she said, "Men can be objectified, too, you know. Of course, that's such a social subversion when it happens in the 21st century that it's almost fetishistic, but you'd be surprised at the mainstream places you'll see it. Look at Fabio—old romance book covers, you know. Why, this story alone! Do you know how many stock photos of shirtless men you get when you look for the words "sexy ironing?" More than anybody would have expected, I'll tell you that much."

A spot! Out, damn spot. Sabine sucked a tooth and, licking the edge of her thumb, rubbed the spot on the collar with a little witch's spittle to get it from her sight. Finally, the shirt looked good as new. Pleased, Sabine picked it up to admire it again, then began, one button at a time, to work it open. "The truth is that the human gaze is sexual. If I show you a cactus that looks like a penis, you'll laugh just the same as a middle school boy. If I were to put a dog in a bikini, my first instinct would be to take satirical pictures of it and give them out to friends in calendar form. Sex sells. Etcetera. But beyond the shallow, commodified, or exploitative relationship Western society has developed with sex, there's something much, much deeper at work."

Upstairs, the house's doorbell rang. Smiling, Sabine put out her cigarette in the nearby wash basin and slid the shirt over her shoulders. While she buttoned a couple of holes placed over her bosom, just enough to give the shirt the effect that it was struggling to stay closed (and, in truth, it was struggling quite a lot over those voluminous but magically perky tits of hers), Sabine took the stairs from the basement at a far more leisurely pace than before.

"I think about the paintings of martyr saints a lot, and not just because I'm a witch, and therefore predisposed to think about spiritual matters all the time. It's not just because I'm a sadomasochist, either, though there's also that. Instead, well, I think about the paintings of martyr saints because—just look at them! Saint Francis reclining with his crucifix erection in his lap, Saint Teresa with her eyes rolling back in her head—ah, ah, ah, oh, angel, stab me with your spear, ah!" Sabine stuck out her tongue and crossed her eyes, panting exaggeratedly, then laughed to herself and dropped the affect when the doorbell rang again. "Coming," she called.

"Anyway—you see, anything's sexual, everything's sexual, and sexuality is intimately linked with the divine. Why do you think Jove is always 'descending upon' helpless women? Why do you suppose sex is sacred in the first place? It's a symbol…a symbol for how your meek, humble little human body is getting God-fucked every single day, whether you know it or not…but especially when you know it."

With a shudder, Sabine ran her hand over herself, smoothed the collar of her shirt, and, smiling expectantly, opened the front door of her house. The cable guy on the other side lifted his head and his eyes lit up.

"You must be here about the set-top box," she said, leaning against the doorway.

Three minutes later they were tripping all over each other on their way into the den, the sweaty repairman's clothes falling off of him and upon the floor in rapid succession. His cock was already hard and the witch laughed to grab it, batting her eyes as the burly young man pushed her back upon the arm of the couch. "I'll bet you've dreamed of this day since the second you were hired to be a cable guy. Aha—" Her hand pressed to his mouth as he tried to kiss her lips. She shoved him down to his knees by the jaw, saying, "Let's see if you can make me cum through the underwear, and if you're a really good boy, I'll let you fuck me bareback."

Oh! He was a really good boy. Really, really good. While the twenty-something blue collar worker tickled Sabine's thighs with his grizzled beard even as his tongue teased her clit through the lacy thong, Sabine clutched the curls of his dark head and kept him pressed down tight against her groin. Those limbs clamped shut on either side of his head and she moaned, gasping, saying while he couldn't hear it amid the pressure of her legs, "Oh, oh—oh, you see, sex, ah, it's a form of—trance-induction, hypnotism, oh, yes, yes!"

Fuck, her pussy was so wet! Thank Satan. It had been a few days since she'd felt really horny. Always such a relief to get all nice and turned on after a dry spell. While she ground her hips against the stranger's face, one foot resting upon his back, Sabine moaned. "Yes, fuck, oh, oh, I get you all good and horny and the more turned on you get, the more your higher-level consciousness falls…gets animal, fuck, yes, oh, reptilian, primitive, fuck, oh, I love it! And when you're in the deep, deep center of your brain I could tell you anything…plant any suggestion, oh, fuck, make you my slave! You want to be my slave, don't you? Sabine's little fuck-slave...well, if you really wanted to be my slave, then you'd spend your money on my stories and the stories about my friends and neighbors without even a second thought. Maybe if you do that, and you're as good a reader as this cable guy is a random lay, then I'll visit you in your dreams some night...we can get personal. Until then—oh, fuck!"

Her limbs tightened further around his head and she gasped, almost sobbing when that naughty tongue of his pushed the thong aside and plunged into her cunt. The sudden invasion after stimulus delivered only through the barrier of lace made her wail with her orgasm, her dripping wet pussy fluttering around the tip of the cable guy's tongue. "Fuck! Fuck! Oh, what a good boy you are...oh, yes, oh, fuck...hold on."

He had been starting to get up but Sabine lifted a leg and pressed her foot to his face. The man groaned and fell back on his haunches, pushing kisses all down the arch of her lovely bare foot. Sighing, spreading her toes, Sabine said, "You'd be a very good dog, wouldn't you?"

"I'd be whatever you want me to be, baby," he said while she laughed.

"That's the attitude! I was just telling a friend of mine how eager men are to be objectified, from a fetishistic standpoint... often it really doesn't matter what the object or even the situation is. It's the mere idea of being degraded by a beautiful woman"—she slid her big toe into his mouth and grinned, flush-faced, while he fellated it—"that causes the enhancement of the erotic experience. Because, of course, beauty is and should be an elevating experience, and the same is true of sex. So, when it's perverted in the literal sense...used to degrade... then it's very, *very* fun and naughty...oh, you're awfully good at that, actually."

Making sure he followed the motions of her hand, Sabine slid her foot from his mouth, then spread her legs as wide as they went. With the black tip of one carefully manicured nail, the witch pulled aside the soaked crotch of her thong and showed the stranger her glistening pussy, bare and flushed as the cheeks of a virgin on her wedding night. "Go ahead…I promised to let you stick it in me…but you have to do me a special favor, please."

He was already standing up, an ape with his hard cock in his hand. Now he paused, trying to brace himself for a strange request or at the very least struggling to parse words at that moment in time. Pouting sweetly, teeth sinking into her lower lip, Sabine asked, "Will you please be sure to cum on this shirt? It's my boyfriend's, see…I love for him to know that I've been fooling around with strangers."

"Oh! Fuck, holy shit—uh—sure, baby, I'll cum wherever you want, but—uh, he's not coming home, is he—"

"Oh, no…not until after you're gone. Go on, oh, please, hurry! My pussy is just aching to be filled. Don't you want to fuck me?"

He sure did. The witch gasped, laughing with unexpected delight at the eagerness the man showed to press his hard cock against her drenched lips. As he teased the hole that did, it was perhaps worth saying, genuinely ache, Sabine moaned and unbuttoned her shirt. The fabric fell free of her heaving breasts as the stranger slid into her. Oh, Satan! His cock was so small compared to yours, Master! Still very fine, though, yes, oh, she appreciated dicks of all shapes and sizes.

"What a good boy you are…yes, that's right, oh, fuck, yeah, give it to me hard, hard—harder! Oh, yes, yes, good and deep, oh, that's how I like it—"

Sabine's back arched and she displayed herself to the stranger who pounded away between her legs. He marveled, one large hand running over her contorting ribs and the tight line of her stomach. "Fuck, oh, baby, you're so hot—"

"You like fucking my bare pussy with that big, hard cock,

huh? Oh, yeah, you like it dirty, don't you—me, too, yes, fuck, oh, yeah, that's right, I want you to get that prick all nice and hard, all nice and big and hard and ready to explode, and then I want you to take it out and just soak this dirty old ma— shirt, this dirty old shirt with cum, oh, yes, yeah, yeah, fuck, you like that? Gonna cum where I tell you to cum, you dirty dog? Yes, yeah, oh, yeah, oh, fuck, pound me harder—"

"You're a real freaky bitch!"

"Fuck yeah I am, fuck, fuck yeah, oh, fuck, I'm about to cum, oh, shit—" The witch reached between their legs and rapidly fondled her clit, those burning green eyes boring up into the stranger's while he fucked her with the shirt pinned between her body and the couch.

"What a dirty fucking pervert you are, too—oh, yeah, that's right. Seeing all these bored fucking housewives all day, all of them just dying for a hot, young stud to fill their cunts up…oh, yeah, baby, I bet you think about it all day long, don't you, you dirty fucking goon…I bet you go home and jerk off all night to what it would have been like if you'd only had the balls to bend Mrs. Johnson over her TV stand and fuck the shit out of her once she's got access to her reruns of *The Days of Our Lives* again—oh! Fuck! Yeah!"

The cable guy had gotten the inspiration to slap her ass and, moaning, Sabine lifted her leg to give him better access. Her hands ran up over her breasts and into her hair while, back arching, the witch panted through clenched teeth and twisted her legs tight around the young man's ass. His dick felt hard as marble inside of her, and at the feeling of it slamming again and again into that sensitive g-spot *Cosmopolitan* magazine so loved to worship, Sabine released a passionate scream of the same pleasure that caused her dripping pussy to convulse.

While her second orgasm shuddered through her, she tugged at her own hair and screamed, "Hail Satan! Hail Satan! Oh, fuck, yeah, fuck me for Satan, baby—"

"Satan? Damn, what is this…oh, man, your pussy feels like paradise—fuck, I don't care—"

"Nobody does, nobody ever does—yeah, yeah, that's right, baby, that's right, oh, fuck, hold on, hold on, take me over the back of the couch—"

Sabine squirmed and whined as the cable guy pulled out of her, but soon enough he tugged her upright—by the collar of that shirt, no less—and pushed her over the sofa as instructed. While, semi-inverted, Sabine clutched at the cushion before her, the cable guy spread her legs and then, experimentally, her ass. His thumb brushed against the hole but, probably owing only to the unprotected nature of the encounter, he decided to continue enjoying the already risky enough cunt that oozed for his attention. While his cock worked into her, Sabine pushed herself up a little and looked into the reflective glass in the center of the coffee table.

"Oh, fuck…of course, the real purpose of a trance state is to maximize one's power over one's own mind. Hypnotism…"

"Are you talking to me?"

"Just keep fucking me, oh, go on, stuff me full—that's all I'm saying, all I'm saying is how much I want your dick, baby—" Rolling the eyes she knew he couldn't see, Sabine looked significantly at the reflection in the glass and went on at a softer volume. "Anyway…oh, um, fuck, uh, hypnotism is really about bettering oneself. Stripping away all the layers of trauma and fatigue and who you *think* you are, and getting—getting to the control-mechanism consciousness in the—the center—oh, yeah, yeah, baby, oh, you love that tight pussy, oh, fuck, yeah, I love that big, hard dick—"

"Shit, you've got the finest cunt I've ever used—oh, fuck, you're going to make me explode, baby, oh, baby—"

"Mm, yeah, that's right…that's right, get yourself right up to that nice edge…oh, yeah, use my cute little pussy to come for Satan, yeah, baby, oh, yeah—oh, yeah, see"—she lowered her voice and peered at the glass again—"I could tell this loser to do anything right now, fuck, yeah, just like I could tell you to do anything, good or bad…I could be really mean, or I could tell you to continue improving as a person. Oh, yeah, baby, it turns me on when you eat right and live healthily…fuck, yeah, ten years from now you'll be eating wholesome dinners every night and asking yourself what happened. Satan was what happened, baby! Remember to thank Satan! Remember to thank Sabine! Praise Satan! Praise Satan! Oh! Fuck! Fuck! Yeah!"

Her back arched as another orgasm came upon her, this fast fluttering of her pussy sufficient to draw a sudden outburst from the stranger's dick. He gasped sharply, working even faster at the pressure, then drawing sharply out of her and capturing his cock in his hand. With a pleasurable gasp, Sabine looked over her shoulder and watched through heavy-lidded eyes as the groaning man jerked off on her ass, the tip of his prick aimed for the fabric of her shirt.

"Yeah, baby, oh, yeah, make it all dirty—that's right, stain this shirt, fuck, oh, give it your cum, go on, cum for Satan. Do it, do it, hail, Satan!"

Her voice rose in a cackle as, with a noise almost of shock, the young man came. A few ropes of white cum jetted across the back of the shirt along with Sabine's thick lily thigh. "Oh, yeah," he groaned while she hid her second eyeroll. "Yeah, oh…fuck, baby…"

"That's all you can say, isn't it? 'Fuck, baby,' very limited vocabulary…just like what most dogs have."

"Huh?"

"You heard me." Cold as ice now, Sabine sat up and pushed her hair out of the back of her shirt. She ran her hand over the fabric and sat upright to let her legs hang free over the edge of the couch. "You're about as much good as a dog…look at you, coming in here and humping me until you're satisfied."

"Hey, baby, don't be so *ruff* with— huh? Rough—*ruff!*" The man's eyes widened in shock, his hand lifting to his mouth even as it emitted another bark. Sabine threw her head back and laughed in devilish delight, pushing the idiot away from her with the flat of her foot.

"No barking in the house…get that under control or I'll start keeping you outside."

"*Ruff! Ruff! Woof woof woof!*"

Soon his legs gave out beneath him and he was on his hands and knees. Sabine cackled in outrageous delight and slid the shirt from her shoulders. "That's right…you didn't think you could just come in here and fuck me for free, do you? A witch? How cute. That's also a very doglike trait…yes, you're cute. And cuter by the second!"

He sure was. Hands and feet quickly became paws; a scruffy beard developed into something more like an animal's mane; the barking became a nonstop panic and within that barking mouth human teeth became the gnashing fangs of a mongrel that snarled furiously at this betrayal. What should it have expected? There are always consequences to casual sex… don't horror movies teach people anything, anymore? Or sex education?

"Sex education never taught anyone anything, Sabine."

At the female voice behind her, Sabine gasped and whirled in delight. "Oh, Master! You're here as a woman today."

And what a woman! Fuck, a real fox. There was no denying that Sabine was one of the hottest witches around…but Satan, when he chose to become a she, was perhaps among the most exquisite of all beings to have ever graced the planet Earth. Lest we forget, we are talking about an angel, here. A fallen one, but an angel nonetheless. And angels are genderless, generally speaking.

"I just thought it sounded fun," said the Prince of Darkness through his female mouth, running a hand over his sumptuous breast and smiling at the cum that covered it. Satan's short black hair, curled in the updo of a kitschy 1950s housewife, even bore a little strand of the stuff; the witch leaned forward and wiped it away with a fingertip, offering it to the Lord of the Flies. Satan's lips parted and the female body's tongue slithered out to lap the substance from the tip of Sabine's nail. "After all! It seemed to me you were going on an awful lot about men wanting to be objectified, and the male gaze—or sexual gaze, if you'd really rather—applying to men in equal measure…this form seemed appropriate, then."

Satan moaned while the witch ran her hands over these wonderful, magical breasts still covered in cable guy cum. While Sabine lowered her head to suckle on a nipple, the Prince of Darkness went on through that supple woman's mouth, "But surely you can't deny, Sabine, that the vast majority of works utilizing this kind of objectification prominently feature women. Moreover, unbelievable women. Women who are either extraordinarily disempowered or altogether too yielding. Too pining. And heaven forfend a woman is herself sexually desiring! That's the greatest sin of all…it's too horrible, too frightening, to think that a woman might encourage the male gaze. Might see the power in it."

"But, Lord…" Sabine slid down between her Master's spread knees. On the floor, the German shepherd whined wretchedly, scratched at its ear, seemed as though to boggle as the witchy woman who had done this to it ate out the even witchier woman who had manifested from the shirt. Ignoring the mongrel, Sabine's fingers trailed along her Master's clearly yearning cunt. She continued on to the Dark Lord, "You forget that women can have plenty of power over other women… why, your beauty is so captivating, especially when you're in this form, that you could make me do anything."

"I certainly could, Sabine! But I could make you do anything any time…you and all the rest of your coven are my devoted slaves—oh, yes! Oh, and talented." Moaning, Satan arched her aching clit up against the tongue the witch liberally applied against it. With one hand extended across the back of the couch, the devil snapped the fingers of the other, then whistled between her moans. "You, dog, come here."

Reluctant, tail and ears drooping with terror, the shepherd that had once been the cable guy edged toward the couch. Satan leaned forward and plucked a hair from the beast's head, blowing it into the center of the room with a puff of unholy air from her ruby lips. As the hair wafted to the floor, from it sprang a perfect replication of the cable guy. This new simp stood, dazed, looking down first at the dog and then at the women playing on the couch. The dog's jaw dropped and a new, sharper set of whines came upon it. It turned and urgently pawed at Satan's bare leg but both women hissed at it, the Prince of Darkness kicking it away.

"Shoo! Scram, go on—you stick around here too long and readers will get the idea you're part of the point. Then we'll be in trouble…we're done with you. You"—Satan gestured at the replica, then at the television—"fix the cable, or whatever nonsense reason he ended up coming here today, then let yourself out and take over his life."

Gasping, the Devil let the female body's head fall back against the couch. As those broad hips bucked up against Sabine's fast-working mouth, feminized demon fingers curled through her hair. "Oh! Ah! Fuck, yes, I suppose you are quite right, though…inasmuch that sex can be used for a motivator, a very helpful motivator, for both sexes. Yes! Oh! Fuck, fuck, your little tongue is so fast, Sabine—"

As Satan spread her legs wider, the witch responded eagerly. She kept the Devil's labia spread wide and suckled on that tiny nub of flesh, somewhat amazed at the flow of arousal that had quickly come to drench those folds. While her tongue then trailed down to probe a few rapid times in and out of the Devil's begging hole, the cable man in the background at last tore his eyes from the scene and bent to fix whatever he'd come to fix. The dog, meanwhile, had crawled off to adapt to the reality of its new existence.

"Don't worry," gasped Satan toward the reflection in the middle of the coffee table, "long-term, the dog will be well-loved…it just needs to be punished right now. Can't get it into its head that this new state is a reward, after all! Though an awful lot of you out there would certainly love to be turned into Sabine's dog, wouldn't you…of course you would. I love it every once in a while, myself." Winking, Satan then gasped sharply. The body wrapped its legs around the witch's head and, in response, her tongue worked all the harder, all the faster, into the Prince of Darkness's sweetly drenched hole.

"Fuck, yes, oh, Sabine, I suppose you're right—I suppose it's right to say that sex is empowering, and that's what makes degradation so exciting…oh, fuck, yeah, that's why men like me like it! Like to be used, even feminized by women…oh, Sabine, Sabine! Fuck, yes, oh, fuck, that's right—"

Sabine knew better, by this point in her relationship with the Dark Lord, than to take her tongue out. She kept it in there, lapping up the rushing splatter of girl-cum as Satan moaned sharply and tugged at her with every limb. "Oh, fuck—Sabine, Sabine, fuck your Master—"

"I'll go get the cock," said the witch brightly, springing up, then stopped by the clutch of Satan's hand tight around her arm.

"There's no time…I need it now, oh, fuck, I've been so fucking horny ever since that boy of yours came all over me—here, slut—"

Tugging Sabine upright by her shoulder, the Devil tore away the lacy thong of Sabine's panties and grinned at her scream. Satan then plunged a pair of fingers into her aching cunt and produced a startled moan. While the witch writhed,

Satan crooked the feminine body's fingers to tickle Sabine's insides, then drew the soaking digits from her clenching hole. Sabine gasped as the touch trailed up over her clit. On this caress, that small nub began at once to grow. Shocked, delighted, Sabine oversaw the development of her own cock while Satan ran female hands all up and down its shaft.

"What a splendid girl-cock you have, Sabine…I love to bring it out of you every once in a while! Oh, it's much better to take your natural one than to take that toy of yours. The toy is just convenient…and I love to snap it off your little cunnies when you're done with it, watch you bleed all over the floor, but that's quite literally another story, isn't it…go on."

Seeing the thing had grown to full length, Satan leaned back in the arm of the couch, legs spread wide. "Fuck your Master, oh, yes, fill me up, Sabine—what a privilege I give you—"

"Yes, yes! Such a privilege—oh, Master, you're so good to me—" Delighted as a girl on her birthday, Sabine passionately kissed the mouth of this beautiful common enemy of man, her tongue plunging in between those luscious red lips and against a matching, waiting organ. Meanwhile, Sabine fondled another organ, the new cock that throbbed between her legs. She moaned to feel it, tugging at it, her eyes fluttering shut with the weight of her hefty sigh. "Oh! Master…yes, oh, you're so kind to give me a thing like this…and your pussy! Oh, you're so wet, Master."

"I love being fucked by you, Sabine," crooned the feminine Devil, one hand up in its body's hair while it gasped. Sabine ran the head of her cock along the dripping labia of the Devil and grinned, beginning to ease in only once the ache became too much. Satan's brow furrowed and a cry rose up, high and beautiful and deadly; Sabine's own scream joined along, the pleasure at once as crushing as a tidal wave. The deeper the witch pushed into her Master's cunt, the deeper she wanted to push—the more rapidly and hungrily that cunt seemed to draw her in, begging her for more, until she was up to the hilt in Satan. Sabine's eyes rolled up into her head and she groaned, her hips beginning to work steadily in and out against the pussy of her dark god.

"Oh! Fuck! Satan! Hail Satan!"

"I have to go get something from my truck," said the automaton of the cable guy, who wandered listlessly off in the midst of his duty and probably didn't even see the outrageous scene unfolding behind him. While the girls fucked away, the sofa squeaked in protest beneath the vigorous activities performed upon its surface. Sabine, finding her rhythm with one foot flat on the ground and the other leg bent to kneel upon the cushion, only fucked harder in response to the furniture's cry.

"Oh, Sabine, that's it, that's right, oh, fuck, give your Master a good pounding—oh, Sabine! None of my girls can fill me up like you...I love the way you stuff my pussy. Fuck! Oh, I much prefer to be a man all the time, oh, yes, but I love being a woman for you because there's nothing on Earth like feeling your dick inside me...oh, yes, give me that witch's dick, Sabine, Sabine! Fuck, make your Master cum!"

Moaning, head thrown back, Sabine worked her hips all the harder against her master's. For her own part, the witch was overwhelmed with pleasure and almost had to struggle to maintain her grip on Satan's legs. It was hard to remember or think of anything else but the feeling, the wet embrace and the pressure that Sabine wanted under any circumstances to increase—both in herself and in her god. She bent down to kiss Satan's moaning mouth, the wet lash of that borrowed tongue sending sparks of pleasure that streaked right down from her mouth to the tip of her throbbing cock. While the member's ache somehow only seemed to increase, Sabine groaned aloud and turned her face away only when Satan smiled.

"And lest we forget, Sabine…not even witches are immune to the trance-inducing powers of sex. All it takes is an overwhelmed moment, and any idea could be implanted—oh, fuck, that's right, oh, all kinds of ideas—that's the real source of a witch's power, yes, yes, that's right—it comes from the things they say to themselves in the heat, the passion of sex.

"Power is begot by simply observing power—that's the real nature of the male gaze. When we catch ourselves following the pattern of the male gaze, we'd ought not to remonstrate ourselves…far from it. We should celebrate it, we should be excited: we find ourselves in the position of power sufficient that we are able to look upon the object of the male gaze and enjoy it, which was once only the privilege of the powerful and wealthy with access to art. Moreover, we have the knowledge sufficient to even know what the male gaze is, or how it impacts society…or is impacted by society. The chicken and the egg. Either way, the education sufficient to recognize that cultural leitmotif is, in and of itself, another sign of power. Of privilege."

Gasping, Satan glanced down from beneath a furrowed brow to watch the witch's cock ram home into that well-used cunt. "Oh! Fuck! So! Oh, fuck, yes, you see, the male gaze is the male gaze because it's really a form of objectification that occurs not based on sex, but based on power; and men are the class with current social control. So in a sense, you are right, Sabine…but you must never discount the power dynamics of sex, and how sexuality factors into social roles.

"While you've got Satan whispering in your ear that sex makes you powerful, remember that many more, far less lucky girls have the Christian monkey on their back. They feel that shame every time they have sex, every time they see an arousing image. Why, soon they've convinced themselves that sex is inherently objectifying when the problem isn't sex, or even sexualization. The problem is what we as a society think sexualization gives us the right to do to another person. We think that just because someone is sexualized or a moment is erotic that it naturally follows that consent is assumed…but, why, it's not, not at all. In fact, I would argue that eroticism is itself a separate issue from sex. Sex is a product of the body—eroticism is a function of the soul. The problem then is not the male gaze itself, nor even the term "the male gaze," as you were focused on at the start of this discussion. The problem is the Western relationship to sexuality, and how disconnected its sexuality has become from—from the soul—oh, Sabine, fuck, you're just so hard, oh—"

"Master! Master, ah, I don't know if I can last any longer—oh, I'm not used to having something like this—"

"That's okay, that's okay, oh, that's right, oh, Sabine, Sabine! Fuck! Cum in me, witch! Cum in your Dark Lord!"

"Fuck! Satan! Satan! Hail Satan! Hail Satan! Oh, fuck, yes!"

While Satan's pussy clenched sharply around Sabine's dick, the witch moaned and shuddered. She caught her Master's soft mouth and plunged deep with kisses, groaning while her hard prick at last burst beneath its pressure and shot a few shockingly pleasurable ropes of cum deep into the Devil's belly. While the women moaned, tangled together upon the couch, the cable guy returned with the new set top box and removed the old, malfunctioning one. "That should do it," he said, hands on his hips, looking satisfied once he'd plugged it in. "I'll go ahead and set up your new remote—oh, you got a universal one?"

"Let me do it," said Sabine woozily, face in the Devil's bosom. Pleased to have his job finished for him, the cable guy nodded, then turned and made his way to the front door. He stopped and chuckled at the dog who whined sadly in the front hall.

"What a cute dog! Who's a good boy? Who's a good boy? That's right, you're a good boy!"

Then, having ruffled the shepherd's ears, the replacement cable guy went whistling off and shut the door behind him.

"The greater problem," said Sabine with a sigh, sitting up and pushing her hair back from her flushed face while her dick once more receded back to normal clit size, "is that Western society—and modern Western art—has become divorced from spiritual matters. What do modern transgressive and erotic writers, for instance, have to say? Nothing! Nothing at all. It's all a bunch of edgy nonsense. Erotica used to mean something. Used to have value just like any other form of literature…just look at the Marquis de Sade.

"Even if he was using sophist nonsense in every argument against faith, the Marquis was still arguing against faith. He still had something to say. Now, with most creatives also identifying as secular or, at best 'not religious, but spiritual,' what is transgressive work going to argue against? Society, itself? Okay, how edgy. How unrealistic! Arguing against society is like arguing against living on Earth. We have to have society if we're going to progress as a species.

"Then, should it argue against modernity? Modernity is everything we enjoy about life at present—convenience, casualness. Cable!" Sabine waved a hand at the television in the corner of the room. "People love modern life. Even the edgy ones who claim they don't like it love it—maybe especially them. So now you've got a lot of graphic fiction that has no real point, and if it has a point, the point is usually just 'Bad people are bad.' How original! Thanks, Bret Easton Ellis."

The Devil snapped her fingers and the pack of cigarettes in the middle of the table manifested itself in Sabine's hand. The witch removed one and offered another to Satan while going on, "But there are still so many interesting questions that sexuality can be used to answer. Questions we're almost afraid of asking for fear of offending anybody. So…well, maybe you're right, Lord."

While Satan lifted a fingertip to light the end of Sabine's cigarette, Sabine continued with a smile, "Maybe my focus on the term "the male gaze" is defensive, in a way…maybe by thinking about it, I'm granting some negative value to society's conception of male-ness and therefore only progressing the argument that male sexuality is somehow different from female. But that doesn't solve the problem of society's very negative view toward sex."

Head tipped back, Satan blew a few smoke rings and laughed. "Honey," said the Devil, legs extending over Sabine's lap, "let's be real…the longer society as a whole views sex in a negative light, the better it works out for me. What time is it—oh! Our stories are on…"

With a giddy noise, Sabine leaned forward and plucked up the remote control. In a magical flash, it aligned its settings to the new set top box, and the grinning witch hurriedly hit the power button to put on her afternoon soap operas. No doubt feeling as wretched as he looked, the cable dog slunk in to droop to the floor at their feet.

"Aw, don't pout." Nudging the animal with her foot, Sabine grinned and said, "I haven't had a dog in years! Let Mommy watch her stories with her friend, and then we'll take you for a walk…you'll see! It's not all bad being a witch's only pet."

The Witch's Guilty Pleasure

SABINE'S OVEN chimed in happy announcement that it had come up to heat, but she wasn't even close to putting in the cookies yet. Cable Dog sat on the edge of the kitchen looking hopeful that she might drop an egg, or maybe enough chocolate chips for him to commit suicide and start again in a new, human body. Someday, Cable Dog! Someday.

But if you had to be transformed into a dog and owned by somebody else, that somebody else might as well be a hot witch who stood in her kitchen wearing black lingerie and a funky apron emblazoned with the words *SAIL HATIN'* in white block letters.

"You know," she said while doling room temperature butter into her KitchenAid mixer, "everybody's been thinking about health a lot lately. Of course, that's good! But amid all this focus on physical wellbeing, it's important to keep your mental health in check, too. Don't you think so, Cable Dog?"

The poor German shepherd drummed his tail once, sadly, on the floor. Laughing at the former human, the witch scooped a cup of sugar into the bowl and said, "It's tempting to claim that times right now are like they've never been, but that's just not true…awful things are always happening everywhere, all the time! It's enough to make a person go crazy if they really think about it." She fit the paddle attachment into the mixer and, letting it run, crossed to the Victorian kitchen's other side to mix her dry ingredients.

"That's why it's so important to find little ways to escape. Fun things, you know! Something just for yourself. Oops!"

Scooping flour was just so dangerous! The white powder puffed out all across the front of the apron and settled with nearly sentient intent across her breasts. While she tutted at the particles falling across her feet, Sabine shook her head and said, "I'm just so clumsy when I bake…but I try not to be too hard on myself. Why be critical of little things? Life's too short for that. We'll sweep up later, won't we?"

Dusting off her hands and rinsing them once for good measure, she returned to the matter of her ingredients and got a few leavening agents prepared. "That's one of the things about anxiety, you know. It's the worst when you're all in a tizz about something you can't control, or some situation you have nothing to do with. Don't you think people would be better off if they could forgive their little mistakes? If they accepted that sometimes their best isn't enough now, but that they could always improve in the future, I like to think society would be a bit more positive."

After a quick stir of the bowl, Sabine returned to the mixer and switched it off. While retrieving a couple of eggs, she smiled at the reflective door of the microwave. "Always crack your eggs into a separate bowl before adding them into your recipe…don't want blood in there, do you?"

With a pleasant hum, she swept the eggs off in the direction of the sink and the small bowl waiting there. Seeing his opportunity, Cable Dog darted past her. Sabine stopped short and one of the eggs dropped from her hand to splatter across the floor, its translucent ooze extending along the top of her pale foot. "Oh, on the wood! You naughty dog."

But he was already going for it—lapping up the yolk with delight, tail wagging like he'd been a dog all his life. Of course, on one level or another, he had been. Sabine stood with her arms crossed, rolling her eyes slightly in the direction of the shining microwave door. "I'd be a hypocrite to be too mad after all I was just saying, but you have to agree that he did that on purpose. Somebody likes eggs, doesn't he? That's a dog for you, though…they'll eat anything you put in front of them—hey!"

Cable Dog's enthusiastic licking had swept across the floor and now over the top of Sabine's foot. She giggled, leaning back against the counter, one egg still treacherously in her hand. "Now, you bad boy…you're going to get Mommy all distracted! She was just giving a nice talk about self-care, and when exactly it is that self-care becomes…oh, self-indulgence…ah!"

Gasping as the dog's tongue curled around the arch of her foot, Sabine at last said, "Well, if you're going to do that, then I'd might as well get something out of the bargain, too."

With a wave of her black polished fingertip, Cable Dog was suddenly a Cable Guy again. Yes, ah, a full grown man lying naked at her feet, eagerly sucking disgusting raw egg yolk from her toes. Sabine chuckled, waiting for him to realize what had happened, and sure enough, his sucking lips slowly came to a shocked stop.

His eyes lifted toward her.

"Eggs are good for a dog's coat, you know," she told him, pushing her toe deeper into his mouth and urging him upon his back with the flat of her foot. "Helps to keep the fur all nice and shiny. Want another?"

"Can I go home," he asked pathetically while she lifted her foot from his lips.

Sabine laughed cruelly at the mere idea. After cracking the second egg on the edge of the counter, she pulled its shell apart to watch the contents drip on his face. He grimaced as it splattered across his nose and mouth, but not nearly as much as he did when her foot planted on his face again. There it worked to smear the substance into his skin.

"You can't go home, little doggie! Your replacement is in your home now. Living your life. Kissing your girlfriend, calling your mother, paying your bills. Honestly he's saving you a lot of trouble…you should thank me. Go on." The pressure of her foot tightened as she put a little more weight onto it. "Say 'Thank you, Madame.'"

Weakly, muffled by the arch of her foot, Cable Guy said, "Thank you, Madame."

"That's a good boy…now, go on, keep cleaning Mommy's toes while she talks to her friend."

Not bothering to question who this friend was or why she sporadically talked to herself while going about her daily life, Cable Guy commenced an admirable job of forcing himself to lick the runny raw egg from Sabine's pale foot.

While Sabine sighed, her head tilting back, she continued, "By far and away, I think the most important factor in mental health—all health, but especially mental health—is the ability to distinguish harmful behaviors from harmless ones. Sounds simple, of course, but really it's just not that way…why, even something innocuous as drinking a soda can lead to diabetes if you do it too often! Look no further than my old friends, the Catholics, to see even prayer can be misused in excess. So it's not as simple as saying, 'This activity is good, that activity is bad.' It's a frame of mind…and what's the killer variable here? Well, as usual, it's shame.

"We started to touch on the issue a little bit last time—you know, the time I made my dog, here—but the truth is that if I really wanted to, I could develop a whole college course on the way shame negatively impacts the human being. What interests me about the power of shame today is the fact that it's such a self-fulfilling sensation. That is to say, when we feel ashamed of a behavior that we enjoy, we tend to do that behavior in secret…and because we can't engage in the behavior all of the time, we enjoy it to excessive levels when we're alone, thus increasing the level of our shame and ensuring we'll keep the behavior a secret. It's a vicious, vicious cycle."

Seeing that Cable Guy's dick was hard after barely a minute of licking her dirty foot, Sabine lifted her arch away from his mouth and stepped back. She wiggled out of her panties, hardly looking at him while she reached beneath the apron to feel her own wet pussy with a gasp of anticipatory pleasure. "Oh! I love a good boy who knows how to humble himself… nothing makes me wetter than seeing a man on his knees. Or his back. Feel like using that tongue of yours on something else, fuckboy?"

"I don't really have a choice, do I?"

Sabine laughed while she stood over Cable Guy's head, then carefully knelt atop him. "Since this is a mailing list freebie, I'm allowed to say—no, you don't have a choice, you absolutely don't have the least choice in it. You're a captive, a slave forever. Now go on!" She leaned forward and slapped his throbbing cock, producing a yelp and a satisfactory lift of his head toward her waiting pussy. "You interrupted my baking, the least you can do is please me…oh, yes, oh—"

Sabine's eyes fluttered shut. Running her hands up over her breasts and into her hair, she ground her pussy and ass back down against Cable Guy's face and now focused, gasping, blushing, on the reflective front of the oven.

"You—you know, oh—shame is such a—a powerful social control mechanism that, rather than trying to liberate others from it, we—we instead—oh, we instill it! We shame others! We make people feel bad for being themselves, for liking what they like in scenarios stretching from sex to food. Isn't it better to treat others the way we want to be treated? Unless you're a witch, of course. Witches are allowed to be cruel to everybody…

bad witches, anyway. Maybe if you're a goodie-two-shoes like Miss Clarinda Lovegood down the way," she said with a jerk of her head and a derisive wave off in that direction, "you have to be more empathetic as a matter of course…but then that takes all the meaning out of the empathy, doesn't it? I think it makes it more special for the people I like if I'm a bitch to everybody else…what is it?"

Cable Guy had been slapping rapidly on her ass and she thought he was spanking her at first—getting into it, you know—but the slapping was a little continuous and starting to seem like an effort at communication. Sabine lifted her hips and he gasped sharply, managing to sputter out the words, "Suff—suffocating—"

"Then you'd better hurry up and make me cum, hadn't you?"

Lowering herself and quickly muffling Cable Guy's cry of protest, Sabine moaned and ground her pussy all across his face. To make matters a little more bearable for her slave, because she was such a generous person, she reached across his body and tugged on his aching cock a few times.

"I haven't let you cum since I made you into a dog the other day, huh? Poor boy! Well, maybe one of these days when I'm in the mood I'll let you take it up the ass from me. You'll like that…oh, yeah, my cute little puppy boy will cum buckets for me, won't he."

Grinning, landing another sharp slap across his cock and laughing as he whined, Sabine lifted her apron to watch her labia grind against his jaw.

"Of course, all that being said about empathy and not shaming other people, shame does serve a valuable purpose. It keeps cultural taboos in order. Look no further than the "#MeToo" phenomenon to see the importance of some good public shaming. A general sense of shame is important to the human being, like a sense of pain. It's a humbling emotion that reminds us to keep ourselves in check.

"But where shame really gets out-of-hand is when we start to apply it to the creative outputs of other people. We talked a little before about the current state of erotic and transgressive fiction, but looking at it in detail, you can see how modern literature really is one of the most brutalized victims of cancel culture. It started with trigger warnings in the early 2000s and went from there. Because, of course, what are trigger warnings but a method of categorization as much as any tagging system? Oh…fuck, yes—"

The Cable Guy's nose was buried in her ass, where one would expect a dog to bury his nose; all the while his tongue, working hard and fast against her clit, was finally starting to get her someplace, and she moaned to rub against the slick organ that worked with such desperation to please her. "Yes, yes! Oh! But see! The problem—the problem with any system of self-labeling—oh, fuck, is that such labeling makes it easy to identify and eradicate undesirable or allegedly harmful objects!

"But who's the fiction really harming? When everything is fantasy and nothing is memoir, what does it matter if— if somebody shows, oh, fuck, I don't know, corpse-fucking, or bestiality, or even the Big One? You know the one…the 'P-word.' Nabokov. Balthus. See? I can't even say it out loud here in the middle of my own kitchen, lest you think I'm advocating it. Talk about witch-hunting! Fuck, fuck, oh, yes, yes, who's a good boy? Who's a good boy? Oh, fuck!"

Sabine gasped sharply as at last her pet extricated an orgasm from her. As she moaned, cunt fluttering, the witch leaned up to let him free and was so busy washing away in the throes of pleasure that she couldn't even manage to laugh at him. "Hm…ah…oh…good boy. But…oh, this being fiction…ah, well, I just don't understand what the problem is.

"You know…the US government was involved in an obscenity lawsuit as recently as 2009. You should look it up.

What was the site called again? "Red Rose," that's right. Some poor, traumatized old agoraphobic lady ran a website where she posted her perfectly fictional stories about perfectly fictional"—she glanced sidelong as though looking around for cops and stage-whispered—"C-H-I-L-D-R-E-N getting brutally tortured and murdered.

"Because she was taking cursory credit card payments from readers in an extremely responsible effort to keep real kids from accessing the site, the government decided that she was pedaling the textual equivalent of—let's just call it, "Cheese Pizza." Let me just tell you…the *actual* victims of "Cheese Pizza" would probably be disgusted and upset by the fiction, sure—but they might be even more disgusted and upset to think that the government was putting the fictional plights of these fictional children on the same level as their own very real, very horrific traumas. Well, anyway, obviously the Feds picked the right test case…this poor old lady was too old and mentally ill to even think about facing down the charges in court, so of course she folded early on. If she'd fought it, though, who knows? She probably would have won. No doubt that's why they picked her, specifically."

Standing up, one foot coming to rest on her slave's stomach, Sabine stretched and let him stare at the jiggle of her breasts beneath her apron. "That's just the extreme, most clear-cut case of controversial content, though. I mean, don't get me wrong. I love consenting adults when it comes to the erotic fiction I prefer to consume. The stuff on that Red Rose website doesn't sound like it would have been my cup of tea, but I'll defend anybody's right to write anything, and I'll defend anybody's right to publish anything, too.

"If a publisher is willing to take the hit on a perverse book, more power to them… Of course, with a monopoly currently providing almost everyone's books, the market has no choice but to conform to the demands of said monopoly. Want your books to get read? Have to put them on Amazon. Want to put them on Amazon? Then you'd better be writing Amazon-approved content, buddy...in the world of taboo smut, that means you'd better be walking some very fine lines."

Based on the repeated trailing of his eyes away from his mistress, Cable Guy was starting to think less about his unsatisfied cock and more about the nearby door to the back yard. With a wiggle of her finger, Sabine lifted her foot and laughed as he began to contort once more into his canine body. "For me, well, I suppose it's a matter of personal taste. Certain subjects are just trashy to write about...but if somebody else writes about them, what does it bother me? Why, if a story I'm starring in is found on the same bookshelf as, I don't know, a book about a slut who gets fucked by a dog—a real book I've read on the Amazon store, by the way—what does it affect my story any? It doesn't...except now I'm jealous that other people are able to get away with dog-fucking in fiction when it's in question for others."

Cable Dog, now reverted to his four-legged and furry form, wiggled his ears hopefully at that.

"Get real," said Sabine with disgust, shooing the dog from the kitchen with a wave of her hands. "Didn't I just say it was trashy? Just because I wish we were allowed to explore any subject on any platform doesn't mean I actually would do the thing if given the chance, you know. Some people!"

Shaking her head, she turned away to the fridge and removed another pair of eggs from the carton.

"Some pets...hold on, would you? This will take a few minutes."

After finally getting the eggs into the mix, adding the flour and throwing in some chocolate chips, Sabine arranged a baking tray with nine beautiful, soon-to-be cookies.

"Sorry for the interruption...I just wanted to get the hard stuff out of the way. A lot of people don't realize how long you really have to cream butter and sugar and eggs together when you're making cookies!"

Sliding these into the oven, the witch straightened up with a pleased smile and set the timer. Then, tidying a little as she talked, she resumed, "A lot of authors who are on the side of restricting the kinds of content available on the mainstream digital stores say things like, "Well I don't want my book to be on the same shelf as a book about incest," or some nonsense like that. But does it affect you, I ask? Of course not. If you are so traumatized that the mere concept of incest is enough to trigger you, then maybe you haven't worked through your trauma enough yet, and you should be watching where you look…not restricting other people's behaviors. That's why children are given adult supervision. They're not emotionally equipped to handle the realities of life and they need an adult to guide them…if you're so traumatized that you're not emotionally equipped for it as an adult, then get yourself a handler instead of crying to Twitter or shaming people on Reddit.

"Then, well, it's like we talked about before: because people can't do the thing that they're shamed for, they do it in secret—or, worse, they do it in duplicitous ways. For instance, instead of incest, right at this very moment Amazon overflows with 'pseudo-incest.' As though that were better! As if forcing people to go through all these contortions just to get the content they desire doesn't simply reinforce the exclusivity and therefore gratification of the fetish. Then, of course, there's the related—and, even by my dirty standards, somewhat excessive—proliferation of ageplay erotica, which…I won't even comment on that one, really. People in glass houses shouldn't throw stones. But do you see what I mean? Do you see how ridiculous it is to tiptoe around these subjects in fiction? Do you see how absurd it is to let your shame rein in your creative work?"

Satisfied that the dishes were at least stacked up to be done in a little while, Sabine removed her apron with a sigh of pleasure. Now clad in underwear and bra alone, she made her way through the kitchen, past the moping dog, and up the stairs of her creaking old house. "The same authors who are on the side of censorship like to smugly point out things like, 'You can write whatever you want. You just can't publish it.'

"Okay, well, sure. I can scream in my basement for hours at a time, too. It's not going to make me feel better—not as much as it would if somebody heard me screaming from next door and came over to say, 'You know, Sabine, I heard your wails of existential anguish, and I just want you to know that I really identify with them. You're not alone: I feel the same way you do.' And if that person pays me money to listen to my screaming, hey, that's just a bonus. I mean, really…why is it fair that the people with the most pain—the artists with the most fucked up subject matter to get out of their brains and bodies—are frequently as subject to public shaming as any movie producer infamous for rubbing up against his starlets?"

In her bedroom, Sabine dusted her arms and chest off. She pulled a black sweater over her head and fixed the v-neck to show off her bust; then, with a pair of jeans draped over her arm, she slipped into her bathroom. "That's the real problem with shame…with cancel culture in general—when you're going around canceling everything, wagging your finger at everybody and 'thou shalt not'-ing all of society, then the gravity of real sins gets lost. Save your grief for actual controversies!"

With a damp washcloth from the sink, Sabine bent to rub away the spots of egg that Cable Dog had missed. "That's what really slays me, you know…the real world is full of real crimes. Real, awful people getting away with awful things all the time. Every day! And there are really people out there who feel like it's the job of fiction to somehow rectify it. Why? Why should an author have to write stories about people who are flawless?

Would you want to read something like that? No, of course not. You wouldn't want to look at a painting like that, either. I don't, anyway."

Finally satisfied, the busty witch slipped her clean feet into her tight-fitting jeans and wiggled the black denim up her thick thighs. "And this has really just covered the topic of creators…God forbid you have the audacity to *consume such works*. Which, of course, people do…talk about dogs! Werewolf fiction, hello? 'Knotting' tropes in stories aren't allowed on Amazon, technically, but just do a search for 'knotted' sometime. You tell me what the market wants. People are out there who want to read this stuff, and shaming them isn't going to make them non-existent.

"But, I have to ask…what's really the harm?" Making her way down the stairs two at a time, Sabine smiled as she hit the landing, then bent over her dog to ruffle his ears. Cable Dog did wag his tail a little, perhaps against his better judgment, but that tail-wag significantly increased when she leaned down to plant a theatrical smooch on the tip of his black nose. "Were J.D. Salinger and Holden Caulfield really responsible for the death of John Lennon and the attempted assassination of Ronald Reagan? Of course not."

Straightening up and strolling into her kitchen with a smile of satisfaction, Sabine rooted around in a nearby drawer for her oven mitt. "John Hinckley Jr. was obsessed with more than Catcher in the Rye, you know. He was also obsessed with Todd Rundgren. There's poor Todd just trying to bang on the drum all day, and here's crazy Hinckley getting hooked onto his music. Was Todd Rundgren responsible for this? No! Of course not. Nobody in their right mind would say that, but still somehow we get it in our heads that the existence of depravity in literature will encourage depravity in real life. The fact is that criminally depraved people will latch onto any justification for their criminal acts. You can't blame fiction or music or anything else when Joe Shooter goes on a spree—for all you know, what really set him off was a coded answer in Will Shortz's New York Times crossword that day."

The timer dinged merrily and Sabine bent to remove her cookies from the oven. Very nice! She used an empty cookie sheet to fan them off a little. "So when it comes to shame, you see, the problem isn't the activity or thought in and of itself. It's the person performing the activity or thought, their intentions with it, the void they're filling with it—etcetera, etcetera. In other words, we all have our favorite treats—a naughty little thing we might like to do or think about that eases, at least somewhat, the pressure of living. But as long as we're not acting those things out in real life, or letting those things impact our health or the health of others, then we should move forward in good faith that any shame we might feel is artificially imposed. That we are, in fact, brainwashed by society into shaming ourselves…a process so automatic that, by the time we're adults, we might not even notice it anymore."

After setting aside the empty cookie sheet, Sabine plucked a spatula from the depths of her drawer and began carefully sliding still soft cookies from their places. As she placed them, one by one, upon a waiting plate, she said, "In fact, a lot of people don't realize that it's the shame itself that they're addicted to… the shame is the real vice. Shame is what makes so many sex acts so much more exciting, after all…that naughty feeling that we're doing something taboo. Shame, as I said before, is self-perpetuating—an invader in your mind, a parasite that encourages you to let it run your entire life.

"But don't you think there's enough to worry about in this sordid world?" Beaming, Sabine picked up her plate of cookies. Rather than sitting down at the dining table with them, she whisked them through to the basement door. "With so much to worry about these days, I think we would all do ourselves a huge favor if we could just let a little bit of that shame go.

What a boon to mental and physical health it would be if we could accept the people we are, whether we're indulgent or ascetic, productive or lazy!"

The cellar was divided into several chambers. Passing through the laundry room and into the storage space beyond, Sabine said above the distant sounds of shouting children, "So, I say, write and draw and read whatever you want! Eat as it pleases you, within the limitations of your health. Have an extra cookie. I won't tell."

Winking, smiling, Sabine unlocked the door to the larder that formed the basement's final room. The cries of the grubby children inside reached a fever pitch and Sabine laughed over her shoulder. "Oh! Did you think these were for me? Gosh, no…all that butter goes straight to my hips. Here you go, sweeties!" With an evil chuckle, Sabine slid the cookies into the center of the dungeon and watched her tiny, tender prisoners dogpile upon the plate.

"That's right…you just enjoy and get all nice and chubby, now."

Shutting the door, she admitted, "Auntie Sabine has a little bit of a sweet tooth."

Her green eyes batted at a dusty mirror, broken and left to lean against the nearby stone wall. "You won't judge me for it, will you?"

The Witch's Garden Hoe

SABINE PERCHED atop the ladder positioned against her backyard privacy fence. She frowned, eyes narrowing through the binoculars as her focus swept across that stuck-up bitch, Clarinda Lovegood, the good witch who lived three houses down. Golden-haired, hardbodied, and so boring it made Sabine want to puke, Clarinda reclined beside her swimming pool with a drink in one hand and a paperback in the other. As the good witch took a sip of her drink, Sabine took a reflexive puff her cigarette, then lowered her binoculars. The reflection in the lenses caught her eye.

"I have to quit," said the bad witch with a sigh, tapping ash from her cigarette and studying the end. "It pains me to say it, but the time is long overdue…and, well, cigarettes are just so *expensive!* It's more than a health issue at this point. Let's face it—if it were only a health issue, there'd be a whole lot more smokers still in the world. No, no…it's just that, well, a witch has bills to pay, and we can't all afford a hot gardener like Clarinda Lovegood can."

Said hot gardener passed the good witch by, his tanned back glistening with sweat from the exertion of his workout. Meanwhile, at the base of the ladder, Cable Dog had sniffed something good amid the dirt and begun to dig at Sabine's rose bush. "Instead I get you," Sabine told the former Cable Guy in annoyance, before adding to the reflective lens of the binoculars, "and you, I guess…that's pretty good, too."

Descending the ladder, Sabine admitted, "Well, my mother has always told me that it's not enough to get rid of a bad hobby…you have to replace it with a good one. Be productive, you know. Not destructive."

Humming, smoke pluming up from the corner of her mouth, Sabine considered the back yard of the renovated Victorian that she called her home. Weeds! Weeds as far as the eye could see—and plenty of flowers, yes, but in no perceptible order or arrangement.

"Too bad I hate gardening," said Sabine with a shrug and a spread of her hands. "And home improvement in general… but, what's this?"

Cable Dog, with a small 'boof' of victory, now wagged his tail. With the tip of his careful snout the transfigured German shepherd pulled something from the ground, and a few seconds later—pop! Up came a human foot, still attached to a leg that was rooted in the earth.

"Why," said Sabine with pleasure, "I remember you! That's right."

Yes, that *was* right! Who had this person been? Brown uniform: a delivery driver? Well, he wasn't much of anybody anymore—as Cable Dog, with several vigorous pulls, managed to pry him out of the ground, the delivery driver appeared to be much more of a skeleton than a man.

Crouching over Cable Dog to praise him lavishly for this find, Sabine then turned her attention to the corpse and, puffing out her cheeks, blew a thick coating of dirt away from the hollows of its eye sockets.

"Don't you just hate when your delivery guy tosses your packages around? So do I…hey! You!" The witch slapped the corpse's bony cheek. She grinned as it gasped awake, dust and debris sputtering from its mouth in a theatrical plume while Sabine resurrected it. "Yeah, good morning! Wake up. Good thing my little dog found you!"

The corpse moved its mouth and stared blindly up at Sabine's face, its tongueless jaw hanging open in shocked and quite horrified recognition.

In a frantic rattle of bones, the dead body leapt up and tried to run away.

"Hey!" Hands on her hips, Sabine scowled after it. Her sharp whistle cut through the yard. "Cable Dog! Go get him."

Bark, bark, bark! Cable Dog may not have liked his new lot in life very much, but he couldn't deny that his canine instincts were impossible to resist. When something ran, he had to chase it—and when Sabine told him to chase it, he especially had to chase it. The hound blasted off after the corpse which had, owing to a lack of tissue to keep its joints together, quickly begun to fall apart anyway. By the time Cable Dog had knocked it down and pinned it amid the weeds of the yard, it had already lost a foot and one whole finger.

"Maybe we got off on the wrong, uh…" She looked at the foot lying severed on the ground. Picking it up with a little slap to dust it off, Sabine chose to avoid the obvious pun. "Anyway, you don't need to be afraid of me! Not anymore, anyway. Why, once I've taught somebody a lesson, I think it's important to be friends! You want to be friends with a witch, don't you?"

The skeletonized head rapidly shook 'No' back and forth.

"Sure you do," Sabine answered for it, nudging its knee before reattaching, with a green bolt of magic, that lost foot. "Why, as cruel as I am, I'm just as generous…think of all the things I could give you if you proved you were worth it. Skin! You want skin, don't you?"

With an empty-eyed glance down at its bony hand, the skeleton looked back up at Sabine and reluctantly nodded. The witch smiled.

"That's right. Skin and muscles and *eyes*. Wouldn't eyes be nice?" Again, the skeleton nodded, now a little more vigorously. Beaming in pleasure, the witch straightened up and fixed the spaghetti strap of her top before her humongous tits could escape.

"Of course, they'd be nice…well, I can give you all kinds of nice rewards if you'll agree to help me with one or two little things around the house…"

By that afternoon, the skeleton's list had grown from 'one or two' items to something more like 'twenty or thirty,' depending on how you counted and which tasks you combined. For instance, one could easily argue that 'power-wash house siding' and 'repaint façade' were two parts of the same task. The skeleton didn't seem to see it that way, judging by the prolonged wheeze of unhappiness it produced once it had studied the list, but Sabine didn't think she was unreasonable. After all—how could you repaint the façade without making sure everything was clean, first?

"I thought you were going to replace smoking with a positive hobby," Satan, wearing his preferred masculine form, reminded Sabine while they watched through the parlor window. The corpse was in the middle of desperately trying to get the rusty lawn mower to start and let's just say that if it had blood pressure, ol' Bonesy might have been on the verge of an aneurysm.

"This *is* a positive hobby," said Sabine, gesturing toward the glass pane. "I'm supervising…that's an awful lot of work, as housewives all across the country will tell you."

"Yeah, I can see you breaking a sweat even now." At last, giving up on the lawn mower, the skeleton threw its hands angrily into the air and did a double-take when those hands quite literally flew off its wrists and into the distance. While it pursued the lost body parts, Sabine laughed along with her dark master, who who smoothed his tie over his chuckling diaphragm while the witch went on in a flirtatious tone.

"That's not the supervising, Master…that's just you."

"Do you mean to say I make you nervous?" His mouth hovered around her ear, the hot breath drifting past his smiling lips enough to provoke a shudder in even the witch. To feel such a tremor wrack her body, the Dark Lord gently chuckled. "Ah, Sabine, now, what call have you to find me anything but doting? Anything but a generous protector toward you and all my other daughters in vice."

While he lifted her hand to kiss it, Sabine followed the motions of the skeleton to the shed in the back of the garden. "I would be a very foolish girl if I didn't fear you, Father, knowing what you can do with the blink of an eye or the wave of a hand."

"Oh, why of course! There's no arguing that I'm dangerous to those of average dispositions or weak morals—but, why, to a well-versed witch, what's even the Devil but just another slave?"

"Just like you to try and stoke overconfidence…" While the skeleton emerged from the shed with a bucket of paint in each hand, Sabine turned back to her master and draped her arms around his neck. "You'd see me lulled into a false sense of security, into thinking myself the guiding font of wisdom… soon enough I'll forget to thank you. I'll forget all my courtesy and all those things you like about me."

"And I'll have the chance to beat them back into you," said the Prince of Hell as he bent to apply his lips down the witch's neck. Sabine moaned and sighed, permitting her master to push her back into the fabric of the overstuffed sofa beneath the picture window of the salon. Soon enough his mouth found hers again and while the fire of his tongue slid into her mouth Sabine groped at his shirt buttons, tugged at his tie—he was half undressed already when Cable Dog's petulant whine reached her ear.

"What's the problem," she asked the dog in a short tone, glancing away while Satan kissed her jaw.

"He's envious, of course…what man wouldn't be?" Cable Dog's ears pinned back against his skull as Satan whistled from where he bent over the witch. "Here, boy. Want attention, do you?"

"No," cried Cable Guy as he emerged from the German shepherd, humiliated at once. He remembered he was naked and threw his hands in front of his crotch. "Shit," he said, then, with a rapid glance at the kitchen and the door to the back yard beyond, "please—"

"If you ask to leave again we'll make you mute, so don't." Pouting over at the handsome Cable Guy who had been made her—we'll say, uh, dubiously consensual—pet, Sabine refrained from openly moaning while the Dark Lord's eager kisses trailed down her breasts. "Don't you like being my doggie, Cable Guy?"

"My name's—"

"I think I treat you very nicely, you know…why"—now she was unable to help her moan, for Satan's powerful hands made short work of her jeans and his lips pressed through the black silk of her panties to leave her gasping for air—"why, why, I give you all the finest kibble and treats all day…I even rub your tummy when you let me."

"I don't think that's what he's trying to get you to rub," quipped Satan wryly, earning a clap over his head from the audacious witch. While he laughed at his servant's temerity, Sabine crooked her finger in indication for Cable Guy to approach.

Reluctantly, hands still folded over his johnson, he did.

When the human was near enough, Sabine knocked his hands away to grab his hard cock.

"Now, come on…why are you so shy?" Sabine's sharp green eyes searched Cable Guy's face while her hand pumped up and down the length of his shaft, his gasps so shocked and desperate they sounded almost like ones of pain. "It's not as if we haven't known each other for—well, at least a couple of weeks now! Trust me, that's longer than most people get to enjoy in my presence." Her mouth twisted into another parody of a pout. "Maybe you don't think I'm pretty."

"No! No, that's not—" Cable Guy's voice leapt to a high tone and broke while Sabine leaned forward to take his prick into her mouth. "Oh! Uh—uh—"

"Perhaps," the Dark Lord suggested while sliding Sabine's panties down, "he finds you altogether too beautiful, Sabine… some men are intimidated by beauty and need to be taken by it, rather than conforming to the standard male role of the dynamic party. Why, it could be that he feels intimidated by traditional gender roles as a whole!"

"Oh, yes." Lifting her head away with a 'pop,' Sabine smiled up at Cable Guy and continued running her hand over his dick while her attention returned to her master. "Yes, Master, you know, they really are such terribly restrictive things… they hinder the imagination. How many men and women throughout history have failed to meet the standards of their true selves, their highest selves, only because society didn't allow them the creativity to envision it!"

"Yes, yes, oh, all the wasted men who'd have made fine dancers, all my lovely female architects and masons born prior to the 20th century or so…it still amazes me that people want to claim I'm the problem. Society does all my work for me! Particularly in the West."

"There's nothing you could do that mankind doesn't eagerly do to itself…oh—" Sabine sighed, shifting in her seat, her legs splaying wider to accommodate the lips pressing between her thighs. As Satan's tongue went to work battering her clit and teasing down between her labia, the witch lifted her eyes to her pet. "For being such an anxious man, you sure do like to look."

"I— I— I don't—"

Sabine laughed at Cable Guy's anxiety and dragged him down into the couch with her, then caught his handsome bearded jaw. "Don't deny it." While she planted a kiss upon Cable Guy's mouth, the Dark Lord's tongue lashed all the faster between her legs; Sabine moaned and arched her hips up against him, leaning back from her pet. "Go on, admit it. You want to watch my master fuck me, don't you?"

"I—" Cable Guy's eyes flickered down to Satan, who paid the human less mind than he might have a speck of dust floating through the air. "Yes," whispered Cable Guy shamefully. "Yes, Sabine, I love to watch it when you let men fuck you."

"I'll bet you like it even more when I'm the one doing the fucking," Sabine enthused, her hands lifting into her hair and pushing the dark strands up from her shoulders. Her fingers tangled amid the locks and she pulled at her own scalp when her master's tongue sped along: teeth clenched, the witch gasped, "Fuck, oh, Master, you make me so horny!"

Glancing up at her with a roguish cock of his brow, Satan assured her, "Of course I make you horny, my damned little slut—how else could I tell you were mine in a crowd?"

"Hail, Satan," Sabine said, gasping with pleasure and flashing the sign of the horns while his finger slid into her cunt. "Oh, fuck! Hail Satan, Hail Satan!"

"I hate it when you start saying that," muttered Cable Guy.

"Hm, poor dog, it makes you jealous, doesn't it—oh, fuck, well, ah—no need, no need to be jealous, oh, Sabine will make it all better! Why—why, oh, there are even things I might do to you that Master doesn't permit me to enjoy with him."

Suspicious but intrigued, Cable Guy glanced between them and reluctantly asked, "Like what?"

"Like sodomy," answered the witch while Satan chuckled between her legs. "Oh! Ah—oh, Master only indulges in such fine arts with me when he's in a feminine mood. Just think of how much room that leaves for you! Oh! Fuck—Master! Oh, Satan, Hail Satan!"

Brow furrowing, feet digging in against the edge of the sofa, Sabine gasped and thrust her hips against the Dark Lord's mouth. Her master's tongue plunged deep into her dripping cunt—far deeper than a human man's might have, it was worth saying, though by the time it slithered back out and into his mouth it was perfectly average in appearance. While her pussy fluttered with the end of her orgasm, Satan stroked her thigh and watched her with unfeigned fondness.

"You are among the best of my creations, Sabine, pretty as a rose and with thorns even sharper. Ah! And no matter what form you take, it's always sublime."

"The same could be said of you, Master…oh, though I wish you would be a girlfriend to me more often! It's such a treat when you come to me as a sister. But it does rather benefit our friend, I must admit…so, dog?" With a bat of her eyes and a winsome smile over at Cable Guy, Sabine ran her hand over her sumptuous breasts and down the slopes of her tight, pale body. "What do you say? Care to enjoy with me the lovemaking whose prototype Ganymede inspired?"

Cable Guy wasn't really well-versed in mythology. "Uh?"

"Sodomy," said the witch. "I'm asking about sodomy."

"Oh! Oh. Uh—yeah," he said without thinking, excited by the idea of an orgasm after weeks spent in the form of a dog with absolutely zero stimulation other than headpats and back scratches. "Yeah, fuck yeah, sounds great, I'm down for whatever."

He might have thought better of his own phrasing, or at

the very least specified a few things that he was "down" with in slightly clearer detail—because, well…we were talking about a witch in the service of the Dark Lord, Satan. That same Dark Lord chuckled and bent his head over Sabine's lap again, spurring a gasp from her plump lips while he sucked and lapped at her sensitive clit.

"Fuck," gasped the witch, "oh! Then—ah, Master, won't you help me, help me introduce this fine young man to the art of anal sex?"

"Wait—I thought you meant"—Cable Guy gestured between himself and Sabine—"you and me."

"She did," Satan deigned to tell him before resuming his work on Sabine's clit. The pressure increased beneath his mouth and the witch moaned, gripping the ruggedly bearded face of the Cable Guy while the Dark Lord coaxed her clitoris into the shape and size of a most impressive cock. Soon what Satan had once been lapping he now fellated, and Sabine grinned over at the shocked, red-faced and, one really did have to admit, rather intrigued Cable Guy.

"Don't worry," enthused Sabine. "Your delicate sense of your own fragile heterosexuality isn't at any kind of risk here… after all! This is a girl-cock, isn't it."

Cable Guy knew better than to argue. He saved his comments for himself, glancing down at Sabine's erection from the corner of his eye while meanwhile the Dark Lord lifted his chuckling head. "Here, slave," said Satan, rising to catch Cable Guy by the short brown curls of his scalp. "Suck your mistress's cock before she fucks you…get an idea for how big it is, aha, see how hard she is for you?"

The bad witch was really very proud that, with only a second of reluctance delaying him, Cable Guy opened his mind enough to drop his head and suck her cock with some real vigor. Oh, yes! "Is this your first time," she inquired between gasps, "because I don't think it is!"

"He does seem very talented," observed Satan, bending over Sabine to kiss her mouth while his hands roved over her heaving breasts. "At least, enough to get the job done."

That was one way of putting it! Sabine's head tilted back against the couch beneath the Dark Lord's caresses as Cable Guy put his all into pleasing her. Maybe he thought if he got her to cum he'd avoid the humiliating fate of being sodomized in front of Satan, but whatever the reason for his avid work over the head of her cock and down the throbbing shaft, the bad witch didn't really care. It was a delight (and something of a surprise, she had to admit) to discover that her adorable pet, manly and scruffy Cable Guy, was just so good at sucking cock.

The beard did tickle a little when he got down to the shaft, though; she giggled and in response Satan pushed Cable Guy's head down farther, an action perpetrated with enough force that the human choked. Fuck, oh, she loved feeling too big for a man to take!

When the Dark Lord released his head, Cable Guy came up wheezing. Sabine laughed, then gasped. Her master gripped her cock and stroked it while staring her in the eyes, each lascivious pump of his hand from base to head infinitely more pleasurable than the most practiced human's fellatio could have been.

"Why don't you two get comfortable," advised Satan, his voice a low rumble between the kisses he pressed to her mouth and her cheeks. "I'll join in once you've found a rhythm."

With a moan of anticipatory, almost fearful delight, Sabine pushed herself upright and, with her free hand, grasped Cable Guy's hair. She pulled the poor (lucky?) bastard up to his feet and, after being again pleasantly surprised by the enthusiasm he showed in exchanging a kiss with her, Sabine pushed him over the edge of the couch and admired the tight swell of his ass.

"How cute you are," she enthused, smacking a hard cheek a few times while he gasped in humiliation and buried his face in the couch. "Beg me to fuck you, dog."

"I—ugh—please"—the word was a muffled grunt of shame beneath the witch's laughter—"please—f—fuck me, Madame—"

"He even calls me 'Madame' so willingly! Much more happily than my little Alma." Sabine smiled over at the doll who watched, a captive audience from where she had been placed that day upon a nearby bookshelf. With a chuckle, the witch turned back and spread Cable Guy's ass. Oh, her cock throbbed just to see that tight little hole! The idea of humiliating him was, generally speaking, the real pleasure of it all—not that sodomy wasn't fun in its own right, but she had to admit she preferred the practice as a recipient.

The real pleasure in fucking a man in the ass was not the stimulation but the mental component. Wasn't it delicious to see a big, burly boy humbled by the tip of a prick poking against his rear entrance! Sabine moaned in sweet anticipation, pumping the throbbing organ against his ass, running her hand over the shaft still slick not just with saliva but with the natural lubricants of her feminine anticipation.

"Beg for it again," she ordered, easing the tip barely in and repressing her moan of pleasure to feel how fearfully tight he was.

"Uh—uh—please, please, Madame—oh, please, let me have your cock, I want to feel it—please, let me cum—"

"Goodness, don't we just want the whole world! Maybe if you're good…" Chuckling, then gasping at last at the pressure that swallowed her dick, Sabine pushed herself deep into Cable Guy's ass. Her eyes rolled in pleasure. "Oh! Fuck, yes, ah—you've never been fucked this way before, have you?"

"No! No! Oh—ah—"

"Probably should have let him practice a little, first," she said, chuckling, patting his ass while beginning to steadily slide out and in.

Satan was by now fully undressed—and quite admiring of the scene, based on the state of his enormous cock. How the Devil thrilled her to look upon! Oh, he was a beautiful being no matter what form he took, man or woman or even animal—once an angel, always an angel, and his brooding features leant an elegance that made the whole rest of his body seem the tool of a grand predator. Yes, ah, it was a serpentine smile the Dark Lord wore to see Sabine burying her cock in hapless Cable Guy, who moaned with his face wretchedly buried in the couch as though in effort to hide his pleasure.

Of course, that natural predatory elegance was as emphasized by the Dark Lord's prick as it was by his wicked smile. Once he had prowled to Sabine's side to kiss her neck and slide his hands over a body swiftly coating in a thin sheen of sweat from her exertions, Satan pressed that throbbing member to her ass and made her cry with desire to simply feel it. Let alone to think of it in her!

The tool of size and scale incomprehensible to man was outfitted with spines and oh, Sabine had been frightened of them at first…only at first. Now, just running her hand along those pulsing points while he fondled her breasts and sank his fingers into the flesh of her ass filled her with anticipatory ecstasy—an intense desire that worked its way into the girlishness of her voice as she turned her head to gaze at him and beg, "Oh, Satan, oh, Master! Would it please you to use me today? How I burn for you! Oh, sweet fuck, this boy's ass is to tight and so wonderful—but nothing on this Earth could amount to the feeling of your cock in me."

"See," the Devil said with a light ruffle of Cable Guy's hair and a grin for his subsequent moan of discomfort. "That's how you beg…Sabine certainly is an expert at making a man feel wanted. Let's see if your body is as desperate as your mouth."

While his tongue slithered along the ridge of her ear, Satan's great hand searched beneath the base of the bad witch's cock and down a little lower in pursuit of the source of moisture dripping there. Her cunt, waiting for use even as she fucked Cable Guy with her transfigured clitoris, was so sensitive to her master's touch that she almost screamed just to be brushed by him. As a finger slid in she bit her lip and moaned, slowing her motions in Cable Guy's ass as if afraid the slightest movement would send the Dark Lord away.

"My, Sabine," the Devil chuckled and worked his fingers steadily in and out of her, following the same pace she used to pleadingly pet his cock. "You certainly are ready for me, aren't you."

"Always, Master! Always, oh, please, use me, use my body—ah!"

Sabine's sharp gasp echoed through the salon: her master gripped her by the hair and pushed her down over the same arm of the couch where she'd bent Cable Guy. With Sabine's body pressed to that of her gasping pet, Satan slid her legs wider apart. The cool air of the house emphasized her exposure—indeed, it felt as though the Dark Lord's very stare plunged into her long before his spined cock pressed to the lips of her pussy.

"This is your favorite part, isn't it, Sabine…" The Dark Lord sighed while working the head of his prick over her hole, the enormous member of such absurd scale that even after all this time and plenty of magical assistance the witch still felt the same old fear, the same old question. Would he even fit in her?

Of course he would…this was Satan we were talking about. He wasn't about to let a little thing like Sabine's discomfort keep him from ramming his thorny cock as deep into her cunt as he could fit on the first stroke. Sabine's eyes widened and her teeth clenched against the initial pain, the feeling of being torn asunder that always came over her before she adapted to being so utterly filled. Then the pleasure set in: then the terrible spines of the Dark Lord's great, throbbing monster of a cock sank pleasurably into the walls of her cunt and made her scream with ecstasy, the organ itself seeming to clutch at her insides as though in an effort to disobey its master's will and remain within her body.

While Sabine screamed—"Yes, Satan! Yes, oh, Master! Fuck, yes, yes, fuck me hard, oh, please, make me suffer!"— the Prince of Hell's broad hand glided down her spine and fit against the back of her neck. Gasping, almost faint with the pleasure-pain of being stretched beyond all reason, Sabine at last remembered to resume the rhythm of her own prick within Cable Guy's tight ass.

Oh, the ecstasy was sublime! In truth, having a cock and a cunt together at once was not all that different from having a cunt and a clitoris. The pleasures had a way of whisking together, sweeping up through Sabine's body until it was simply one great euphoric wave of stimulation. Until it seemed as though the boundaries between her and the rest of the universe would be dissolved if the pleasure reached enough of a peak.

Certainly it had a way of transforming the rest of her body into one great sex organ, for oh, wherever Satan laid his hands upon her, she moaned with high delight. The pressure of Cable Guy's ass around her cock seemed ready to squeeze it off and drove her on, deeper and deeper into the hapless pet-boy's sphincter. All the while, each time she drew back, she impaled herself all the farther upon the Dark Lord's shaft. Satan groaned with delight, his nose and lips nuzzling fondly against his servant's neck.

"That's right, Sabine…ah, what a pretty slave you are to me—that's right, what a dripping wet slut you are for your master's thorny cock…"

"Oh, Master—yes, yes, fuck, oh, nothing makes me wetter than when you fuck me with that big, big dick! Oh, Satan!"

Moaning, one hand upon the shoulder of writhing, panting Cable Guy, Sabine reached down with the other and grasped his cock to produce a whimper. "Maybe someday you'll let my good doggie feel what a fun time you can give a willing soul."

The Dark Lord's chuckle was as low as it was pleasing to Sabine's ear. "Someday you'll learn, Sabine, that not everyone is equipped to appreciate the lessons I impart. I'm not so sure your pet is one of them."

Fuck! Oh, how anyone could resist the Day-Star was beyond Sabine, whose soul had long ago been committed to his service. She supposed it had something to do with the general view the world had of Satan…or at the very least, it had something to do with the general sensitivities possessed by the average person. Sabine herself had been forced to get used to a few things when she joined his ranks, after all. She had just come such a long ways that she had forgotten.

For instance, well, she wasn't always such a fan of that gigantic, spiky prick…but then again, she'd rather been taken aback by the sight and shape of a human penis the first time she saw one. What was *really* the difference? Wasn't like she was looking at it when it was plowing into her womb with such force that her mouth hung open with her panting and her eyes filled with the same tears of pleasure that furrowed her brow. As her body clutched around his member and her sensitive pussy was overwrought with ecstasy to have its walls raked by the spikes, the tension spread to Sabine's cock and she marveled at Cable Guy's sharp gasp—his almost boyish whimper. Chuckling, the witch twisted his head to the side and kissed the fuzz of his bearded cheek.

"Who's a good boy," she asked against his ear, stroking his cock in time with her fast pumps in and out of his tightly gripping ass. "Who's a good boy? Are you going to cum for me, baby? Going to cum for Madame? What a good doggie you are, that's right, oh, I feel it, you love it, you love getting fucked by my big, hard girl-cock…oh, fuck, you love it, you love it—oh! Fuck! Master!"

Sabine's orgasm wracked her so suddenly that she was almost shocked—but it was just that talented prick in her! It was impossible to feel the battering of that terrific mace of passion into her g-spot more than once or twice without experiencing an explosive climax that dissolved the very matrix of reality. While this fluttering, feminine orgasm worked its way through the new avenue of her transfigured cock, she gasped and rammed herself home to the base: now Cable Guy gasped sharply, crying out, his body stiffening as his cock beneath her hand. They came together while Satan pounded on relentlessly, oblivious to the humans' pleasure when his own was so powerful.

"Sweet fuck," gasped Sabine, "oh, fuck, oh, Master—"

Cable Guy, meanwhile, sputtered as though for air. "Hah! Oh, Sabine"—she was so busy in the throes of her own passion that she wasn't fully aware that the dog had misspoken and disrespectfully called her by her name until long after she emerged from her orgasm—"oh, oh—"

"She is good, isn't she." Head thrust back, powerful hips working at twice the speed, Satan grasped the witch by the pelvis now that he was liberated by the rhythm she maintained while fucking Cable Guy. "Yes, oh—yes, she's very good, ah, tender Sabine, what a hot little bitch you are, come here—"

Sabine's eyes rolled up into the back of her head as the Son of the Morning drew her up into his arms, her cock jerking out of Cable Guy's ass and reducing beneath her master's hand to the size and shape and high sensitivity of her normal, aching clit. One hand on her neck, the other holding her arm hostage behind her back, Satan fucked her so hard it hurt—but a woman's relationship with sexual pain was so very complicated.

Especially this woman. You couldn't be Satan's lover without being a masochist, and Sabine was certainly that. The sharp bursts of pain and the tight cramping of her cunt as it spasmed at the scratching of his spines only sweetened the ecstasy, every burst of stimulation a privilege when it was granted to her by her dark god. She even propped her leg against the couch to assist him, begging him, "Deeper, Master! Oh, fuck, kill me with it, yes, oh, strike me through with your arrow, oh, joy! Oh! Fuck, oh, Satan, oh, dark seraph!"

"You're as good a pet to me as the dog is to you, Sabine… go on, cum for me, where's that spot, aha, ahaha, ah, that's how you like it, isn't it—"

Sabine screamed in horrific agony as, meeting no resistance that could have restrained him, the Devil plowed deep enough into Sabine to burst through her cervix. The pain was so absolutely horrible that she couldn't have enjoyed it if she wanted to, but somehow the thrill that this gave her was a superior pleasure to any base physical stimulation she could have felt. Sabine's screams rattled through the house and Satan pounded all the deeper into her uterus for it, his cock throbbing with the clamp of her organs around him.

It was a paralyzing agony and she became as still in his arms as a corpse might have been, submitting fully to the sensation of being obliterated by his dick. Oh, that great big devil dick! What a privilege it was to be brutalized by him.

As great a privilege as it was to see him, truly see him: what he really looked like beneath his human skin. The hand around her neck tilted back her head. Sabine gasped with captive delight at the shining black skull of his face—the rotten tongues flowing out of his fanged mouth like a heinous nest of serpents to plunge into her throat, her ears, her navel, her soul.

Yes, her soul! The Dark Lord's organs pushed through the mere vehicle of her human body and beyond, into other, all-encompassing dimensions, and Sabine saw in such moments that her body was the vehicle of something far greater—that her entire physical self was nothing but a cunt, a means of interfacing with reality in the way the vagina was the means of interfacing between the sexes. While botflies swarmed out of his empty eyes and, somewhere off in the background, Cable Guy shrieked with mortal terror when he made the mistake of looking in the direction of the buzzing, Sabine's pain turned inside out.

Her body became absolutely enraptured by the ultimate pleasure, by this absolute use at the hands of pure evil: she was so mesmerized, so awash with euphoria that she didn't even laugh when Cable Guy was reduced again, by the wave of Satan's clawed hand, to the form of Cable Dog. The poor German shepherd bolted off through the house to hide beneath a bed, yelping the whole way, tail tucked between its legs, not even pausing to throw a look of sympathy in the direction of the doll who, owing to her placement, was forced to watch every second of a sight that most men would have lost their minds to behold.

Sabine was not most men, or most women. Her eyes fluttered while the Common Enemy of Man penetrated her every orifice and a few that did not even exist on this dimension, her mouth hanging open to accommodate the tongue that plunged into her throat to fuck her lungs, her stomach.

In the center of her consciousness the flaming light of her awareness broadened like an explosion: that explosion, she slowly realized, was a chain of orgasms that continuously rolled through her while her Master provoked this symphony of pleasurable suffering.

Her meaningless human body aflame with desire, Sabine rolled her nearly blind eyes back in the direction of Satan.

Somehow, the sheer beauty of the face—the true face that replaced that odious demonic visage which cast the frightened dog from the room—was so much more infinitely terrifying to Sabine than his rotten flesh or his botfly choir. No, oh!

There was nothing more frightful for the human mind to behold than the face of an angel, if angels could have been said to have faces.

Her eyes burned with tears beneath the vision, beneath Satan's natural appearance. Even though his hideous tongues and spiked cock still plunged into her from all directions, Sabine moaned, her vision clearing, his hateful disguise rendered translucent by the clarity of her witch's consciousness. To simply look upon him with her human eyes in such a state as this was to risk the destruction of her mind, but she didn't care. Oh, how she stared into his plethora of eyes, into the cosmic fire that burned about his head in the kind of aura that men called halos! How she wept with pleasure, with joy, with the divine union for which she was, truly, unworthy.

At last, looking so long into him as she had, the fire of his appearance immolated her mind like the sun blinding a pair of human eyes.

Sabine awoke to Cable Dog anxiously licking her face.

It always took a few seconds after waking up from once of the Dark Lord's ravishments to remember what had happened, which Sabine suspected had less to do with the blackouts and more to do with the lack of consequence. The first time Satan had visited her, in fact, she had thought it was a dream…until his next visit, and the next, and the next. Soon his companionship became so normal to her that she thought nothing of being eviscerated by the fallen angel and restored to one piece only after he was finished. She wasn't sure if she literally died during these encounters, or what…she did know he loved to make her suffer with the cervix thing, but that when she woke up she had no lasting physical effects from all the grotesque penetrations she'd endured. No longterm effects, anyway…there was always a little bit of an ache, but that was sort of nice.

"Don't slobber on me," Sabine muttered to the dog, sitting up and propping her hand upon the mattress where she lay. A bed? Uh-huh, master bedroom. Guess he'd moved her…and left flowers?

Aw! Sabine's hand had hit a cellophane wrapper while she braced upon the mattress. She turned to blearily assess them, this generous gift from her dark god. Withered black roses and the wrinkled mouths of dead Venus flytraps. Gasping, laughing with pleasure, Sabine drew the flowers into her arms and said to the empty air of the room, "Oh! Master…thank you, how wonderful these are."

The dog, who still sat at the edge of the bed with his front paws propped upon the mattress, looked worriedly at the bouquet. "Get down," Sabine told him, pushing him off. Then, stretching, she slid out of bed, herself. "What time is it? I guess it must be tomorrow already…"

Now that the rest of the context returned to her, Sabine remembered something else. "Oh! Bonesy. Have you seen him?" She looked at Cable Dog before, deciding she was silly to talk to a dog and expect a response, Sabine set off to find her slave.

"*Some* people can follow directions," said the witch, looking at the dog once she'd thrown open the front door and squinted into the morning sunlight.

Sure enough, there was the skeleton hard at work in the garden. A neighbor passed by pushing a baby carriage and, caught as she was staring at the house for some reason, waved pleasantly to Sabine. The witch waved back, then explained at the double-take the woman gave the witch's new gardener, "Oh, don't mind him, he's an immigrant. You know how different other cultures can be."

This non-sequitur was so bizarre and so matter-of-fact that

the neighbor clearly had no way to argue with it, despite the fact that the gardener in question was obviously a skeleton. Americans just hate conflict, though—at least, they hate their own conflict even if they love reading or hearing about the conflicts of others. Accordingly, the woman assumed it must have been her own fault that she was perceiving this hard-working immigrant as…uh, an undead skeleton, and she even told her baby, "Wave 'hello' to the nice man, angel."

The baby made a coo that was absurdly cute even to Sabine, and Bonesy lifted his skull from his work to wave a skeletal hand. Once mother and child had continued down the sidewalk and Sabine stepped down into her yard to inspect Bonesy's work, however, she discovered that the skeleton wasn't the only thing the neighbor lady had been staring at.

"Oh, shit," said Sabine, whose peripheral vision had been caught by a strange shade and who now turned.

The façade of her Victorian had been painted matte black from top to bottom.

"Oh, shit!"

Bonesy stared vacantly up at her while she gawked at the house, one hand on her forehead. Fuck, dude! That was as black as her robe. She tightened the garment reflexively around herself. "Guess I should have looked at the paint, first…Master got me all distracted."

Bonesy watched her, preemptively cringing until she patted his skull, then frowned down at the dirt left on her hand by the action. Sabine dusted her palms, saying, "Can't expect a skeleton to tell one color from another. We're lucky you can see at all…I guess it does look pretty metal, huh?"

The Victorian had always had a super goth vibe—frankly, a few gargoyles and the place would have looked like the Addams Family's summer home—but now, well…it had *attitude*.

"Yeah," Sabine said to herself. "You know…I actually kind of dig it! Good work, Bonesy." Patting him on the back of the worm-eaten delivery uniform, Sabine put her hands on her hips, nodded, then looked down at the dog who had come to stand beside her and panted as if in substitute for human laughter. "Just wait until the girls get a load of this next Sabbath!"

Oh, yeah. Those bitches would love it! Pleased as punch, Sabine left Bonesy to his work and went inside to take her morning shower. The whole day she was so happy that she could have almost whistled if her mother hadn't taught her it was bad luck to whistle in the house. Nothing like getting laid while your slave—er, handyman—does all life's hard work for you.

However…not everyone was as thrilled with the house's new façade. Bonesy might as well have been invisible while working beside the towering black Victorian. Everybody passing by openly gawked at the house, and some discussed it at a volume that carried through its open windows to delight Sabine with the horrible neighborhood scandal this change apparently represented.

She supposed she understood. The building had been there for years. It was pretty awful to take such a beautiful house and paint it totally black. Plus, well, people were always freaking out about property values and shit. Now that, Sabine definitely didn't understand—but that could have been because she got the house for such a steal. As in, she literally stole it…but you didn't want to hear about that, reader. Not today.

You wanted to hear about everything that happened—or started to happen—when, three days later, somebody knocked on her front door around noon.

Having expected no one that day, Sabine was forced to put a pause on her baking and shut off the mixer with a glance of consternation for the preheating oven. Alma the doll was once again today's captive audience from where sat upon a bookshelf in the den, her resin doll-eyes almost focused as Sabine crossed through the house to respond to the interruption. Sunlight flooded into the foyer and the witch blinked rapidly, making out amid the inundation of light a hint of golden curl, a daisy-fresh smile, a flushed cheek made extra cute by a pair of cherub's dimples.

"Well hello, neighbor!" Clarinda Lovegood the Good Witch's voice was an annoyingly cheerful sing-song tone while Sabine's vision revealed the hot little blonde bitch in all her obnoxious glory. "It's so nice to see you, thanks for coming to the door! How are you on this blessed day, Sabine?"

"Hungover," answered the bad witch, assessing her neighbor with the usual hint of a leer she had a way of wearing whenever Clarinda was around. "Want to come in and hit the hair of the dog with me?"

"Oh, I never hit dogs, or any of the wonderful creatures God put on this Earth—oh! You mean *drinking.*" Laughing, waving a hand, falling back a step and flattening that hand on her heart, Clarinda enthused in her cute southern drawl, "Gosh, no! I don't drink, either…maybe you'd feel better if you cut back a little."

"If I'm not going to be allowed to smoke tobacco, I have to at least drink."

Eyes widening, the good witch asked, "Are you really quitting cigarettes? Oh, Sabine, that's such nice news, congratulations! Are you proud? *I'm* proud of you. It can be awful hard to kick an addiction like that one."

"Uh-huh." Now leaning against the frame of the open door, Sabine rested her cheek upon her hand and tried as hard as she possibly could to see through the fabric of the good witch's pink dress, a kind of pale peach that was almost translucent in the sunlight.

What a fuckable fox! Eyebrows high, Sabine stared at Clarinda's adorably small tits while asking, "So have you finally come to your senses and decided to go left-handed?"

Left-hand path, that was—witch slang. Sorry, reader. Clarinda was very familiar with these terms, enough that her bright and cheery sense of positivity dropped into a petulant snort. "No, thanks," the stuck-up brat responded, "I'm happy being right."

"Cute pun."

"Thanks. Cute, uh…" Clarinda looked around, desperate for something to compliment. Seeing Bonesy washing windows up on the ladder beside the porch, she completely switched tactics mid-sentence. "I mean, nice—skeleton."

"I made him myself."

"Huh!" Appearing as if she were in physical pain for as badly as she wanted to turn around and go back to her own, brightly colored home down the lane, Clarinda nonetheless managed to invoke a smile. "Say…do you have a minute to chat?"

Sighing, Sabine stepped aside. "I get the feeling that wasn't really a request. That word, 'chat,' it's the fucking worst… HR-type shit. Sure, come in. I was just baking some cookies, actually."

"Oh *are* you? What kind?" Then, without stopping to wait for the answer as she stepped over the threshold and slipped out of pink flats matched carefully to her dress: "You should come and join the neighborhood bake sale with us sometime! We never get to see you!"

"I'm not really a people person," Sabine said while shutting the door.

Cable Dog, desperate for someone to free him from his new life of servitude, charged from the den to bark excitedly and run circles around Clarinda. Oblivious to the human's suffering, (or even that he was a human at all—shows you what a lot of good right-handed magic does), the good witch gasped in delight and knelt to ruffle his ears.

"Oh! Oh! I didn't *know* you had a doggie, Sabine! What a

handsome boy! Oh he's so handsome! Yes, hello! Yes, hello! Aren't you handsome! Yes, hello!" Sabine exchanged a wry sidelong glance with the mirror over the keyhook and then the doll in the den. On the floor, Clarinda let Cable Dog lick her face and paw at her tits as though he were simply an enthusiastic and innocent canine.

Yeah, uh-huh. It was all complaints about being made into a dog until you realized the kind of sugar it got you. Sabine saw your pervert ass, Cable Guy…that was why you were in this situation in the first place.

"So," said Sabine, leading the way into the kitchen without waiting for the good witch to extricate herself from the affection of the dog, "what's the situation? Somebody hex you, or something?"

"Oh, no, the Good Lord wouldn't allow something like that to happen to me…hexes aren't real, anyway. That's just silly heathen talk."

With another, far more prolonged glance at Alma—whom Sabine swore made a noise of derision, trapped as a doll or no—Sabine shook her head and resumed the process of making her cookies. Looking all around the house through which she wandered, Clarinda caught up and made herself at home in the beams of sunlight pouring upon the kitchen table. She cleared her throat before beginning in a delicate tone, "No, Sabine, I'm afraid to say I'm here today in…well, something of an official capacity. It's just—I'm the president of the neighborhood homeowner's association, and—"

"Of course you are," said Sabine out loud before she could stop herself, laughing in undisguised disgust. Even Cable Dog made a noise like a snort as he came to sit at the good witch's feet, probably hoping that she would offer to take him off of Sabine's hands. Instead he had the pleasure of having his back rubbed by Clarinda's adorable foot.

Sabine asked herself why she was jealous of a dog as the

perfectly innocent good witch went on, "You didn't know that? I guess I haven't seen you at any of the meetings, huh…"

"I would rather put a gun in my mouth than go to an HOA meeting for two minutes, babe, I've got to tell you."

Gasping sharply, leaning forward in her seat with one hand slapping flat upon the table, Clarinda said, "Don't say *that*, Sabine! Suicide is nothing to kid about."

"Who's kidding?"

"You don't have to be so *dramatic.*"

The good witch settled herself back down a little. While Cable Dog's head rested upon her knee and she doled out some ear scratches to the happy hound, Clarinda scowled primly. "HOA meetings can be fun, you know…it's a good way to meet your neighbors if you're not social enough for bake sales."

"I'm not social enough for bureaucracies, either.…HOAs are just fascist control mechanisms, an artifact of the patriarchy's obsession with having power over other people's lives."

"They serve an important purpose, Sabine! HOAs keep neighbors happy and property values in check…and that's why I'm here."

Pushing the snout of the dog back down to her knee once it had gotten somewhat too friendly, if you get the drift, Clarinda sat upright in her seat. The good witch said imperiously, "You can't paint your house without HOA approval, and you *certainly* can't paint it black. That's just not right. Think of the Broadstiens up the block. They've been trying to sell their house for two months! Do you think they'll have a prayer with this place looming down the street, looking so—so—ugly?"

Sabine laughed at the amount of force behind the word, as if producing an adjective that was the least bit judgmental caused the good witch physical pain. Oh, yeah…Sabine had to admit she loved the thought of Clarinda in pain, terrible pain.

If only Master would come by! Fuck, Sabine would have

sold her soul a second time for the opportunity to watch him go to town on Little Goody-Two-Shoes over there.

"Did you hear me, Sabine?"

"Huh?" Jarred from her fantasies, Sabine shook her head, laughed, and threw a few eggs into the mixer. "Yeah, yeah, sure. Ugly house, Broadstiens can't sell. Sorry. If you care about the neighborhood so much, why do you want people to leave it? Surely you'd want them to stay and be part of the community."

"*Nobody's* going to want to be part of the community with a big scary mansion like this one on the block! Do you think we're living in a Shirley Jackson novel?"

"Fuck, I wish."

"Oh, I know, don't you just love her—" Catching herself mid-distraction, Clarinda cleared her throat and continued, "Anyway! While I sure do admire your...uh...your *bold* devotion to being yourself no matter what other people say, even you have to admit that painting your whole house black is taking it a little too far."

"Well, Clarinda, I'll be honest with you...I wasn't sure I liked it at first, but now that I know how much it pisses you off, I think I might actually love it."

Her petulant scoff interrupting her petting of the dog, the good witch folded her hands in her lap. "Is that so?"

"Uh-huh. I was kind of thinking about having Bonesy change it back...but since you went out of your way to interrupt me in the middle of my day for a totally unwelcome lecture, now I'm asking myself what else I could do. Oh! Maybe a big mural. Satan fucking me up the ass, the whole thing emblazoned with big block letters that read, *MORE, DADDY, MORE!*" At the absolutely scandalized, wide-mouthed expression of the good witch, Sabine cackled—but when her cackling faded and she noted exactly how red-faced the good witch had become, well...

Sabine had to wonder about Miss Innocent over there.

"You—you *certainly* can't do a thing like that, Sabine—"

"Will you relax? I'm kidding. Don't get excited."

"I'm not *excited*, I just—I just wish you'd take some of this seriously. We're talking about the impact you're having on other people. Real people with real properties and real money on the table. Do you really want to be the reason the Broadstiens take a big financial hit?"

"Gosh, well—I just don't really care very much."

"How can you not *care*?"

"Uh…I'm evil?" Spreading her hands, Sabine started the mixer and admitted, "I guess I'm a little disconnected from material bullshit—money, or whatever. It's just another control mechanism, like an HOA. Doesn't it ever trip you out to think about what humans will do for some scraps of paper?"

Rolling her eyes, Clarinda said, "How high school of you."

"No, for real. People literally kill over this shit. They lose their whole lives. Think about all the businessmen who've cracked under pressure and murdered their families because it was easier than admitting they'd lost a job or couldn't send their kids to college."

"I try *not* to think about such things, generally."

"Maybe if you did, you wouldn't be so fucking patronizing."

"Patronizing! You're a fine one to talk—for as long as I've known you, Sabine, you've talked to me like I'm stupid. Just because I love God!"

"Loving God is pretty fucking stupid, Clarinda."

"Don't you *dare* say that."

Oh! There was the spice Sabine knew the good witch had inside her. Repressing her grin at the sharply appalled tone, Sabine settled for lifting her brows. "Well? It's true. You're just mad because you know I'm right. Everybody wants to blame *my* master for the bad shit in the world, but who created my master? Who gave my master free will and let him fall from grace?"

Ugh, smug Catholics. They always got the same look, the same tone when they said things like, "But free will is just why it's not God's fault. Sin is *mankind's* fault, the sinner's fault. Your—'master' is the most prideful sinner of all. That doesn't reflect on God."

"Oh, I'm sorry, are we all not part of the same fucking divine godhead expanding across the universe in infinite forms of being and expression? Furthermore, is this not the same guy who's always letting Job get boils, or turning women into salt, or, you know, *flooding* the fucking earth because He was butthurt about His angels coming down to fuck humans? I love how you good witches always conveniently forget that passage of the Bible."

"It's a metaphor!"

"Okay," said the witch who was still walking with a bit of a limp after being fucked by Satan the other day. "Look: regardless, my point is that you get all high-and-mighty about religious shit and it oozes out of your every pore. You are *super* patronizing and unrealistic."

"Is it unrealistic to ask that you not paint your house black?"

"It's certainly fascist," said Sabine. "I own this house, and—"

"Because you stole it."

"That doesn't make it any less mine now," the bad witch bandied back. "Not that the HOA cares. It's ridiculous! Regardless of how I got this place, I pay property taxes, don't I? Then your stupid organization turns around and charges me even *more*, and levels fees, and does all this other nonsense. If other people having money was so important to you, why are you letting the organization charge us? So we can—what, add a bench to the empty lot at the end of the street?"

Shaking her head, Sabine tided up a few dishes and cooking implements to dump in the sink.

"It's amazing to me you're as young as you are, Clarinda. Usually the president of an HOA is somebody in their fifties or sixties. What does your boyfriend think about your control problems?"

Scoffing, Clarinda looked down at the dog and resumed tickling his ears, clearly unable to resist those eyes or that hopefully wagging tail. "I don't have *control problems*—or a boyfriend."

Right into the classic trap. Oh, Clarinda! You naïve spring flower. Sabine scrubbed flour from her wooden spoon and examined it in the light to ensure it was clean. "Really? You mean you're not fucking that hot gardener of yours?"

Clarinda's voice had a way of leaping in pitch when she was embarrassed, and now was no exception. Sabine bit back a laugh while her rival sputtered out the words, "Wh—*well, good*—of course not, of course that would be—that's just not—the Bible—premarital sex is, it isn't right, it's a sin, of course, Sabine, and—"

The bad witch's eyes widened and, spoon still clutched in her hand, she whirled on her surprise guest. "Are you trying to tell me you're a *virgin, Clarinda?*"

"Of course I am, silly!" Coiffing her blonde curls to have an excuse to look off to the side, Clarinda cleared her throat and insisted to her Satanic neighbor, "The Good Lord created—*sex*"—Sabine inhaled to hear how difficult the word was for the good witch to even say—"as a gift, a celebration of marriage between—between a man and a woman—what? Why are you looking at me like that?"

It was sort of appropriate that unicorns had such a notorious interest in virgins: in the 21st century, virgins *were* unicorns, at least so far as the bad witch was concerned. Who still waited for marriage? Holy shit, Sabine was tripping out just thinking about it—it totally blew her mind to even remember that virginity was a concept. Boggling, the bad witch said, "This makes so much sense."

"What does?"

"You! Your HOA thing. No wonder you're the president of the homeowners' association! You have nothing better to do! Oh man, I totally understand now."

"That's—one doesn't have anything to do with the other!"

"Yeah, yeah!" On a roll, Sabine pointed the spoon at the good witch as though it were a magic wand. "Oh, wow, I get it! I totally get it…and your power trip thing? Shit, of course! No wonder you're such a slave to social control mechanisms."

"What on earth are you talking about?"

"Virginity's not real," said Sabine flatly, crossing back over to turn off the mixer and throw in her dry ingredients. "Like, I mean, it exists as a concept—but *only* as a concept. Like zero. You ever gotten into a debate with somebody about whether zero is a number or a concept?"

"No, because I fill my life with wholesome and productive activities instead of getting into pointless arguments with people."

"Hah, yes, because your HOA is so wholesome…because this isn't a super pointless visit."

Although—Sabine now had to wonder if it was really pointless. Did you send Clarinda over here, Master? Why… glancing over to the kitchen window where Bonesy appeared with the rag clutched in his spindly fingers, Sabine couldn't help but think that this was exactly what had happened. Had the Dark Lord not distracted her while Bonesy got the black paint out of the shed? If she hadn't been fucked unconscious by her master's tendrils she might have gone outside soon enough to notice the color and put the brakes on.

Was all of this nonsense Satan's will?

"I just can't believe you're a virgin," said Sabine, dusting off her hands and removing her black *SAIL HATIN'* apron once she'd added the chocolate chips.

"How can you stand it? Everybody in the world is out here having fun. Meanwhile you're just sitting in your house, watching your sweaty gardener glisten all over your yard, hot and buff and fuckable."

"Well—well I just don't *think* like that, I suppose—I do have fun, you know—"

"Uh-huh. Like what?"

"Like—oh, well!" Sitting up, beaming, Clarinda said, "Like having the girls over for Bible study on Sundays, that's always a blast. You should come, Sabine! We'd just love to have you. There's a potluck, oh! And sometimes we play White Elephant."

Gag! Oh God, the worst and most corporate game of them all. Sabine would rather her master turn her eyes into spiders so they could crawl out of her head while he gave her a good frontal lobe fucking like he had on his birthday that one year. (No, not June 6th, although that would be cute.) The bad witch was just about to politely refuse when Clarinda continued, "And jigsaw puzzles! I love a good jigsaw puzzle. Oh, and crosswords. And, of course, I love to read."

"What do you like to read?"

"Romance novels, mostly."

"Oho! You dirty girl."

Blushing, Clarinda sputtered, "Why—what do you mean?"

"Because! When you're reading something, your brain responds as if you're actually living it. It's basic neuroscience… the narrative structure of traditional fiction appeals to the human brain in some very specific ways. In other words, when you're reading a romance novel, your synapses are firing to produce a simulation of romance, and you're even getting some of the same chemicals. So, really, reading sleezy romances, you're being as much of a slut as me."

Appalled, Clarinda insisted, "Of course I'm not!"

"You are, you bad girl…instead of actually taking a big, hard dick like you're too scared to, you're reading about all kinds of other people doing it. Why, you're practically a philanderer!"

"That's a ridiculous thing to say." Cable Dog audibly sighed while, with a stomp of her foot, Clarinda rose from her seat and seemed to almost bristle. "Reading is just *dreaming!* There's nothing wrong with dreaming. Fiction is—human creativity is a gift from God."

"Yeah, you're right. When you're reading a book you're engaging with the fruits of somebody else's creativity... receiving it into you, if you will. Partnering with someone for a temporary length of time to experience the ecstasy of romance...huh, what does *that* sound like..."

"Reading somebody else's writing is *not* the same thing as having sex with someone."

"After a certain level of abstraction I defy you to prove there's any difference."

"Oh, that's silly. You could say that about anything."

"Yeah—I could, couldn't I! Good and evil, black and white, God and Satan...it's almost like the whole universe is just one object dispersed into a multitude of symbols across spacetime as a result of the inevitable emergence of consciousness!"

Clarinda had stopped listening about two sentences in. "Excuse me! God and Satan are *not* the same."

"Well, not linguistically, and not when they're physicalized...but what's the difference between the numbers 1 and 2, really? It's either a unit of '1', or an *infinite* number of steps. Everything and nothing. It just depends on how many numbers you're willing to acknowledge stand between them. And when one alternative is infinity, well...then a difference of a single unit might as well be zero."

"That logic is so flawed I don't even know where to begin."

"Not really...it's a difference of perspective. It depends— perception is relative, like time. Consciousness is a function of discernment, this thing from that thing. Without consciousness, everything would be unified. *Solve et coagula.* Dissolve and coagulate. Consciousness and unconsciousness. I know we can at least agree on alchemy, Little Miss Catholic."

While Clarinda watched with her arms still crossed, Sabine set down the wooden spoon she'd used to gesture while she spoke.

She began plunking chunks of cookie dough upon a nearby pan, observing, "For instance, at what point does this collection of ingredients start being cookie dough? Does its current state as cookie dough negate the fact that it is also, strictly speaking, a chemical combination of flour, butter, eggs, sugar, all the other things I threw into this bowl? Does its future state as completely baked cookies negate its current condition? Are these things, these definitions, not just units on the scale of physical assessment?"

"Of course, but in that case, one thing is turning into the other. There's no evidence that God and Satan are part of the same entity, the same structure."

Sliding the pan into the oven and hitting the timer, Sabine asked, "So angels just appeared out of nowhere in your version of the Bible? They don't have any divine substance to them at all? Angels—like, I don't know, Metatron, the literal voice of God—aren't a part of God just like you and me?"

"Satan is *not* God." Clarinda's tone was the salty Catholic one that indicated she wanted the conversation to be over. Arms folded, she crossed the kitchen to stand before Sabine, eyes blazing as if she weren't a full head shorter. "Black is not white, and your house is not acceptable in its current condition. You can change it, or you can move—but you absolutely, unequivocally cannot keep it the way it is."

Blame the bad witch's poor impulse control. Probably had something to do with whatever led her to selling her soul in the first place. One time when Sabine was a kid she had a nickel in her hand: a strange compulsion came over her and, right in front of her father, she wound up like she was pitching a baseball and hurled the nickel dead into the front door. It didn't leave a dent or anything like that, but it made a considerable, bullet impact sort of noise, and her father had asked her, baffled, "Why did you do that?"

She had no idea. She'd done it because her brain had told her to do it. And in the moment she snatched up her wooden spoon to smack Clarinda Lovegood's tight little good witch ass, Sabine was once again just doing what her brain told her to do.

Some compulsions were too natural: certain targets, too tempting. Sabine realized what she was doing only as the sound of Clarinda's sharp gasp leapt into her ears. Then, deciding her only choice was to double down, Sabine did it again, harder, the *crack* of the spoon's back against the good witch's ass like thunder in the kitchen.

"What—"

At the connection of the third strike, Clarinda shrieked and automatically reached back to try to cover her ass. Can't have that! Sabine didn't want to break her hands, after all. Helpfully catching Clarinda's wrist with one hand, then momentarily putting down the spoon to nab the other in the same grip, Sabine soon went to town on the blonde's adorable backside and cackled evilly all the time.

"Stop! Ow! Sabine! Oh, ow! Ow! Quit it, let me go—"

"You're just getting what you deserve—you can't come into *my* house, insult my skeleton's hard work, tell me to change my paint or get out—"

As Clarinda hissed and bounced from foot to foot in an ill-fated attempt to escape the rapid onslaught of the spoon, conflicted Cable Dog mirrored the motion as if trying to decide whether to break it up. His tail was wagging a little too hard to justify intervention and eventually, settling on his haunches, the dog produced a happy, high-pitched yawn and enjoyed the show. Bonesy, too, had abruptly stopped his work. One skeletal hand cupped around his eye sockets, he peered into the kitchen through whatever magical means permitted him even the slightest vision.

Who could blame either one of them? It was what you were doing right now, in a way.

And, anyway, there was a lot to look at. Sabine's grin as she brought the spoon down at a painfully fast tempo was only rivaled in intensity by Clarinda's shocked expression of pain and embarrassment, her face as flushed as her plump, open lips. "Oh," whined the good witch, wiggling in Sabine's grasp, "oh, oh—stop, please, Sabine—"

"Are you going to drop this shit about my house?"

"But—but the bylaws—oh!"

Sabine's spoon sped its pace and tears filled Clarinda's eyes—but, soon, something about her cries changed. Her squealing and shrieking reduced to whimpers and, although her struggling continued, the glassiness of her eyes altered from tearful to something Sabine couldn't even recognize in the good witch's face. She paused the assault to examine Clarinda's features more carefully, unable for a few seconds to identify what she saw there...until, at last, a victorious gasp erupted from Sabine.

"Are you getting *turned* on?"

"What?" The word was so sharp and panicked it might as well have been an avid, "Yes," or even, "Hell yes." While Sabine gaped, Clarinda at last extricated one slim wrist from her grip while insisting, "Of course not—of course not! Why would you say something so—ah!"

"You *do* like it," Sabine said, applying the spoon a few more times, faster and lower across the back of Clarinda's pink dress. "Yeah, you do like it, you dirty girl...no fucking wonder! All Catholics are perverts, that's why they're always in confession—they're always thinking of so much fucked up—hey!"

At last, teeth clenched, Clarinda managed to snatch the

spoon from Sabine's grip. "I am *not* "turned on," and I'm not a pervert, and—how do you like it!"

In what was quite possibly the greatest mistake of her adult life thusfar, Clarinda liberally applied the implement to the bad witch's ass. Sabine laughed at first, but soon the hot sting elicited a moan of pleasure. "Oh," she said, "I don't just like it! I love it. Fuck—spank me, Clarinda! Oh, yeah, I've been a bad, bad witch, that's right, I'm naughty—"

"Wh—what's wrong with you?" Stopping, shocked and appalled, Clarinda looked down at the spoon in her hand and said in a tone even sharper than her denial, "What's wrong with *me!*" While Sabine cackled, the good witch tossed down the spoon and recoiled from it like it was a viper poised to strike.

Looking with terror between that spoon and the moaning, snickering bad witch, Clarinda stumbled back to the threshold of the kitchen. Appearing by the second all the wilder, all the more desperate to escape, Clarinda stared as Sabine, tears of her hysterical laughter in her eyes, enthused, "What's wrong with *me?* At least I don't lie to myself."

"I—I don't—I don't know what you mean—"

"Oh, yeah! I'm so sure…oh, but." Her eyes lighting with sadistic fire, Sabine grinned at the good witch and assured her, "Maybe you don't really know. Gosh, it's no wonder you keep waiting around and dreaming of love…do you even realize you're into chicks?"

"I—I— Repaint this stupid house!"

Clarinda's command came with such an abrupt, childlike stomp that Sabine could only laugh again. The good witch turned on her heel at the sound and stormed out, Sabine calling after, "Aw, babe, don't be like *that*, don't worry! I won't tell…"

The front door slammed and Sabine, alone in her kitchen, laughed herself to tears.

Go figure! All this time, Sabine had thought Clarinda was a stuck-up bitch…turned out she was just shy, or in denial. Also kind of a bitch and definitely stuck-up, but now some aspects of that made more sense.

If anything, Sabine felt bad for the good witch. It must have been so hard to be a bisexual Catholic! Or a gay one. Sabine wasn't sure which Clarinda was but, judging her interest in trashy romance novels, Sabine had a sense that this was a "swinging both ways" kind of situation.

The question was, how much of the rest of her coven— sorry, "Bible study group"—was the same way?

Next Sunday, Sabine was again perched atop her ladder with that pair of gleaming binoculars. Hazel, who had come a few minutes earlier than the other members of Sabine's coven, perched a rung lower with her red curls pulled up and her hand shielding her pretty green eyes. As similarly ponytailed Sabine said, "Look, look, they're starting to arrive," and passed the binoculars down to her friend, buxom and bleach blonde Gina began to fidget from where she held the base of the ladder for the other two.

"When do I get a turn," complained the bimbo while Hazel zoomed in on the binoculars.

The elder witches ignored their slutty friend. Still peering through the lenses, Hazel enthused, "Dark Lord, there must be seven of them!"

"Six plus Clarinda, yeah, that's about right."

Several houses down from the black Victorian, the good witches were beginning to gather for their usual Sunday brunch. One by one they cluttered up the street parking and went around to Clarinda's side gate, letting themselves through familiarly to kiss and hug and contribute their variations of fruit salad to the prearranged table in the back yard.

"I can't believe there are still seven Catholics left in the *world*, let alone millions…ugh!" Thrusting the binoculars back into Sabine's hand, Hazel shook her head. "They really are brainwashing experts."

"Guys," called Gina up the ladder as a sleek silver car rolled around the corner to slide alongside Sabine's house, "can I see?"

"You can see if you go let Bernice in," lied Sabine, who lifted the binoculars to her eyes and swept their focus from the Bible study's guests to their hostess.

Damn, Clarinda was fine. Those curves! That smile. Very George Petty. Sabine hated to admit it, but for a good witch, Clarinda really turned her on. And now that she seemed so corruptible, well…

"Does Master really think we have a—a prayer, if you'll excuse the pun—of getting through to these spoiled little bitches?" Peering beneath the shade of her hand, Hazel glanced up to Sabine.

The foremost bad witch was busy trying to zoom in and see down the cleavage of Clarinda's white, lilac-printed summer dress. "Don't know," she said, deciding the task was impossible from that angle, "didn't ask him. But I feel it in my gut."

By the time Sabine had finished explaining the business about Bonesy and the distraction that had kept Sabine from noting the black paint, Gina returned while leading Bernice. The Haitian witch's braids were elaborately arranged atop her head in a sort of crown that earned her a call of delight from Hazel, but Sabine couldn't stand to lower the binoculars for longer than a few seconds. She was too busy leering with jealousy every time Clarinda so much as put her hand on a friend's arm.

"So what's this emergency meeting about," Bernice called from the bottom of the ladder. "Sunday is my 'me' day, you know—I thought our next Sabbath was next weekend, anyway."

"It is," agreed Gina, who looked hopeful as Hazel descended the ladder. Bernice didn't wait before barging past the instantly pouting bimbo, scaling the rungs and sticking her artfully decorated head up over the top of the fence. Meanwhile, one guest had gone to Clarinda's front door. As a result of having her attention drawn inside by the doorbell, Clarinda disappeared from view.

"You know me," said Sabine, at last relinquishing the binoculars. "I lose interest in a plan if I don't go through with it when I get the urge."

Bernice scoffed. "What the hell is that over there? Some kind of baby shower, or something?"

With a snort of her own, Sabine answered, "It's about as interesting—Clarinda Lovegood's Bible study group."

"Ugh!"

While, at the base of the ladder, Hazel mimed gagging just to hear the words aloud again, Bernice's lovely mouth curved into an exaggerated sneer. The Haitian witch turned her face from the binoculars only as long as it took her to spit on the ground. "Bible study! That fucking book, it's good for three things. Rolling joints, swearing oaths in court, and subjugation."

"You forgot about Psalms," said Sabine. "Like the hyssop one we use all the time."

"Tch! Whatever. Four things, I guess. So—we're going to break it up, eh?"

"If that's all we do, I'm going to be very disappointed. I think we might be able to convert them—one of them, anyway."

Still at the base of the ladder, Gina gasped. Hazel folded her arms and arched a brow up at the witches who, one at a time, descended the ladder.

"Really," said the redhead, both eyebrows now lifting with

the comic articulations of her lips. "What are we going to do? Knock on the door and ask if they've heard the Bad News?"

"No, you bitch." Shoving her laughing friend once her feet were upon the earth, Sabine folded up the ladder while ignoring Gina's complaints about never getting to look. "We're going to demonstrate. Let's just go over there and summon Master."

"Oh, come on." Bernice leaned back against the fence while Sabine whistled for her slave—uh, handyman—who came rattling out of his storage space in the shed. (What? Skeletons don't need beds to sleep in, or bedrooms. Don't feel bad for him, he earned this just like Cable Dog.) "If there's anybody who already knows Satan exists just as well as we do, it's the Christians. They practically invented him. A demonstration isn't going to change their minds."

"Satan's way older than Christianity," corrected Sabine, hands on her hips. "And it's one thing to just know that Master exists in an abstract way. It's another thing entirely to actually meet him or see what he can do."

Hazel mirrored Sabine's posture, ignoring Bonesy as he collected the ladder from his mistress. Gina, the newest witch of their coven, openly marveled at the skeleton while Hazel asked, "You just want to ruin their brunch, don't you?"

"That Lovegood bitch wants me to change my house or move out of the neighborhood." While all three witches made appalled noises, Sabine, validated, continued, "I think we need to show her who's really in charge around here, HOA or no."

"Ugh," said Bernice, voice overflowing with disgust, "HOAs!"

Hazel added in a supportive tone, "I meant to *say* how much I love your new house color."

"Yeah, well, apparently it's "against HOA bylaws,"" said Sabine, making air quotes with her fingers. "And it's "damaging to property values" and "an eyesore.""

"Fuck that," said Bernice.

"Right?"

Gina, in a mousy little voice, began, "It is maybe just a little—"

Three heads whipped in her direction.

Stuttering, Gina corrected, "Uh—uh, that is, uh—fuck them!"

"Fuck it," said Hazel, heading toward the yard's side gate. "Let's set them straight."

Setting them 'straight' wasn't what Sabine had in mind, exactly…but, well, she wasn't going to correct her friend's figure of speech. "Hold down the fort, you two," said Sabine to Bonesy—and Cable Dog, who sat panting happily under the shade of an apple tree. "And prune that tree," she added to the skeleton, whose bones rattled as though in lieu of an eye roll or a muttered comment. "Don't think I didn't hear that!"

Out on the street, Sabine admired the sky. Beautiful, blue, perfectly clear. A great day to do some light home invasion.

"So," said Hazel as the foursome made their way down the sidewalk, "how are we going to summon Master today? A spirit board? Playing "Stairway to Heaven" backwards six times? Another game of *Dungeons & Dragons?*"

"Don't be ridiculous," answered Sabine. "You know we don't have time to start a whole campaign in Clarinda's basement before she discovers us. I have something better in mind."

"What's that?"

"Virgin's blood."

The bad witches stopped before the Lovegood residence.

Ugh! Just look at it. Standing in front of the good witch's house made Sabine sick to her stomach. The back yard ruckus of happy, laughing, Bible-thumping young women was the only imperfect thing about it. As much as Sabine's house resembled, say, a cool old-fashioned dollhouse hand-carved of wood, Clarinda's was like a tacky, cheap, overly cheerful

Fischer-Price alternative. The white siding gleamed as brightly as the blue accents, and the very windows seemed to smile in welcome.

Sabine exchanged a glance of horror with her friends. Bernice, looking particularly disgusted with the building, asked, "That's all well and good, but how are we going to get inside?"

"I'll just do an unlocking spell or whatever," answered Sabine, quietly mounting the stairs of the porch and then, with one more glance around, resting her hand on the knob.

Of course—imagine her surprise when the thing turned beneath her hand without her even having to hex it.

Hazel rolled her eyes to see it was unlocked. "Oh, Dark Lord's sake—these naive good witches…"

Sabine had to repress a spate of cackled laughter. "But it's such a *safe* neighborhood,'" said Sabine in an nasally impression of Clarinda's southern belle accent. "'Who'd lock their doors on a blessed day like today?'"

"Richard Chase would go into houses that were unlocked and kill everybody inside," said Gina, who, despite her stereotypical appearance as an overinflated bimbo, was a veritable encyclopedia of macabre knowledge that had made her a fantastic fit for their coven. "He felt like he was invited. That was why they called him the Vampire of Sacramento."

"I thought that was because of the blood-drinking," said Bernice.

"That, too."

Annoyed, Sabine shushed both her friends. "You want to get us caught? Come on…"

With a shake of her head, Sabine pushed open the door and slipped into the Lovegood home.

Boy. Oh, boy. If the outside was nauseatingly cute, the interior was…we'll be generous and call it "old-fashioned." Talking, crucifixes decorating walls-, samplers reading *HOME*

SWEET HOME-, afghans on every surface-"old-fashioned."

Sabine wrinkled her nose just to look around the place while Gina, with a delighted, "Ooh!" went straight for the little black cat sleeping contentedly in the corner of the striped divan. "Kitty-kitty-kitty," she sang while Hazel scowled at a particularly detailed crucifix hanging over the same sofa.

"I feel like I'm in my grandmother's old house," commented the redhead while Bernice came over to tickle the ears of the cat. It had permitted itself to be cuddled in Gina's arms and even stuck out a pair of white fangs in outrageously cute approximation of a smile.

"I didn't realize that good witches kept black cats," remarked the braided witch.

"Oh, sure. Good witches like all animals…and, anyway, they're still witches." Sabine delivered this answer absently, looking around, deciding how best to lure the brunch's hostess back into the house. She had tried to think this out beforehand but, never having been in Clarinda's house before, she wasn't really sure of their options for mischief.

Rubbing her jaw and thinking as she was, she barely heard Hazel ask, "What are they doing practicing witchcraft, anyway? I thought the Bible is all anti-magick."

"If the Bible were as anti-magick as people seem to think it is, transubstantiation would mean nothing…"

"Speaking of transubstantiation"—Hazel had found herself before a liquor cabinet and cackled to open the glass door—"look at all this! I'm amazed she's been able to keep her virginity with this stuff around."

"Catholics practically invented alcoholism," answered Bernice with a husky laugh.

Sabine was just looking up the stairs, formulating a plan, when the back door opened. All four witches froze, exchanging a quick look of semi-panic while, laughing gaily, a cute brunette trotted in with her keys in her hand. She was obviously headed back to her car to fetch something she'd forgotten, but she stopped dead on the edge of the living room.

This stranger looked between the busty goth girl and her friends, then smiled. That was, of course, the Christian thing to do.

"Why hello! Are you ladies here for our Bible study group?"

Not very long later, while the gagged brunette's desperate protests were muffled not just by the rag in her mouth but also by the hall closet into which the bad witches had stuffed her, Sabine said, "Okay, this is perfect. Now, let's see—Gina, will you put that cat down?"

"But he likes me!" Yes, it was true. Clarinda's purring black cat looked very happy in the pouting witch's arms—but who wouldn't be? Annoyed, Sabine strolled over and extricated the feline from the bimbo's grasp.

Upon setting the cat down on its feet to let it wander back to its warm spot on the divan, Sabine said, "We don't have very long before somebody, hopefully Clarinda, comes in looking for that one. Let's do something about the lights. Does she still have a landline phone?"

Of course Clarinda had a landline phone—it was what a person was supposed to do, after all, and good witches did what they thought people were supposed to do. While Gina hurried off to the garage to find the fuse box and kill the lights, Hazel cut the phone lines.

Bernice joined Sabine upstairs. The witches shared a horrified look at the sheer number of doilies accenting the darkened master bedroom. Hard to decide if it resembled an old lady's room or a little girl's. Though, pursuant to her kitchen conversation with Clarinda, the only real difference between a little girl and an old lady was relative location in spacetime.

"Not a single human skull," marveled Bernice while Sabine used her left hand to cross herself in reverse.

"There but for the grace of Satan go we." After looking around and finally deciding with a shrug that there was no point in being shy, Sabine crossed to the antique white dresser beside the plushly made bed. While Bernice asked, "So, which one's a virgin," Sabine laughed and slid open the top drawer of the dresser.

"Are you kidding? These girls are the squarest of the square—they're spending a day of their weekend attending a women's Bible study. They're *all* virgins."

Jackpot! Sabine beamed at Clarinda's frilly underthings, reaching right into the drawer of panties and pulling out its contents by the handful. Without having to be asked, Bernice hurried over to take a few armfuls of her own. "You never can tell with those Christian girls, though," she was saying, snatching a few bras for good measure. "Like, what about the ones who take it up the ass or give out handjobs?"

"They're already slaves to Master, just like every other hypocrite in the world. Wait—" Bernice had been turning away but, with a gasp, Sabine reached into the now mostly empty drawer to push aside a few loose socks. Beneath all those frilly underthings there sat a hand-carved cigar box, and so far as Sabine knew, the good witch didn't smoke cigars. What was Clarinda keeping in this little wooden box hidden in her underwear drawer?

The skunky smell hit both witches as soon as Sabine cracked open the top.

"Clarinda Lovegood smokes *weed?*" Sabine marveled at the sight, almost unable to compute the contents of the stashbox in the given context. Bernice laughed with delight into the wooden container while, temporarily dropping her armfuls of underwear, Sabine lifted the box to her nose and took a sniff. "Oh man! Good shit, too. I would have been less surprised to find dead body parts in here! What the fuck?"

"Guess she's cooler than we thought," Bernice answered

while Sabine slipped a paper out of the screaming orange Zig-Zag pack. "I mean, it's not that surprising. The Bible doesn't say anything about it—and it's legal in this state, after all. All the moms who used to drink a glass of wine every night are sneaking joints now."

"Guess so…"

With a well-practiced hand, Sabine crumbled a sizable moss-green bud into powder and sprinkled it along the paper she then twisted shut. The common magician trick was to light your joint with your finger, but Sabine preferred blowing across the joint's tip and watching the cherry spring to life—it had such a nice, neat symmetry with blowing out the flame of a candle. After offering Bernice the first puff, Sabine stuck the cannabis cigarette in her mouth and said, "Man, nice flavor… you know they say pot actually improves your lung strength?"

Hm…and she was just talking about replacing her bad habit of tobacco. Thanks, Satan! Good idea.

A footfall drew Sabine's attention. While stooping to pick up the abandoned pile of panties she turned, then grinned to find Hazel and Gina had appeared in the doorway.

"What are you doing," asked Gina while Hazel laughed at the sight of two witches with armfuls of panties.

Sabine grinned. "Just getting the homeowner's attention…"

With Bernice and Sabine overburdened, it was up to Hazel and Gina to find a window that overlooked the garden party. It wasn't long before they found a suitable one in a guest room. Before it was opened, Sabine peered out through the glass and down upon the lawn.

Her eyes narrowed.

There she was: Little Miss Perfect. Smiling happily between all her friends.

"Okay," Clarinda could be heard saying while Hazel pushed up the window with a grunt, "who wants to say grace?"

"What about Martha," asked one of the good witches.

"She's been gone at least five minutes! She didn't leave, did she?"

"Huh! I guess she has been gone an awful long time…hold on, let me see what happened to her."

Now or never! Already grinning to see Clarinda leaving her place at the table, Sabine asked Satan in her heart to help her with her timing. Of course, wasn't the Dark Lord always guiding his servant's hand? Especially in matters of interference with all people who were kind and decent: then, Satan was especially present, especially able to whisper in Sabine's soul that now was the exact right second to dump her armful of panties out the window to cover Clarinda in the maximum amount of lace and cotton.

"Wha—"

Baffled to be smothered in an avalanche of her own underwear as she was, Clarinda was certainly not anticipating a second armful to be dropped by Bernice. Very obviously, Clarinda wasn't even sure what the garments were until a bra landed right on her head.

While the bad witches cackled from their vantage in the upstairs window, Clarinda yanked the B-cup from her face. The elegant hostess gawked up at the jeering women who had crashed her garden party but only seemed to fully comprehend what was happening when she saw them passing a joint back and forth.

"—will you ladies excuse me," the good witch said through a painful grimace, an attempt at a smile that made her look like she was baring her teeth—like she was experiencing an emotion that wasn't some variation of feigned cheerfulness, however the expression attempted to remain pleasant. "I have to—I'll just be right back."

While Clarinda peeled a pair of panties off her shoulder, then stormed into the house, the witches shared another spate of laughter. Together they retreated back into the room.

"Her face," enthused Hazel. "I think she was literally turning red."

Sabine wiped a delighted tear from her eye, hooting. "She probably was, only because she's so embarrassed... probably doesn't want her friends to know that she has to wear underwear. I bet she wants her friends to think she's all smooth like a Barbie doll—sh-sh-sh, hold on—"

Angry footsteps were crossing through the house, intent on the stairs. They stopped when attracted by the sounds of struggle coming from the hallway linen closet. A door opened. "Martha—*Martha*, oh my God! What happened?"

Again, the bad witches were unable to help themselves and exploded into tearful laughter. The outraged good witch downstairs grumbled, "No, never mind, of course I know what happened—" and, too angry to think, shut the door again while her friend's screams reached a high pitch on the other side of the gag. On her way up the stairs, Clarinda swore at something, and then, after a great deal of tromping, the guest bedroom door flew open.

Bristling like her cat, Clarinda the Good Witch demanded to know, "What on God's green earth is going *on* here!"

"More like what are you doing smoking pot, you bad girl!" Sabine laughed and accepted the joint back from Gina while the other members of her coven giggled with her. "Naughty, naughty! Didn't you take the D.A.R.E. program in middle school? Before too long you'll be selling that cute virgin pussy for smack."

Instantly as red as a strawberry, Clarinda produced a few incoherent stutters while she looked around the room as if for help. Finding none, she rested her hands upon the backs of her hips and, blinking rapidly, managed, "It—it—if you *must* know, I do smoke—sometimes. For menstrual cramps."

"Uh-huh...far out, man." While the other witches laughed at Sabine's hippie voice, the neighborhood's native bad witch slithered over to offer the joint to Madame HOA President. "Come on, take a hit! Relax a little, we're just teasing you."

"I understand *teasing*," said Clarinda, glancing between Sabine's sharp eyes and the red tip of the joint. At last she snatched the cigarette from Sabine's fingers and the bad witch grinned at her coven, then savored the downright shocking sight of the good witch's lightly rouged cheeks hollowing while she angrily puffed the pot between her words. "But there's—there's a line between teasing and—and being downright rude, Sabine, and—and I'll have you know that I work hard to make my Bible studies nice, and—"

Choking on smoke, Clarinda covered her mouth with her fist and passed the joint back to Sabine. While she accepted it with one hand, the goth patted Clarinda on the back and repressed a shudder of appreciation for how warm, how soft, how lean was all the flesh beneath. As the choking spell cleared she kept her hand there and the good witch was in too much of a tizz to notice or comment.

That, or she liked it.

While the good witch passed the joint to the bad one, she asked through her clearing throat, "Did you cut my *power?*"

"We can't summon Master with the lights on. In fact, most electronic equipment is verboten. Your girlfriends will have to leave their cellphones at the door."

"Wh—" Clarinda recoiled but, much to the bad witch's delight, not fully from reach of her hand. Pretty face paling beneath her light make-up, the good witch clasped the golden cross hanging by the chain around her neck. "You mean—Why, what nonsense, what a load of nonsense, that's just ridiculous—"

"It's true." Hazel sashayed up and draped her arms around Sabine's shoulders. Only now did Clarinda step back and away, glancing down at Sabine's hand as if just realizing it had been there. That hand folded back over the one Hazel had draped upon Sabine's heart. The redheaded bad witch said with her chin upon the shoulder of the goth, "Our sister received a message…I'm convinced of it. Our Master is the one commanding you to give Sabine such a hard time about her house."

"What an absurd thing to—" The gears turned in that Catholic brain. "—What an absurd thing to say."

Catholic brain, remember. Clarinda still had a ways to go in her understanding of the occult. Poor good witch! They always made it so hard for themselves.

Clarinda crossed her arms. Her hands, neatly painted in soft pink gel polish, drew unconscionable amounts of attention to her petite bust as she carried on. "Look—I respect your right to be wrong, but I'm a human being with free will. I know Christ has already saved me, and I'm sure you girls believe what you believe for very good reasons, but I'm not *interested*."

"I'm never this polite to the Jehovah's Witnesses who come around," remarked Sabine to Hazel, who laughed while Bernice sidled up to sling a friendly arm around the good witch's shoulders.

"Well, baby, if you're already saved, why don't you try living a little?" Bernice accepted the joint from Hazel. After effortlessly inhaling and passing the cigarette to Gina, the braided witch blew a smoke ring past Clarinda's taken aback face. "Christ is all about forgiveness, don't you know?"

"That's right," said Clarinda, red-faced and frightened, her eyes rapidly moving from one set of wicked eyes to another before settling helplessly on Sabine's. Surrounded by the bad witches now, the good one seemed to shrink in fear.

There was a plea there, and Sabine would answer it…but she wanted Clarinda to sweat a little, too. And wanted to think about how, after they got the matter of her virginity out of the way, it would be awfully fun to run a train on her some Sabbath.

Seeing her plea was not about to be imminently answered, the intimidated good witch cleared her throat and forced herself to explain, "But—but you see, you see, you can't consent to sin and then confess knowing that you intend to sin again. It's disingenuous in the worst possible way. It's a mortal sin. What is it? Therefore—um, whoever—

""Therefore whoever eats the bread or drinks the cup of the Lord in an unworthy manner shall be guilty of the body and the blood of the Lord." Gina repeated the quote with a crooked grin. At Clarinda's open surprise that the sluttiest-looking bimbo of the group had produced such a rapidfire Bible reference, said bimbo explained, "My parents sent me to one of those pray-the-gay-away camps."

"Oh"—Clarinda's brow furrowed—"those places are just horrible! I'm so sorry they did that to you."

Gina shrugged. "It's cool. Daddy saved me."

"She means Satan," helpfully explained Bernice, waving a hand toward her and then toward Sabine and Hazel. "Just like Christ saved you, Satan saved us. The difference is that Satan is willing to do it in this life and the next."

"But look at all the things Christ and God the Father have given me in this life! A house, a group of friends who are waiting for me downstairs, the fortune to be—privileged." She couldn't stop her reflexive glance toward the dark hand of braided Bernice: a hand that clearly only stopped itself from grabbing a palmful of Clarinda only by virtue of not having received Sabine's permission.

Bernice, who was very patient, did not show offense if she felt it. "I grew up very privileged, too, but you're right. God privileged us both in different ways. Accepting the invitation of a relationship with Satan is not the same thing as denying God. In fact, some would say a relationship with Satan is predicated upon a relationship with God."

"That's right," said Sabine. "I grew up Catholic, and—"

Gasping, Clarinda asked, "You did? I didn't know."

"Well, I'm not, like, confirmed or anything. But obviously, having thought about a lot of the doctrine, the Virgin Mary, how Christ is by definition the physical embodiment of a specific archetype of high and perfect clear light consciousness, I acknowledge that Catholicism is correct. There's no doubt in my mind that it's correct. But it's what a person does with that faith that begs the question of the soul, because, well…what does that book say, faith without works, Gina?"

""For as the body without the spirit is dead, so faith without works is dead also.""

"That's right. And "works" can be charity or whatever…but "works," that's an interesting word. That's what we call what we do, spells and all…we call it working, "magickal working," "works." Sometimes "fixing" or "tricking," but of course"— Sabine chuckled—"that last one also means something else in modern American culture."

"Though it's very appropriate," offered Hazel. "Because, of course, witchcraft has always had its sexual associations, but for very, very early pre-Christian and even pre-Hebrew faiths, sacred prostitution and general sacred sexuality play important roles in magickal and religious rituals."

In the taut, slightly unsteady tone of someone who was listening but still clearly on the defensive side of a confrontation, Clarinda asked, "What's the difference between a religious ritual and a magickal one?"

"Whether or not the venue is taxed," answered Bernice.

The other three laughed and Clarinda sputtered, eyes fluttering as if out of some kind of daze. Rejecting the joint with a palm lifted flat, Clarinda said, "This is out of hand. Look, I really have to get back to my guests, and—oh! By the way, whose cat is that? I wish you'd left it at home. I'm allergic, you know, and—"

"Wait"—Sabine glanced sharply up at Bernice, who had

frozen and looked at Hazel, who had tightened her grasp around the goth and looked over at the shock-parted love doll lips of blonde Gina—"that's not your cat?"

You could have heard a pin drop, as the saying went, but only for a sliver of time equivalent to the width of that same pin. While good, sweet, pious, suntanned Clarinda turned lily white, then corpse green, Hazel and Bernice and Gina all screamed like teenage girls learning that Elvis was in the building.

"Master," they cried, abandoning laughing Sabine and sickened Clarinda to dash from the bedroom and greet their hidden god. "Master, oh, I want to hold him first— No, me— Fuck you, bitch—"

While they all tripped and tackled and strangled one another, falling down the stairs as they vied for the right to be first to knowingly snuggle the Devil in his adorable cat form, Sabine laughed and glanced at Clarinda.

"The last time I made a doll, Master told us we were terrible at sharing…maybe he's right."

The good witch was having none of it. Her thumb and forefinger worrying back and forth over the cross at her neck, she insisted, "I really don't want to have to start writing crazy letters to the Vatican begging for an exorcism, oh, please—"

"Just relax, Clarinda, hey—look, I'm sorry for my friends."

As if this had been their idea! As if they'd pulled Clarinda's undies out of the drawer and invited all this chaos. After casually strolling over to shut the door, Sabine leaned back against the striped wallpaper and extended the joint still on the offer. Looking relieved and, as a consequence of this, not nearly as intimidated by Sabine as she probably should have been, Clarinda edged forward and took the joint from her hand.

"I wanted to come by and tease you a little, but, well. We get together and just egg each other on. You know how it is!

I'm sorry, we'll fix everything at the end, really. We can even make it so your friends don't remember anything."

Sighing in relief to hear that, Clarinda glanced toward the still open window and walked over fast to shut it. She put out the joint in the dirt of a potted cactus on the sill and turned back to Sabine with a nervous expression. "I don't want to ask you to—to do anything to my friends against their better interests, of course. I mean, I don't want you to *hurt* them—"

"Oh, no, this sort of thing happens all the time, it won't hurt them. You wouldn't believe how many people every day have some kind of alien encounter or see something they shouldn't and have a little bit of a memory correction. Ever walk into a room and forget why you're there? That's all."

Though Clarinda managed a relieved nod, her hands still worried their assortment of rings and art deco bracelets. The bad witch felt almost sorry for her. Actually—well, strike that. Sabine did feel sorry for Clarinda, though not because of anything the coven had pulled that day.

Sabine rested her ponytailed head back against the wall. "Can I just ask you—are you gay, Clarinda?"

Looking almost affronted, then afraid, the good witch glanced at Sabine's black boots before consulting her own pointed blue heels. "N—no, well—I think I'm bi, but—"

"It's hard to tell when you can't experiment, huh."

"Well—but it's okay to *be* bisexual or gay. It's perfectly okay to have the thoughts and the urges because gay people are perfect just the way God made them. It's just—two gay people can't get married in the eyes of the Church, so—"

"So all gay sex is fornication by the Church's standard. Yeah, I know. Like I said, I grew up Catholic, too."

"Sorry…you probably had *your* parents telling you that stuff all the time, too." Laughing a little, Clarinda rubbed her hand back and forth across her forehead and eased herself down upon the edge of the bed. "Well, just like you believe there's…

some benefit to just, I guess, "taking it easy" in life, I think it's the responsibility of the human being to rise above that instinct and to live as Christ said we should live."

"But—I mean, you know what it *really* is to be Christ-like, Clarinda. He walked into the temple and found the money-changers and made a whip to beat them with. He made it, with his hands. He put his creative energy into it. Fuck, I'd love to own that whip, can you imagine being beaten by it? Oh…maybe if I'm a good girl, Master will make the Krampus leave it for me this year."

Sabine couldn't help the twinkle in her eye any more than Clarinda could help her shudder—her faint flushed affect. The bad witch prowled across the distance and continued, "He was a man who never married but traveled with twelve men and a former prostitute."

"There's actually no evidence that Mary Magdalene was a prostitute."

"That's such a long rabbit hole of an argument that I don't even want to touch it, but it's definitely moot at this point because the cultural, psychological, and spiritual association of Mary Magdalene is inherently intertwined with the image of the fallen woman or the prostitute. They fulfill the same purpose from an archetypal perspective…just like Satan plays the role for me that Christ plays for you. And that's okay."

"Maybe," agreed Clarinda, "I mean…I guess if you accept Christ as the Son of God, God on Earth, then there's no conflict with venerating Satan in—in a pre-fallen, angelic form, but—but it's one thing to venerate a spirit and another thing to compare it to Christ. Or to, you know, say that *I'm* being influenced by it."

"But you are! You were. That was why you were sent to my house—why the Dark Lord lured you to me. I only missed that Bonesy was painting the house black because Master was distracting me…want to guess how?"

Furiously blushing, truly shocked, Clarinda asked, "He has—sex with you?"

"Uh-huh. Jesus of Nazareth isn't half as fun in this life…of course, well, that's what they call nuns, right? Brides of Christ. Maybe Christ really is a party animal."

Chuckling, Sabine let down her hair and clicked her tongue at Clarinda's displeased noise "Oh, come on. If he was a man on earth, he had male urges just the same as any other man. But you're right…he chose not to act on them. He rose above them, because that's the Christ-like thing to do…because it's Christ's job to save humanity, just like it's humanity's job to be guilty of profaning his flesh. We *all* crucified the Redeemer. That's the whole fucking point of the story, Clarinda—people want to argue about the Jews and the Romans and this and that and Pontius fucking Pilate and King Herod and fuck you."

While Clarinda almost physically jolted at the profanity, snapped as if out of a form of mesmerism, Sabine sat upon the bed beside the good witch. She leaned close enough to smell the floral perfume behind Clarinda's perfect ears. Oh, Sabine's mouth ached with desire as it whispered the terrible truth of Catholicism.

"It was humanity. *We* crucified Christ, Clarinda. All of us. It was one big, horrible, cruel team effort. We lined up in the streets to watch him drag that fucking cross to Golgotha—we threw rocks at him and let the Romans scourge the flesh from his muscles and we laughed. Some of us were shocked and sad but more of us said, "Good, one less criminal in the world." Because that's what mankind always does when a criminal is killed. You see it on the Internet all the time in true crime articles about executions, or sex criminals getting murdered in prison. People celebrate. Whether it's the Messiah or a contrite thief or an unrepentant thief, we're all treated the same by our fellow man. And Christ came here to prove it—to show us what we're really like. He came here to be Christ so we would never have to be—so we could be thieves, as long as we agreed to come back to the Lord when all was said and done."

Clarinda was listening closely now—oh, so closely, braced still as a prey animal before the maw of a predator. A delicate gazelle. Sabine was more a lion every second. "But we can't be absolved of sin when we intend to sin again," protested again the good witch.

"We're not intending to sin," Sabine answered, listing slowly toward the still, innocent woman whose eyes, less innocent in their bedroom affect, flickered between the bad witch's hypnotic green gaze and her artful red mouth. "At least, you're not. You're just intending to be human. God created you as a human woman with bisexual urges—not as Christ."

This at last seemed to reach the good witch, who glanced away for a brief second before Sabine went on. "That means you don't have to be like Christ. You can be like Clarinda. You can do the things Clarinda would do if she would only let herself."

Sabine's nose brushed Clarinda's—but, much to the bad witch's surprise, she did not initiate the kiss. The good witch shut her eyes and leaned in first, her pretty cupid bow mouth opening just before contact.

Oh, Master! Feel through her: wasn't this fresh girl as soft as a feather? As a flower. Yes, yes, Satan! Her very tongue was a scrap of silk. Sabine moaned against Clarinda's mouth and swallowed the humid breath of her gasp.

"I'm afraid," whispered the virginal blonde, lips twisting away from Sabine's.

The goth tried not to laugh at the woman who had read too many romance novels. She caught Clarinda's face in her darkly manicured hands. "That's all right…you can be afraid. That makes it fun for everyone. I love it when people are afraid just because they want to be afraid; just because they want to be absolved of their desires…isn't that why bodice-rippers exist?"

In that captured face, Sabine read all manner of silent pleas. "I understand, baby," she said to Clarinda, leaning in to let their lips brush between the words. "You want to be taken, but you want to be *taken*…it's all right. It's all right. I understand, and so does Christ."

"Oh," whimpered Clarinda even as she melted into Sabine's arms, "I just don't know…I just don't know, Sabine."

"I'm not asking you to know, Clarinda…I'm just asking you to be human. Just be human with me."

"I almost don't know how to be."

"Let me show you…just relax…let me kiss you, Clarinda."

The good witch stared deep into Sabine's face, her face flushed and her lips tense with consternation. At last, the tip of her pink tongue darted across that evocative mouth. She shut her eyes and offered those splendid, just-parted lips again, and Sabine took full advantage of the invitation. Her tongue slid past perfect teeth and over a cool reflection of that same organ, and while her hands slid over the good witch's back to the zipper of her dress, Clarinda gasped softly.

"I've really never done anything like this," whispered Clarinda, gasping again all the more sharply as Sabine's lips trailed down her neck. "Oh, God, forgive me! I was afraid this would happen—"

"You've been thinking about that spanking, haven't you…"

Biting her lip, breath hitching as the zipper reached her lower back and Sabine peeled open the dress, Clarinda softly confessed, "Yes, it's true…oh, I've always thought you were so beautiful. I just never imagined—this, all this. It's so fast—"

"Better to keep you from changing your mind," said Sabine with a laugh, pushing her fretting neighbor back amid the pillows. "Don't be shy. I want to see you…I bet every inch of you is beautiful, too."

Oh, and she was. She had a little freckle on her right set of ribs and another on the matching breast, and her stomach was tight as any athlete's. A dancer, maybe. Sabine moaned to pull the dress down around Clarinda's thighs and have her at last down to her undergarments, her lacy white panties and matched strapless bra so reminiscent of her untouched condition that Sabine salivated. "What a cute little snack you are! Fuck, I bet your pussy tastes like candy floss. I'm so glad those bitches left…but you should come play with all of us sometime. I promise I won't tell…your priest probably won't even be mad when you confess. 'Say 5 Hail Marys and swear you'll come back next week.'"

"I hate the lecherous priest stereotype," complained Clarinda while Sabine laughed and apologized with kisses.

"I'm sorry, I'm just teasing…Catholics are so sensitive."

"Bad witches are so *insensitive*."

With a sudden look of inspiration, Sabine asked, "What are you going to do about it?"

Clarinda's eyes flashed in lurid question and immediate response. Gripping Sabine by the arm, Clarinda sat up amid her pillows and said, "Bend over."

"Oh, Clarinda"—in a tone of mock surprise, Sabine fell over and even wiggled a few degrees to improve her captor's grip—"oh, no, don't *spank* me, goodness, oh!"

That was quite a sharp hand Clarinda had, jeans to strike through or no. While Sabine gasped and arched her rear against the oncoming strikes, Clarinda went to town and insisted sternly, "You've been so—so *disrespectful* to me, Sabine! I'm trying to do a community service—"

"Ow, ow, oh, ow! You're right, of course, you're right—"

"And I didn't do anything unreasonable by asking you to fix your house. A color that you admitted you didn't even like—"

"Ow, oh, I just don't like being told what to do!"

Voice raising louder over the rhythm of her sharp claps, Clarinda said, "That's just it! You're immature. It's why you're just so—so *edgy*. You're such an edgelord!"

"An *edgelord!*" Shocked, appalled, laughing openly while Clarinda bit back her own mirth and obviously struggled to contain it in her voice, Sabine looked at her with one hand poised over her shirt depicting the hideous teeth from the cover of her favorite SWANS album, *Filth*. "Me?"

"Yes, you…you try-hard! Making a skeleton paint your house black…fornicating with the Devil! Probably eating kids, too—"

"Only the bad ones who don't go to bed on time or talk back to their parents— ow! Ow! Don't you know, it's the circle of life?"

Tsking, Clarinda reached around her waist and unbuttoned the bad witch's black jeans. Sabine tried not to look too eager. "Could you be more of a stereotype? I think I need to be even stricter with you, if you're saying things like that…oh! Sabine…" She had gasped at the sight of the bad witch's perfect, pale ass, its peach shape so distinct and lovely that it didn't need the slightest hint of color to make it any more alluring—but the pink flush from the spanking certainly didn't hurt its effect. To find these spankable cheeks peering at her through the black lace thong, the good witch swatted all the harder, all the faster. Soon enough Sabine was moaning and Clarinda struck her with increasing frequency to no avail.

"Fuck, oh, lower—spank my pussy a little bit, oh, Clarinda, that's right, give it to me, yes, yes, I love to be punished—"

"You're a degenerate," said Clarinda, nonetheless obliging her. "This isn't supposed to be fun for you…this is a punishment, for seducing me and for—for being a bad witch!"

"Oh, yes, fuck, I *am* a bad witch. A bad, bad witch—that's right, oh, fuck! Have you ever fucked yourself, Clarinda?"

"Wh— what kind of question is that?"

"So, no…that's okay, I'll be gentle. Thanks for the spanking, but I don't think I can stand to wait anymore…you got me so fucking hot and bothered, I want to fuck you right this very second—take off your bra, I want to see those little tits, let me see your pussy, here, here—"

Her lips pressed hungrily to the gasping good witch's and, while Clarinda reached around her back to unclasp her bra, Sabine hastened to slide her lacy panties down her firm golden thighs. She moaned at the sight of the tanlines, the evidence of Clarinda's regular sunbathing distinct against the pale phantom of her bikini. "You cute little tart, oh, fuck—oh, even your pussy is blonde? Oh, baby, let me taste it, oh, let me have some honey—"

Fuck, oh, Satan, it was a good thing gay Catholics couldn't marry in the church! Sabine might have converted then and there…a shocking thing to so much as think, but you understood all about temptation—and angels understood all about the power of a cute human pussy. Clarinda's was the absolute cutest, at least to Sabine, and she moaned just to see that the blushing pink flesh in that hot little valley already glistened.

"Fuck, you like giving spankings, don't you…or you just like me. You should come over and give me a whipping some night. Especially if I do get my Saturnalia present! That would be so hot…can I kiss it?"

"Oh—" Hands covering her face, blue eyes peering shyly through her splayed fingers, Clarinda silently nodded. Sabine grinned and thought about telling her to beg, but ultimately she wanted Clarinda to think fondly of this encounter. Didn't want to push her past any unknown limits. Sabine simply gave into her urge and leaned down to taste Clarinda's wet cunt.

The good witch's gasp was so sharp that it was almost indistinguishable from Sabine's moan of desire on first contact. Gently running her fingers down the plush lips that she then carefully spread, Sabine looked up past the powder pink nipples crowning Clarinda's goosebump covered breasts. There, the bad witch found pure blue eyes haunted by desire.

She held that eye contact as long as she could while lowering her tongue to the pink bud of the good witch's clit, a nerve no doubt aching with desire and hyper-sensitive at its first contact from another human being.

"Oh! Oh, God—Sabine—"

"Hail Satan," Sabine murmured softly under her breath, not wanting to incite another metaphysical argument with her preferred sexual invocation. "Oh, Hail Satan…what a sweet pussy, poor neglected thing, Sabine's here…you've waited so long, Clarinda! Doesn't it feel good?"

"Yes! Oh—fuck—"

Sabine moaned to hear the good witch profane and lowered her head to lash all the more rapidly at her begging clitty. While the good witch gasped and spread her legs wider, Sabine pursed her lips to suckle the adorable nub. Her tongue teased it even amid this vacuum and all the while more sweet nectar flowed from that virgin hole. By the time Sabine's tongue had edged down to explore the possibilities, a veritable waterfall had coated Clarinda's pussy along with the bad witch's saliva. This audacious tongue probed in over and over, lifting away only to permit the tease of a fingertip.

"Wait," whispered Clarinda, gasping, "wait—will you kiss me while you do it?"

The bad witch, who had been poised to overcome any protest, was instead left gently chuckling at a sweet request. "While I take your virginity, you mean? Of course…oh, baby, of course…"

After sitting upright to remove her own t-shirt and bra to the sound of Clarinda's appreciative gasp, Sabine moved in to please her with a few long, patient kisses.

Downstairs, Sabine's sisters had surely begun the ritual. She had no telepathic knowledge of such things, but Satan always saw to matters of divine timing, and when the time was right for Sabine to take Clarinda's virginity, the chanting witches arranged in a triangle around the smiling black cat would have reached the appropriate peak on the lower floor of the home.

The truth was, Sabine didn't really care. Clarinda's private downstairs was currently the subject of attention, and the bad witch's fingers took up the work of teasing the good one's clit. She watched the blonde's gasping face and felt an imminent orgasm in the tension of her body. Exploiting that tension would paradoxically relax her for the big moment. While Clarinda gasped and received the eager lashing of Sabine's tongue against her own, she reached up and experimentally slid her hands over Sabine's sumptuous breasts. The bad witch moaned and the good one became bolder, reaching down to grab a handful of well-spanked ass. Sabine gasped with pleasure and her finger's circles grew more rapid; soon, body taut as a spring, Clarinda cried aloud and arched her hips up toward those wicked fingers.

"Oh, fuck, that's right, Clarinda—cum for me, pretty girl, that's right, oh, doesn't it feel good, isn't it fun to sin—"

"Oh, oh, of course—that's the point, oh—oh! Sabine!"

Gasping, her fingers sinking deep into the flesh of the goth's thick ass, Clarinda came with a high cry and an all-body shudder. The fluid leaking from her cunt became all the more obvious a few seconds before she came, and when the climax hit her, her legs tensed around Sabine's hand. The bad witch grinned to kiss her, her seeking tongue sliding against that thrashing, gasping organ. Clarinda grasped her by the face to keep her there for the duration and remembered to relax her grip only when her thighs released of their own accord.

"Oh! Sabine! That was—oh, oh, it felt so good…I've never felt an orgasm like that before…."

Aha, so she *did* masturbate…well, Sabine would leave that alone for now. "I know you haven't, baby…get ready. The next one will be even better. Don't be nervous…"

Her fingers trailed down to the tight mouth of that virgin

territory that Satan urged Sabine to claim in his name. Nothing if not obedient to her Dark Lord, she gazed into the eyes of the good witch and teased that sensitive entrance as she teased a gasping mouth with her smiling one. "It's better to get it over with, poor thing…you'll be less nervous. And who better to help you through the process than another woman? Here, lay back…you can touch me, too."

Though still visibly anxious, Clarinda did as she'd been told. Easing into the pillows beneath Sabine's urging, Clarinda slid her hand over the busty goth woman's tits and toward the dark thong concealing her throbbing pussy. "You'll tell me if I'm no good, won't you?"

"Just do what feels good to you…don't worry, I trust you. I don't need you to fuck me…when Master shows up, he'll give me what I need. You can try it when you're ready. For now… just relax. Kiss me again."

Though still adorably shy, increasingly bold Clarinda offered her mouth to the bad witch. Sabine captured it in her lips. With that savage kiss she muted somewhat the good witch's cry of surprise at the sudden, hard penetration of the bad witch's finger—but oh, it was still evident. Sabine moaned at her noise of shock and pain; with a sadistic rush, the bad witch glanced down and slid her fingers out to examine their faint coating of blood. "Hail Satan," she whispered, her voice a thick murmur of longing that was soon replaced by a grin. Downstairs, the rest of the coven shrieked with delight.

"What was that," asked Clarinda as if from the distance of a dream.

"Just Master arriving," she said, wiping the virgin's blood in a brisk cross over her forehead and, before she could be stopped, Clarinda's. "There, the worst part's over, now, lay back again—"

Clarinda moaned with far more pleasure than with pain the second time Sabine slid her fingers in. The deflowered girl even leaned back against the pillows and spread her legs in welcome. As the bad witch fingered her, Clarinda dared explore the dark forest of her pussy and slide her fingers over Sabine's clit.

The goth moaned into her mouth while working fingers in and out of a channel so tight she could think of nothing else but how it would feel around her cock, if Master would have been good enough to permit it sometime.

Again, probably not that first time…some hardcore futanari fucking would have been a bit much for Clarinda, poor delicate flower that she was. Soon, though, she'd be an eager whore just ready for Sabine's enchanted cock…why, as it stood, she was certainly ready for Satan's.

Sabine moaned at the embrace of the pussy that dripped around her fingers, her own cunt wetter by the second for the sensation, the satisfaction that came with fucking such a cute virgin. Oh, Clarinda's flesh was so soft and smooth between those blushing labia! Soft as her tongue, smooth as her mouth. Sabine moaned to hear the way pleasure sharpened Clarinda's voice to a desperate, adorable whine; to see how one hand lifted into her blonde curls and caused the jiggle of one small breast. Sabine descended upon that breast and its hard pink nipple while she finger-fucked the slut-in-training to orgasm, taking her from cloistered virginity to Sapphic bliss.

"You're a good little slut for me, aren't you…oh, yes, that's right, you're so fucking hot—"

"Oh, no, Sabine, I'm not a slut, please—"

"It's a good thing…you're *my* slut, Clarinda. You'll fuck whoever I tell you, won't you—I know you wanted it from all my friends, you want to be gangbanged by a bunch of bad witches, oh, it's okay, fuck! Fuck, that made you so wet—oh, don't worry. We can pretend to force you, if that's what you want…we'll hold you down and take turns on you, you'll love the way I fuck. Oh, baby, I'll make you feel so good—"

"You already do—oh, Sabine! Sabine, that feels so good—oh, God—"

"You should let my master fuck you," Sabine begged. "Not with his real cock, I don't think you could take it yet—or ever. But he has a man's cock, too, because he often uses the body of a man, of course…you'd love it, he's so good, oh, he'd be perfect for your first time!"

"I don't know, I don't know—"

"Please? Please? Come on—don't you want to feel the tender embrace of an angel? That's all he is, an angel. A fallen one, fallen to earth like you and me. Oh, fuck! I know your want it, this pussy doesn't lie—"

"I do—oh, God forgive me, maybe I do, but—but I don't want to be damned—"

"Nobody's going to damn you…oh, it's bliss, go on, cum for me, get that pussy all nice and soaking wet and ready to receive my master's wicked angel-cock—that's right, oh, fuck, you love that thought, yeah, I want to watch him fuck this cute little puss—"

Two fingers rapidly pumping in and out and the flat of her hand thereby able to slap repeatedly against the adorable pink clit, Sabine worked Clarinda to a blasphemous orgasm that rocked her body and produced a high-pitched scream of pleasure. While Clarinda's arms tightened around Sabine's shoulders like her thighs tightened around her wrist, Sabine marveled at the greedy clutch of the puss around her fingers. Cooing, kissing, Sabine murmured, "Oh, Clarinda…oh, baby, that's right, oh yeah…yeah, you want him to fuck you so badly, oh, just wait…he's got such a big cock…"

"Why would any angel want to consort with mortal women?"

Chuckling, Sabine kissed her recovering mouth and said, "We'll use magick to give you a cock sometime when you're ready…then you'll see. Come on"—ignoring the look of hilarious scandal that crossed the good witch's face at this suggestion, Sabine pulled her delirious friend to her feet and dragged her to the bedroom door—"let's go. I hate to keep him waiting no matter how patient he is."

"Wait—but—but what if my friends—"

"They won't remember any of this, right? And anyway, they probably won't even see you…or me, for that matter."

This was very true. The brunch party had gotten curious about all the noises coming from both the upstairs and the downstairs of the house: by the time Sabine and Clarinda made it down the stairs, an assortment of cute, tight, innocent Christian coeds had assembled on the edge of the kitchen to whisper about the impossibly handsome man and three sexy women who made out in an armchair on the edge of the living room. Even as his hand continued its slid up Gina's skirt, the Devil lifted his head from Bernice's mouth to offer the assembled guests, then Sabine and Clarinda, a charming smile.

"Ladies," he said, ignoring the whispering of the group. A lot was being exchanged between the brunch members ("He looks like the way I picture Christian Grey." "Christian Grey! Holy cow, he's hotter than that." "The way I *picture* him—from the book, I mean." "I think he looks a little like Ted Bundy. But on the good days, you know." "That's a weird thing to say, and he's hotter than that, too, but—speaking of weird, has anybody seen Martha?") and the Son of the Morning ignored all of it to extend a hand toward Sabine. "Sabine, come kiss me! Your mouth looks in want of love."

"It's never lacking when you're around, Master…but it wasn't lacking today, either."

"So I understand—ah—"The Dark Lord sighed and smiled at the taste of her lips, of virgin's cunt and unabashed lust. "How delicious your kiss is to me, my daughter in obscenity."

"And how happy the taste of yours makes me! Oh, but Master, we summoned you here to thank you today. Look at all these virgins! We offer them all to you, Lord—and this one, my favorite, most especially." Sabine gestured up to the blonde on the stairs; Clarinda gasped and covered her heart, her hand closing around the crucifix she still wore around her neck. A slave's yoke around the throat of a naked animal. The Dark Lord assessed the exposed good witch with a contemplative, appreciative eye.

"She wants it, does she?"

"Who could help themselves but crave your cock, Master… look at how these sluts are reduced to beasts to see you. Which of you wouldn't love to do as we do?" Demonstrating, Sabine slid into Satan's lap and caressed his face, her ass grinding against his tented pinstripe trousers while his hands slid over her body and tore away the pitiful lace of her thong. "Angel cocks are second to none…oh, it's so big. Can't I have it, Master, oh, just a little? Just to demonstrate?"

"Of course, Sabine…go on, go on…"

Grinning, Sabine arched her hips to eagerly unzip Satan's trousers. Soon she freed his throbbing organ, his massive red dick of inhuman proportions even when it was of human anatomy. No spikes today—it was almost too bad, but oh, it stretched her so wide and filled her so deep as she impaled her wet cunt upon it that it really didn't matter. Yes, the Devil's cock curved sweetly against her g-spot and caused a seizure of pleasure to rattle through her body until her tongue lolled from her mouth with her scream. A tidal wave of ecstasy crashing through her and erasing all logic, the bad witch pounded up and down on Satan's massive prick and made eye contact, not with anyone in the watching crowd or with one of her sisters, but with shocked Clarinda.

The good witch watched, lips parted in shock and wanton desire. Enchanted by the sight of Sabine being openly penetrated by the Day-Star, Clarinda no longer remembered to cover herself and instead gripped the edge of the railing.

She leaned toward the scene with hunger in her eyes while Satan's great hand landed upon the back of Sabine's neck. The other fit to her hip while the Dark Lord worked the bad witch up and down his cock like a fuck doll. Soon none of the effort was hers at all; Sabine's eyes rolled up into her head and she groaned, begging, "Yes! Fuck! Use me, Master! Use me, Satan! Harder, harder, Master, fuck me harder, oh, fuck—"

"What a horny bitch you are, Sabine…there's no limit to how often you want my cock under the best of conditions, but you really do love it in front of these tender young virgins, don't you."

"Not—*all* of us are virgins," suggested the Christian Grey fan, a cute brunette prep in a polo shirt and pearl necklace with 'horseback rider who has huge Daddy issues' written all over her.

Her suggestion earned a few clearing throats and nervous glances among the throng, but no real protests.

"I know," said the Dark Lord, exchanging a grin with Hazel. The redheaded witch slithered across the floor and into the crowd to clutch this boldest girl.

A few of the other members of the Bible study gasped, slightly appalled, but a dark magick had settled over the room and relaxed all inhibitions. There was no escaping. All those who had been unable to help themselves but watch were subject to this celebration of their true desires, and soon Hazel, Gina and Bernice were among the good witches, making out with their favorites and egging others on. It wasn't long before the clothes started to go: soon the Good Witches' Bible Study had devolved into an orgiastic tangle of limbs all across Clarinda's sitting room.

At the head of it, Satan rewarded his loyal servant with a fucking as hard as the nails that pinned Christ to that cross. Sabine whimpered with pleasure so great it practically left her blind. At Satan's urging, she forced herself up off of his prick with a whine—only to be bent over the arm of the chair by his firm hand.

"What a wicked bitch you are for seducing these poor innocent souls…bad Sabine." He spanked her a few sharp times before slamming his twitching cock up to the hilt in her drenched pussy. While he fucked his slave like he was trying to bruise her, the Devil glanced up to study Clarinda. "Don't worry, loyal servant of Christ…I can be gentle, too. You know, Clarinda—I can call you 'Clarinda,' can't I, Miss Lovegood—Clarinda, I think I'm very misunderstood."

While a collective moan rose from the orgy on the floor, the Dark Lord adjusted Sabine's pelvis. The bad witch groaned, stupider by the second. Oh, she loved being fucked by Satan! It was the only time she didn't have to think—the only time she wasn't hyper-aware of the state of mortal suffering that was reality. Satan provided her a pleasure that cut it all away and left her shuddering with the first of many orgasms: a chain of climaxes that crashed like waves one into another and left her twitching endlessly around the giant prick that split her in two.

Satan spoke on. "All that in the desert with Christ, for instance…I was just giving him an opportunity to take a way out. Helping him exercise free will. Seeing if Jesus of Nazareth really had it in him to be Christ. That's what I'm all about…my every temptation is a celebration of human will. The rush of power I put into your heart every time you get to tell somebody what to do, Clarinda, in your HOA or your Bible study or the dance classes you teach…that's my gift to you. If you understood how many good Christian men and women are unconsciously in my service, your head would spin. At least Sabine here has given you the opportunity to do it consciously—willfully. Come here, trembling little lamb. Come to me, Clarinda…let me make love to you. Let me show you that the Devil's not so bad."

The good witch's frightened eyes swept from Satan's face to Sabine's blissed one. The bad witch was too busy cumming to urge her neighbor to make the right choice—and, anyway, Clarinda was smart enough to see an opportunity that would never come again. God would probably forgive her, anyway. What human could resist the opportunity to be fucked by an angel, so handsome and dark in the suit he straightened once he drew his prick from Sabine and shoved her from the chair.

The masochistic witch, laughing, gripped the arm of the seat to pull herself to her knees and watch the show. It was tempting to join the orgy, but orgies were just a normal Saturday night for her. Better to stay around and support Clarinda as, amazingly, she took a few nervous steps down her stairs, then edged into the room. With an uncertain glance into Sabine's flushed face, Clarinda reached out and took the offer. She slipped her hand into Satan's extended one and gasped as he yanked her close.

"I know I said I'd be gentle…but I can tell you like it a little rough." The good witch's body pressed to his, the Dark Lord caught her golden curls and craned her head back for his kiss. Clarinda moaned in shock, then shut her eyes and went totally limp in his clutch. "Make sure this virgin is ready for me, slut," Satan commanded without looking at Sabine, who thrilled to be derided by her beloved Master.

"Oh, yes, sir, yes—" Moaning with eager delight, Sabine crawled over to run her hands up Clarinda's legs. The gasping good witch glanced down, then swiftly had her gaze corrected by the hand on the back of her head.

"Don't mind my fucktoy…I just want to make sure you're good and ready. Feel how hard my cock is?" Clarinda gasped to have her hand fit around the massive organ, its length still wet from Sabine's pussy. While it pulsed in her tight grip, Satan brushed his nose against Clarinda's and assured her, "I only want to hurt those whose souls beg to be hurt, of course…

you beg to be taken, not hurt. I can oblige, but first you have to relax."

"I'm frightened—oh, I'm very frightened, I never thought it would be like this—ah!"

Sabine had parted the good witch's pussy lips to give her head. Clarinda stared in shocked pleasure up at the contemplative face of the God of this World—who, studying her in return, said, "No one's first time is ever what they thought it would be…but you have to admit, this one makes an awfully good story."

Satan chuckled at the gasp the good witch produced; Sabine's fingers had slid into her cunt even while her tongue teased that eager clit and, standing, the effect was overwhelming. Clarinda swooned in the Dark Lord's grip and soon had to be eased into the divan where her limbs naturally splayed in invitation. As though her body were more educated in these matters than she was…that was the purpose of genetic memory, wasn't it?

"You picked me such a pretty flower, Sabine…here. Help me undress and stay with us. Comfort her." While Satan swiftly unbuttoned his dress shirt and slid his tie from his neck, Sabine delighted in the removal of his belt, the further opening of his trousers. "She'll need it. I don't think I'll be able to keep myself under control for very long."

Only the briefest flicker of hesitance crossed Sabine's features, but she didn't argue and was soon rewarded by a broad hand that swept down her cheek and under her jaw to tilt her head up. Somehow she managed to stare into his face rather than at his cock, maybe because his human prick was old news compared to that demonic spiked pecker he pulled out when they were alone or on a Sabbath night. "No need to fret, daughter. The girl will still be yours when I'm through, and even still in one piece. But you know how I am, because you're the same way…oh"—the house rattled with his chuckle, his thumb slipping into Sabine's lips and eliciting a moment of bliss to have any part of him inside of any part of her—"I'm sure the first time you get your cock into her, you'll have a little sympathy for me."

With a coy grin at that on-the-nose reference and half an eyeroll at his wink, the bad witch drew his trousers and boxers down, then helped him step out of his socks. Naked and beautiful beyond compare with any mortal being whether man or woman, Satan stood in the center of the room and with both hands slid his black hair back upon his head. His glacial eyes bored into Clarinda, who had covered herself again—at least, she had rested a hand upon her bosom upon the sight of the naked Devil, clearly shocked. Overwhelmed by his perfection. She looked as if she just barely resisted her urges to fight or flight and as a result she had settled on freeze. Satan bent over the good witch and, with the same hand that had caressed Sabine's cheek, now took his fill of innocent flesh.

Still on the floor, one hand poised upon the armchair to brace herself, Sabine watched with bated breath. Only as Clarinda's eyelids fluttered beneath his touch did the bad witch remember she had been called to assist. Pulling herself from her state of enchantment, Sabine hurried over to obey— to bend her head and press kisses to Clarinda's mouth as Satan lowered his head and kissed a heaving breast. When his lips grazed the crucifix, Clarinda gasped like she'd been struck by lightning.

"Oh, God, oh, what am I doing—"

"Having fun," answered Sabine.

"That's right, Clarinda…having fun. Using that pretty human body as God intended." Satan's tongue slithered out along her flesh, its length bearing a hint of the same inhumanity hidden beneath his ungodly perfect features. Clarinda again shut her eyes, a little whimper on her lips. "You don't have to be afraid of me, Clarinda. I'm a child of God just like you are…more. As much his Son as Christ."

"Please, please don't—"

"It's true. You remember Job—my father called to me and all my other siblings, and I came late. From going to and fro upon the earth, and from walking up and down upon it. Every family has a bad child, Clarinda. A black sheep—a prodigal son. You can't have a model Redeemer without a model Sinner."

His kisses migrated over her stomach and Clarinda gasped in fright while his tongue flickered against her navel. She looked helplessly into Sabine's face and Sabine made no response; only bent her head to kiss the good witch, who had, funnily enough, gone from busybody to friend in less than an hour. Maybe she'd always sensed the friend potential there, and that was why Clarinda so annoyed her.

Either way, Sabine really put her heart into the kiss and was pleased that the good witch responded in kind. Clarinda reached up to touch her face, to keep her held close—especially as Satan pushed her legs wider apart and poised himself between.

"Now, Clarinda…I won't lie to you." Satan's thumb rested upon the mound of her vulva and his thumb gently lifted her labia apart, the open appreciation of his gaze lost on Clarinda when she could stare nowhere but the bad witch who kissed her. "This is going to hurt. But, you know, really that works out for you…I like a girl in pain. So, if you think about it, the more pain you feel, the faster I'll cum. It'll feel good, though, too… and I love a girl who loves to feel good as much as I love a girl who loves to scream in agony."

The Dark Lord inhaled sharply and Clarinda did, in fact, scream out loud. Sabine turned with a gasp of pleasure to watch the Devil's huge prick penetrate the innocent witch. Clarinda's sweet blue eyes filled with tears and her smooth brow contorted with the incredible discomfort of taking such a big cock for her first time ever. While Satan's eyes closed in appreciation and his big hands came to rest upon her hips to promote a better angle, Clarinda gripped the couch with one hand and Sabine with the other.

"Oh, God, oh, oh—it does hurt, ow—"

"Master's got such a big dick, doesn't he…" While, behind them, the orgy was a wild, writhing rat king of tongues in cunts and fingers in assholes and mouths on mouths and grinding and moaning and wet, wet ecstasy, Sabine eschewed her own bodily pleasure. She was more than content with the sight of the good witch's bitten lip—the sounds of her pretty whimpers as Satan plowed the field of her unused body. "That's right, oh, don't worry, you'll love it soon…you'll love it very soon. Soon all you'll be able to think about is when you can have it again."

"Fu—fudge—oh, God, I hope I don't—"

"Then you'd better pray, Clarinda," advised the Devil, his voice dark as it was almost unnervingly gentle. Oh, Sabine loved it when he spoke gently. There was nothing more frightening in the world than the gentleness of an angel, especially Satan. Their immortal concerns were simply beyond worldly issues and their empathy was therefore an alien quality among aliens—and with Satan, there was always the tacit assurance that his empathy was a tool like any other.

There was nothing empathetic about his gentleness now and oh, Sabine the Bad Witch was terribly wet as her Dark Lord, pounding into her adorable friend, commanded that same girl he fucked to pieces, "Pray! Pray for God to save you from me. I know you know your prayers so well, Clarinda, I hear you say them all the time. Ah! How horrified you would be if you knew what I do to myself while I listen to you recite them before bed at night…"

"Oh—oh, Christ—Our Father, who art in Heaven—ah! Oh, ah!"

"Good, good, that's good, Clarinda, oh, that's right, keep praying, do it, 'Hallowed be Thy name.'"

"You can pray?" Clarinda gasped at the Dark Lord's

guidance, her voice inundated with the greatest horror yet.

Sabine exchanged a laughing glace with her master, who assured the good witch, "I've taught more than one man how to pray, Clarinda…go on, go on. Let me hear if you can remember it with my prick so deep inside."

"Ah! Ah! Oh—God, it does feel good—oh—Our Father, who art in heaven, hallowed be Thy name—ah ah ah ah!" His flash slapped against hers and Sabine moaned. Unable to take it a second longer, she reached down to slowly finger herself and ease the ache. Clarinda gripped her free hand like she was trying to break its bones and Sabine's pleasure only increased. The good witch's hips arched up and, amazingly, her legs wrapped around the Devil's waist. He glanced with an approving grin over at Sabine, who blew him a kiss as Clarinda continued reciting the prayer. "Good girl," said the Lord of the Flies, "good girl, oh, that's so good, you pray as well as any angel—again, again, let me hear it again, oh, fuck, ah, there's nothing on earth that gets me harder than hearing a virgin pray—well. A recent virgin, anyway…"

Biting her lip, Clarinda obeyed—if only because it was a meditative exercise to help her get through what surely had the hue of a nightmare. As, from within the orgy, a few climactic moans began to daisy-chain up, Satan sped his pace and clenched his teeth in his dark smile to force a few interrupting moans from Clarinda.

"My cute little vixen, I feel how close you are…you're going to cum for me, aren't you? Yes, you are…the first cock to make you cum will be Satan's cock. Remember that, good witch, my little servant of Christ…" The wet slaps of flesh were muffled beneath Clarinda's cries, beneath the squeak of the couch upon which she arched, beneath the husky laughter of the bad witch who still lapped up a few kisses from time to time. "Remember, this pleasure you owe to Satan; remember, this liberation you owe to Satan."

"Hail Satan," gasped Sabine, lifting her fist in praise of her master and forcing Clarinda's hand unwillingly up with it. "Hail Satan!"

From the throng of bodies, the bad witches keened with their own calls of pleasure. "Hail Satan! Hail Satan! Hail Satan!"

The Devil smiled in his work. "That's right—Hail Satan. Oh, fuck, Hail Satan—say it, Clarinda."

"No! No—no, please, not that—"

"Say it…say it"—he rotated her hips a few degrees higher and the good witch's eyes flew open in shock at the inundation of intense pleasure—"say it to me, slut."

"Oh! Oh! Oh! God! Help me, oh, Christ—"

"I don't think he's making any cameos today. The last time Christ showed his face down here, you naughty children did this to him." The Devil flicked the cross upon Clarinda's breast and, as she gasped with fright and excitement, he gripped her face. "I know you want to say it. You haven't even said my title yet. Say it for me—say it."

"Satan," she gasped, the word of blood-curdling horror but breathless with pleasure once it flooded from her lips. "Satan," whispered Clarinda again, more avidly, pushed to the brink of orgasm by the very word, "oh, Satan! Oh—Hail Satan—"

"That's right…Hail Satan. But I'm no adversary to you, Clarinda…I'd like it much more if you considered me a friend. And friends tell each other about themselves. Satan's just a title…nobody knows my real name. Not except for the witches who serve me. All the theological experts of the world would die to know it."

The bad witch gasped with pleasure at the expression of pained curiosity on Clarinda's flushed face. Bending down over her, the Devil smiled, his teeth glittering and perfect even in the dark living room.

"Do you want to know my real name, Clarinda?"

He didn't wait for a response. The Dark Lord continued leaning and, as he fucked her to orgasm, he whispered it in her ear.

Sabine had it on personal experience that the hearing of the name itself was sufficient to produce the kind of orgasm that Clarinda subsequently experienced. Sabine also had to wonder, however, if Clarinda wasn't having some kind of vision—or if, perhaps, she did not at least briefly perceive Satan in his true form, as Sabine did so often. It was hard to tell with angels. They could walk into a room full of people and every human being could see something different if that messenger of the divine was in the mood for mischief or secret missions. Satan was generally consistent…but there were moments like this where he couldn't resist revealing himself selectively to someone, if only so he could appreciate the result in front of company.

A sharp gasp tore up from the good witch's lips. Her eyes widened even as her pupils shrank, then disappeared entirely upon the rolling of the orbs up into her head. While Clarinda's mouth contorted in cosmic seizure, her four limbs clamped as tight around the Dark Lord's body as her cunt did around his giant schlong. The Day-Star laughed while the scream of Clarinda's ecstasy rose so high that Sabine would have been surprised if the whole neighborhood hadn't heard it. Bonesy and Cable Dog were probably both well aware it was tied somehow to their mistress…but wouldn't they have been jealous to think of what they missed out on!

While the nuclear explosion of an orgasm tore through the innocent good witch, her scream dissolved into hyperventilation. "Satan," she screamed, "Satan, Satan—oh—"

Her head dropped back, mouth open, eyes shut. Sabine gasped slightly and touched her face, her mouth. Still breathing! Oh, phew.

The pleasure had just been too much for her tiny human

brain. Happened to Sabine all the time.

The bad witch released an exhalation of relief and patted poor Clarinda's sweat-beaded forehead. She smiled as the good witch moaned in her enchanted sleep.

"How cute you are, Sabine…it's not like you to worry. You really like this one, don't you? Anyway, I told you I'd leave her in one piece for you. You should have more faith."

Grunting slightly to draw himself out of Clarinda's unconscious body on the divan, the Dark Lord bent to collect Sabine in his arms and set her in the adjacent armchair. While he caught her face in one hand and aligned his cock to her very ready channel with the other, the Devil arched his brow. He flashed Sabine the teasing, wolfish grin that drove her absolutely wild.

"After all…when have I ever lied to you?"

In the end, the witches didn't need to do anything to erase the memories of the Bible study group. Satan did it all, and when everyone woke up fully dressed at the brunch table with no bad witches in sight, the orgy had been reduced, at best, to a pleasant shared dream far too scandalous for the individual members of the group to share. The coven even remembered to let Martha out of the closet before they left. Eventually.

But the one thing the Devil didn't fix was Clarinda's memory, which Sabine had been nervous about. Dressing, he had said, "Well, so few people know my name…I hate to lose even one. I need more friends in the world."

So did Sabine. After leaving the good witch's house, she saw her friends off, kissed them, and thanked them all again for coming to help her. Once they had driven away she turned to face the black Victorian looming over the neighborhood. The bad witch sighed.

A trip or several to Home Depot later, Cable Dog happily panting out the window the whole way there and back again, (and trying to jump out at a few red lights—uh-huh, nice try, Sabine was ready for you, buddy, that harness was for more than leashes), Sabine returned home with a fresh collection of paint cans that she set before Bonesy.

He looked between them reluctantly, clearly unable to tell the difference.

"Don't worry," said Sabine, trying to keep her tone from sounding too gruff. "I'll help you this time."

Yes, ugh. Ugh! Fuck.

Sabine hated work more than anything in the whole world, which was why—among other reasons—she sold her soul to Satan in the first place. Her Big Bad Daddy gave her all the money she needed, often in weird and synchronistic ways that caused terrible problems for others, and she used that monkey's paw money to pay people who ensured she had to work as little as possible.

But…well. There was something to be said for the sense of satisfaction that came with painting one's house oneself…she guessed. Fucked up her neck, though. And, to be fair, she spent a lot of it in a supervisory role…but she *did* help, and hey, that was pretty mature of her, or something. Whatever.

In fact, she and ol' Bonesy were both hard at work when, on Wednesday mid-morning, Clarinda's call from the end of the walkway drew the bad witch's attention.

"Oh my *goodness,*" said the chipper good witch, hands on her hips and the lips of her smile red as the rims of her crimson sunglasses. "I love it!"

Hiding her smirk and her eyeroll, Sabine descended the ladder where she'd perched to apply an extra layer on the white trim. "Sorry I didn't submit an approval form before I decided the color, but I thought the soft blue siding would look nice with your house down the street."

"No, it looks great! So great, Sabine."

The good witch removed her sunglasses and came over to admire the work a little more closely, the glasses' arm poised against her lower lip. "I like it."

"Thanks. Your house is really cute, too, by the way. I didn't even say anything."

"Well thank you! Yeah, that was kind of a busy day, huh…" Looking like she didn't want to say what she had to say out on the street, Clarinda waved a hand. "Don't worry about that silly old approval form. It doesn't matter, everyone will just be glad you've fixed it up. And anyway…well, between you and me," she dropped her voice, "I think I'm going to be stepping down as HOA president."

Trying not to audibly gasp, Sabine nonetheless couldn't hide all her surprise and did, with big eyes, ask, "*Really!*"

With a sort of crooked smile, Clarinda looked up at the house again. She slid her folded sunglasses over the bust of her polka dotted dress. There they rested next to the crucifix still shining around her neck. "Yeah, well…I don't know, I just don't really have a lot of time for it anymore. It's just such a commitment and—really I need to relax. Um—"

Glancing down at her bright white patent leather purse, Clarinda opened the bag and showed the contents to Sabine. The bad witch recognized the plastic dispensary bottle of primo ganja and, pleasantly surprised, smiled down at it the way most people smiled at newborn babies. Smiling wryly, herself, Clarinda asked, "You want to hang out and watch a movie or something?"

"Fuck yeah! Do you like David Lynch? I've been in an *Eraserhead* mood."

"What's *Eraserhead?*"

"You mean you've never—all right, well, if you thought I showed you some fucked up shit on Sunday, get ready. This is about to be way, way worse…come on, it'll trip you out."

Grinning, Sabine caught Clarinda's golden hand in her fingers, pale white and stained with light blue paint. Hand-in-hand, the witches went inside as friends and Sabine shut the door.

The Witch's Milk Jugs

SABINE THE BAD WITCH was in the bad habit of checking her phone first thing every morning…but, weren't we all? Sometimes she was glad for it. The news that day made her laugh and, after she'd spent some time in the shower lathering every curve of her luscious lily body, she moisturized her youthful skin in the fat of children, slipped into her black robe, and made her way downstairs with a skip in her step.

"You know, some things in life are just givens. The rule of cause and effect, for instance. A Cable Guy comes to my house and thinks he's in for an easy lay—and he does get laid, but then he's turned into my dog forever. A sexy Latina objectifies me, so I make her a doll. A careless delivery driver becomes my skeletal slave for eternity and keeps up my garden for me. A hot little good witch from down the street judges a little too much and is judged in turn. That's Karma—that's *really* how Karma works. I'm sure you, like me, have been thinking an awful lot about Karma in the past few days. Now…why would that be, I wonder?"

Sabine chuckled to herself, then stopped with a gasp and looked down at her reflection in the otherwise empty face of her smartphone. "What—*really!* Is that what's happened in your universe? My goodness, what an idiot…well, yes, that is an example of Karma, but I was talking about a news story I was reading this morning. It was about a group of stupid rich people who forced the conductor of a train to let them bring their orangutan on board. They were all killed when the orangutan got up to the engineer and—well, I won't really go into details…but you just wouldn't believe it! The orangutan went free in the end, but of course, in a way, it's really less the ape's fault. More the now-dead rich people who thought it'd be funny to let their ape pretend to drive the train for awhile…hm."

Sabine tapped her chin with the tip of her finger, pausing on the edge of her kitchen.

"I guess it really is sort of the same thing, isn't it? Funny how parallel universes work out that way. Huh? Oh, *our* president? Haha, oh, no, no. You see, in our universe, Hilary Clinton won the election, and as a result all witches everywhere were able to claim ritual human sacrifice as a tax write-off. Finally, equal representation! I love democracy…oh, that's a meme in your world?"

She gasped as your mind made the natural connection. "He made *prequels?* Oh, no…you poor things. Disney! Disney bought them? You really are in Hell, aren't you? Well…don't worry. Stick with me long enough and maybe I'll break you out of there some time. Poor little demon! And speaking of little demons…who wants nummies? Who wants nummies? Who's a good boy? Who's ready for breakfast?"

Sigh! Cable Dog wanted nummies…although he wouldn't have admitted it at gunpoint. You know, if he were still a human capable of speech. As usual, his dog instincts were greater than the human he was in his soul, and the transfigured Cable Guy dashed over, an excited prance in his step at the promise of a huge bowl of dry kibble Sabine thrust down beside his water dish. The German shepherd even gave a bark of appreciation while Sabine stood, one elbow propped against the back of the kitchen table's chair.

"The lesson for both of us, no matter what universe we're living in, is that if you want to keep your train or your country or—your house, say—in order, then you have to be proactive. When you see a threat coming you have to deal with it, whether it's a presidential election, a pandemic, or a literal orangutan skull-fucking the train engineer to death while some rich people laugh. Should I have said that out loud? Well…we'll put it in horror. The book, that is."

Cable Dog wiggled his ears. Sabine grinned to see his obvious consternation. It drove him crazy! The thought of him dying to ask who she was always talking to made her laugh out loud. She did a lot of thinking out loud, but every once in a while she got into a patter of actually *talking* to somebody. Who, who?

She should have turned him into an owl instead of a dog.

Nah—flying was much too fun.

"Was that good? Num num num." Cable Dog had wolfed his food down while she drifted into outer space. Now, her robe falling open to give a scintillating peek down the rolling curves of her over-sized but gravity-defying tits, Sabine ruffled his ears, kissed his cute nosey, and swept the empty bowl up. "Don't stare," she added with a tap of his nose. "Bad dog… what do you know about any of that? You're a dog right now. You don't want me to neuter you so you've got no balls when you're in this form, do you, Cable Guy?"

The dog whined, his tail dropping sharply between his legs. The bad witch patted his head and watched more approvingly as the hound took out his angst by filling up on water, lapping mightily with a few anxious wags of his tail as he showed her what a good, good doggie-boy he was. "Good boy," she said with a pat of his back. "Good dog. Don't worry…I can make you a man later, as a great transvestite from Transsexual, Transylvania once punned. Wow! You're sure thirsty. Guess that's a pun, too, but I mean it."

Yeah, boy! Cable Dog was really going to town. Guess it was that dry kibble. Did he really deserve wet food, though? "Nah," said Sabine out loud, turning with a wave of her hand and going to tend to her own breakfast as the dog lapped on. "Dry food is fine. It's what my family fed all my dogs growing up…"

After dumping the empty dog bowl in the sink, Sabine washed her hands and got an empty bowl of her own. Her stomach grumbled. Time to eat! She snatched a spoon and grabbed a box of her favorite cereal, "Daddy-Os." *Tastes* like cream pie, promised the box, which bore a caricature of her one and only Dark Lord pointing at the viewer with a wink and pair of finger guns.

"Oh, Master," said Sabine with a chuckle, kissing the sexy cartoon drawing in his dapper suit before brusquely tearing open the box and jerking out the crinkling bag within. The cereal inside rattled like a groaning man stirred from sleep by a handjob. Sabine's practiced fingers slipped inside the cellophane and gaped it wide open to permit the thunder of a torrid avalanche of sugary O's into the receptive bowl. That naughty, naughty dish took every one of those little holes into its waiting mouth, but, of course, one or two managed to bounce off across the kitchen counter. "Oops," said the witch in a breathy tone, gazing at the caricature of her Lord and Master while she lifted one of the lost loops to her lips. "I'm always dropping things in the kitchen these days, aren't I…"

Slowly, maintaining eye contact with the cartoon, Sabine extended her tongue. The house rattled upon its foundation while, with a moan of pleasure for the sweet, crisp taste of the cereal, the bad witch put the first escaped loop upon her tongue with all the euphoria she'd normally reserve for a tab of acid or a sacrilegiously received Communion wafer.

"Mm, mm," she said, crunching up the piece of cereal. She swallowed it with a groan of ecstasy, a pat of her stomach. "What a nice, yummy box of cereal this is…I hope Master leaves more for me soon, this one's almost emp—oh!"

Naughty, clumsy Sabine! There went the other lost loop, slipping from the fingertips that tried to pluck it from the counter. Must have been staring too intently at the cartoon… the Daddy-O fell to the floor and, pouting, Sabine shrugged. "Oh well," she said, slowly lowering her foot upon it to grind it beneath the bare heel. While the loop shattered to pieces between her foot and the floor that was in need of sweeping, (Lazy Bonensy!), Sabine ran her hands over herself through the robe.

All the while, the bad witch gazed into the Devil's smiling, two-dimensional face. "There's more where that came from, anyway…"

Pinching her nipples in expectation of the pleasures to come, moaning slightly to think of eating her delicious Dark Lord, Sabine resisted the urge to finger her pussy only because she still had to finish preparing her breakfast. Humming, she went to the fridge, saying, "That's sort of how Karma works, too. After all—"

She reached in without looking and grabbed a much too light gallon of milk. Frowning, then looking in with a noise of shocked displeasure, the bad witch summarized absently, "The universe always has more lessons to teach…damn! How did I let myself run out of milk?"

Yes—want to talk about keeping a house in order, well, Sabine was only an expert on what it took because she was so very lazy. It was much easier to be an expert on what other people should have been doing than to do those things oneself.

Sucking a tooth and glancing over at her leering cartoon god, Sabine shook the two tablespoons of milk still sitting in the bottom of the jug, remembered all the times her parents ever tore their hair out because of this bad habit of hers, and tossed the container away with a disdainful slam of the trashcan lid.

"Well, I'm not going to choke down dry cereal…ugh! Is this about Cable Dog? Whatever." Rolling her eyes, Sabine lifted her hands and said, "Well, it's too early to go to the store. You're going to have to wait, unless you want me to knock on a neighbor's door this early in the morning."

Hey, seven in the morning *was* early for a bad witch! Just you try doing ritual incantations and crazy lesbian orgies into the early morning hours without coming out the other side a bit of a late sleeper. Frankly, seven was almost insanely early to her, but she had a lot of baking to do if she was going to get the kids locked in her basement fattened up for Saturnalia. And what were they going to do without milk? Fuck. She was probably going to have to go to the store later, after all… but that didn't solve her immediate problem. Her stomach rumbled again, and with more than just anticipatory lust for a little weird vore with Satan.

"Seven in the morning, seven…who's up at seven? Schoolkids and the parents who have to get them there, people who work for a living, you know, squares—oh, of course. Clarinda!"

Yes, yes! Clarinda the Good Witch was up bright and early every morning. Right at the ass crack of dawn or, more often, hours before. Sabine knew this because once or twice, after spending all night awake, she got up on her spying ladder sometime around four or five in the morning just to see what was what before she finally got some shut-eye.

There, peering over her privacy fence, she watched the good witch a few houses down turn on her bedroom light and get dressed to do morning aerobics. Had to love those workout leggings…and a sports bra had a way of somehow flattering the blonde's tiny, perky tits, rather than wholly eliminating them. They, like Clarinda, were sleek and cute whenever she worked out—but now Sabine couldn't help thinking how absolutely smoking hot the athletic good witch would have looked with a big rack of magickal bazongas.

Oh yeah. She had gotten that hot little bitch to strip down and give her virginity in the name of Satan, and once her cherry was broken, the befriended good witch had permitted some measure of making out, feeling up and general fooling around during what was swiftly becoming a weekly movie night. Yeah, Clarinda was one hot number, and Sabine knew that if she would just let herself be a little more of a bimbo, why, she'd be even hotter.

Maybe this was an opportunity to kill two birds with one stone. "Thanks, Satan," said Sabine unironically, hurrying up the old Victorian house's stairs and throwing open the door to the library.

Sabine, who was not generally humble, would have not shied away from telling you that her library was one of the coolest on earth. She had a collection of real badass occult texts going back to the dawn of the written word, and she was diligent in their keeping and cataloging as a librarian. Whether it was written by a mad Arab and bound in human flesh or produced by people in their sleep with the help of a thought-to-text device, if it was a strange occult work, it existed in Sabine's library.

Therefore, it was easy enough to find the books she wanted, but harder still to settle on a spell. Hm, hm…checking the index of *How to Seduce Friends and Curse People*, Sabine took a peek under 't' for transformations. So broad! Did all these animals really need separate categories? "Cow, cow…hm—no, not a real cow."

Though it would have been funny. Humming, flipping back to the index again, Sabine now tried a few others. No milk under 'm.' Inflation under 'i,' well, that was something different altogether. Related, but different. Finally, dissatisfied, Sabine drummed her fingers on her chin and had an inspiration just as she was peering under 'F' for fertility spells.

Flow! Flowing spells. That was what the ticket. See, sometimes things in the universe got blocked by unexpected forces. Sometimes life seemed to hit a ceiling or go nowhere or just turn bad in general. In that case, what was really needed was something to get the flow back in its groove again. Sabine had used it on everything from frozen gutters to making her period come on time, but this was a much better purpose. Just had to hope it was going to work, since she wasn't sure Clarinda had ever lactated before.

"Only one way to find out," said the bad witch, shutting the book once she'd reviewed the page and hurrying to carry out its instructions before she really got hangry.

Pretty easy spell, all things considered. Didn't even require human blood or anything! Very cost- and time-effective. This was just one of those things where you lit a few candles, ran some water, and washed your hands with black salt while thinking of the situation that needed a bit of help flowing. A pail of the used water had to be taken to a nearby crossroads and dumped, which was a bit of an extra step, but it was still easier than going to the grocery store for someone as antisocial as a bad witch.

And, anyway, those extra steps were where the magick happened. Sabine had no sooner gotten back from her trip to the end of the block—had in fact just put her bucket away and picked up her phone to see the time—when a knock rang out on her front door. Bingo! Trying not to look excited or expectant, Sabine hurried to answer and promptly struggled to keep her tongue from lolling out of her mouth a la Tex Avery.

If there was one thing better than Clarinda's new tits, it was the sight of the tears springing from her innocent blue eyes as she kept folding and re-folding a housecoat clearly intended for a petite woman of her more usual proportions. "Um," began Clarinda, trying to smile and failing, eyes whipping wildly up and down the street, the blue curlers still wrapped in her blonde hair bobbing slightly with the motion. "um, Sabine! Hi! Gosh, sorry, you're not even dressed yet! Is it too early?"

"No, no, you're just on time. Come in!"

Clearly so distracted that she didn't even catch that comment, Clarinda edged in with a nervous smile. Sabine shut the door after her and willed herself to avoid staring at the obvious protrusion in the top of Clarinda's housecoat. "Whatcha need, neighbor?" Pleasant, smiling, Sabine lifted her eyebrows at the good witch and fought back a smile. The blonde worried her hands, used to turning her glamorous rings but, so early in the morning, consigned to rubbing her knuckles.

"Well! Well—well, it's just—I—I wouldn't really normally go to one of *you* for anything, uh, magickal, but—"

"'One of you?"

"Oh, just—a bad witch, you know."

"Even after you let my master fuck you, you're still so nervous about us!"

Looking aggrieved to have the inciting incident of their friendship brought up, Clarinda said, "I'm nervous about my soul and not so much about you or your friends…but you're right. Of *course* I'm nervous. I mean—I mean, we're talking about the Devil here, aren't we?"

"Sure, but society has tricked you into assuming 'the Devil' is a synonym for 'evil.' That's just not the case. There's nothing inherently evil about opposition…in fact, when the dominant force is oppressive, opposition is just called 'revolution.' You smuggling melons under that robe?"

Sabine hooked a finger beneath the fabric and lifted it away a degree to peer inside.

Clarinda stepped away quickly, arms still crossed tightly over her chest. "That's just it! Oh, I'm so embarrassed—I don't even know how to say this. Really, I don't know what's going on…"

It was awfully hard to maintain eye contact—especially as, Sabine noticed, a small pair of stains had already dampened the fabric of the robe. Keeping her tone innocent, the bad witch asked, "What is it? Ghosts in your basement? Bats in your belfry?"

The good witch threw around a shifty look, as though for observers. Evidently deciding that Cable Dog—who had trotted up with a wagging tail for the nice lady he hoped would someday rescue him from the mean one—didn't qualify, Clarinda admitted with a bit of humiliated shifting and shuffling, "It—I seem to be—" She dropped her voice and whispered the word like an obscenity: "Lactating?"

Sabine was on track for Best Actress, no question. Her eyes widened and, hands on her hips, the bad witch enthused, "Really! Are you pregnant?"

"N—no! Of course not—well—" Looking startled by the revelation that she was, of course, no longer a virgin and therefore perfectly capable of pregnancy (especially when this was Satan's dick we were talking about), Clarinda drummed her fingers on her chin, looked down at herself, then decided more firmly, "No, no, I'm not pregnant. It's not that. I think."

Terror filled the blonde's hot face and Sabine felt a little bad. Shit, well, she couldn't let the good witch think she might be pregnant…Sabine was a bad witch, but not a total *bitch*. Sympathetic in an instant, she draped an arm around her friend's shoulders and, while guiding her into the salon, used the vantage to stare down into the beautiful bazongas distorting the fabric of the too-small robe. "There, there, I'm sure it's nothing like that…maybe you were just hexed."

At Clarinda's skeptical noise, a high laugh of pettish

Catholic annoyance, Sabine arched a brow. "You've had sex with Satan and you *still* don't believe in hexes?"

"Well—it's just sort of silly, isn't it?"

"But the Bible's full of hexes! God is facilitating the curses of His prophets all the time. Look at the Egyptians…all those plagues Moses called. Frogs raining from the sky? That's a classic hex if I've ever heard one. Oh, and, uh, you know… murdering all those firstborn children…"

Sitting her friend down, Sabine perched on the davenport beside her and reached forward while delicately asking, "May I?"

With a bashful frown down at herself, Clarinda relaxed her arms. Sabine's body warmed with anticipation as she gingerly peeled the milk-stained robe away from Clarinda's swollen tits.

And *how s*wollen! The good witch was a B-cup on the best of days, but clearly a bra was out of the question at the moment… frankly, these bazookas looked like they weren't long for staying in the nightgown that battled for their containment. Golden flesh pulsing with aching veins overflowed from the bust of the nightgown, the fabric's straps barely sufficient to keep the dress together. Sabine thought, in fact, she saw a hint of pink nipple peering at her over the lace of the bust…hard to focus on that aspect, though, when the cotton of the nightgown was so wet with milk.

"Oh, yeah," said Sabine, leering openly now while Cable Dog, curious, trotted over and did a doggie double-take. While the pervert Cable Guy wagged his dog tail all the more furiously, his mouth hanging open in an expression of open delight that only Sabine could appreciate, the bad witch adopted the concerned expression of an I.T. expert doing tech support for somebody whose problem was obvious but who was paying by the hour.

"Yeah, you're definitely hexed, all right. When did this start?"

"This morning! Oh, I didn't even realize it. I was all—*achy* while I took my shower. I thought it was PMS. But then when I got out to dry myself off, I looked down and—oh, they're just huge! I feel ridiculous. And they hurt."

"I bet they do! How about this?" With a bold hand that was not to be stopped despite its gentle pressure, Sabine caressed the shocked good witch's left breast. While Clarinda gasped in surprise and her face grew all the redder for it, Sabine stared into her desperate blue eyes with the anticipation of Harvey Weinstein at a casting call.

"How about when I touch you…does it hurt?" Sabine's thumb drifted over a stiff nipple straining against its cotton prison. "Or does it feel good?"

"Uh—uh—oh—" Clarinda gasped all the sharper, eyelids fluttering as Sabine gently pinched at the tempting bud. "It—it does feel sort of good…oh, I'm so *sensitive.*"

Yeah, she was. Oh yeah, baby…Sabine leered with deeper predator relish while the good witch squirmed in her seat. Whining, whimpering, so fucking cute. Ugh! Sabine really hated how hot she found this goody-goody former HOA president…but, fuck. What could she do? Leaning in, nose brushing Clarinda's paralyzed cheek, Sabine murmured as she pressed a kiss to unready lips, "I like you sensitive, though."

Gently, sweetly, Clarinda moaned and opened her mouth to the bad witch's kiss. It had taken some getting used to—and more than one movie night spent getting high together on the salon sofa—but slowly, slowly, Sabine conditioned Clarinda to accept her own sexuality. Before, getting so much as a few kisses from the shy good witch had been like pulling teeth. But now, oh, that soft mouth yielded with steady passion, the good witch's supple tongue rollicking out from her mouth and into Sabine's with the pace of her moan. While Sabine sipped the good witch's sweet breaths, her thumb worked gently over that concealed nipple.

Then, trying not to startle Clarinda, Sabine drew a thin strap of the nightgown down its suntanned shoulder.

"Oh!" Clarinda's embarrassed gasp arose with the freeing of one great breast and she lifted a hand to try to stop Sabine. The bad witch caught that interloping hand, still kissing her friend, and turned it into an opportunity to intertwine their fingers while she steadily slid away the other strap.

"Don't be shy," whispered Sabine between the soft, crystalline laps of their lips. "You came to me for my help…I have to look at the problem, don't I? Just think of me as a doctor…a witch doctor…a nurse…"

Both voluminous globes free of the nightgown, Sabin looked down and gave into her urge to groan appreciatively. "Oh, baby! Baby…you *must* be sore. Look at these big things! They're overflowing."

Gently as she could stand to, Sabine placed one hand on each breast, firm with their inundation of fluid just dying to be released. Yet the skin itself, so soft…soft as Clarinda's nipples were hard. While the good witch moaned, squirming into the caresses and shutting her eyes to block out the humiliation, Sabine lightly rolled one nipple between her thumb and forefinger. Talk about stacked! A bead of white liquid appeared at once.

The bad witch moaned at the image as much as at the sharp inhalation of the good witch before her. "Feels good, huh…"

"Uh-huh…" Whining, whimpering in girlish embarrassment, Clarinda gasped, then moaned at the unexpected shock of Sabine's damp lips around that same nipple. "Oh! Oh—"

Gently, carefully, but oh, very eagerly, Sabine tried the fruits of her labor. At her first slow suck a stream of sweet milk filled her mouth, the fluid as anxious to be released as Clarinda was to be relieved.

Fuck! All Clarinda's squirming and whining was really

getting Sabine super wet…at this rate, she wasn't even going to get around to breakfast. And the thought of humiliating the cute good witch, turning her into a hot little hucow—damn! That was a pretty sexy idea, actually. Sabine learned something new about herself every day.

"You like that, huh," whispered Sabine, her hand sliding up the good witch's firm dancer thigh and under the fabric of her nightgown.

"Oh—oh, it does feel relieving, but—but—"

"It's embarrassing, huh? Embarrassing to admit you like having milk sucked out of your hard little nipples…it's okay… it's fun to be embarrassed sometimes. And so nice to be emptied…"

To Sabine's delight, Clarinda's thighs spread as she whispered, "Uh-huh."

"That's a good girl…my good witch…just lie back, now. Let Sabine take care of you…"

While the bad witch's fingers trailed between the welcoming thighs and beneath the surprisingly wet crotch of the panties there, Clarinda moaned in obviously intense pleasure. Sabine's mouth returned to its work of relieving her friend, all that warm, sweet milk flowing from the breast and over her palate. Her fingers, meanwhile, tickled the good witch's damp clitoris and steadily grew firmer in their pressure.

"Oh—oh, goodness, I—oh, it really *does* feel good. What a relief! Oh, yes, Sabine—oh, Sabine…thank you…"

No problem! No problem at all…the bad witch teased Clarinda's sensitive clit while her mouth worked harder to draw milk from that swollen breast, streams jetting out from the nipple in a veritable fountain. As her tongue teased, her fingers found their way down to the valley whose honey flowed as readily as did the good witch's milk. Maybe the bad witch should have been more specific about what she wanted flowing from the good one…but, no, who was she kidding?

Sabine wanted Clarinda to be a whining, horny, desperate bimbo.

Middle finger teasing just barely inside that tight little hole that was no less tight for being used by the Dark Lord's gigantic cock just a few weeks before, Sabine pulled a few more mouthfuls of fluid from the swollen tit she suckled. At the good witch's lower, more desperate moan and splaying legs, Sabine couldn't help but lift her head to deny relief a bit. While her other set of fingers pinched the nipple her lips had just abandoned, her exploring digit probed deeper into Clarinda's soaking cunt.

"What a horny slut you are, Clarinda!"

"Oh, God—I hate it when you call me that—"

"Then why do you get so wet? Come on, admit it. You love it…you love being my slut and you love being my cute little cow. Sweet Satan, I could suck on these tits all day…especially with you moaning like this." As her finger was joined by another and Clarinda opened herself to the experience more by the second, Sabine tugged lightly at the leaking nipple still poised in her fingers. Clarinda gasped sharply, moaned, whined, squirmed with absolute desperation.

"Oh—ow, Sabine, they're so sensitive, be careful, please!"

"Poor thing! You really do need relief…well, I'll help you more if you tell me how much you like it. If you beg me. Say, 'Please, Sabine, please suck my cute, milky tits and tease my pussy until I'm dripping wet.'"

"Oh, God! I could never say that."

The bad witch stared expectantly into her friend's face while curling her fingers. The wet chamber gripped them all the tighter and Clarinda thrashed, moaning sharply as a particularly mean pinch of Sabine's fingers elicited an unexpected stream of milk. While the witch laughed to have her own robe splashed with the stuff and decided it was better to slide out of the black fabric entirely, Clarinda panted, head back against the couch. The bad witch slowly removed her fingers and, as the good one realized what was happening, she gasped sharply. "No," she begged, "please, keep going, oh, I'm so close—"

"Then you better ask me nicely," commanded the bad witch. "Tell me what you want, slut."

"Oh—oh, God—oh, Sabine, please, will you fuck me? Please—please, milk me! Oh, I'm desperate! It *hurts*, Sabine… it felt so good when you were sucking the milk out of me and fingering me like that—ah!"

"Tell me you're my slutty little cow, and I'll do it."

"Ah—ah—I'm—I'm your slutty little cow—oh, yes! Fuck, I'm a dirty, dirty slut—your little milk-whore—"

Haha, getting weird with it! Sabine loved it. Clarinda was such a cutie…Catholics were all such fucking freaks in the universes of their own skulls. Probably because of the shame— it had a way of making hot things all the hotter, like when Clarinda got a guilty tone while calling herself a slut but that fine fanny absolutely flooded with lust at the admission. "That's right," said Sabine, squeezing that nipple, then working her hand over the breast to tug a stream from it.

As Clarinda gasped sharply, another jet of milk burst from the sore nipple and relieved her by pouring forth. It shot into Sabine's mouth, over her lips, across her neck and breasts. While the bad witch was bukkaked with breast milk, her fingers began a steady pumping in and out of Clarinda's drenched pussy. The good witch's back arched as if to encourage Sabine to apply her lips to the task; she obliged, her mouth enclosing that stiff nipple and briefly twisting into a smile to find the flow had only seemed to increase in intensity. While her fingers worked at a faster pace, her tongue and lips coordinated to coax as much of the sweet, warm milk from Clarinda's swollen breast as possible, and Clarinda whined Sabine's name at an increasingly high frequency.

Seeing the neglected of the two nipples overflowed with sympathetic output, Sabine lifted a free hand but didn't touch the sensitive spot herself. Instead she placed Clarinda's hand upon the breast and silently encouraged her to work it over. Milk spurted out beneath Clarinda's fingers and the good witch gasped in shame to splash her wicked friend's face in the stuff—but soon enough that gasp became a moan of pleasure to match Sabine's. While Sabine worked the milk out of one breast, Clarinda squeezed the other and coated her bad influence in the rich white fluid.

Groaning, eyes practically crossing with pleasure, Sabine rapidly pumped her fingers in and out of that slick pussy. Very soon, between the two intense flows to which Clarinda submitted herself, the good witch was wracked with a more powerful orgasm than Sabine had yet had the privilege to see in her.

"Oh! Oh—oh, God, Sabine—"

True to the flowing spell's implications, the good witch even squirted! Sabine laughed in dark delight as the good witch's cunt clamped rapidly around her fingers, milking them the way the bad witch's lips worked over Clarinda's leaking nipple. A few desperate squirts of ejaculate burst from the twitching labia, rewarding Sabine for having removed her head from her thirsty work to watch the show. While Clarinda screamed for Sabine and for God and gasped wildly, milk still trickling from her swollen breasts, Sabine wiped her mouth and grinned.

"You're too fucking hot, you bitch…" Snapping up the good witch's arm, Sabine landed a few playful, rapid spanks on Clarinda's ass. The good witch moaned in shock but was soon consoled by a sweet kiss and the assurance that, "Those were just for being so irresistible to me…you naughty slut. My sexy little cow!"

With an embarrassed look down at herself, then at Sabine's naked body—beautiful and pale and unfurled before her like the very hills of Eden—Clarinda uneasily stroked the bad witch's knee. She asked in that uncertain virginal tone still had for sexual matters, "Um—should—should I—are you—"

"Oh, I'm horny as fuck now…but before we mess around some more, could you actually do me a favor?"

If Clarinda had looked uncertain before, she looked ready to back out while standing in the kitchen before Sabine's bowl of Daddy-Os. "You—you mean you want me to put it in *there?* In your cereal? Yuck!"

"What do you mean, 'yuck!' It's milk, isn't it? Anyway, don't knock it 'till you've tried it. Here, don't be nervous." Rolling up the sleeves of her replaced robe and stepping behind Clarinda, Sabine enfolded the good witch in her arms and pressed a kiss to her ear. Clarinda gasped in shock, then obvious humiliation as Sabine slid her hands up over the good witch's tight stomach. "Just relax…think of how much better you'll feel. My hot fuck-heifer…just relax…"

She tried, bless her heart. While Sabine's hand slid over the more neglected of those two aching breasts, Clarinda moaned again. The good witch rested her head back against the bad one's shoulder; she seemed to melt into Sabine's arms, and Sabine took that as an invitation to go on. With great pleasure, the bad witch did, her other hand cupping its partnered breast.

One overfull bag at a time, Sabine made eye contact with cartoon Satan on the nearby cereal box and squeezed milk from her friend's enormous tits. The first jet sprayed in a few directions and landed nowhere near the bowl of cereal. The girls laughed, Clarinda more shyly than Sabine's wicked cackle. Much to the bad witch's delight, the good one nervously suggested, "Um, maybe if I bend over a little—"

"It's so hot when you play along with me," Sabine said encouragingly, helping her bend forward over the bowl. Yeah…talk about cows. Now *this* was milking—Sabine wished she had a straw hat and a piece of hay in her mouth or some shit. Repressing her grin lest Clarinda think she was teasing her, (And wasn't she at least marginally? You couldn't tease a good witch, though…they were so fucking sensitive), Sabine resumed her careful caressing and squeezing of those two sumptuous bosoms.

That was more like it! "What a good idea my cow had," said Sabine approvingly, admiring the ease with which she could now aim the multi-headed streams of milk into the bowl with very little splash-back. Worked like a charm…or a hex. While the good witch moaned to be relieved of the pressure in her aching breasts, Sabine monitored the level of milk in the bowl to make sure the Daddy-Os didn't get too soggy; then, when it was just enough, Sabine released her friend with a lascivious kiss and said, "Thanks, babe."

Dazed from the interaction and the kiss, Clarinda barely realized that there was no further sexual action immediately happening—not until Sabine more or less ignored the almost hypnotized woman and sat down at the breakfast table to *finally* eat her fucking food.

Shit! She'd been starving. The bad witch moaned from the first bite, and not just for effect.

"Uh—" Clarinda laughed. "You really *are* going to eat it? Right now?"

"Well I can't wait to let it get all gross and mushy," said Sabine, glancing at the leering illustration on the box before lifting the spoon toward Clarinda's mouth. "Want to try it? It's really good."

"W—um, I guess—" With an awkward, somewhat befuddled look down at the spoon of milky cereal Sabine lifted up to her, Clarinda fixed her nightgown back over her overgrown breasts and bent over to open her mouth. Sabine stared down that swollen cleavage while sliding the spoon into her friend's mouth, pleased by the sight of a drop of liquid dribbling down the good witch's plump pink lip.

"Say!" Pleased, Clarinda stood upright and chewed with her hand poised before her mouth so she could talk while she ate. Sabine tried to glance past her hand and swore that the Satanic mascot had altered his gaze to watch the good witch chew him up, but she could never be sure about such details. "That *is good!* What is that—Count Chocula?"

"Nah, Daddy-Os."

"I've never heard of that one!"

"It's my favorite. You want some?" At Clarinda's pleasant acceptance, Sabine sprang up from her seat to get a bowl and a spoon. Then, without thinking, she said, "You're going to have to provide your own milk, though…I'm all out this morning."

"Oh, well, it's a good thing I came over then—wait! Wait a minute!"

Ah, shit. Busted! Sabine, pre-grimacing, turned back with the bowl and spoon in her hand. The good witch's wild-eyed and shocked expression said more than the hands on her slim hips ever could.

"Did *you* do this to me, Sabine?"

"'Do' is such a *strong* word when it comes to magick, don't you think? Like, it's not causal, it's synchronistic. I always think about Shakespeare. The Wyrd Sisters in *Macbeth*, you know…'I'll do, I'll do, and I'll do.'"

"Sabine!"

"Hey! It's not like there's any harm…you got to have fun, didn't you? *And* you're getting breakfast out of the deal!" At the tap of Clarinda's impatient foot and her petulant scowl, Sabine spread her hands. "Oh, don't worry, you'll be back to normal by tomorrow…anyway, it's a valuable lesson."

"About?"

"Hexes! And Karma," added Sabine with a glance into her reflective microwave door, setting the empty bowl and spoon at the seat beside hers. "But that second one's a lesson for me and not for you quite so much. Well, come on! Are you going to stand there being pissed off at me all day, or are you going to eat breakfast? It'll do you good. What's the commercial say? 'You're not you when you're hungry.'"

Looking more aggrieved by the second, Clarinda regarded the empty bowl, the box of Daddy-Os, and then, from the corner of her eye, the bad witch who sat to resume eating breakfast. Shaking her head, Clarinda snatched up the box and roughly opened the bag inside to dump the remaining cereal in her provided bowl. "I can't believe you would do this to me."

"I didn't, really…Master did, by making me forget to get more milk. He must have wanted you here."

"Satan again." With a roll of her eyes and a look of annoyance, Clarinda slipped her sorer left tit from her nightgown and bent over with a grumble. "What a load of—well, don't stare!"

"I can't help it!" Sabine grinned while the streams of milk dripped down into the Daddy-Os, all those desperate cereal mouths open and more than receptive to the inundation of fluid. "How often do you get to see a woman eat cereal with her own milk…especially this cereal."

Sniffing, sitting primly and crossing herself to swiftly mutter grace, Clarinda crossed herself again, snatched up her spoon and claimed a scoop of the cereal. "What makes this stuff so special, then?"

"It's Master's, of course."

"He owns it?"

"More like, he *is* it."

The good witch had only just taken the spoonful of cereal and breast milk into her sulkily pouting little mouth. Now she choked, sputtering, and managed the word, "What!" around the bite. While Sabine cackled, Clarinda stared in shock and horror down at the bowl, then up at the caricature. By the time she had looked back down at the table, both bowls of cereal had disappeared along with their contents. Clarinda gasped with horror, reflexively swallowing the food in her mouth when Satan dropped a hand on the back of her neck.

"Now, Clarinda, don't be like that…you were enjoying me just a few seconds ago."

"You! You—you evil man, you—*Devil*—"

"That's what they call me," said the Dark Lord with a chuckle, accepting Sabine into his arms as she stood to kiss his mouth. His nose brushing hers, he said, "Bad girl, teasing your friend…she didn't have to know."

"You know how weird people are about consent these days," said Sabine, nose wrinkling as they pulled apart from another kiss. "Even if it's horror…ah! Oh…"

Satan landed a few brisk swats on the bad witch's ass. His hand remained to fondle through the fabric of her robe. "That may be, but you're still getting a flogging later."

"Oh, I *hope* so."

Unable to enjoy the scene of the busty bad witch being groped by her Dark Lord, Clarinda reached reflexively for the crucifix she hadn't yet put on that day. Finding her neck bare, she instead rested her hand over her heart.

"So Sabine was right! Did you lure me here? What do you *want* from me?"

"All kinds of things…well, let me rephrase. I don't want from you anything that somebody else couldn't give me just as well…but my pretty little Sabine's just so fond of you, Clarinda. I love to watch you girls play together…and, anyway, Sabine is right. You both have your own lessons to learn."

While Sabine nipped playfully at the fingertip her master used to tickle her chin, Clarinda folded her arms over her breasts and said, "I really—*really* wish you would at least pretend you aren't…observing us."

"At least I'm honest about it, unlike my upstairs neighbor… honest when pressed, anyway. Oh, now"—at Clarinda's scowl, the Lord of the Flies transmuted the smile of his handsome lips into a flirtatious pout; Sabine swore the good witch's eyes filled with immediate weakness and that the roll of her shoulders up and back was a kind of shoring up, a resistance to how obscenely hot Satan was in his human form—"don't be like that, Clarinda! I have feelings, too, you know…after what we shared, are you really going to reject me out-of-hand?"

"We didn't *share* anything. You two manipulated me! I was seduced! I—I—"

While watching Clarinda, listening with active interest, Satan was nonetheless using the hand on the bad witch's ass to pull up the black fabric of her robe. Soon that big white peach was bared and he sank his fingers into the flesh, drawing Clarinda's eye and provoking a sharp inhalation from her flaring nostrils.

"Everything in life is a form of seduction," Satan assured the good witch while the bad one stroked his chest and gradually trailed her fingers toward his belt. "Every interaction… especially romantic ones. After all! If there's no seduction involved, why, that's awful…for instance, there's nothing worse than a man who thinks he's entitled to the bodies of women with no work owed on his part. Any decent kind of man recognizes that sex is a gift…that he'd ought to get down on his knees to thank the woman who gives it to him."

"And instead you encouraged Sabine to—do *this* to me." Annoyed, Clarinda waved down at her tits, leaking once again through the cotton of her gown.

"It was all Sabine's idea, of course. I rarely suggest anything specific…you'll know when I do because it'll make the news." At Clarinda's slightly pale features and the hand that she extended to support herself against the back of the chair, Satan chuckled, then groaned as his wicked slave slid his cock out of his trousers. Sabine got on her knees to suck him hard, grinning all the while.

As her expert mouth worked the Dark Lord's shaft, her

jaw sometimes backing away to permit her tongue's rapid flicker along the underside of the glans, Satan exhaled low and stroked the dark locks of her head back from her face. He gazed into the eyes of beautiful Clarinda, who now struggled mightily to keep her gaze level with his.

"But I hate the thought of you two arguing now…especially over, ah…something so harmless…and so sexy…come now, Clarinda—let me make right what my servant did. I know you've been thinking about this cock since you had it last time. It's certainly been inducing me to think about you."

Biting her lip, one arm still folded over her swollen breasts while the other supported her against the chair, Clarinda permitted herself the briefest of glances at Sabine's bobbing head. As the bad witch's tongue swirled up and down the Devil's throbbing cock, he groaned and tilted back his head. Oh, the ecstasy written across his hard face would have been irresistible to the very saints themselves. Clarinda Lovegood, who already knew the abominable pleasure provided by Satan's dick, stood absolutely no chance.

Nervously tugging on the strap of her nightgown, Clarinda admitted with a shy glance at the cereal box that was now missing its mascot, "Well—well, I am *very* sore…and if you could fix it, I would be very grateful. But—this is the last time something like this can be allowed to happen. Understand?"

"Of course!" While wearing an angelic expression truly worthy of his origin, Satan jerked his servant's head roughly from his prick. He pushed Sabine aside while she choked and laughed, and by the time the bad witch had recovered enough to watch, the Dark Lord had crossed to take Clarinda far more gently into his arms. "Wouldn't want that pure soul of yours to be sullied by my wicked influence, now…here, Clarinda. Don't be shy. Let me see what my servant has done."

Sitting Clarinda down in the breakfast nook near the table, Satan knelt beside the bench and reverently slid the straps of her nightgown down her shoulders. Though the good witch at first stiffened beneath the Devil's sensual caress, she exhaled and forced herself to relax.

Soon enough those overflowing breasts were revealed again.

"Oh, my," said Satan, his voice low to see the bead of white fluid that, clinging to Clarinda's left nipple, also drew Sabine's attention. "That does look very uncomfortable…you poor girl. Hard enough going through PMS once a month…"

The good witch sniffed in displeasure. "What would you know about it?"

Sabine slid out of her robe and let it fall upon the floor to leave her body once more utterly naked. "Oh, Master manifests as a woman every once in a while." At Clarinda's visible surprise, the bad witch snuggled up beside her in the breakfast nook, stroking her face and trailing her fingers over those golden athlete's thighs. Satan, meanwhile, chuckled to lower his head in a long chain of kisses down Clarinda's neck and the bust of her aching upper half.

"Angels are genderless, of course…but you knew that, my Bride of Christ. Ah! Poor lamb."

His tongue slithered out along the pulsing veins of her full jug and down to the hard peak of a weeping nipple. While Clarinda moaned, riveted by the sight just as much as Sabine, the Devil gazed up at her and slowly enfolded that nipple in his lips. One large, firm hand settled gently upon Clarinda's breast and worked the flesh with far more expertise than even Sabine had showed.

While the good witch gasped in surprise and arched with pleasure into his touch, staring down into his ice blue eyes, Sabine reached down into the Dark Lord's lap and tugged on his pulsing member.

"Isn't Master good at everything? There's no one who knows how to please a woman better…oh! Master, your dick is so hard."

"As I said—seeing you girls play together has an irresistible effect on me. And how sweet this milk is!"

Having removed his mouth to speak, a few beads of white liquid trickled down Clarinda's nipple and over the swell of her breast. Sabine's head ducked and she hurriedly lapped along the trail and the soft, hormonal flesh, moaning when Satan caught her to lift her mouth to the nipple, proper. As she latched at his silent behest, his hand fell to the rhythm of stroking her head for a few seconds. It released only to permit him to adjust his attention down to Clarinda's once more splaying thighs.

She looked as though ready to protest but, at the tenderness of his hand trailing over her limb, the good witch relaxed back into the nook. She even sighed softly.

"There"—the Devil kissed to the apex of Clarinda's thighs while Sabine worked the milk from her still overfull breast—"there, just let us take care of you, Clarinda…what a good girl you are. Yes, a very good witch…"

That good witch moaned wildly from the first second that Satan's lips landed upon her pussy. Her legs spreading wider, Clarinda's eyes flickered from Satan to Sabine and back again. Why, her hand even landed upon the back of the Dark Lord's head! Sabine was so proud of her friend. Yes, it was just a matter of time and effort. Someday, the good witch would be fully committed to the Dark Lord's service…and then, a good witch no more. For now, the still rather innocent mite was overwhelmed with bliss and soon screamed with ecstasy beneath Satan's touch.

"What a drenched pussy you've given your girlfriend, Sabine…she's begging to be fucked already. Should I oblige her?"

"I don't know," whimpered Clarinda. "I don't know—"

"Poor shy girl! Well…why don't you watch me fuck Sabine, and you can decide if you want to take your turn."

Eager as a girl on the playground invited to play her favorite game, Sabine sprang up and helped her master to undress. Ah, she loved his kisses! They alone were an overwhelming pleasure, but soon the bad witch was subject to a far more infernal ecstasy. With her long hair like reins in his hand, Satan turned her around and pushed her down to Clarinda's breast. The bad witch, still standing as she bent, moaned to latch back on and suckle another stream of warm milk from her friend's aching tit. Satan, meanwhile, positioned himself behind his slave, pressing to her ass for a contemplative second before sliding his enormous prick, hard as a steel rod, deep inside her dripping cunt. While Sabine moaned in high, almost pained pleasure, the Devil groaned, found his rhythm, and, one hand on the back of Sabine's ass, bent to kiss Clarinda the Good Witch on her gasping mouth.

The pride! Clarinda's head tilted back and, whimpering with the strange pleasure of being drained by her friend, she offered her mouth fully to the Dark Lord. As Satan's tongue fucked her throat not quite so deeply as his cock fucked the bad witch's pussy (for it could have if he had willed it to, but clearly he didn't want to scare the good witch off before she could be thoroughly corrupted), his hand lifted to her untended breast and began again its slow massage. Sabine moaned around Clarinda's other tit, watching from the corner of her eye as the Devil slowly, carefully urged white milk to dribble from the good witch's pink nipple. While the beads of fluid ran down her nightgown and dripped upon her thighs, Satan groaned appreciatively and doubled his pace inside of Sabine's cunt.

"There's really nothing wrong with enjoying a thing like this, you know, Clarinda…" The Devil lifted his tongue from the good witch's mouth to peer intensely into her eyes, his milking hand extracting pulse after pulse of sweet white liquid. While Sabine commenced to once more tease and tickle her friend's sensitive clit, that friend almost screamed with pleasure and stared helplessly back into Satan's hypnotic stare. "Why, it's just a sensation as abstract as any other…it's the value, the taboo that humans ascribe to it that makes it sexual. I'm not the one saying sex is bad…not even God is the one saying sex is bad. It's humans. All humans."

"It's not that it's bad—oh, oh—it's—oh—ugh, ah—"

"Can't speak, eh? Well, that's all right…don't worry. I know what you were going to say. You were going to correct me and say that the sin isn't sex, but sex before marriage. Right? But sodomy is sinful in and out of marriage in the eyes of the Church, so not all sex is acceptable. Yet why is it fine to go to the doctor and get a pap smear, a colonoscopy? Do you mean to say that intimacy isn't just as much a requirement in human life as a bland, cruel, cold medical procedure from a near-stranger? Is it really so much worse to be fucked in the ass or have your cute tits milked than it is for a man to accidentally orgasm and spill his seed when the doctor sticks a finger in a surprising place?"

"Ah—ah—"

Clarinda couldn't respond, clearly already nearing another orgasm. Sabine was close to one herself, especially with as hard as Satan's big prick was inside of her. Eyes rolling into the back of her head, the bad witch moaned and panted and excitedly lapped at the flow from Clarinda's bosom.

At last, that point of incredible suspension was reached. Time itself seemed to halt, as it did at the top of a roller coaster's hill—the second before that cart was overcome by gravity and crashed down through the ride. Sabine screamed with a particularly hard stroke of the Devil's and the orgasm was upon her, rattling through her body and boiling her brain with ecstasy so great that its mere observation proved the cause of Clarinda's own orgasm. As the bad witch lifted her head and, in the midst of the kiss she doled out, poured breast milk into the good witch's gasping mouth, Satan slowed his strokes to guide his servant through her climax and watch the kiss with appreciation.

"What good girls you are…you play so sweetly…that's right, isn't that nice…oh, Clarinda—"

"Will you—fuck me, please—" Gasping, barely able to produce the word, Clarinda looked urgently into Satan's eyes, then into the bad witch's face as though to search for permission. Both evil beings laughed with pleasure, exchanging a tender glance of affection for Clarinda and a passionate kiss with one another. The Dark Lord slowly drew his length from Sabine's cunt and smiled as she stepped aside, her hand running along the member to offer it to Clarinda.

"Of course, Clarinda," answered Satan, bending down to kiss her. "Here…I was rough with you last time when I was doing the riding. Why don't you get on top. And you, Sabine! You've been an obedient slut to me today, so you can sit on my face if you'd like…"

'If!' Consent was never a problem for Sabine, baby. Clarinda slid up from the nook and, once the Devil had arranged himself amid the green cushions, Sabine hurried to take him up on the offer. While she knelt over his face to brush her pussy lips against his waiting mouth, Clarinda stripped out of her milksoaked nightgown and crouched uncertainly over Satan's throbbing erection.

"Oh, God," whimpered Clarinda, looking at the evil thing she was nonetheless compelled to caress with soft fingertips, "I don't even know how to put it in…"

"I'll help," said Sabine, gasping not just with eagerness but with the sudden pulse of Satan's tongue deep into her cunt. Oh, far deeper than he had permitted it to delve into Clarinda's throat! While Sabine moaned to be fucked by her Dark Lord's flexible, inhumanly long tentacle of a tongue, she braced one hand upon the cushions and used the other to prop up his prick. The weapon twitched in her grasp, especially as she teased it against the dripping wet lips of Clarinda's pussy. The good witch's eyes met hers and she grinned into them.

"Say 'Please put Satan's big dick in me, Sabine.'"

"Now, Sabine," the Devil began to say, his tongue sliding away, "don't tease your poor little—"

"Please!" Brow furrowed in desperation, hands rising up into hair and pulling away the blue curlers that soon left her blonde locks in wild disarray, the good witch moaned. Clarinda looked down at the giant prick teasing her hole and begged, whined, cried, "Please, please, oh, put Satan's big dick in me, Sabine! Oh, fuck, I want the Devil to fuck me in front of you—yes, oh, God, forgive me, I want the Devil to fuck me, fuck me, please—"

Satan and Sabine moaned in mutual pleasure, absolute delight. "Maybe she's further along than I thought," Satan said with a chuckle, kissing the bad witch's pussy with appreciation and landing an affectionate swat on her ass. "Maybe, maybe… only God knows all in this life…"

As his tongue went again to work in Sabine's cunt, faster and harder now, she shuddered and stroked his shaft a few times. "You beg so nicely," said Sabine, lining the tip of the Devil's aching dick up to Clarinda's glistening puss. "Go on… impale yourself on my master's cock. Do it, witch."

Moaning, Clarinda obeyed. Sabine's eyes glittered with pride at the absolute ecstasy crossing the good witch's face when she was filled. The sweet hole, so tight and unused to any stimulation let alone from such a big tool, nonetheless proved highly receptive. Perhaps this was owed to that flowing spell… 'Thanks, Satan?' More like 'Thanks, Sabine.' You're welcome, Master! Without getting Clarinda all good and wet there would have been a lot of unpleasant whining…but, dripping as she was, the good witch was able to soon figure out the basic mechanics of girl-on-top and freely ride the Devil's big, throbbing dick for all she was worth. She moaned, drowning in bliss, her hands moving over her pleasure-wracked body and worrying over those aching breasts.

Sabine, gasping with her own excruciating pleasures from her master's tongue, leaned forward to kiss Clarinda's mouth. While the women made out, Sabine lifted a hand to help her friend milk those glorious tits. Soon, white fluid poured in streams from Clarinda's aching nipples and splattered all across Sabine's tight stomach. The milk dripped down the length of her body, into her navel, along her mound and down into the Devil's mouth. After wetting his fingers with the fluid to slid them with greater ease into the bad witch's tightly grasping asshole, Satan removed his tongue only to say, "You know, Sabine…I think maybe you need a taste of your own medicine."

"Oh, yes! Yes, Master…oh, yes, give me what I deserve, ah!"

It was funny to say but, as big as her tits were, Sabine had never tried this sort of thing with herself before. Hey, she was down to try whatever, though. You never knew what you liked until you'd given it a shot…glass houses, throwing stones, Karma, whatever. She would have lectured you about metaphysics or something, reader, but, um, she was a little busy moaning while her already expansive breasts began to inflate even more. Clarinda gasped at the sight but was much too lost in the pleasure of repeatedly hammering herself down on the Devil's big red dick to speak to it. While his other red organ went back to work on Sabine's pussy and his finger worked in and out of her anus, his other hand lifted to blindly find Sabine's growing left breast.

With the slow, steady touch of an expert, Satan worked the bad witch's globe as confidently as he had Clarinda's. The pressurized ache that had started with the inflation soon overwhelmed Sabine with the release of the first few drops of liquid, and thereafter her breast was as much a font beneath Satan's hand as Clarinda's had been beneath Sabine's. The witches moaned together, their tongues intertwining. They giggled as their streams of milk interfered, splashed together, dribbled across feminine bodies and Satan's cut stomach. With a bold look into Sabine's face, Clarinda pulled from the kiss and, making eye contact as long as she could, lowered her head to run her flat tongue along the swell of Sabine's throbbing breast.

That overfull tension really was something terrible, but oh, it was all worth it to watch the good witch's lips clamp to her nipple and suckle as eagerly as Sabine had earlier. And it was different, that feeling! Very different—very exposing, somehow, to be fucked below and suckled above. Yes, it made Sabine even wetter, and she groaned while Satan lapped up the sheen of her arousal, to submit to the pleasure of the good witch sucking milk from her leaking tits.

The hand the Devil used to milk his slutty cow lowered only to toy with Clarinda's clit, then to brace against her thigh and encourage harder pumps. She obeyed his silent command and Sabine, consumed by the pleasure, drenched the Dark Lord's chin with her own squirting orgasm as his tongue pounding against her g-spot combined with the sight of milk-dripping Clarinda and her own creamy relief to great effect. While her pussy clenched as rapidly around his tongue as her asshole did around the Dark Lord's fingertip, Sabine moaned and drew Clarinda back from her breast to snatch a kiss from her.

Moaning to taste her own milk on the good witch as she did, Sabine almost missed the start of that good witch's orgasm, but the climax as a whole would have been impossible to miss. How she screamed with the Devil's prick inside of her, milk jetting from the breasts she massaged! The image resembled the cum that shot from that wicked organ of diabolical lust— Sabine moaned to see it twitch and pulse with semen when he shoved gasping Clarinda from his lap. The bad witch leaned over the groaning Devil's organ just a second before his climax. She was subsequently blasted in the face and eyes with his unholy seed…which wasn't acidic that day, she was glad to note. He only did the acid thing sometimes, when she'd been disobedient or forgetting to pray. That was maybe a mailing list story, though, reader.

Oh, shit! Reader. Fuck. Haha, Sabine almost forgot about you! She grinned into the feng shui mirror suction-cupped in her breakfast nook window and winked a cum-tangled set of eyelashes. Don't forget to leave a five-star review, you dirty bird.

"Ah, Sabine…Clarinda…you ladies…" Satan stroked Sabine's thigh while, panting, the bad witch fell aside from his face and offered Clarinda her lips. The good witch, still rippling with pleasure's aftershocks in the face of such demonic euphoria, pressed a kiss to Sabine's mouth without the least delay. Pleasure rumbling in his voice when Clarinda boldly licked a string of semen from Sabine's smiling cheek, the Devil assured them, "I've not seen a finer pair of girls in centuries…even among witches, you are both exceptional."

Slowly gasping herself back to reality, back to Catholic beliefs and the fact that she was a good witch who had just narrowly avoided being inseminated by the Devil—and only by virtue of the Devil's decision to push her from her mount—Clarinda panted down at herself. "I should go," she whispered, then, gasping in surprise, "oh—"

Her breasts had reduced in size while her consciousness exploded in the annihilating orgasm, her attention therefore impossible to maintain. Yes, an orgasm was a moment when any small alteration in reality was simple…especially for a being as powerful as Satan. (Why did you *really* think masturbation was a metaphysical no-no, reader? Wonder what changed in your room while you were hard at work reading this story? You'll never know.)

Noting the obvious adjustment in Clarinda's bust, Sabine

glanced down to find herself in the same condition, and laughed—harder still when Clarinda's attention returned to the Devil to find he had vanished. Well—not vanished. A fresh cardboard box of Daddy-Os sat on the kitchen counter, just as Sabine had requested. Sweet!

"He disappeared," Clarinda commented unnecessarily while Sabine laughed at her.

"Aw, don't worry! He'll be back…I'm sure if he felt like he wanted you to stay, he would have." Indeed, Clarinda looked hugely relieved, and Sabine could already see her trying to write the memory off as some dream or hallucination. Rubbing her cum-covered cheek across the good witch's mouth, then nuzzling those same sticky lips, Sabine murmured, "He just doesn't want to scare you away…neither do I."

Exhaling shakily, the good witch looked just a little longer into Sabine's eyes. "I should go," Clarinda at last repeated, collecting her nightgown and standing up.

Sabine didn't mind for her own sake—she had errands to run and, as she had said earlier, there was a lot of baking scheduled for that day—but, worried that they had pushed the good witch too far, she did grab Clarinda's wrist and kiss her hand. "Sorry I turned you into my human cow."

With an annoyed arch of her brow and twist of her lips beneath a disarrayed lock of blonde hair, the good witch tugged her damp nightgown over her head. Once it had fallen around her knees again she leaned down and, catching Sabine's face in her hands, kissed the bad witch hard upon the mouth. Sabine moaned softly, tongue taking a real beating from the one that lashed it as savagely as she could only hope the Devil would lash her later.

"Ask me first next time," flush-faced Clarinda chided, tapping Sabine on the nose as Sabine herself affectionately rebuffed Cable Dog. "Are we still on for movie night on Friday?"

Sabine grinned ear-to-ear. "Hell yeah!"

"What are we watching?"

Her grin widened. "How about *Rosemary's Baby?*"

The bad witch laughed to see the good witch actually flipped her off on her way out of the kitchen. Ah, progress! Sabine loved to see it. Yes, Clarinda could be very fun when she set her mind to it…and Sabine could be reasonable.

Reasonable! Yeah, yeah…she got it. The bad witch rolled her eyes at the box of cereal and, sighing, turned off the kitchen light. While the front door shut after Clarinda, Sabine made her way to the second floor and said into the reflective corner of an old oil painting (a suicidal clown putting a gun to his head) framed at the top of the stairs, "That's the important thing to remember about Karma, reader…it's okay to enjoy the justice inherent to someone else experiencing Karma in front of you—as long as you realize that *you* are the one who's supposed to be learning the lesson. Not them. Karma is what happens when somebody can't learn a lesson…and you can avoid a similar trap by learning a few lessons, yourself."

After another shower and a quick change into a turtleneck and black jeans, Sabine returned downstairs and whistled for Cable Dog. He scrambled in at her behest, looking surprised to find her with the lead in her hand and the garage door open. The dog looked suspiciously at her, probably owing to her earlier comment about neutering, and she laughed while putting on his harness.

"Don't worry, we're not going to the vet…"

On the way to pick up milk at the grocer, Sabine stopped by the pet store. There, she let Cable Dog sniff out his own preferred brand of wet food while he all but danced with joy. The cute high school student working part-time there (still in braces, Satan love her adorable heart) said, with an approving smile for the alleged shepherd's happy tail wags, "You're such a thoughtful owner!"

"You know," said Sabine, beaming at the nearby can of Daddy-O brand dog food giving her a thumb's up, "I really do try."

The Witch's Filthy Habit

SABINE PERCHED ON THE HOGTIED PRIEST while, at the altar, the Devil cut up a few more lines of Communion wafers. "

You sure you don't want any of this, babe?" He rubbed a little on his gums while his bad witch tried on the naked, panting nun's appropriated veil.

"You remember the nosebleed I got the last time you made me try that? No thanks, Master."

"Suit yourself."

Retrieving once more a rolled up check made out for a thousand dollars to the Catholic Church, one among many checks and bills and coins that they'd dumped from the collection plate after the evening Mass, Satan snorted a line and sat up with a grin while both Catholics moaned in a combination of horror and supremely depraved arousal.

"Oh, yeah," he crooned, "you fucking like that, don't you… look at how wet she is. You like to watch me, don't you, Sister."

The firm, spry young nun writhing naked on the floor

worked a crucifix in and out of her own pussy while Satan and his witch leered on. "Yes, yes! Yes Satan, yes!"

"Hail Satan," said the witch, while the Dark Lord chuckled and bent to do another line.

"Hail Satan," he answered, groaning a little as he sat upright and wiped his hand against the back of his nose. "Oh, buddy, Jesus, I miss you. Fucking damn! Come back and see me soon."

"Fuck that, Master, I don't think he's ever coming back. Would you?"

"Look at me! I'm here all the time…I love it here, this place is a madhouse. And when you're a sane man in a madhouse, the difference between you and the position of director is just a matter of time and money. Get the camera, baby, takes some pictures while I fuck her…you want this big Devil dick? I bet you think you do…"

Satan turned and sprang upon the nun, yanking the crucifix out of her cunt and sliding his huge dick out of the black folds of his cassock. While the Dark Lord plunged to the hilt in screaming Sister Ignatia, Sabine cried in delight and scrambled up for the SLR.

As she snapped off a few solid shots, she and Satan laughed together—as one does while laughing in a group, she glanced at the other members and saw the nun was having a grand old time but that the priest, for whom fucking women was the only boundary they had been able to find (not because he was more interested in men but because the Good Lord commanded it, understand), averted his eyes by turning his face toward the marble floor. His dick was as hard as a rock when Sabine turned him so that he was forced to view the debacle unfurling upon this sacred ground. Sabine laughed in his face, flicking him in the nose and commanding "Watch, you cuckold, come on, you loser piece of shit, just watch—"

As she rubbed her foot back and forth over his dick through the black fabric of his trousers, the gagged priest produced a muffled set of noises and Sabine increased her pressure to something closer to a stomp. "Unless you want some CBT, you'll be good and give in. Just relax! You were so into it before…you consented then, didn't you?"

Weakly, the priest nodded. Sabine smiled at that and rubbed his dick a bit more longingly with her foot.

"You know, Father, you're pretty cute…want to hear my confession sometime? It's a long, long list…oh, it'll make your dick so big and hard. I'll have to figure out where to start, though…examine my conscience, as the Catholics say. Want a blowjob?" The priest shook his head and she laughed nastily. "Into edging, huh? Some weird tantric thing…whatever, I get it. As long as it's consensual, it's all cool with me."

"That's my girl," said the Devil with approval, groaning and grasping the nun's face. "See, Sister? We're not so bad…I only give the people what they want! Consent is hot…that's what they say. And baby, I agree."

"Choke me," begged the nun, gasping with the instantaneous tightening of his hand around her windpipe. "Choke—oh—!"

Honey locks tumbling around her face making her flesh look all the redder, Satan slammed his fingertips over her artery and groaned as her eyelids fluttered. "Oh, baby, baby! Even tighter…cum for me, baby, cum for Satan—yeah, yeah—sh!"

While the asphyxiating nun writhed on the floor, mid-orgasm around his dick, Satan lifted a free hand and looked up at his bad witch. Sabine had just taken one last good picture but paused with the device still raised; the priest made a muffled noise and Sabine stepped on his face to shut up him while footsteps edged into the church.

"If you say a word," Sabine whispered to the priest, wagging a finger in his face before drawing it across her own throat. "Sh."

"Hello?"

Sabine tried not to gasp too loud in her delight and glanced sharply over at her generous master, who had noticed when he released his hand the nun had gone very still and now leaned down to ensure that she was still breathing. "Is it my *birthday?*" The bad witch's voice, an urgent whisper, was tinged with her delight of recognition. That bright 'Hello' could have only belonged to one tight, easy-to-torment good witch: Clarinda Lovegood.

Extricating himself from the nun with a chuckle, Satan whispered to the bad witch, "Let's do some rearranging."

Sabine, meanwhile, wiggled quickly into the nun's abandoned habit and donned the veil straighter this time. With a tap of her finger to the tip of her nose she made a slight alteration to her face and, voila!

Meet Sister Nadine.

Grinning wildly, Sister Nadine batted her brown eyes, said to Satan, "Thank you, Daddy," and appreciated the sight of his ass in the cassock while he hurried over to the priest to collect the bound man in his arms. The nun lay blacked out on the floor, still as a corpse.

Oh, don't worry. That was just a metaphor. She was alive. Everybody was going to live tonight. You're welcome.

Sabine and the Dark Lord had just loaded the priest into the confessional when Clarinda appeared on the edge of the chapel. "Father," called the good witch from across the church, unable to see around a column that blocked them at her distance.

"Impatient," muttered the Devil to his servant before adopting a parody of the priest's Irish immigrant accent. "Be with you in a moment, love, just give me a second ta finish me paperwerk."

"Oh sure," said Clarinda, who, as a former HOA president who had denied many requests to alter houses owing to shoddy paperwork, understood the importance of thoroughness in bureaucracy better than any other sort of person. "Sorry, I just wasn't sure you were—I thought I heard a strange noise—"

"That was probably just me," said disguised Sabine, plucking up her camera and hurrying down the aisle to see her naïve friend. Not recognizing her neighbor in this state of imitation, Clarinda gasped, then smiled to see a new nun.

"Why, hello Sister! I don't believe we've met, have we?"

"Not us! I'm Sister Nadine. And you are—?"

"Oh! I'm, uh, Clarinda Lovegood, I used to work here part-time." Fun fact! Sabine didn't know that. She also learned another fun fact: a far, far more fun fact considering Clarinda introduced herself this way even given what Satan and Sabine had already gotten her to do. "I'm actually kind of a lay nun, in a way, uh—a consecrated virgin."

So that was what a good witch was! Of course. Sabine had always wondered about how all that was structured. Funny to learn how the other half lived. You know, reader, this was why it was so important to talk to your neighbors, your colleagues, everybody you had a chance to meet in life—if you didn't open yourself to meeting new people and expanding your worldview, how could you learn new things to fetishistically exploit?

"How interesting," said Sister Nadine, lifting her camera and adjusting it for portrait mode. "My father and mother died when I was twelve, then my auntie sold me off to a deacon. He shipped me to a convent when he was done with me. Say 'cheese!'"

Eyelids batting, mouth open in shock, Clarinda was clearly unable to process this information. It showed in the series of pictures the grinning bad witch managed to snap off in the midst of all this fluster. "Uh—oh, uh, you mean…when he was done—educating you?" Clarinda took a guess at the meaning of this, especially in the context of Sister Nadine's enormous grin.

"Yeah, sure," said the alleged nun, "you could say that. You're pretty cute for a consecrated virgin, you know. That is, stylish." While the good witch laughed awkwardly at the extremely, bizarrely forward Bride of Christ, Sabine thumbed through the photos she had taken and smiled warmly at the best one. Oh, Clarinda! What a cutie-pie. Master really was too kind to Sabine, giving her a gift like this!

The thing was that Clarinda Lovegood was just so thirsty. Oh, man. The closer the two neighbors got as friends, the more Sabine saw it all the time. They had started to trade books and, uh, suffice it to say that Clarinda's favorite titles were, one might say, *saucy*. Not throwing stones, of course, but Sabine was actually pretty shocked to discover what passed for a romance novel these days. Maybe she would have been less so if she thought about some of the old vintage sexploitation novels that still floated through used bookstores now and then, but since she was effectively living in one, she guessed she didn't really think about them much.

The point was that, after deflowering her at an orgiastic sacrifice of virginity during her Bible study brunch, then going on to give her a little hex on a morning when Sabine had discovered she had no milk for her cereal, Sabine was one hundred percent sure that Clarinda was an absolute freak with a capital 'F.' That was why she was so uptight, of course, but it was one thing to know something in the abstract and another thing to sit on Satan's face while your moaning "consecrated virgin" is riding his big, throbbing dick and blasting breast milk in your face. Haha, what a weird morning.

Not that this was normal, per se…but it was more normal by Sabine's standards.

"So," said the disguised bad witch, still beaming through the sunshiny innocent face of tender young Sister Nadine, "you wanted to see Ma— uh, Father—Father—"

Fuck, what was the priest's name? Luckily, the good witch was kind enough to step in and help this new nun rather than let her make a fool of herself. "Father Tristan," she supplied, smiling in relief to have even a half second of normalcy. "Yes, I had an appointment to, uh—to speak with him."

"Oh! You're here to confess your sins privately, are you?" While the good witch cringed at hearing the words said out loud, Sabine grinned within her disguise. "Well, why don't we go and see if he's ready?"

"That—really won't be necessary, I'm sure he's all set up by now—"

The good witch, smiling politely, began to extricate herself from the conversation by saying how good it was to have met the new nun, but that new and naughty nun wasn't having it. "You know, if you want to be free of temptation, you could always come join me and my sisters in the convent…who needs men, right?"

"Well—well—oh, look—"

The door to the distant confessional cracked open and, still in the priest's accent, the Devil called, "I'm ready for ya now, love! Come on up."

"Thank you," said Clarinda, meaning it in more ways than one, now shining an obviously relived smile over at the weird nun. "Well! It was sure nice meeting you…Sister Nadine?"

"That's right, that's me. Sister Nadine."

"Guess I'll see you around," said Clarinda, suffering inside and sighing audibly when at last she could hurry away from the conversation to meet the "priest." Still with her shark's grin across her crafted features, Sabine left the camera upon the nearest pew and raised the hem of the nun's tunic over her ankles. Naughty! Chuckling to herself, the bad witch waited for Clarinda to disappear into her side of the booth, then dashed quietly up the aisle.

She paused only long enough to remove her panties and stuff them into the unconscious nun's mouth, using that same nun's own bra as a makeshift wrist tie. With another second of consideration she set the gag in place with the nearest rosary, nodded in approval at her work, then hurried to the Dark Lord's side of the confessional.

Ugh, just look at that Devil! Fuck, she loved him. Sometimes the lighting was just right and the turn of his face was just so and the shape of his hand was maddening, and all of it combined to make him almost hard to look upon. He glanced briefly at her from where he sat upon the exposed priest, one hand running over the true Father Tristan's tormented cock while his other, elbow poised against the grill, rested lightly against the sculpted lip of his imitative mouth.

"Go on, my child," Satan crooned, rectifying his gaze to the grill while Sabine dropped Nadine's face and knelt between his legs. As she pushed away the fabric of the cassock and freed once more that throbbing, giant dick, the Devil bade contrite Clarinda, whose head was low on the other side of the lattice, "You don't need to be afraid of me. God's grace is for all who confess."

Clarinda exhaled shakily. Already crying? Man, Sabine got so wet when Clarinda cried. "Oh, I know…I know that, father, but I'm just so ashamed." While Sabine stared up into his face from beneath the white brim of the veil, Satan lowered his hand from his mouth and caressed her cheek. "I've behaved just unconscionably these past few weeks…it's why I haven't been able to see you until now, why I had to make an appointment. Oh! It's awful."

"What have you done that could be so abysmal, lass?"

"Oh—I'd might as well just tell you—I broke my vow to be celibate, Father, I'm sorry. It's awful!"

"How sorry I am to hear you're ashamed, my child. We're all only human in this world."

"Yes, but you know how I pride myself on my behavior."

"Pride is the most insidious of all sins, Clarinda…you would do well to remember that, always."

He did an admirable job of keeping his voice level while the bad witch's cowled head bobbed up and down his dick. As he slowly stroked the priest's more normally sized cock, Satan continued with his voice, "How many times have you sinned, my child?"

"Well—well, I don't really know what to say about that. Only a few times, I guess, but it seems like so many already."

"A few? How much is that."

"It's hard to say."

"With a man, or a woman?"

"—Both."

"Clarinda," chided the Devil in the priest's stolen voice, admiring the pentient's pretty profile while Sabine's grateful tongue slithered up and down his cock. "Oh, Clarinda…what a pity to know the deceiver has provoked you to a period of such self-torment."

"I know!" Good thing she wailed as she did, for hearing how she wept made Sabine moan around her master's dick. While she pulled the nun's tunic high, Satan lifted one elegantly polished shoe. He permitted his slave to grind her soaking pussy and hypersensitive clitoris over the leather toe while pushing her head down harder on his dick. As Sabine choked, Satan's eyelids fluttered, but he committed himself to watching the good witch as she wept, "Father, oh, Father, you can't imagine how true that is…I've been seduced, seduced by Satan!"

"All sinners are."

"No," she said more firmly, "no, you don't understand. I've been—*literally* seduced. Oh, I sound crazy! But it's true."

He lifted Sabine's head from his dick lest the sound of her choking give the game away. The bad witch's eyes rolled in ecstasy to grind her slick cut up and down her master's leg like the horny bitch she was, her drenched hole aching to be filled by the dick that she diligently serviced no matter her own personal desires. "Tell me more," said Satan to Clarinda, encouragingly patting Sabine's head. "I'm listening—I understand how difficult it is to say these things, my child."

"So difficult—oh, Father. It's—it's this neighbor of mine, this woman, she—she's so beautiful, but she's a witch, a bad witch. She dabbles in black magick, you see."

Excuse, as they say in French? 'Dabbles!' While Sabine scoffed at the insulting choice of word, Satan narrowly avoided laughing. He did in fact fail to keep his smile entirely from his voice while glancing at the vain witch from the corner of his eye. "Does she, really."

"Yes! She's an extremely—treacherous woman. She uses her looks and her knowledge of the occult to do all kinds of things. Awful things!"

"What kinds of things are those?"

"Oh, it's hard to say. She summoned Satan in my *house!* Of course…none of my friends remember it but me—but—I sound crazy, don't I?"

"It's a rather outrageous tale, my dear, even for a good witch."

"It is! But it's true—the Devil himself came to my house and deflowered me."

Holy shit, she really did sound crazy. Sabine had a hard time trying not to cackle and, in the name of assisting her, the Devil rammed his dick even deeper down her throat. "The Devil comes in many forms…how did he appear to you, my child?"

"In the form of a man, a handsome man—oh, the most beautiful! Like—like Jon Hamm, or Cary Grant, or—"

"A young Hugh Hefner," suggested the flattered Devil, rubbing his jaw with a thoughtful smile.

"Yes, exactly! I—how did you know?"

"Just extrapolating, my girl, merely theorizing…" Sabine grinned around his pulsing member as he dropped the 'h' of 'theorizing' amid his (some might say slightly offensive) Irish accent. So cute! Damn, she really wanted to fuck him. Reading her mind, Satan pulled her head from his dick and tugged up at her arm. She beamed with delight and pressed a long kiss to his cheek while climbing into his lap. Her slight addition caused the weighted down priest, pinned upon the bench, to groan in the ecstasy of shame. As Sabine's eyes crossed and her tongue lolled from her mouth just to be penetrated by the first few inches of the Devil's giant dick, the Lord of the Flies cracked a little. He exhaled amid the pleasurable grip of his slave's tight cunt.

"And what did this hateful Day-Star do to you, my girl, Clarinda, oh, my poor good-hearted lost lamb? Did he make you sacrifice?"

"Only my virginity, Father."

"Ah, aha, I see…" While Sabine rocked up and down upon his stiff rod, leaning back to stay out of sight of the grill and to increase her own pleasure by permitting him to stab again and again that high-pressure g-spot, the Devil moved his hands over her body and up beneath her tunic. While filling his hands with her heaving tits and caressing one hard nipple, he asked, "Ah—but no people, though? No goats, no children? Not even any money?"

"No, Father. Nothing like that."

"So he asked you less than our Church does, then…"

"Excuse me?"

"Nothing, my girl, nothing. Go on, tell me more. Unburden your soul to the merciful and forgiving ear of the Good Lord."

"Well—well—" Chalking up whatever she had thought she'd heard the priest say to the humiliation of having to outpour the catalogue of her sins, Clarinda cleared her throat and meekly said, "This is going to sound—oh, very embarrassing, I don't know how to say *this*, either."

While Sabine tickled her own clit, keeping the tunic up

high around her stomach to both facilitate the action and to admire the sight of Satan's tool cleaving in and out of her soaking puss, Satan placed her other hand upon the priest's twitching prick and tried not to laugh as Tristan, having been tormented all night, immediately came.

Sabine moaned at a hush to collect the spilled seed: she sucked it from her fingers before working to immediately torture Father Tristan's sensitive member back into working order.

"Just say whatever you need to say," Satan encouraged Clarinda. "I'm listening, I promise you."

"Well, this—bad witch, there's a lot I like about her, and I'm very attracted to her…she's nicer to me lately, and we're very, um, *friendly.*"

"You mean to say you've indulged in a second licentious relationship already! Fornicating with a bad witch, are you? Certainly not a consecrated virgin anymore."

"No," agreed Clarinda miserably. "No, I'm certainly not."

"All this indulgence in the flesh is a symptom of human weakness, my child…it's forgivable, if you'll but repent and forgive yourself."

"But how! How can I repent with that wicked woman living down the street from me? Oh, it's awful. Why, just the other day—this one is just strange, I don't even believe it, myself."

"Try me, I'm open to many ideas."

"Well! I was minding my own business in the morning, getting ready for the day, and to make a long story short, she cursed me so that I started—lactating."

"Really! Strange! Is that so!"

While Sabine bounced more vigorously on her master's stone hard schlong, Clarinda sighed and said, "I know how it sounds, but it really happened, and it was very strange…worse, I think I enjoyed it somehow. Ugh, I don't know, I don't know what's wrong with me. Why is God letting me fail these trials?

Oh, what am I saying—it's not God's fault. It's not even the Devil's, it's *mine*. I just can't resist Sabine!"

"Who can," asked Satan lowering his head to slip his tongue into the bad witch's mouth. While her eyelids fluttered beneath the kiss he reached down and pulled the gag out of the priest's lips. Before Father Tristan could scream the Devil grabbed his cock again and, with a few pulls of this male anatomy, spoke through the sinful priest's mouth like he was a ventriloquist dummy.

"That is, I mean to say, who can resist the dark forces when they set their sights upon us? There, there, my child." While Sabine's body was coaxed into orgasm by the tentacle of the Devil's tongue whipping fast down into her throat to fuck her like the cock that battered her insides, the horrified priest went on to say on behalf of Satan, "Not even I could resist if the Dark Lord so chose to make me fall from grace."

"I know…but it really is my fault. I mean—I *like* Sabine, like I said. I like to hang out with her and watch movies with her. It's just that, at least half the time, she's up to no good. I don't want to lose my friendship with her but I don't know if I can maintain it in good conscience when she's doing these wicked things all the time. Leading me astray."

"Love the sinner, hate the sin, my child."

"That's what they say…but it's hard to tell where the sinner stops and the sin begins, especially with a bad witch."

"What was it that finally made you return to Confession, my child?"

"Oh, well…it's just a little thing—honestly, it's silly now when I think about it. I guess I got a little offended by something she did. The straw that broke the camel's back, you know."

Recovering from her orgasm, Sabine's ears perked. Her hips slowed their gyrations upon the Devil's prick. While his hand released the priest's cock to replace his gag, Sabine commenced his manual work for him. Father Tristan was hard again and Sabine worked her hand up and down the aching length while the good witch said, "It was just the other day…"

Maybe it was a bit stereotypical to say this, her being a witch—even if a good one—but Clarinda *loved* Halloween! It was her favorite holiday after Christmas and Easter, and dressing up was always such a fun creative problem. What would she be this year? The question popped into her head sometime around July and, by the first week of September, was an urgent priority if not already answered.

This year she had intended to go as Violet Beauregarde from *Willy Wonka and the Chocolate Factory*, but then she had gotten to know Sabine, and, well, things had started to change. Painting herself purple sounded like such a chore, after all! Why do that when she could do something more specific? She'd only settled on the previous costume because she hadn't been able to come up with anything thematically appropriate.

Now, though…now, the choice was obvious. And plentiful. Witch costumes were always in-demand, although it did take Clarinda quite awhile to find one that wasn't either extremely cheap or embarrassingly slutty. Finally she found a fun and funky one that was maybe just a little risqué owing to its leg slit but otherwise pretty modest. And it had a fun cape attached! One pointed hat later and she looked at herself in the mirror of her bedroom with a grin of pride.

"Who's the bad witch, now," she said with a laugh, looking approvingly at the purple sheen on the fabric of the fairly reasonable bodice that cut straight across her chest and kept her cleavage from popping out. It could have been her imagination, but her breasts were still just a little too big after that business with the lactation the other day.

Well…there were worse things in the world, she supposed, then getting magickal plastic surgery you never asked for. Still! It was pretty rude, so maybe Clarinda would have done well to focus on that, rather than denying that her Halloween costume was entirely intended to tease.

It wasn't long, after all, before she stood on Sabine's porch with a cheeky grin and her costume's cape blowing in the breeze. "Hey, Sabine," she cried when the bad witch opened the door, "I'm all ready to join your coven!"

The bad witch, who always seemed to be briefly stunned by the glow of even dusky sunlight, blinked rapidly and struggled to make out Clarinda's outfit. Her brow furrowed when it did and her lips twisted into an unexpected scowl. "Lame," said Sabine, trying to close the door in the good witch's face.

"Hey!" Gasping, Clarinda stuck her boot into the doorway to keep her friend from shutting her out. "What do you mean? I thought you'd think it was funny!"

"Cultural appropriation is *not* funny," lectured the bad witch, her expression sour and her weight shifting to one foot. While her German shepherd hurried up to say hello, panting happily as Clarinda bent down to rub his ears, Sabine continued, "Pointed hats? Come on, way to stereotype. You might as well have just showed up at Bernice's house in blackface, or made an appearance at a burial mound wearing some fucking feathered headdress."

"This is *not* cultural appropriation," defended the good witch, somewhat shocked by the response. "It's just a costume."

"That's what people always say when they're appropriating somebody's culture."

"Oh, what, next you're going to say I can't eat Chinese food because I'm not Chinese?"

"No, bitch, I'm not saying that! Trying other cultures' foods and even religions with an honest and open mind is an excellent way to broaden your horizons and make new friends.

Don't come bringing that fallacious, conservative BS argument into my house, I'll throw your hot ass out…even if it does look pretty good in that tightass little gown."

The bad witch slapped Clarinda's backside, provoking a shriek of semi-outrage.

"So you're perfectly fine with objectifying me, but not with the same outfit you're objectifying me in?"

"I'd objectify you no matter what you wore," rightly countered the bad witch while the good one rolled her eyes. "You're just hot to me…but, look—you have to admit it's pretty freaking rude, dude."

"I was just teasing," insisted Clarinda with a pout. "I thought I'd make you laugh, come on. Don't be so serious! You're usually the one telling me to lighten up."

This was maybe weird to say, but sometimes Sabine reminded Clarinda of her father…mostly because Clarinda's father had never been able to resist her girlish whims once that pout came out.

"I don't mean to be lame," said Sabine, slinging her arms around the good witch's waist and looking like she wanted to lean down for a smooch. "I'm just sensitive. I got into an argument with somebody a few weeks ago about whether or not the movie *Hereditary* represents cultural appropriation of Western occultism and seeing you in that outfit just rubbed me the wrong way." Nose brushing the good witch's, the bad one asked, "Want to see if you can rub me the right way? I need a good fucking."

Such language! Sabine spoke in ways that made Clarinda blush but, well, she was just so refreshing somehow. It was very flattering, after all, to be desired by the bad witch in such an open way—that was even accounting for the fact that the bad witch seemed to be willing to fornicate with just about anybody if it served her ends.

It was the way Sabine looked at her: oh, that hungry passion made the good witch shiver. She draped her arms around the bad one's neck, lips grazing against lips.

"You just want me to take off this costume, huh…"

"That's definitely a fringe benefit…have you ever used a strap-on before? I'll let you keep the hat on if you'll give me what I need."

Well…Clarinda didn't want to admit it, but the truth was that she was more than willing to try anything. This strap-on was kind of intimidating, though. "This is the starter one," Sabine advised Clarinda, drawing up her costume's outfit to secure the dildo to the good witch's hips when they stood a few minutes later in the luxurious master bedroom. "I've got a special one, too, a magickal one, but I don't think you're ready for it yet."

"I'm barely ready for this! Look at this thing." She laughed at the purple schlong and tapped its head, watching it wag back and forth from its mount upon her pelvis. "How do men go around without feeling silly?"

"They're not hard *all* the time…and they're usually not this purple, either. There!" Grinning with pride, Sabine swatted Clarinda's ass again and stepped back to admire her work. Her hands on her hips, she nodded, then at once sprang forward to savagely kiss the good witch. Clarinda produced a noise of surprise but very soon submitted to the bad witch's velvet tongue—to the hands that traversed beneath the silly costume and groped and pinched and fondled. As Sabine savored a few palmfuls of Clarinda's ass, she enthused, "You're such a cute little slut, Clarinda…well, if you're going to dress up in this outfit, I suppose I'd better give you what a bad witch deserves."

Perching upon the edge of the bed, Sabine clutched Clarinda's unready hand. The good witch cried out to be jerked across the bad one's stockinged knees. With a practiced hand, Sabine flipped up the back of Clarinda's skirt and went to town laying a series of hard, fast smacks flat across her bottom.

"Oh, oh! Sabine—"

"You didn't think you could just show up, flaunting that ridiculous outfit, and *not* get a spanking from me, did you? You're lucky I don't pull out the paddle for you…and anyway, you like it, huh? You bad witch."

A grin in her voice, Sabine lowered her blows and Clarinda couldn't help her moan. She had to support herself against the floor with her hands and as a result couldn't stop Sabine from roughly jerking her panties down. As the good witch gasped, the bad witch resumed the spanking with a new, lower target, the flat of her hand cracking sharply across Clarinda's labia. "Oh, Sabine! Oh, that stings—"

"But it sure does make you wet, huh? You love being all exposed to me, don't you…fuck, I love it when you're helpless, Clarinda! It's a good thing I already put this big dick on your, otherwise I'd be the one doing the fucking for sure…but I want to ease you in, huh."

The spanking hand relaxed. As the good witch gasped for air, the bad one's fingertips trailed lightly down her parted pussy lips. After lightly fondling Clarinda's clit for a few seconds, her index finger teasingly invaded the wet interior of her cunt. Clarinda moaned in miserable shame, thrilled to be touched but never any less guilty for it.

"That's right," continued Sabine, pushing her finger deeper by the second. "Oh, that's right…want to take it nice and slow with you. Turn you into my cute little fucktoy…that's right, that's right, baby."

"Oh, Sabine! Sabine, you say such dirty things…"

"I'm a dirty girl. It's a filthy habit, but I just love to corrupt hot young virgins for Satan's pleasure with nothing more than a few choice words. Magick words…"

Chuckling, Sabine withdrew her finger and began to spank again. Now the slaps were short and slow-coming, aimed entirely at the swollen pussy emphasized by the black straps of the strap-on that framed it along with Clarinda's perky ass. When Sabine's hand did raise to that backside, the good witch swore she felt a fingertip occasionally graze her tight rectum. The thrill this wicked sensation provoked was enough to leave her absolutely flooded.

Soon she writhed in the bad witch's lap. When those practiced fingers slid—two at a time, now—into Clarinda's cunt, all she could do was pant and moan and spread her legs in eager welcome.

"What a wet whore you are for me, Clarinda…what a bad, bad witch. You know why they say witches melt when we get wet, don't you?"

Oh, fuck, she did! She certainly did. Clarinda melted then, cumming with a great, almost disruptively sudden orgasm as the angle of Sabine's fingers produced a particularly sensitizing clench of the pussy they worked. While Clarinda's legs bucked up against Sabine's with the climax, the bad witch laughed in delight and reduced her pumping fingers to a gentler tease.

"There, there…there you go, baby…oh, doesn't it feel good to be bad?"

Soon Sabine was splayed upon her bed and, unsteadily upon her feet once having recovered, Clarinda bit her lip to look across the displayed body of the naked witch. Her pussy glistened in the light beneath its patch of dark curls and, moaning low to see her touch herself, Clarinda bent her head to apply a shy kiss there. Sabine adjusted the tilt of the witch's hat upon her blonde curls so she could watch Clarinda eat her out, her pink tongue working uncertainly against the target of her passion.

"Oh! Fuck, you're getting really, *super* fucking good at that, Clarinda—oh, yeah! Fuck, oh, you've been paying attention… ah!" Sabine moaned while Clarinda's fingers explored her labia, sliding just inside the pussy beneath the clit her tongue assailed. While Sabine writhed and arched her back, gripping the pillow around her head, the bad witch moaned unnervingly, "Satan, Satan, Hail Satan, oh, fuck! I must have been a good witch if Daddy sent you here to me today—oh, yeah—"

Yikes! Sabine sure did say some weird stuff during sex… but what did you expect from a bad witch? Clarinda had to admit, when she thought about it, that it was awfully weird for people to cry God's name during lovemaking…yet, something about Sabine's screams for the Devil had overtones of ritual. Sometimes, in fact, Clarinda got the idea that she was an unwilling—well, semi-willing—participant in some kind of sacrifice to Satan every single time she made love with the bad witch.

Silly as it was, the thought spooked her. She tried not to think it, then…tried not to think of much of anything but the intensity of her own pleasure while her tongue and fingers urged on the inundation of Sabine's soft cunt. Soon Clarinda's efforts were rewarded: soon the bad witch clamped around her with a gasp, hips bucking, eyelids fluttering. Clarinda lifted her head to watch the beautiful ripples contorting like waves across Sabine's frame. The bad witch gasped her way through the climax but halfway through those gasps became soft words. "Clarinda! Clarinda, oh—fuck, kiss me—"

With a tender smile, Clarinda wet her lips to find them already soaked with the bad witch's softly flavored arousal. Sabine moaned to taste herself on the good witch and the women embraced for a time, tongues intertwined and legs rubbing together until at last the bad witch begged, "Fuck me, Clarinda, oh, Clarinda, I need you to fuck me right now—"

Talk about performance anxiety! Clarinda totally understood why guys felt so much pressure…suddenly she was all but sweating as she looked down to the apex of Sabine's splayed thighs. The pussy there that was so dripping wet the bad witch didn't even need to spread it with her fingers for it to look wanting. With another furtive glance up to her friend's green eyes, Clarinda took the purple dildo in her hand and lined it up to the bad witch's cunt.

"Right in here?"

"Right there, go on…don't be shy, fuck me for all you're worth, Clarinda…oh, Clarinda—fuck! Yes!"

The good witch gasped to feel the tug of Sabine's body: as if the good witch's false cock didn't even need nerves to transmit to her brain the desperation, the grip, of those powerful muscles. Clarinda gave into this pull and buried herself to the strap in Sabine's pussy, astonished at the arching hips and groaning mouth this simple action provoked.

"Oh, my," said Clarinda, hand coming to rest upon Sabine's splayed thigh. As, steadily, she began to work the dildo in and out of the bad witch's cunt with the mere swaying back and forth of her own hips, Sabine moaned and bucked some more. Clarinda couldn't help her grin, saying, "This actually *is* fun! Goodness gracious…you make such cute noises when I'm inside you, Sabine…"

"Fuck! Oh, fuck, oh, keep fucking me like that and I'll make all the noises you want…ah! Yeah! Fuck, give it to me, fuck me harder, oh, Clarinda, yeah, yeah—"

Feeling only moderately silly to use a thing like this when it produced such intense pleasure for the bad witch, Clarinda found a rhythm she could maintain and began to pound nice and deep into Sabine's body. The bad witch's hands tangled up in her own hair before roving over her magickally swollen breasts. One remained there while the other slid further to toy wither clit. Those beautiful green eyes of hers, when not fluttering with pleasure, were locked on one of either two places—the dildo slapping rapidly in and out of her dripping wet pussy, or the flushed face of the good witch who admired the effect she could have.

"You're a natural," assured Sabine, squirming, then gasping as the dildo found a particularly sensitive spot. Her bare feet bracing against the bed to permit the arch of her hips up against the toy, Sabine encouraged Clarinda to strike the spot again. The good witch obliged and the bad witch screamed, "Oh, yes, yes! Fuck, oh, Hail Satan! Praise Satan for sending you to me, yeah, yeah, I needed this—oh, fuck, sometimes I just need something in my pussy, Clarinda, oh, fuck, I need it so bad—"

"And you call *me* a slut!"

"Oh, oh, uh, fuck, you are one, of course…but it's okay, it's okay. We can be sluts together. You can be a hot little bad witch with me…fuck, yeah, you bad, bad witch, oh—fuck! Keep going, keep going, oh, Satan, don't stop—"

Throwing her back into it, as they say, Clarinda hastened her pace and braced one hand against Sabine's hip to keep her pelvis propped up. The bad witch's leg lifted up and draped over Clarinda's shoulder, making the good witch first laugh, then moan as she discovered the ease of access this gave her to plunge deep into the bad witch's pussy.

"That looks like it hurts," said Clarinda with undeniable pleasure.

"It does," whined Sabine, fingers tangling again in her hair. "Yeah, yeah, fuck, yeah, it fucking does, I love it to hurt! I want it big and deep, oh, fuck, I'm a size queen—shit, oh, you're almost as good at fucking me as Satan is, oh, Clarinda, Clarinda! Fuck!"

The bad witch gasped, eyes boring into the good witch's. This time, Clarinda didn't have to be asked. She dove upon her wicked friend and held open her mouth for a kiss, her tongue sliding right away into Sabine's open mouth and battering back toward her throat. The bad witch moaned and the good one moaned with her, and soon, the orgasm ending, Sabine reached down to slide the dildo gingerly out of her clenching puss.

"You want a turn?"

It was so hard to admit these things! But oh, Clarinda *did* want a turn…she wanted to know what it was like to be fucked by Sabine the way the Devil fucked her. Biting her lip, still wearing her bad witch hat, Clarinda nodded shyly. Sabine delivered one last tender kiss before sitting up to help her out of the strap-on.

Soon enough the wicked witch wore the thing herself, the big purple dick bobbing from her pale pelvis. It shone not just with its rubber material but with Sabine's glossy coating, and the thought of having the bad witch's fluids fucked into her was enough to make Clarinda dizzy. She fell back, legs spread, and gasped while Sabine lined the toy up to her cunt. Its head teased her clit for a few seconds, at least until she produced a whine.

"So cute," said Sabine with joy, chuckling to herself in her dark way before at last teasing the tip of the dildo into Clarinda's body. The good witch gasped and whimpered while the bad witch gave her more, one hand caressing her breast while the other guided the toy inside. "I love it when you get all cute and fussy and whiny, Clarinda…my hot little would-be virgin. The Catholic Church makes it so hard to be a slut! But it's sure fun, huh…"

"Uh-huh, uh-huh—oh, Sabine!" With a gasp of joy to find the toy inside of her was a far better, far less painful fit than the Devil's enormous dick had been on the two occasions she'd been invited to take it, Clarinda arched her hips higher and caught one of her friend's dexterous hands. "Sabine, Sabine! Fuck me as hard as you want, oh—like a bad witch deserves to be fucked!"

"I love hearing you say dirty words," Sabine had said, sliding her dildo as far into Clarinda's cunt as she could make it fit. "Say it, baby—go on, say it for me, say it for my master."

She hated to say it. "No," whimpered Clarinda, gasping as Sabine sharply hurried her strokes. "Oh, no!"

While the bad witch caught the good one's face, Clarinda moaned and shuddered. "You know you want to, bitch. Go on—say the words that make you cum. My favorite words to hear you say, go on, go on—"

"Hail Satan," whimpered Clarinda, trying to avert her eyes, then gasping as her gaze was corrected by the firm grip of the witch who fucked her. "Hail Satan," she repeated, staring with terror into the bad witch's face. Sabine smiled and lowered her head for a kiss.

"Hail Satan," agreed Sabine, then sitting upright to work the toy more deliberately into Clarinda's pussy. The good witch gasped, all sensory input except for pleasure at once unintelligible. "You're my little slut for Satan, oh, yes you are, Clarinda…fuck, yeah, Clarinda, oh, I think I know what Daddy wants to do with you, and it makes me so fucking excited…"

Pale with terror even as the pleasure built in her taut tummy, the good witch begged to know, "What do you mean? What does Satan want with me?"

"Nothing unreasonable. Don't worry. Something you might even like. Oh! Oh, fuck, Clarinda, oh, fuck, you just pull me in and in and in—especially when I talk about my master, huh? Don't worry, oh, fuck, don't worry…keep letting me fuck you like this and soon enough he'll be your master, too. You'll love being his slave, oh, his cute little fuck-slave…yeah, oh, it'll be so much fun, I love it when he arrives in the night to use me… you will, too, yes you will."

"Oh, God, God, oh, help me—I can't believe the things you make me say—"

"It's just what you want to say, Clarinda…oh, it's just what you want. This is Satan's pussy…he's so nice to let me fuck it. Oh, fuck, Satan! What a generous master I have, yeah, yeah, yeah—"

The bad witch bore her teeth with the vigor of her pounding while Clarinda screamed in ecstasy. Her limbs spread, save for one hand that kept the hat pressed upon her head for Sabine's appreciation, Clarinda moaned and arched her hips against the thrusting toy. One leg wrapped around Sabine's waist. In response, the witch doubled her pace and soon Clarinda's drenched pussy teetered on the precipice of orgasm. It wasn't long at all before she went tumbling down, her voice rising in a high cry of, "Oh, Sabine! Sabine, you make me feel so good—oh, Satan, Satan, if I had to worship Satan to be with you, I would—"

"Aw! Honey."

Laughing, slowing her strokes to guide her gentler friend through the climax, Sabine lowered to kiss Clarinda's gasping, moaning mouth. "He wouldn't make you do a thing like that," Sabine assured her, sliding the dildo gently from the good witch's quivering pussy. "Satan's much more compassionate to the spiritual needs of men and women…you can believe whatever you want, baby, worship however you want. You can still have me…you don't have to be a bad witch. In fact"— removing the silly hat and placing it atop her own head with a grin that made Clarinda laugh—"one of the things I like about you is that you're a good one…don't tell anybody I said that, though."

Shucks! Sabine remembered that afternoon. *That* was what sent the good witch to Confession? The harmless strap-on play, not the Satan fucking?

The Devil seemed affronted by this failure on his part to break the good witch's mind with his dick alone. With Sabine still riding his dick for the duration of the story that Clarinda had told in a cleaned-up, detail-skirting way, the Lord of the Flies said in the priest's borrowed accent, "Well that doesn't seem so bad compared to the other things you described to me…why did that send you here, and not the lactation or the business at your Bible Study?"

"Because I fell asleep after we—finished," said Clarinda, her tone taut with annoyance, "and I woke up to the smell of smoke. I found her burning my costume in the fireplace!"

"What a bad witch! You can't burn those things, not in the house…lucky you both weren't poisoned."

"Yes, well, she made me walk home naked—"

Satan accidentally laughed, then caught himself and grinned at Sabine while turning the noise into a cough. "How cruel," the Devil said while Clarinda huffed in annoyance.

"Yes, it was totally obscene. I don't think anybody saw me because it was already dark outside by the time I went home, but they easily *could* have, and it was cold. What if a cop had driven by or something? I would have been in so much trouble. It's just so ridiculous. So rude! It made me wonder if our relationship is really equivalent at all. What I did by wearing the costume doesn't compare to any of the things she does to me on a regular basis!"

"But did you get wet," asked Satan, bracing his hand against the front of the bad witch's abdomen to feel the thrust of his cock in her belly.

"I—excuse me, Father?" Clarinda's tone was so shocked that Sabine didn't need to see through the grill to know the wide-eyed, fast-blinking expression that the good witch wore. Sabine bit back her laugh only barely; only by focusing on the outrageous pleasure throbbing through her more with every stroke.

"Did your pussy get wet," asked Satan more clearly now, his Irish accent fading into the usual timber of his human speaking voice. "That tight little virgin cunt, that despoiled puss, did it get all hot and dripping wet with humiliation when she pushed you, naked, onto her lawn?"

"Father! What's gotten into you?"

"Into *me?* Oh, nothing yet, my child, not today…but the night is young." Chuckling, tugging the real Father Tristan's aching cock, Satan braced his head back against the booth and groaned while Sabine neared an orgasm. "Maybe soon enough I'll let you meet me as a woman and you can watch Sabine give me a fucking like the hot one she gave you…wish I hadn't been busy at the time, or I would have made an appearance."

Gasping sharply, Clarinda peered through the grill. Her eyes certainly *were* wide! Sabine cackled madly while the good witch, outraged, said, "You!"

All in a tizz, Clarinda slammed out of the confessional. Sabine and the Devil howled with mutual laughter while the priest protested not his treatment but the violation of the sacred rite of Confession. This, combined with the opening of the door and the inpouring of light into the stall, made Sabine cum with a high scream that timed out well with Clarinda's second, more furious gasp.

"Sabine! How could you! I—what on *Earth* are you wearing?"

"Oh, fuck! Fuck, oh—" The bad witch couldn't answer and, braced against the door as she'd been, fell backward off of the Devil's dick even before her orgasm was complete. "Fuck, fuck…oh…just my—Sunday best, babe…"

"This is unbelievable, I can't—oh, Father Tristan! What have you done to the priest?"

"Nothing he doesn't beg for in his prayers every night," said the Devil, putting the shamefaced clergyman's dick away while the bound participant protested lightly for effect in present company. Patting his resealed trousers, Satan then stood upright and smoothed his own cassock. "Much like someone else I know…hello, Clarinda."

Sniffing primly, Clarinda forced herself to say, "Hello," before looking down at Sabine with her arms irritably crossed. "So it's fine for *you* to dress up like a nun, but the minute I put on a pointed hat, I'm appropriating your culture?"

"Can you really appropriate a culture as dominant as the Catholic Church's," Sabine asked, openly staring up Clarinda's light blue dress and gingerly raising a finger to the hem in aid of the task. Realizing what the bad witch was up to, Clarinda kicked her lightly, slapped the interloping hand, and began to step away.

Though laughing, Sabine nonetheless affected a pout and rolled over to hastily crawl after her. She caught the good witch by the ankle, begging, "Aw, come on! Don't be like that…we went too far in our teasing again, huh?"

"This isn't *teasing*. This is blasphemy. It's awful. I can't believe—I just can't believe," she said, glancing behind Satan and into the confessional that he shut.

Father Tristan made a few real noises of protest from behind the closed door and Satan assured him, "Don't worry, Father. Someone will be back for you later…"

"He can't *want* this," insisted Clarinda. She ignored Sabine as, still in the habit, the bad witch pressed a few pleading kisses over her ankle and the top of her foot within the blue patent leather of her pump. "I know Father Tristan! He's a nice man."

"Nice and sexual aren't mutually exclusive qualities," Satan rejoined, fixing the collar of his outfit before striding over to sling an arm around the good witch. She permitted it, perhaps only because of the bad witch lying at her feet and now eagerly running a tongue along the surface of her shoe.

The Devil watched with a low hum of approval, his cock having been put away for the good witch's sake but visibly tented within the confines of its black fabric prison.

"Society has systematically brainwashed generation after generation of human beings to believe, even unconsciously, that sexuality is vulgar or wrong. But, why, if everyone consents, it can be elevated to an artform. The only thing that's wrong with sex is when it's inflicted upon somebody who doesn't want it…

and that can be said of anything. Knives are great tools until somebody's sticking one into you without your permission."

"But a knife isn't meant to create life," insisted Clarinda, visibly irritated even as her eyes kept dropping to the disguised witch. Still on the floor, Sabine reverently helped Clarinda out of her shoe and, finding no protest, kissed the tan stockings covering her toes. The good witch blushed, bit her lip, and insisted on, "Sex it—it has a positive purpose…an intimate purpose, oh—it's a symbol—"

"A symbol of humanity's relationship with the divine," Satan agreed, his arms sliding around Clarinda to embrace her tight body to his. The good witch moaned, helpless in an instant while the Devil's big hands lifted to cup her tits and tease her nipples through the fabric of her dress. "The intersection of matter and consciousness, yes, that's the symbol, all right…the sacred creation of life, there's no denying it's the most important thing in the world. Without mankind to experience, consciousness would have no host on Earth…we'd all be plunged into a state of nothingness, unobserved and therefore unable to observe. Unable to party."

Slowly, carefully, while the good witch gasped and glanced down at the bad one now sucking on her toes, the Devil drew up the pale blue fabric of her dress. "But the paradox lies in the orgasm…the temporary annihilation of everything, the dissolution of experience into bliss…why, Clarinda…"

The good witch's gasp drew Sabine's eye. She twisted her head, tongue still lashing against Clarinda's dainty dancer toe, and grinned as Satan's fingers disappeared into cute white panties. "You're dripping wet, my good little witch… confessing all those wicked things to Father Tristan sure did get you ready to be fucked."

"Oh—God, help me…" While the good witch swooned back against the Devil's chest, Sabine grinned and reached down between her own legs to tease herself. The Lord of the

Flies hooked his index and middle fingers up into Clarinda's cunt, chuckling at the ease with which he violated her yet again.

"That dissolution is part of the inherent bad-ness the human being feels toward sex, you know, Clarinda…"

He went on lecturing, his head lowering to plant a few kisses down her neck while she moaned in the ecstasy of his attention.

"They sense something frightening deep within it. The same pit that they spend their lifetime seeking to avoid, it's a boon in sex—practically the only goal the modern person sees. Sex for procreation is so 1900…in vitro fertilization was the real liberator, not birth control. Now that heterosexual intercourse is no longer the only means of creating life, now that science is just as sacred as sex, people can't help but see how ridiculous the Catholic Church is being on this matter. Especially when you've got a church just full of horny priests."

"Stop it," begged Clarinda. "Please, I love the Church—I love God."

Cooing in a patronizing but truly fond way, Satan assured her, "I know you do," and kissed her on the mouth. He slid his fingers out from her and said, "Unfortunately, if you keep things up, the Church isn't going to be able to love you…that's the cruel thing about it. Everybody claims that *I'm* the bad one, when the truth is that organized religions specialize in making human beings feel bad about being human. There's nothing wrong with a little enjoyment of your flesh during your short span of mortal life on Earth…anybody who tells you that there is something wrong is just trying to bend you to their will."

"You say it's fine," said Clarinda, staring defiantly into the Devil's face while he ran his tongue along his glistening fingers. "But you and Sabine both try to—to "bend me to your wills" just the same, more than the Church ever did."

"Maybe, but we're not lying to you about it. You know when the Devil strikes up a relationship with you that there's something in it for him…but when Father Tristan strokes his cock on the other side of the grill as you recount your confession, well, baby, that's the *real* sin. That's a sin against you, against God. These hypocrites and blasphemers fill the Church all across the world. What I do, these faint and small protests against the unreasonable fetters of a two-faced faith—it's nothing. A blip of light in the black cover of an unwholesome shadow. The trouble is that, of course, the Catholic Church is right about the faith…but it's the organization that's gone rotten."

"Master loves the Good Lord," supplied Sabine helpfully, removing her mouth from Clarinda's foot but still lying there upon the floor. "One might call him a big fan of His work."

"Too true! He has an imagination of such sickness that I dare not even aspire…I just wanted his attention a little too badly, and, well, you know how that story went. But do you see, Clarinda?" His fingers tangling into the golden curls of the good witch to draw back her heavy head, Satan stared into her face and lifted his brows. "I'm not a hypocrite…I'm a man of faith as much as any priest. More, for being an angel. Don't you think that makes me perfectly qualified to grant you absolution? To hear your Confession and prescribe a recompense?"

Inhaling sharply, staring into the handsome Dark Lord's expectant features, Clarinda forced herself to ask, "What do you think I should do?"

"Well…the Catholic way is to encourage you to mortify yourself. Whip yourself until your perfect, golden back is running red with welts and blood. And I won't deny"—the Devil smiled, a twinkle in his cold blue eye—"that image does strike me as being quite a fine one…but I'd rather be the artist behind such a painting, if you could stand to wait. Instead, I should say the natural solution is for you to take your power back."

A flash of green light blinded the witches and Clarinda gasped at its source. The leather scourge that now snarled from Satan's hand looked cruel indeed and Sabine, moaning with delight to see it, moaned all the more when her master turned the thing around to offer Clarinda its handle.

"Seems to me the only way to make peace with your sinful nature is to punish the witch who brought it out of you."

Sharply, fearfully, Clarinda inhaled, her eyes fixed to the tongues of the cruel device waiting patiently in the Devil's loose fist. Sabine, who enjoyed pain in all its forms and *really* enjoyed the thought of getting whipped in the middle of a Church by Clarinda, didn't even bother to hide the glow of girlish anticipation from her face. Incensed by Sabine's obvious enjoyment—nay, hope—Clarinda snatched the scourge from the Devil's grip and told Sabine, "You better start praying for my soul, because knowing you has made it filthy."

"Oh, of course! Of course, Clarinda, oh, poor Clarinda—" Springing up at her cute friend's behest, Sabin hitched up her hem again and dashed to the kneeler near the altar. There, at the same place where so many, more absolved souls consumed the flesh and blood of Christ one time a week like the happy little cannibals they were, Sabine knelt as though to pray and even crossed herself. Her hands clasped and her eyes turned dutifully toward the rolling ones of Christ sweating and bleeding upon his cross at the head of the chapel. Sabine was so excited for her whipping that she had all but forgotten about the real nun, who, unconscious, drew Clarinda's attention just as she came looming up behind the wicked witch.

"Oh! Sister Ignatia, what did you do to her?" Gasping in horror, Clarinda hurried forward a step, begging to know, "Is she—"

"Perfectly alive," said Satan in the kind of casual tone he

used to pretend he remembered something he'd really long since forgotten about. (You try being an angel of his stature relegated to Earth and see how many places your mind takes you at once! He had a lot to think about, at home and abroad.) "See?" With a glance around, he grabbed the flask of the consecrated blood of Christ that had been previously removed from its sanctified storage space for fun and games with Father and Sister. Now the Devil splashed the ruby substance across the unconscious nun's face and she came alive with a gasp, a sputter, a shocked, wet cough.

"Hallelujah," cried Sabine, "praise the Devil!"

Satan grinned down at the nun. "She is risen. Good morning! Feeling better?"

Ignatia, who batted her burning eyes rapidly and wiped her encumbered fist across them, looked like she barely even remembered where she was. Sputtering, she yanked the gag from her mouth with her bra-bound hands. "Wh—wh—oh!"

The nun's eyes had fallen on Clarinda Lovegood. At once her hand flew up to protect her bosom from the appalled eyes of the good witch, who had just watched a terrible profanity committed in the spilling of the wine and seemed far more distraught over this than the condition of the nun.

Seeing Sister Ignatia's appalled face, Satan offered, "Oh, don't worry, why—strictly speaking, transubstantiation doesn't occur until the blood and body is consumed. That's just wine right now. So"—smiling back down at the nun, Satan removed his dick and let his smile widen at the hungry eyes she had for it—"ready for round two, Sister?"

With one more reluctant glance to the good witch with whom she was acquainted before receiving the assurance from Satan that, "Clarinda's cool," Ignatia wiped more wine from her face and got on her knees. The Devil and Sabine both groaned to see the young nun crossed herself before, red alcohol staining her sweet honey hair, she leaned forward with her eyes fixed upon the entity to whose cock she eagerly applied her mouth.

"Oh, good girl…blessed are the meek, they say, but I say fortune favors the bold. Should have brought Father out to make him watch—oh, well. Go on, Clarinda."

His blue eyes lifted and shocked the good witch out of her stupor, Clarinda's own wild eyes narrowed at the contact with the Devil's. He looked away only to admire Sabine, who grinned openly as he commanded the good witch, "Punish my slave and prove your commitment to salvaging your immortal soul."

Jaw clenched, teeth bared, Clarinda gestured with the whip. "Don't tell me what to do," she said even as she rounded back on Sabine. "Take off that stupid costume! Oh! But the cowl—leave that cowl on."

"Yes, Madame," said Sabine with thorough delight, springing up and wiggling from out of nun's uniform. Soon naked and left in only the veil, Sabine's pale, curvy body was a very pretty sight, and even the nun fellating the Devil couldn't help but openly admire the rack she sported when free of all clothes. Then, crossing herself, Sabine knelt once more and affected a nervous glance over her shoulder. "Won't you forgive me for leading you astray, Clarinda?"

"When you're ready to seek forgiveness," said the good witch, drawing back her arm as Satan watched.

The first thunderous *crack* of the leather thongs against Sabine's back was accompanied by only the sweetest of gunfire pains.

Ah! Like being clapped in the back with a round of birdshot. The scourge stung deliciously as its tails landed from the tops of her shoulders to the Venus dimples positioned just above her hips.

Sabine swore, as her ringing ears cleared, that she heard Clarinda gasp worriedly—but soon enough, emboldened, the second stroke came, and the Devil groaned, one hand on the back of the real nun's head while he watched the scene unfold.

"That's right," Satan encouraged the angry good witch. "That's right, Clarinda, give it to her nice and hard…ah, it feels good to mete out justice in the world, doesn't it! I never have understood how the Nazarene could resist the urge to come down from his cross and annihilate with the blink of an eye those very persecutors who put him up there…but I suppose that's why he's Christ, and I'm the Devil."

If Clarinda was listening, she wasn't about to respond. Sabine did however notice that the more her Master spoke, the harder that whip came down against her hide. She groaned, pitching forward against the kneeler while Clarinda's third and fourth lashes came in rapid succession, one thong wrapping around her waist to lick across her skin with the first wicked welt. Speak on, Satan!

"Of course, there's much in common between the two of us…it's hard to deny. I could turn water into wine just as easily as he could, for instance…or I could turn it into snakes, or fire, or poison gas, or a virus. I could do anything. I could turn this hot little nun inside-out, Clarinda—"

"Don't you dare!" The good witch paused before the next lash, gasping, looking sharply up at the laughing Devil.

"You worry too much…I'm kidding. Only kidding." Removing his cock to admire the sight of his hard dick against the delicate face of the gasping nun, Satan went on, "I only mean to say…miracles are miracles. Good or bad, it doesn't matter. All magick is the same. Good witch? Bad witch? Please…whatever you tell yourself, you're just as wicked as my little Sabine."

"That's not true! I help the poor, I donate time and money, I teach dance to young people, I serve my community!"

"Yet here you are…punishing my Sabine instead of spending the night at a soup kitchen."

With a hard slap on the nun's ass, Satan pushed her toward the altar. Soon he was upon her, his demonic dick fitting comfortably between her thighs before getting on with the main show. As excited Sister Ignatia moaned and ground on him with even more abandon than she had when it was just the Devil and Sabine there corrupting her, Satan stroked her hair with the fondness of a man for an animal.

"You think being a good witch or a bad witch is about miracles, morals? Oh, no…it's about guilt, Clarinda. The whole world is upside-down. The guiltier you are, the more sinful you know you are, the better a person you are in the eyes of the Church. Father Tristan only thinks he wants you to be good. He doesn't realize that if he didn't sit here listening to all the filthy, depraved things the upstanding members of his community do and think about, he wouldn't just be out of a job…he'd be out of jerkoff material right fucking quick."

The nun screamed with ecstasy while Satan shoved deep into her pussy and, groaning at the sight, Sabine slipped her hand down against the hand-carved kneeler to touch herself. A tinge of jealousy about her, not just at Sabine's appreciation for someone else but at the Devil's use of the nun, Clarinda busied herself with more, harder, faster whipping.

While the wicked witch screamed in pleasure beneath the blows, Satan watched and fucked the moaning nun hard over the altar. One hand pressed into her back to keep her still while his hips slammed against her hot, round ass over and over, the Devil assured the good witch, "Have to keep those pews filled, Clarinda…you know what it's about? Not saving your soul, no, no. If your soul were saved you wouldn't need the Church. You'd be at peace with everything you are and do. For instance, Sabine's soul is saved. No fire and brimstone for her. She's eternity-approved: going to take that big golden escalator up into the proverbial sky when I'm finally done fucking her senseless…if that day ever truly comes.

"No, Clarinda, baby, my cute little good witch…you know what it's about? All this." Satan lifted the curled check he'd used to snort the Communion wafer, waving it in the air before dropping it back amid the pile of money they'd dumped across the altar during their first, unrecorded round of festivities. "*All* this, all this, Clarinda…and all this isn't really about helping the poor, is it? Huh?"

Yanking sharply on the gasping nun's hair, Satan stared down into her face and grabbed some fistfuls of money. "This is what you fucking Catholics like," he told Ignatia, cramming dirty dollar bills into the Christ-Bride's mouth. While the nun coughed and sputtered, Satan responded only by shoving in more bills: soon Ignatia moaned more wildly than ever, totally enraptured by her profane treatment at Satan's sensual hands.

"That's what you like," he said again, slapping her ass a few sharp times before cramming more money in her now receptive mouth. "Money, money, money, oh yeah…render unto Caesar what is Caesar's, yeah, baby, you say that a fucking lot and then you drive off in your fucking Bentleys to go interfere with some altar boys. Very fucking easy to tell people "blessed are the meek and the poor" when you only help them some of the time…and don't ever get me started on the Crusades, or the Inquisition, or the concept of martyrs in general. Oh, fuck! I love a good Catholic martyr, yes, I do, I certainly do—"

Gritting his teeth, Satan went to town on the nun. Sister Ignatia screamed in pleasure-pain to be so deeply used by the Dark Lord's human cock. Clarinda wore a similar expression to that of the Devil while she brought the whip down again, again, again upon Sabine's back, utilizing her ass and thighs only when the bad witch's stinging flesh was painted bright red in every other place that could be seen. A euphoric glow of lust had washed over Sabine, the effects of a good beating tending as they did to resemble a post-orgasmic haze without need for orgasm…not that she didn't seek one, her fingers working slowly over her clit and sometimes teasing down to the slick chamber of her pussy.

Soon enough, arm aching, out of breath, Clarinda dropped the whip and closed the distance in two short steps. Sabine, who had collapsed against the kneeler to catch her breath, was not expecting the good witch to yank her upright with such force—no more than she was expecting to be the recipient of such a passionate, hungry kiss from the tender girl.

"Now, that's nice," said Satan with approval as the bad witch's tongue battled back, her hands hastily rushing over Clarinda's body to free her from her pretty blue dress and leave her, gold and naked and infinitely more beautiful than even the hot nun playing the part of Satan's living fleshlight. "Kiss and make up, that's right, let's not fight…Daddy wants his girls to get along, oh, yes he does."

Clarinda was perhaps too busy to be taken aback by this. Sabine had gotten her out of her dress and, having stripped off the good witch's underwear, pushed her back upon that same altar where the Devil fucked the nun. Poised up beside gasping Ignatia, Clarinda ignored it all: she only had eyes for Sabine and watched, entranced as the bad witch pulled back from the kiss and knelt between Clarinda's legs. The good witch spread her thighs awfully wide for somebody with any remaining reticence about exploring her sexuality, or the joys of blasphemy—and that pussy was awfully wet for somebody who wasn't enjoying herself. Safe to say little Clarinda was less innocent by the day, and Sabine loved every second of the transformation. Fingers spreading the pretty blonde puss just dying for attention, Sabine leaned in and hastily lapped an orgasm from this still relatively untrained clit.

Back arching, Clarinda released an explosive cry from the first contact. Satan groaned with pleasure and redoubled his pounding of the nun, waving the scourge across the floor and up into his hand. It whizzed through the air and, once in his grip, seemed itself to thrill at the chance to dig its tongues into the soft skin of Ignatia's back. Each time its tails landed the Devil moaned, occasionally commenting, "Fuck, you know, it's not penance if you like it this much, Sister…"

As, with one hand, the Devil whipped the nun, with the other hand he reached over and gently caressed the back of Clarinda's neck. Though the good witch gasped and hesitated, soon she leaned back into the touch. Her eyes burned with hatred even as she offered her mouth to the handsome fallen angel, who smiled crookedly to lower his head over hers. "You'll like me someday," he told her, lips brushing hers, tongue slithering into her mouth while her eyes fluttered shut. "Someday you'll beg me to eat Communion wafers out of your pussy like Sabine here…oh, baby, baby, you'll be such a good slut for me."

"I'd rather fuck a goat," said Clarinda, spitting in his eye when he pulled away from the kiss. Sabine laughed against Clarinda's pussy and slipped a finger in while, groaning with pleasure to have been so audaciously mistreated by the good witch, the Devil wiped her spittle from his eye and smeared it on the Ignatia's cheek.

"Be careful what you wish for," said Satan, wiggling his eyebrows, leaning back in for another, far more savage kiss of the good witch. "Oh, baby, baby, Clarinda, I'll help you do all kinds of things you never knew you wanted to do…I'll show you what you love, baby, we both will, won't we? That's right, that's right…Sabine's such a good mentor. You want to give her a nice fucking for me, don't you, Sabine, baby?"

"Oh, Master! Yes, but—" Gasping slightly, head lifting from her work, Sabine bit her lip and gazed up at Clarinda. "But I don't want to scare her."

"There's no difference between a girl-cock and a strap-on, really, is there? Only that one feels better for both…more intimate. Go on…" Satan waved a hand and the bad witch glanced down, gasping with delight at the sight of the same throbbing member that clearly stunned Clarinda with not just its sudden appearance, but its scale. "Let's show her what you can really do when you've got the equipment, Sabine."

Was this really the time? They were already crossing a lot of Clarinda's lines, after all…oh, but looking up into the good witch's face, Sabine was surprised to find no scandal there at all. Only intrigue. Only lust

"You want my cock, don't you?" Sabine ran her hand over the clitoris that had been transmuted by Satan's magick into a throbbing prick. "I can see it…see it in your face."

Clarinda bit her lip, boldly glancing down at Sabine's steadily moving hand. "Yes," she murmured, foot worrying back and forth against the altar's edge. "Oh, Sabine—you were just so good with that toy before, and—please, please! I want to feel you inside me—*really* feel you inside me."

It was enough to warm a bad witch's wicked heart! Grinning, Sabine rose to her feet, her hard cock bobbing up against her taut stomach while she caught the good witch's face in her hands. Clarinda moaned into the kiss—not only that, but reached down and ran an experimental set of fingers down the shaft of the penis. Finding that Sabine released her own groan on the contact, Clarinda grew bolder and soon, with an increasingly confident grip, she stroked the pulsating tool from stem to stern.

The bad witch threw back her head and practically screamed in ecstasy, extolling, "What a soft hand she has, Master!"

"Yeah, wait until you feel that cunt…oh, such a cute, tight pussy, fuck, I love virgins—"

Sabine could take 'em or leave 'em. They were fun to corrupt, but she had to admit that she preferred a woman who knew what she was doing…and Clarinda knew more what she was doing every day. Their eyes locked, Sabine lined the head of her cock up to Clarinda's aching cunt and soon the mutual teasing of such frottage grew irresistible. The throbbing magickal member slipped into the good witch. Both women's mouths parted in shocked pleasure, Clarinda gripping Sabine's face with one hand and reaching back to clutch at Satan's arm with the other.

The Devil chuckled in low approval while the bad witch dropped her head to suck a kiss from Clarinda. "That's right," said the Devil, "oh, isn't that nice…"

"So fucking nice," gasped Sabine, finding a pace she could withstand without blowing her load right away. Holy fuck! Okay, maybe Master had a point after all…oh man, what a tight fit! Shuddering to feel her rod so savagely strangled by Clarinda's barely used pussy, Sabine rested her forehead against the good witch's and only then realized she still wore the veil. She laughed to yank it from her head and slide it over Clarinda's; before the good witch could protest, Sabine pushed her back upon the altar and held her down in place.

There, fucking Clarinda, she could easily look up from her work and watch Satan nail the nun from the other side of the altar. He caught her free hand and kissed it, sometimes drew her across to take a few seconds with his mouth. Every time, her cock throbbed with an additional degree of euphoria, another pound of internal pressure—but oh, those kisses were nowhere near as pleasurable as those seconds when some particularly sweet combination of stimulated nerves made her hyper-conscious of fucking Clarinda's tight, consecrated pussy. The good witch moaned with wild abandon, her brow furrowed and one hand braced upon the altar while her hips lifted toward Sabine's.

"Oh! Oh, God! Sabine! Oh, it's just so big—so good, oh, Sabine, it feels so good—"

"I know! I know, it's what you've waited for…oh, baby, yeah, yeah, I know, yeah, you like it, fuck, oh, a pussy so wet you just can't hide it, you must be so embarrassed—"

"No! No!" To Sabine's shocked laugh, Clarinda gasped out the words, "No, I don't want to be embarrassed anymore! Oh, Sabine, Sabine, I love it when you fuck me! I love to play with you—oh, God, you make me say such vile things but I think I love that, too, I love it all—oh, God—"

As Clarinda's pussy tightened up around Sabine's hard shaft, the bad witch groaned. "Cumming already?"

"She's so sensitive." Smiling fondly, the Devil glanced down at the nun. "And so are you…you going to cum for me, baby? Oh! Ignatia—yeah, you sure are…" While the nun produced her muffled screams through the wads of cash overflowing from her mouth, Satan groaned low and gripped her by both hips. "Fuck, fuck—oh, baby, so am I, so am I…you don't want that big Devil load boiling in your pussy, though, honey. Oh, fuck, you'd better cum quick, come on, cum for Daddy, cum for Satan—Hail Satan, baby—"

"Hail Satan," screamed Sabine, throwing up horns in the direction of the crucified Christ.

"Hail Satan," moaned Clarinda, wracked with her own sharp climax.

"Hail Satan," garbled Ignatia, body pitching into completion seconds later.

Fuck, man. Watching Clarinda and the nun cum at more or less the same time was hot enough, but it was watching the Devil jerk his cock out and blow his loud across Ignatia's naked body that gave Sabine the last throb of bliss required for her own orgasm. It was just so intense! Two women moaning along with one devious fallen seraph; all the writhing; the hot, white jet of Satanic semen spilling out across the nun's soft belly! In a few seconds Sabine was groaning, the pleasurable sight filling her up so that her own girl-cum had nowhere to go but out into screaming Clarinda's fanny.

While the moaning good witch took her first-ever cream pie like a good little bitch, Sabine steadied her with one hand on the abdomen and moaned amid the pulses of high octane lust that fueled a faster, harder orgasm than the one she was used to from a clitoris or a pussy. While her semen jetted out of her and into Clarinda, Satan watched, his orgasm wrapping up along with his low moan of artistic appreciation.

"Oh, ladies! Fuck, that's beautiful…oh, I love my girls. You could be one of my girls, too, you know," he said, grabbing Ignatia and kissing her sharply upon the mouth. "Always room for one more in any coven of mine…you'd like that, huh? Come and find me sometime. Just look for your nearest crossroads, baby, I'll be there…"

Sabine tuned back into reality somewhere partway through the Devil's pillow-talk to the nun from whom he extricated himself. Ignatia winced, eyes filling with tears of pain at the sharp emptiness. She gazed sweetly up at Satan while he plucked the money from her lips. "Please," whimpered Ignatia, "I think I'm in love with you."

"Haha! Wow, look at the time." Looking at the naked wrist upon which he wore no watch, the Devil laughed, slicked back his hair and smiled charmingly at Sabine. "Not to mention the word count. You want to let Father Tristan out before you go?"

"Of course, Master, I'd be glad to."

"That's my girl. Come here, sugar." Leaning across the altar to catch her face in his hands, Satan pressed an all-consuming kiss to Sabine's moaning mouth. The witch exhaled with delight while they parted, eyes linked, and felt her body return to its usual state as she leaned back.

"Be a good bad witch, now," Satan urged her with a playful wink as he disappeared into smoke smelling of frankincense and myrrh beneath the notes of brimstone. "Don't forget to say your prayers tonight."

Funny to think that was why Satan had told her they needed to go to Church! Sabine forgot all about that after the exciting surprise of the good witch's appearance. The Dark

Lord works in mysterious ways…now Sabine chuckled at his joke, knowing now he had only brought her here to play with Clarinda, and looked down at the girl who slowly recovered from their fucking. The good witch gazed up at her with a wry, albeit sleepy look, bliss having leant her features a laconic haze that was imitated in the dreamlike lifting of her hand to Sabine's face.

"Just what am I going to do with you, Sabine," asked Clarinda while the bad witch smiled.

"Whatever you want," the bad witch answered, "as long as you promise to help me drag this priest out of the confessional before you leave."

The Witch's Bad Seed

SABINE GOT THE FOUR-STAR REVIEW from Kilnor when she was trying out the deck her skeleton slave had built from scratch over the past forty-eight hours. The buzz of the phone caught her attention and, upon checking the notification, her foot went straight through Bonesy's hard work while she almost snapped the device in her hand.

"Do it again," commanded Sabine, waving a hand toward the hole she'd stomped in the porch, then storming off without even becoming conscious of her limp. "Four stars," she shouted on the way into the house, gawking incredulously into the nearest reflective surface—a pan that gleamed in the light, where Sabine paused to stare at her reflection in amazement.

"Which one of you brats was it? Huh?" She waved her phone with one hand and pointed with the other. "Four stars? That's more passive aggressive than one star. The only worse thing, in fact, is a two-star review. One of you little demons working with Kilnor inspired him to leave this—look, this trash. Ugh!"

Scowling, scrolling back and forth over the app dedicated to her bookbinding business, Sabine stood with one fist on her hip. "They didn't even make him leave an explanation! That's the worst. At least justify yourself…everyone's a critic, man! Ugh."

This was just like Kilnor. When the bad witch's increasingly close friend, Clarinda the Good Witch, came over to hang out that day, Kilnor was the subject yet again. While Sabine ranted on about Kilnor's annoying traits in general, Clarinda stopped her.

"I'm sorry, who is this person?"

"Zonama "Zon" Kilnor, the sorcerer. He's an old client of mine," complained Sabine. "One I've been trying to please for years. He's never fucking satisfied, though! Oh, it drives me apeshit. It's never good enough. I wouldn't even take his jobs anymore if he didn't pay so well, and if the rest of my business wasn't so unreliable. He's super finicky and ridiculously arbitrary and I never know what he wants and it's just—this sounds stupid."

"Stupid? No, I wouldn't say stupid. It just sounds like office drama."

"Exactly, stupid. Stupid horseshit. Bend over, I want to do things to you while you pretend like you don't consent."

"Oh, no," said Clarinda weakly, obeying right away, hastily lifting up the hem of her white dress and adding, "Don't *spank me.*"

Of course…can't really show *that* on mainstream platforms, reader. Consensual non-consent has gotten plenty of people in trouble. Best to be on the safe side. Blame crybabies.

Anyway, you didn't come here for that. No, no. You didn't come here to see two hot witches get up to lesbian shenanigans while one protests and the other takes charge. There are other stories for that.

You came to hear about the time Sabine turned a loser into a pumpkin.

Satan was the one who suggested it the next day—albeit

in that usual, indirect manner of his. The Dark Lord stuck around for once after finishing, which was actually pretty nice. Yes, for once it didn't seem like he wanted anything from her at all…for about ten minutes of pillow talk, until he said, "So what are you going to do about Kilnor?"

Sabine tried not to openly sigh to have the man's name brought up now, of all times. "What do you mean?"

"I see how he's bothering you lately. I know you want success with all your clients, but there are some people who just get off on withholding."

"So you're saying I should punish him?"

"Of course that's what I'm saying."

A twinge of fury boiled up in the bad witch's heart. "This was *you* again, wasn't it? You inspired him to do this to me!"

Sorry, reader. Sabine sighed and looked into the vanity mirror. Sometimes she forgot…when bullshit happened, usually her Dark Master was behind it. The real truth was that he was probably also trying to teach *her* some lesson, too, but she was too pissed off at Kilnor (and now at Satan) to care too much. While she hit him with a pillow and he lifted his hand with a patient chuckle and a fast immolation of the feather-stuffed casing in her hand. As the Dark Lord delivered third degree burns as casually as a parent might swat a child around the head for indiscretions, Sabine screamed and careened over amid the agony of her scalded flesh. It might not have been hot if he didn't soon heal her, but frankly the stinging sensation was actually pretty erotic all on its own, heal or no heal.

It was all the more pleasant when the Devil resumed caressing her.

"Now, Sabine," said the Devil to the witch, who gasped as his hand traversed the length of her leg, "remember, it never does to be angry at *me*. That's such a very Catholic mistake of you. Aha." He chuckled and slid his fingers into the dark valley between her thighs, noting, "Still wet, though."

"For you, always…oh, Master."

Sabine gasped and let her legs part beneath his heated grip. He looked vaguely Latin today, as if he had just come from South America—which he had, as there were more opportunities for unrecorded trickery and much violence for him to savor. For the same reason, he was spending much more time in the United States of America these days. The bad witch was glad, of course, because he dropped by whenever he was in the country and therefore she got to see him frequently, but that wasn't the kind of thing you went around saying to the average Tom, Dick and Harry. Talk about the Devil too much in mixed company and sooner or later people started to wonder if you had some kind of a mental problem.

Except other magicians, of course. Other magicians understood what it meant to commune with the Devil. They understood, too, that it was a delicate, sensitive process: one reliant on emotions in general and, more specifically, emotional resilience. The Devil knew all men's emotions, knew what was in their hearts; he knew what they needed to learn, but only some magicians acknowledged that they were the servants of the Devil. But, whether good or bad, in the service of God or Satan or something else entirely, other magicians understood…and occasionally, magicians—good witch or bad witch or sorcerer or warlock—liked to fuck with each other's emotions. Had to keep up a rivalry, you know?

Now that Sabine had become friends with Clarinda Lovegood, she should have expected the energetic vacuum to be filled by some cumnozzle like Kilnor the Impregnable. Yes, that was his title. The title he chose. She wasn't sure he knew what the word actually meant at first, but these days she just had the suspicion that it was a pun. A wry joke about how his mere presence impacted the uteri of the women around him. Then again…that was probably too self-aware for Kilnor.

Sabine and Kilnor had known one another for years now—

they were in the same Dungeons & Dragons party in high school, and then, as now, Kilnor loved to passive aggressively cut Sabine down. For awhile she had thought about pity-fucking him because, despite being kind of a pasty nerd, when they were teenagers he was actually sort of cute and might have made a good himbo (no, that's not a typo, Sabine loved a good reverse *My Fair Lady*, but that was a story still to come, so be patient and join the mailing list).

But the truth was that Kilnor never would have opened his mind to the experience—not to mention he'd really let himself go. Grown a neckbeard and everything…though she had to hope he'd left the fedora behind in high school. Yes, much as he'd been a vicious rules lawyer during D&D, Kilnor was now a know-it-all douchebag: the kind of whining, wheedling incel who no doubt only got laid when he put down the cash for it. Otherwise his personality was too repellent for any woman to give him the time of day as soon as he introduced himself and said anything at all.

"I don't even like to be in the same room with this dude, though," protested Sabine, who had been thrown out of the Dungeons & Dragons group when she team-killed him for the second time—thus proving that she couldn't even function in the group environment of a roleplaying game let alone an office or organized religion. "Kilnor is a super-rude asshole. I'd rather just ignore it and move on."

"And get four-star reviews with no explanation? Do you really want to give him loosh for the rest of your life, Sabine?"

'Loosh' was magician slang for an abstract emotional property that was used as fuel by Internet trolls and emotional vampires as much as by creative individuals getting back-pats or hard-working magickal freelancers getting (in theory) five stars. Think of it like the magickal equivalent of oxytocin and/or dopamine, though with more of a deliberate purpose. There was no way to literally measure it but anybody with a narcissistic family could tell you that it was easy to tell when you had been in contact with an energy vampire or other loosh-stealing asshole. Loosh could be positive or negative, and being a good magician or a bad magician didn't have anything to do with what kind of loosh you used to do your magick.

In fact, Sabine would have ventured a guess that most so-called "good" witches and sorcerers were getting off on watching people squirm within the arbitrary restraints they established for those people. It was why "good witches" like Clarinda Lovegood ran Home Owners Associations, or why Kilnor was strictly speaking an uptight scholar who loved to correct pronunciation at every chance he got, or annoy his local bad witch by routinely giving her four-star or lower ratings despite continuing to use her work. The emotional energy stirred up was just too lucrative for these pricks to resist taking out their control freak tendencies on the unassuming.

And normally Sabine would have preferred getting her loosh by, say, resolving the emotional angst of Clarinda after introducing her to sodomy, or taking Cable Dog to get micro-chipped in case he ever did succeed at running away. But Satan said to do it, you know? The Devil told Sabine to punish Kilnor. You couldn't say *no* to that, could you? Especially not when he made her imagine what it would be like to give Kilnor loosh for the rest of her life. Ugh, no wonder that asshole kept using her services. It was too easy for him to get a book repaired and get off on her annoyance all at the same time. She really did have to figure out how to control her emotions.

Or she could just give Kilnor what was coming to him and make him admit who the better magician was.

"What do you think I should do, though? I don't want it to be a reward."

"Any attention you give him will be a reward, Sabine, at least a little bit...but there are some things that humble even the most arrogant glutton for punishment. Why not try something seasonal? That's always nice. The girls will love it when you tell them about it at the next Sabbath."

"Hm...maybe."

"Come on, you know I'm right...just use that creative head of yours. I'm sure you can carve out something good."

Not very subtle, Master...but a good idea nonetheless. She did hate trying to pick out pumpkins from the grocery store, after all.

Soon Sabine stood on Kilnor's porch. Like most sorcerers and warlocks, Kilnor had a high sense of drama. He owned the dark tower overlooking the college town where Sabine and her friends all made their livings. As she approached it, the sky went dark and ravens' croaking filled the air: soon she stood on a welcome mat that said *NO SOLICITATIONS* and shifted the fat volume in her grip from arm to arm.

The gargoyle-shaped knocker rang out beneath her hand and soon enough footsteps made their way across the stones of the floor. The heavy door cracked open.

"Sabine," said Kilnor in surprise, his nasally voice unusually pleasant due to having been caught unawares. Soon that tone grew guarded; his eyes narrowed in the dark light of the tower's entry hall.

"What do you want? You never come to visit me."

It was true. She preferred to stay as far away from this loser's tower as she could. Like, a tower? For real? Dick replacement, much? Might as well be driving a giant truck.

"You know I'm just always so busy," Sabine nonetheless said, forcing a semi-pleasant smile across her face. "I must work twenty-four hours a day doing everything I do...and then, of course, there's Master always visiting me. It takes up so much time to entertain him..."

As she batted her eyes, Kilnor batted his own, more out of shock than out of any kind of willful flirtation. "Uh," he stuttered, not knowing what to say to a beautiful woman implying anything sexual at all, "uh. So what's up?"

"Well," she told the slightly chubby sorcerer whom, these days, she would have never fucked in a million years, "I have this book, see, and you know I'm just no good in Latin. Would you read a few pages for me? I'm trying to parse out a spell."

With a suspicious second glance at the volume in her hands, he asked, "This isn't going to be one of those spells where you trick me into reading it aloud and I end up cursed because of it, right?"

"No, no, of course not…you know I'm just all about consent." So hard to say these things without rolling her eyes…but business was business. Focused on being in business-mode, she gestured into Kilnor's tower with her free hand and let her lips contort into the pout of a damsel in distress. "Maybe you could let me in and I could just show you?"

Exhaling, glancing back over his shoulder, Kilnor opened the door wider to let Sabine inside. Yikes! The stones across the entry way's floor were dusty with neglect. Sabine had to wonder how often Kilnor even walked down the spiraling stairs to come or go. Not often enough to keep it clean, evidently… some people just didn't have any pride.

"I have to say I'm surprised, Sabine…you've never asked me for help with anything before."

"Oh, well, you know me, Kilnor…I'm just too proud." It was hard to bite her tongue and say shit like that, but at least, with Kilnor's back to her while he led her up the stairs, she could now make faces of disgust with impunity. Nose wrinkled with disdain for her own words, she sighed and lied, "It's just so hard for me to admit I need help…but not even I'm perfect, you know."

"Learning how to admit that is all part of becoming a great

magician," Kilnor agreed, nodding sagely while he pushed open the door to the apartment of his tower.

Ugh…holy shit. Weeaboo, much? Taken aback by the contemporary lighting and furnishing of the living quarters after that gloomy, old-fashioned stone foyer, Sabine took several seconds before she recognized the pieces of art on the walls weren't what most Westerners traditionally considered "art." Scantily clad, big-tittied anime girls winked down at her from all angles, proudly displayed above the overwhelming collections of DVDs and videogames and more than a couple figurines that, in the same style as the posters, saluted or waved from their artfully organized shelves. They were even dusted.

Amazing! Maybe Kilnor did care about something.

If that wasn't enough to keep her from making fun of him, well, imagine her surprise—

"You have a doll," enthused Sabine, hurrying over to see it with a look of eager delight. A ball-jointed doll, too! Very cute. The miniature blue-haired girl beamed up at Sabine, her fingers poised in the 'V' of high-spirited anime mascots everywhere.

Kilnor flinched, expected the mean girl treatment, and began, "Actually, she's a resin—"

"You don't have to mansplain ball-jointed dolls to me, dude. I own, like, twenty." She left out the part that most of hers were actually the dollified personages whose offenses were so grievous but aesthetics so fine that they merited eternal punishment as one of Sabine's playthings. Instead she went on, "Mine are realistic and not anime-style, though…I love her!"

Suddenly far more comfortable—comfortable enough to be a douchebag—Kilnor puffed himself up and hurried to Sabine's side to admire his doll with her. "That's Tentacle Girl Ami-Chan," explained Kilnor with a gesture toward one of the posters upon his walls.

"Is this your waifu?"

The nerd sputtered a little at that, glancing reflexively into the face of the blue-haired doll as though for help. Ami-chan stared back, her tiny anime mouth eternally frozen in the vapid and patient sort of smile that weebs loved their agreeable cartoon women for.

"You don't have to be *embarrassed,*" insisted Sabine, nudging her dumpy rival before flinging herself into the nearest couch. She grimaced and shoved away a videogame controller on which she'd almost sat, glad she'd barely noticed it before her ass landed on it: Kilnor would have had it mounted and displayed after she left, no doubt. You know, if he still had the ability to do such things…she'd see about that. Thumping the book down upon the coffee table, Sabine continued, "Waifus and husbandos are different when you're a magician, as I'm sure you know. All multi-dimensional friends give us power… or take it from us. Do you ever summon her? I guess you probably prefer her 2-D, though, huh. Most weebs do."

"Look," said Kilnor, annoyed, so defensive after years of being torn apart even within his own nerdy circles that he couldn't see Sabine—whose own beloved Satan fulfilled the same role to her that Ami-chan filled in Kilnor's life—was really trying to relate to him for once. "Why don't you just tell me why you're here? I'm sort of in the middle of something."

"Uh-huh," said Sabine, looking briefly up at the videogame paused on the wall-mounted television. While scowling Kilnor shut the TV off, Sabine cleared her throat and flipped through the leatherbound volume to the page she'd previously marked. "Well, it's just this spell, really…for some reason, maybe it's the dialect, I just can't seem to read it! Could you help me?"

Sit by a hot babe or continue awkwardly standing? Never one to miss an opportunity to act like he knew more than everyone else, Kilnor eventually gave in and hurried to Sabine's side. The neckbeard lowered his girth uneasily into the couch and bent forward to study the spell on display there, eyes scanning the page, lips frowning along with the low tone of their, "Hm…'Gourd Soul.' Gourd? What is…"

Kilnor squinted at the page a little longer.

"Is this a spell to turn somebody into a *gourd?*"

"I don't know, is it?"

"It is—but it's one of these spells where you have to have… what? A build-up of—semen!" His face reddened just to say the word. "Is this a book of some kind of sex magick?" Scoffing, brow furrowing, Kilnor held their page with one hand and used the other to lift the cover of the tome. The gold-embossed title proudly gleamed the words *LIBER FORNICATUS.*

"It *is,*" said Kilnor, looking a little appalled but somewhat intrigued. "But what's a spell like this doing in a book about sex magick?"

Sabine's eyebrows lifted. "Whatever do you mean?"

"I just mean—it's not very sexy to be turned into a *gourd, is it?*"

"Of course it is! Oh, it's one of the hottest things I've ever heard."

Most people would probably be worried about laying it on a little thick, but those people hadn't been in a room with Kilnor and seen the look of thirsty desperation he shot Sabine at the high sigh. Her hand sliding over her heart and coming to rest upon the magickally perky swell of one oversized tit, Sabine bit her lip and crossed her legs while she said in an increasingly breathy voice, "Why, just *thinking* about it turns me on…I love a man who's confident enough in his masculinity to consent to turn into a squash for me."

If Kilnor's face blushed before, by now it was red from forehead to bearded chin. "But—but you can't *do* anything about it. If somebody gets turned into a gourd of some kind, they won't have sex organs, for starters."

"Sure, but there's more to sex than just putting your dick

into a vagina." By now Kilnor looked like he was going to pass out and, fighting her urge to grin, Sabine instead threw back her head and theatrically moaned. "Oh, just the thought! Having a cute little gourd-boy able to fit in both my hands… mm, so *sexy*. Why, just think! If you were a gourd, Kilnor, I could touch you almost everywhere at once. You'd still be nice and sizable but small enough that I would seem like a big, sexy goddess. Giant, really. And some gourds still have stems, you know. A man can rest in confidence that his big, hard stem might still satisfy his mistress…if nothing else, she could rub up against his shell until she was all dripping wet. Oh, but I'm making you uncomfortable."

She had looked up to find him all but hypnotized by the eager tone of her voice alone. Snapped out of it by that pouting claim, Kilnor wiped the back of his hand across his drooling lower lip and cleared his throat. "No! N—no, of course not. I just—I guess I'm still not sure how something like that could be, uh…could be very exciting to anyone."

Hands running over her own gourds, now, Sabine lifted her eyebrows expectantly. "I could show you…"

"I—I—what's come *over* you, Sabine? You've never acted like this before. Did somebody ensorcell you?"

"Of course not. It's just, oh, thinking of how hot it would be to have a sexy pumpkin boy to tease and carve into a jack-o-lantern…mm, it makes me so wet, oh, nothing would make me as hot as having a hot stud with a big stem and—"

"*Mecca lecca hi,*" Kilnor hastily recited, sweat pouring down his red face and upon the surface of the book from which he read. "*Mecca hiney hojotoho*—"

Sabine's head tipped back with her cackle as plumes of purple smoke at once burst around Kilnor and obscured him from sight. By the time the witch's high spate of laughter had cleared, so had the cloud: and lo, a helpless pumpkin sat, as shiny and orange and horny as a pumpkin could look.

"You're so *desperate*, Kilnor," said Sabine, touching the tip of her finger to the tip of the pumpkin's stem. "I hope you don't really think I'm going to put this thing into me…oh, it's so rough, it'd hurt no matter how wet I am! And anyway, silly boy, pumpkins aren't for fucking are they? Especially not this time of the year."

With a lurid grin at the staring eyes of Ami-chan, Sabine plucked the pumpkin up and did it the courtesy of holding it against her enormous knockers. "But, don't worry…you'll still have plenty of fun."

The pumpkin, being a pumpkin, did not reply. Sabine lightly patted its surface and hummed in thought while making her way back down the curling stairs from the tower's apartment. "After all, it's fun to be objectified every once in a while… awfully nice of me to do anything with you at all. Why, after that last four-star review you gave me just to piss me off, I can't help but think the right thing to do is smash you. That would free you, though, and we don't want to do that just yet…not until I know you've learned your lessons and I can expect five-star reviews from here on out."

If pumpkins could complain, this one would have no doubt been doing so vociferously. Sabine wouldn't have cared if she could hear it, however, and continued fondling the gourd all the way home. Soon enough she had that naughty pumpkin sitting in the middle of her kitchen floor, displayed upon a layer of unfolded newspapers where she assessed it contemplatively with Satan at her side.

"What do you think I should do this year, Master?"

"So hard to say! Maybe something in my honor." The Devil ran his hands over Sabine's bosom, looking pointedly at the gourd.

True, to be an actual cuckold one technically had to be in a relationship, but the principle was still the same level of humiliating. If only pumpkins could blush or whine or argue!

It would have been funny to hear the fat incel complain about Satan openly caressing Sabine right in front of him, as if he had any say or stake in the matter.

Sabine had to admit, though…she loved it when a man was transformed into something nice and inanimate and mouthless. Men always wanted to *talk*. Even with a gag in, there was a lot of whining and complaining, and sometimes it was cute but other times she truly enjoyed denying them even that level of autonomy.

"In your honor, hm? Sure, maybe I could do a sigil or something…will you get my carving kit out while I get undressed? I don't want to get pumpkin guts all over my clothes, after all."

"Of course, Sabine, of course…you're so prudent."

"I do try."

The bad witch grinned after her wicked master, then turned that grin upon the pumpkin. "You don't mind, do you," she asked while sliding her shirt up over her head and freeing her breasts with a bounce that, even within the confines of the bra, could have given any oppai onee-chan girl a run for her money. "I don't mean to embarrass you…I know you're probably still a virgin and all, but I hate getting all *messy* and dirty when I carve a pumpkin. It's much better to do it naked…in my underwear, at least."

Soon she did stand in her underwear, and she could have sworn that the surface of the pumpkin had gone from orange to red. Grinning, Sabine pushed her long black hair back over her shoulder to let the transfigured sorcerer get an eyeful of her sumptuous curves…however he saw while in such a state.

"Just how *do* you boys see when you're like this," she asked the Devil when he returned from her garage with her carving kit, which he placed upon the kitchen counter.

"Same way we always see…in color, unless we're colorblind. Ah! Sabine." While the witch rolled her eyes at his wry joke and bent to place the retrieved kit upon the floor beside the pumpkin, the Devil slapped her ass with a look of appreciation and pressed against her, his hands on her hips. "What a sexy bitch you are."

"You can't fuck me yet, Master! I have to at least get the pumpkin gutted…hold on."

Then, upon her knees, the bad witch picked up a knife and contemplated the top of the pumpkin. Her hand slid over the curve of its stem, those long, pale fingers folding around its rough surface.

A little moan rose up from her.

"Oh! Just thinking of how afraid our little pumpkin must be—doesn't it make you horny, Master? Don't worry, Kilnor… it won't be so bad. You'll be back to yourself whenever the pumpkin rots. Maybe by then you'll be ready to give me a better review. If you don't, well…we'll just have to try this again until you agree."

The tip of the blade had penetrated beneath the pumpkin's orange skin less than a millimeter before Satan was already groaning with appreciation. "You are the queen of torture," the Devil assured her, his arms folded over his chest while he leaned against the kitchen counter to watch her at her work.

"You think I'm doing this too slowly? Oh, but I want to take my *time*, Master…why, pumpkin carving is my favorite Halloween tradition! And, anyway, it's good to be careful."

The witch leaned forward to apply some force to the knife which, beneath her weight, impaled into the flesh of the gourd and straight through to its center. Satan inhaled sharply as he might have while watching her get fucked by another man… or while watching her fuck another man, anyway. "Give it to him, baby," he told her while she grinned.

"If you take the top of the pumpkin off in the wrong way," she continued lecturing, wiggling the knife back and forth, then jerking it out of the pumpkin entirely to stab it in again at a new angle, "it'll slide into the damn thing and smother the candle…and rot faster, too. Really, the top is the hardest part. And the cleaning, of course. Ah! Slippery."

The knife had glanced off the tight skin of the gourd and she had very nearly cut herself. Tsking, the bad witch shifted so as to hold the pumpkin still between her thick, white thighs, its cool orange surface pressed against the damp crotch of her panties. As those generous limbs enfolded the pumpkin the way they might a man's very lucky head, the witch used both hands to stab the knife in and out of the pumpkin's top around the circumference of the stem. Once or twice the slam through to the other side was so satisfying that even she moaned; she lifted her hooded eyes toward Satan on the final stroke in, lips parted for a kiss that he bent to deliver upon her longing mouth. Sabine moaned into her Dark Master's consuming lips and against the probing of his human-length tongue—oh, those hands that ran over her cheeks, up into her hair and down the back of her neck! Fuck, he made her so horny. She hadn't been super into the idea of doing anything with or to Kilnor, yet Master really did have a way of making it not just bearable but enjoyable.

"You want to please me, don't you, baby," he told her gruffly as they parted from the kiss.

"Oh, yes, Master, yes—oh, all men are just unworthy tools, imitations of your glory. But that doesn't mean they aren't good for at least one or two things…"

Grinning evilly down at the pumpkin still squeezed between her thighs, Sabine set her knife aside and gripped the stem in her hands. She clenched her jaw, thinking for a few moments that she might have to go back over some of her old cuts, but soon enough, with a little bit of wiggling back and forth, she was able to yank the pumpkin's top off with a noise as satisfying as the sloppy crack of a man's spine.

Viscous strands of orange-colored innards oozed back

down into the center of the squash, each and every thread overflowing with obscene seeds. With a high cackle, Sabine set the top aside and wiped her hands off on her thighs. The pulp stained her pale skin orange and she moaned at the effect while sinking both hands into the inside of the pumpkin.

"Oh," she said, gasping breathily, eyes lifting to her watching master as pulp squelched through her fingers, "why, this poor pumpkin is just *full* of seeds…oh, Master, it was a good thing we picked it to carve. Why, it's so full of seeds it might have just burst if it had to wait any longer. Yes, exploded those nasty, dirty seeds all over its garden patch…poor pumpkin! Well, it's all right…now you're getting the attention you need, aren't you?"

Her fingers tangling through threads of pulp and scraping along the fleshy rind of the gourd, Sabine let loose another pornographic moan to pull her stringy fistfuls of pumpkin pulp out of the interior of the transfigured squash. She gasped as a few seeds fell free to cling to her thighs and chastised, "So messy," while flinging the orange guts off of her fingers and upon the newspaper.

While her bare foot shifted to rest in the squishy substance, she dug in again, her ass flat upon the newspaper and one leg extended around the pumpkin to keep it in place. This time the bad witch came up with even more gooey pulp, whose cool texture made her gasp as she smeared it over her heaving breasts.

"What a dirty girl you are, Sabine," lightly remonstrated the Dark Lord while beginning to unbutton his shirt. "Whatever you're doing, you always end up covered in something… with baking, it's flour; with pumpkin carving, it's pulp; with sex, well…"

Sabine giggled naughtily, biting her lip and groaning to run her dirty hands down her stomach and thighs.

"Oh, I know, but life's too short to be fussy about getting a little filthy…that's what showers are for, after all. And, anyway, I'm sure the pumpkin likes it…sure he finds it satisfying to see me all covered with his stringy ropes of pulp…mm, especially my feet."

Rubbing her foot back and forth in the gooey pile of pulp, Sabine grabbed the nearest spoon and reached into the pumpkin to vigorously scrape down its flesh. Ropes of orange innards tore away from the interior and soon she was able to pull out massive hunks of pumpkin guts: this time she didn't hesitate to slide it over her breasts and stuff a little in her panties, but mostly she let it fall over her bare feet. The goo squelched between her toes and over her arch while she giggled wickedly, one dirty foot lifting to rub against the side of the pumpkin. "Yeah…you do like it, huh? Like me squishing your seedy pulp all beneath my cute bare toes…I'll bet if you had a dick it would be hard as a fucking rock right now."

"God knows mine is," extolled the Devil, unbuckling his belt and swiftly unzipping his trousers. Sabine moaned, sliding her fingers into her panties to touch herself with slimy pumpkin hands and laughing with surprise at how wet she already was. Must have just been the Dark Lord's eye on her. He could have watched her while she fixed an engine and it would have made her wet—actually, the more she thought about getting all covered in oil and grease in front of him, the more she realized it totally would have made her wet, and she laughed at herself again. Reading her thought, the Devil laughed with her and pushed aside his pile of clothes to stand naked before the scene.

"You don't have to be embarrassed, now, Sabine…why, one of the things I love most about you is your liberated sexuality. You can appreciate anything in this world! Anything at all… that quality is so important in a bad witch. All reality is an act of lovemaking, isn't it, angel?"

"Of course it is, Master! Oh, yes, oh…and everything I do,

I do in your name, for your pleasure…I love to think about you getting off to me doing normal things around my house."

"And I do. I just love to watch you, Sabine…my dirty girl." With the smirking Devil bent and plunged a hand into the open top of the pumpkin. Sabine gasped, her green eyes flashing questioningly up at her master.

"Is our pumpkin bi, really? I should have guessed…"

"Curious, anyway…don't worry, Kilnor, we won't tell." Chuckling, lifting a fistful of the pulp out of the pumpkin, Satan then smeared it across Sabine's face while she gasped and moaned. "Oh," said the Devil while bukkaking his bad witch with orange pumpkin-spunk, "that's right, that's fucking right, what a wet little whore you are for our nice pumpkin here…that's right, baby, oh, suck it from my fingers."

As Satan's index and middle finger plunged into Sabine's plump mouth, she did as she was told and moaned while her master's free hand lowered to flick open the clasp of her bra. When he slid his fingers from her squash-flavored mouth it was only to push that bra away and free her bouncing breasts from the cups that, like her flesh, had been stained orange by their amusements.

"I just love to see you covered in cum," Satan enthused, his voice a low growl of pleasure while he gave his hard dick a stroke or three. It twitched as he released it to draw more guts out of the pumpkin: while he smeared this prize all over Sabine's body, the Devil continued, "Human, vegetable, it doesn't make a difference to me, baby…all of it makes me ready to fuck you. Oh! Look at you."

Sabine had moaned and reached up to smear the stringy pumpkin cum all across her face and neck. Now she ended her self-caressing only as long as it took to push her orange-stained panties away from her dripping cunt. The Devil stooped to help her free the cotton from her limber legs and soon, theatrically displayed, Sabine parted her thighs and fell back into the pile of gooey pumpkin pulp. She moaned to smear the substance all over her tits and down her stomach, her ass and feet both rubbing in the orange piles with particular relish. The Devil groaned at the sight and bent down to kiss her, holding her jaw with one hand while using the other to extract another tangle of pumpkin guts. With a low hum of appreciation, Satan crammed her gasping mouth full of the stuff, then rubbed the rest into her neatly trimmed vulva before teasing her aching clit. Sabine moaned at a high, desperate pitch, spreading her legs in obscene ecstasy while her master rubbed her most important nerves back and forth.

"That's it, you dirty slut, that's it…oh, yeah, you love it, don't you, love cucking this pathetic pumpkin-boy with me… fuck, yeah, you love humiliating yourself, debasing yourself for me, don't you…I love it, love that you don't let your pride keep you from getting good and dirty for your dark Daddy."

"No, Master! No, oh, it's my favorite thing. Oh, I love to be a dirty, shameless little whore for Satan—oh, fuck! Master!" Her nipples were hard enough to cut diamonds and she moaned to run her fingers over them, tweaking and playing with the orange-stained areolae while the Devil watched. Soon his middle and ring finger had slid into her soaking cunt and, throwing back her head with a high keen, the bad witch bit her lip and arched her hips up into his caress. "Master! Oh, fuck, I'm going to cum already—"

"So sensitive tonight, Sabine…you love being a nasty, messy girl, don't you…" While with one hand he finger-fucked her as she gasped and moaned, Satan used the other to lift her delicate, pulp-splattered foot to his mouth. As Satan sucked pumpkin cum from her toes, Sabine gasped all the higher.

Oh, fuck! What was the use of denying it? She really fucking loved it when he played with her feet…all her body was outrageously sensitive when in the presence of her wicked Lord of the Flies, but when he touched her feet he might as well have been licking her clit. He flicked this same clit with a rapid finger when he slid his knuckles out of her aching little hole and commenced to batter more directly that efficient source of feminine pleasure. Sabine's pussy dripped while she screamed, her tight cunt aching to be filled again, that ache transmuting along with the steady suck of the Devil's mouth around her toe into a cataclysmic orgasm whose rush practically left her blind.

While Sabine thrashed in the pile of newspapers and pumpkin spunk, Satan watched with a chuckle and lowered her dirty foot to his cock. He used that filthy arch to jerk himself off while appreciating her violent orgasm and so as she began to rise out of her climax she was first aware of Satan's hard prick throbbing against her flesh. Groaning, pouting, Sabine spread her other leg and braced herself against the floor, one hand landing upon the pumpkin that she pressed to the curve of her waist.

"Oh, fuck, Master—please, please, will you fuck me now? Oh, I need your dick in me so badly, I can't stand it!"

"Ah, Sabine, my delicious little whore…so desperate for me, aren't you?"

"Yes, yes! Please, oh, Master, I'm such a horny slut for the Devil's giant cock! Fuck, fuck, I want the whole town to know, oh, make me *scream* with it—fuck, fuck, wake Clarinda up with it, make me the instrument of your pleasure, your living Fleshlight! Master, oh, fuck, fill me up with cum, more cum than our little pumpkin has smeared me with—"

"Well! You really are horny tonight…I suppose it would be cruel of me to deny you too much longer. But I do love to be cruel."

"Master! Please?" Whining, Sabine rolled onto her tummy to present her ass to her Dark Lord. Satan groaned and reached down to grab a handful of it, smacking it once or twice while Sabine gripped the pumpkin beneath her orange-stained breasts. She put the lid on to help her brace herself and gasped with pleasure to find how well the rough stem fit just between those big tits. Reaching back with her sticky fingers, Sabine spread her ass cheeks and displayed herself, begging, "Please, oh, I want it in any hole you'll give it to me in—please, please, Master?"

"All right," said the Devil with an indulgent sigh while kneeling between her legs, "just a little…but I have something in mind for the end, so as much as I know you love to have your cute little guts filled with my cum, that'll have to wait for another day."

"I understand," she said, gasping with pleasure just to feel him pressing against the screaming nerves of her valley. Oh, fuck, he was too hard to stand! Just feeling the press of his head against her throbbing pussy made her nearly weep with desire. Sabine bit her lip, dying with anticipation until the moment when the Devil, at long, aching last, rammed his big hard human dick up into the bad witch's cunt.

"Yes," she screamed at once, "oh, yes! Master, Master!"

"Fuck, ah, Sabine—and here I thought you were wet *outside…*"

Slowly, one stroke at a time, the Devil's stony dick found the rhythm of its stabbing. Sabine moaned, eyes rolling into the back of her head as her master gripped her hair with one hand and her fat ass with the other. He kept her held in place while hammering home, the tip of his tool banging again and again against that sensitive internal target that made her feel especially full—especially aching. Especially wet. His cock grew all the harder as her grip grew tighter, each scream from her yielding another, more vigorous stroke. All the while Sabine embraced the pumpkin to her soft belly, her tits bouncing up and down around the gourd's rough stem.

"Fuck! Oh! Master! You're so fucking rough with me, yeah, I love it when you're rough! Fuck me, fuck me, oh, I'm your bad little whore, I'm a bad, bad witch—"

"You certainly are, Sabine…you naughty girl. You prideful girl! Humiliating this pathetic little cuck just because he left you a four-star review instead of a five-star…what would you have done if he had left you a one-star?"

"Oh—oh, fuck, fuck—it would have at least—ungh, been honest—"

"Liar." Satan slapped her ass and she gasped sharply, groaning as the pumpkin slipped from her grip and rolled away. The Devil pushed her down into the pile of pumpkin pulp upon the newspapers, that fist around her hair yanking her face back and forth to grind her cheek in the pumpkin goo. "Lying little slut, ah, you think you can deceive me? You may be the Queen of Torture, but I'm the King of Deception. You would have been even angrier…you're a prideful cunt, Sabine, ah, ah, in earlier times you would have ended up in the town square on display in the stocks…ah, fuck, that would have humbled you, wouldn't it? But you probably would have loved being available for everyone's free use…fuck, ah, you get so wet when I remind you what a vain slut you are—"

"Hm, hm, hm, yes! Yes! Oh, Master, you're right, of course— oh, fuck, yes, I have no business being so vain, I'm sorry, sir—"

"Louder, slut."

"I'm sorry! Oh, fuck, I'm sorry, you're right, I'm a very bad witch! I should be happy that he took the time to give me even four stars! Oh! I'm an ingrate! I'm a dirty little ingrate for thinking it's beneath me!"

"That's right, that's right…after all, you disgraceful little bitch, you're covered in his pumpkin cum now, aren't you? He gave you money, didn't he? Isn't that enough? You should have thanked him for his four stars…"

"Oh, fuck! Thank *you* for correcting me, Master! You're right, you're right!"

"Of course I'm right…" His pace only sped and Sabine

practically sobbed with it, groaning as he turned her face to the side to lick pumpkin from her cheek. Soon he pressed his lips to hers in a ferocious, bruising kiss that left her moaning all the more desperately. Oh, fuck! He was so hard, and his fucking so fast, that she swore she could feel his dick up in her stomach. Her rolling eyes fell upon the pumpkin and she moaned, grinning, wishing it had eyes for her to make eye contact with while Satan's fast-working dick yielded a second orgasm from her. While Sabine screamed and writhed beneath him on the floor, the Devil shoved her face back down into the pile of pulp; he groaned amid her gasps, sighing as her pussy tightened rapidly around his dick. When, toward the end of her orgasm, she tried to push back against him, Satan slid free of her and ignored her whine.

"Now, Sabine…what did I tell you? I want to make use of all this material…there's just too much pulp here to avoid it, so we'd might as well play with it. Why don't you use those pretty feet of yours? Here…come sit on Master's face."

While the Devil rolled upon his back, Sabine cried out with pleasure and soon straddled his head as she'd once gripped that pumpkin. While her dripping pussy lowered over his open mouth and his tongue sprang to immediate work toying against her clit, Sabine braced one hand back upon the newspaper-covered floor. With the other, she smeared a few handfuls of pumpkin guts over the Devil's tight stomach and throbbing dick. While it twitched beneath her touch at the odd sensation, Sabine grinned and found new balance. Both hands supporting her in her mission to stay balanced upon the Devil's eager mouth, the bad witch lifted a foot to his throbbing cock.

"Oh! Fuck, Master, what a depraved devil you are…you love my feet almost as much as I do, don't you…"

It was true. His diabolical device twitched beneath her arch and she moaned, smearing pumpkin pulp and seeds up and down the ultra-hard length. The slick strands of goop made it easy to slide her foot over the organ and served not just as lube but a kind of sensational accent—an extra layer of degradation that left him enthusiastically lashing his tongue in and out of her aching hole to convince her to keep it up. While, moaning, Sabine ran her foot over her Master's cock and down to balls as full of seed as the pumpkin was when this strange process had started, she turned her head to gaze at the pumpkin lying upon the floor.

No emotion legible upon its surface, the pumpkin said nothing.

"Look at what a mess you've made," the bad witch said, reaching over to teasingly flick the tip of the pumpkin's stem. "With a load like this you could practically be a porn star... but you're too shy, aren't you, Kilnor? Well...it was very nice of Master to suggest this for you, so you'd ought to thank him later with a nice offering. Burn some—some oh, some frankincense for him, or just piss on a Communion wafer— Oh, fuck! Fuck, oh, Master, your tongue—"

Sabine's eyes fluttered and she gazed toward the ceiling as the Devil's wet instrument hastened its rapid battering of her clit. Whining when she realized the pleasure had made her stop, she had to consciously recommence her foot's stroking up and down his fat, wet cock. With a gasp, Sabine worked her foot back and forth over the Devil's member and soon was twitching against it, herself, kicking out and stepping straight on the big thing while her third orgasm washed rapidly over her. "Fuck! Fuck! Oh, Master..."

"What a horny witch you are tonight," he commented, groaning low as she pushed herself down a few inches to sit upon his chest. "Fuck, ah...and talented."

Grinning, still with the last pulses of her climax throbbing through her body, Sabine braced herself upon the floor again and now ran both feet back and forth over Satan's messy cock.

He was harder than ever beneath the teamwork of her heels, which she ground into his glans and teased along his shaft… oh, but when her toes tickled his balls, he let out an irresistible groan that was so hot it left her fingering herself again.

"I so love to please you, Master," gasped the bad witch, dripping girl-cum upon his chest while she toyed with her clit and admired his pained throbs between the embrace of her arches. Running her feet up and down his pulpy prick, then tightening the grip as his tool grew all the harder, Sabine grinned to slide her fingers into herself. "Oh! You get so hard for me, fuck, oh, I love to see it…this little fuckboy does, too. Oh, don't you, Kilnor?"

The pumpkin continued to say nothing. Soon Satan also said nothing intelligible, and even Sabine was quickly overtaken by ecstasy—especially as her Master's hips arched to let his cock fuck the hole between her pulp-smeared feet. Sabine moaned, her fingers faster than ever as she squished the Day-Star's aching cock against his stomach.

Soon the pleasure she derived from pleasing him in turn was in excess of anything she could have given herself. She stopped touching herself and rose, one hand upon the nearby counter to support her while she trampled that big, hard dick beneath her bare foot, smearing the sticky ropes of pumpkin pulp all over his dick and up along his stomach. The Devil throbbed, watching her, enthusing, "Sabine, ah, fuck, Sabine, my hot little slave, that's right, oh, you do know how to please your master so well—fuck, yes, both feet, slut—"

Groaning, Sabine sat again and took his aching member in both her dirty feet. One on each side, the bad witch worked Satan's orange-stained cock between her arches, marveling at the ease with which the pumpkin jizz let her slide over her master's flesh. Maybe that was just how hard he was…hard as marble, hard as glass, hard as the orgasm that tore through him with his gasp of infernal pleasure.

"Ah, fuck," he shouted, "Hail Satan!"

"Hail Satan," screamed the bad witch in delight, moaning, caressing her teased pussy to a quick orgasm spurred by the sight of the Devil's fat white load springing from his dick. Nothing made her cum as quickly as seeing Satan's orgasm, but her orgasm only extended when, much as he had with the pumpkin's pulp, Satan drew Sabine down into his arms and smeared his cum all over her gasping, moaning face.

"There we go, baby, oh, that's better…that's what our painting needed a little white. Don't you look cute."

"Master! Oh, thank you for your cum, Master…oh, Hail Satan…"

"Hail me, baby," agreed Satan, drawing her pulp, cum-covered mouth to his smiling one for a long kiss. "Ah! Sabine… Hail me."

"Hail, Hail! Oh, Master." Biting her lip, grinning, Sabine lay her head against his chest and gazed sweetly up at him before glancing at the nearby pumpkin. "And good job, Kilnor."

"Did you learn your lesson?"

Sabine laughed at the Devil's question. "Uh—sure. Pride is bad?"

"Something like that," agreed the Dark Lord with a chuckle, head laying back in the pumpkin goo with a thump. "Normally I'd be leaving about now…but you know, I think I should probably take a shower first."

"What about Kilnor? Usually you turn people back the way they were."

"Yeah, but he's super into it. See?"

Satan caught Sabine's pale hand in his and, after kissing it, pressed her palm to the pumpkin. At once her head was filled with nerdy screams of ecstasy, vibrations of lust, hot impressions of throbbing desire. "Wow," enthused the bad witch, laughing, "I guess Kilnor is into edging, huh?"

"Sure is, baby…he's a regular loosh factory in there."

"Well, who am I to spoil the fun? Let's keep him that way and take a quick shower…then I'll give him the pleasure of being properly carved. Oh, yeah…that's what he wants, isn't it? Wants his rind cut into and little parts yanked out of him. Yikes, what a gross, *weird* pumpkin he is…ugh, so pathetic."

"Boy, he really likes it when you call him pathetic."

"All pathetic men do…come on, Master. Now that you've shown him how a real man fucks a woman, let's leave him there for later…"

"Ah, you know…he does have some businesses to run. Hold on." Plucking up a pumpkin seed, Satan blew the breath of life across it and soon a vacant replicant of Kilnor stood staring into space, oblivious to the hot naked goth that the real Kilnor would have killed to see. "Go home and take care of your original's business until his pumpkin rots," commanded the Dark Lord, waving the magickal duplicate away. "At least, answer the door for his trick-or-treaters so nobody think he's died or something."

Sabine beamed with pleasure as the copy shuffled away, relying on Kilnor's memories to navigate Sabine's house and the town through which it was soon to wander.

"Why, Kilnor," enthused the bad witch, beaming down at the captive pumpkin who had made the mistake of consenting once, which was more than enough for the Devil and his ilk, "aren't you excited? Now there's nothing stopping you from playing the part of my pumpkin for a few days. Don't worry, it's almost Halloween…you won't be here very long in the grand scheme of things. But just think how good it'll feel when you're human and can jerk off again! And you think you were full of cum *today*, pumpkin-boy…just you wait…"

The next afternoon, Clarinda—looking particularly blonde and sweet and fuckable in that tight, hardbodied way of hers—came over with a spring in her step and a potato salad she'd made too much of, which was her usual convenient excuse for coming over to fool around with Sabine unscheduled. She stopped halfway up the path with a gasp of delight. "Oh! Why, Sabine, I thought you didn't like Halloween."

"It's such a stereotype for witches to like Halloween…you have to carve a pumpkin, though. Jack-o'-lanterns keep away bad spirits."

And bad reviews. Clarinda smiled and handed over the dish of potato salad that Sabine pretended to like because she wanted to get laid. Then, hands free, the good witch bent down to smile at the pumpkin's front.

"Is this some kind of cartoon character? She's cute! Who is she?"

"Oh, she's an anime girl…Tentacle Girl Ami-Chan."

"Huh! Is she some kind of squid person?"

"Oh, no, she's a regular magical girl."

"But then what are these tentacles doing coming out of her dress?"

"Haha, they're not coming *out* of her dress, baby…come in, I'll show you an episode or two. I just started watching it! It's not half bad, really…more satirical than I expected."

Grinning with pleasure down at her jack-o'-lantern, Sabine blew Kilnor a kiss and swore she heard an incel's moan of argumentative anguish while shutting the door after her friend. Probably wanted to argue about the show being much better than "half bad," but what could you expect from a sorcerer so prideful? Some people never learned their lesson…

While Sabine carried the potato salad to the kitchen, her phone buzzed in her pocket. Humming, she emptied her full hands and slid the device from the back of her jeans. She glanced absently at it, ready for a call from her Dark Lord or a funny text message from Gina…and instead she got a notification that she'd received another new review.

"What"—the bad witch swore—"*one star?* These ungrateful little—"

Ugh! No…some people really *didn't* learn. Annoyed, flicking a glance at her faded reflection in the window where Bonesy worked hard to finish the deck she hadn't even really thanked him for, Sabine sighed and put her phone away.

"Just a second," she called to Clarinda, waving a hand toward the living room while striding toward the back door. The wooden portal groaned beneath her hand and the skeletal slave who had once been a delivery driver of some sort jumped to attention, almost dropping his hammer in the process.

"Hey," said Sabine, looking at the nearly complete deck, "good work."

Bonesy relaxed a her praise. She glanced coolly over her shoulder. "My friend and I are going to watch this funny anime," said Sabine. "Do you like cartoons? You can take a break if you want."

After a few seconds of pause—probably trying to determine if this was some kind of trap—the skeleton nodded his dusty skull. Sabine stepped aside and held the door for him. "All right," she said, "well come on, then…just one episode. Maybe two, if Clarinda's cool with it."

While Bonesy rattled past her, looking as pleased as a magickally enslaved dead man could look, Sabine's phone buzzed in her pocket again. She glanced at it, braced for more annoying news, and instead sighed in relief to read the words *Your review has been edited!*

Look at that! Five stars.

You know, sometimes Sabine really just had to give people the benefit of the doubt.

The Witch's Eldritch Wingman

WHILE TENTACLE GIRL Ami-Chan really lived up to her name amid the brightly flashing colors of the anime unfolding on the television screen, Clarinda passed the joint back over to Sabine.

"I can't believe they put this stuff in a *cartoon*," said the good witch, scandalized as always. "I mean, it's just so—"

"It's not a *kids'* cartoon," Sabine pointed out between puffs of the joint. "And anyway, it's just a running gag or whatever. It's satirical. It isn't like it's a hentai, where you're seeing full tentacle-in-girl penetration."

"Why would I ever *want* to see that?"

"Uh…because it's hot, obviously."

Clarinda's cute little nose wrinkled in disgust. "Not *really*. I mean, it's very weird. Who on Earth would ever want a tentacle inside of them?"

Reminded her that Satan hadn't been by to see her in a few nights. "Master fucks me with tentacle appendages all the time! It's great." Sabine grinned, wiggling her eyebrows and luridly assuring her girlfriend, "They're awfully flexible."

"Blech! I don't know. Penises are already weird-looking enough. Thinking about a slimy tentacle, I just don't understand how anybody could find that exciting."

Clarinda was really going to have to learn to not tell Sabine these things.

Historically speaking, the bad witch took such claims as a challenge. It seemed to her that the lady doth protest too much—like, why would Clarinda make noise about it at all if she weren't at least curious about the whole thing? That was what questions were for…sating curiosity.

That night, after walking Clarinda home to the bright and cheery house down the street, Sabine returned to her brooding Victorian and considered the contents of her library.

Tentacles, tentacles! Maybe she could send Master over to give Clarinda a good, hard seeing-to…ah, but Satan's tentacle-like appendages only became apparent as he drew closer and closer to his true form. Seeing him in his aspect as Lord of the Flies would have probably cured Clarinda of any and all interest in messing around with the Devil and his bad witch.

So they were going to have to employ the help of a third party. But who? This was also tricky. Clarinda was so up-tight that, well, anything done to her would probably be…well. 'Non-consensual' was such a strong, controversial word. Why, you could hardly even get away with that kind of thing in *fiction* anymore, which really just blew Sabine away. She drummed her finger upon her chin and reclined back at her desk, the reflective face of the nearby clock drawing her attention.

"*You* don't mind non-consensual activities in fiction, do you, reader? I mean…it's horror we're talking about here. Erotic horror or regular horror, it's all the same—and, let's face it. All horror is somebody else's erotica, whether you want to think about that or not. Just look at slasher movies… the Alien franchise. Horror is just an inherently eroticized genre, especially since it so often deals with the breaking or justification of various taboos. Is it really the writer's fault if somebody is getting off to something they've written?

"Oh, sure…rape is lazy writing if it's poorly handled, but why is showing a character being raped any worse than showing a character being tortured in any other way? Murdered? All these things happen to both sexes, so I don't buy the misogyny argument. And don't even get me started on rape in erotica. If you don't like it, don't read it. It's just that simple."

Humming, flipping semi-consciously through the gigantic tome bound in human flesh and inked in blood currently open across her desk, Sabine suggested, "And anyway, this wouldn't really be *rape* we're talking about…more 'dubious consent,' as they say now. I guess 'coerced' sounds too much like 'rape.' Whatever. Anyway…things happen to us with dubious consent all the time in this world. Why, the whole book *Green Eggs & Ham* is about dubious consent. And, of course, what ends up happening at the end of that book?"

Sabine paused at a page depicting a slithering black abomination, a beast that resembled more a knot of hideous limbs than any discernible being.

"The protagonist decides he likes it, of course…of *course.*"

Tapping the image, Sabine rose from her desk and carried the book to her attic. There, she opened it back to the page and followed the instructions.

It was easy! The hardest ingredient to find was the fresh blood of a child, but it just so happened she had a whole gaggle of those down in the basement. After dragging the screaming wretch upstairs (talked back to his mother, the little bastard, and Sabine happened to be walking by at the time—the Devil sent the poor lady a replacement who was practically eager to do its chores, and so far as Sabine knew, everybody was happy but the real kid) and slitting its throat over her floor, Sabine kicked the limp body aside to smear a sigil from the blood. Fun! Like finger-painting.

Soon she had the Seal of Nyarlethotep smeared across her attic floor.

After appreciating her handiwork for a few seconds, Sabine wiped a bit of sweat from her brow with the back of her wrist, washed her hands, tossed the kid's body out into the hall so she could remember to bring it downstairs for butchering later, and set about preparing the rest of the ritual devices.

Candles, check. Black salt, check. A picture of Clarinda, recently published in the local paper for her success at a bake sale for somebody's hospital bills or something? Check and check.

Then, Sabine began the incantation.

The lights flickered as she pronounced ancient, alien words and soon enough even her vision failed, but she carried on. The souls of the dead screamed in her ears, howling that she cease at once the summoning of any eldritch abomination let alone one that might take the form of a man—but she ignored them all and continued, continued praying until, at last, a small explosion brought her vision back online and inundated her sinuses with the scent of brimstone.

"What mortal would summon me upon this disgraceful material plane yet again?"

As her senses cleared somewhat, Sabine managed to focus on the swarthy man now towering over her. Damn! Fine as fuck. Look at that hard jaw; those glittering eyes, black as his skin. Why all these evil elder gods and angels tended to appear as well-dressed, sexy men, Sabine wasn't sure...but she wasn't complaining, either. In fact, it was worth noting that most good angels, like the big JC, tended to resemble the modern perception of a hippie. Probably said something about capitalism...and yuppies.

Sabine lowered her head to avoid staring like a teenage girl. "O Ancient One! O custodian of the Old Ones! O Mighty Messenger, I bring you here for a request of great import."

"Name it, then. But be forewarned: the price for dealing with a being such as myself is high, indeed."

"Oh, I know all about that. My Master is the Dark Lord, Satan." While Nyarlethotep looked somewhat taken aback by her blase attitude, Sabine reached into the circle and snatched up Clarinda's picture. "I actually just have one small little favor to ask of you…see this chick here?"

The dark messenger of the elder gods took the photograph from her hand and carefully assessed it.

"I want you to fuck her," Sabine said, yielding a laugh of surprise from the immortal being. "Like, super graphically and super deep in every hole. Oh…no cervix stuff, though. I don't think she'll ever be into cervix stuff."

"My! This is…*quite* an unusual request. Generally cultists want to end the world or gain complete power over it. At the very least, they crave wealth unending or some other such thing. Are you sure this is all you want?"

"Oh yeah, that's all. It would be great if you could, you know, get some tentacles involved or something. You do have tentacles, right?"

"In some forms…" With a stroke of his beardless chin, the tall, thin man who reminded Sabine of an elegant Pharaoh leaned down to pass the photograph back to her. "So it's a matter of revenge, is it?"

"What? No, just for fun. Like a prank."

Nyarlethotep blinked in faint confusion. "You—you want me to fuck your friend for a prank."

"That's right."

"Against her will?"

"Uh-huh!"

"So you want me to *rape* your friend. For a prank."

"Not *you*, too!" Huffing in annoyance, Sabine propped her fists upon her hips and said, "Look, don't get all PC and weird about this. I don't want you to rape her, I want you to ravish her. She's always reading skeevy romance novels where women are getting *ravished* by, like, big burly Fabio guys, but she doesn't understand that sometimes it's just as fun to be ravaged by big slimy tentacled guys! I just want you to prove to her that she'll like it."

Considering the picture that Sabine had let fall to the floor, the dark entity suggested, "You know…there *are* sex toys for this sort of thing. It is the 21st century in which I presently stand, is it not?"

"*Yes*"—Sabine resisted the urge to roll her eyes—"it is, of course, but there's a huge difference between a toy and a real tentacle monster. And, honestly, she's not super into dildos."

"But you think she'll be into tentacles once she tries them, do you?"

"Exactly! Thank you. Yeah, just—you know, give it the ol' college try. Exude some kind of aphrodisiac or something so she'll be *really* into it. I don't know…just see what you can do. I summoned you to help with this, you're the expert."

"Of course, of course. Well…" Nyarlethotep smoothed his tie and said with a chuckle, "I suppose I can see about fulfilling your request."

Excitement blazed in Sabine's heart. She clasped her hands, asking, "Will you, really!"

"Certainly. As I said…most cultists call me upon the earth to ask for some humdrum, boring favor. This is at least amusing—though there is still the matter of your price."

"Well, Master already owns my soul, so you're going to have to pick something else from me."

"Nothing like that…but do you happen to know any authors, artists? Creatives of any sort?"

With a wry, sidelong glance at the dusty but still reflective glass of the old homeowner's portrait propped up against the wall—and the readers perceiving her through it, along with all the other panes of glass or mirrors in her house—Sabine said,

"Maybe. Why?"

"Well…knowledge of my being is not as prominent as it could be. I think it's time that I become more readily represented in art and fiction again. I'd like someone to resume spreading the word, as it were."

"Uh-huh, representation in fiction is very important, it's true…all right, yeah, I know somebody. So you'll do this for me if I get her to put you into a story?"

"Of course. I always honor my bargains."

"Yeah, so does Master…" Chuckling, Sabine rose to her feet and offered Nyarlethotep her hand. They shook on it and she said, "It's a deal! I'll have my author work you into a little something, and you work yourself into my friend."

Chuckling, Nyarlethotep said, "Lovely. Remind me of your name again?"

"Sabine the Bad Witch—Sexy Sabine, if you'd rather." She added this with a wink and a pop of her curvy hip, engendering another, lower chuckle from Nyarlethotep.

"Well, "Sexy Sabine," consider it done. Your friend will be taught a little lesson by the end of the night."

Yes! Sabine loved seeing people learn a lesson…especially when she wasn't the one with something to learn. Which, of course, she definitely wasn't…right?

Whatever. Being a bad witch was all about watching other people get karma so you didn't have to. That was what she told herself, anyway…but it turned out not even bad witches could behold the transformation of an eldritch abomination from beyond the stars. Sabine watched with a grin as Nyarlethotep's flesh peeled back from his face—

And that was the last thing she remembered of the night.

Meanwhile, a few houses down the street, Clarinda Lovegood finished saying her prayers. As a Catholic, she tended to stick by the standard, structured Catholic verses—she had always sort of turned up her nose at people who thought it was enough to lie in bed asking God to bless them, their parents, their pets, on and on and on. Prayers were standardized within the Church for a reason. It was a form of meditation. The words distracted your consciousness so that your will could be unhampered by ego or inattention.

But—well, it didn't seem right somehow to pray for Sabine's soul within the context of actual, wholesome prayers that Clarinda was used to saying. Not to say that the bad witch wasn't worth salvation, but, well…call it a form of containment. Clarinda didn't feel very comfortable praying for Sabine during the same prayers she used to contemplate, say, her own sins, or her ancestors' souls.

Still, she had to pray for Sabine sometime—*somebody* had to, anyway—so she would generally remain kneeling for an extra minute, telling her cross something like, "…And please, Lord, forgive Sabine for her practices of black magic, and for seducing me, and for summoning the Devil, and for eating children, and for transforming the body You gave her with black magic—oh, and for the time with the lactation, and…"

It was getting to be a long list. Maybe someday she would just write a generalized prayer of her own to try to contain all Sabine's sins. But wasn't it sacrilegious to write one's own prayer? Ugh…being a Catholic was so hard. She would ask Father Tristan whenever he got back from his stay in the mental health ward to which he'd temporarily retired after the incident with Satan, Sabine and Sister Ignatia up on the altar of the church there.

Prayers finished, Clarinda smoothed her cute pink nightie, shut the window curtains, and made her way into the bathroom with a cheerful hum.

You know, though—for all the sins she'd committed, Sabine wasn't really *all* bad. Why, just that day she had shown Clarinda another handful of episodes of that goofy anime show and hadn't even tried to put the moves on her while doing it. It was so refreshing to get a little respect for boundaries! She'd bake Sabine a cake to encourage her. Why, maybe one of these days she'd even get the bad witch going to church!

You know…for non-sexual purposes.

Daydreaming about Sabine repenting her sins, Clarinda spent many minutes doing her hair and putting it up in curlers. Had to keep looking fresh!

Smiling, lightly patting her tight-wound coils, Clarinda shut off the bathroom light and strolled back into her bedroom with a shudder for the cold night air blowing in through her curtains.

Why—had that window been open when she left the room?

Clarinda's stomach tightened in a,fearful knot. A chill rolled down her spine.

She was almost sure the window had been tightly closed.

Of course, it weren't as though she had any *proof.* It could have been her imagination, she supposed.

Still…

Clarinda scanned the room. Nothing out of place. Frowning, the good witch made her way over and stuck her head outside before shutting the window. Nothing was amiss in her rose bushes down there and no footprints stuck out on her lawn.

Yes, her imagination for sure. All this hanging out with black magicians! It made a person paranoid.

With another chuckle for herself, Clarinda shut off the bedroom light and climbed into her bed with a sigh of pleasure for the cozy warmth.

Yes, going to sleep in clean sheets, now that was one of life's simplest joys! And she was good and worn out from her visit with Sabine that day, so all of two minutes had passed before she was drifting off to sleep…which was why the slithering beneath her bed seemed like part of a dream to her.

Just my imagination, the sleepy good witch told herself.

Yes, just her imagination. The same overactive imagination that tried to warn her about the open window was what produced the strange sensation of pressure across the bottom of her bedspread. It alone was responsible for the bizarre, musty smell spoiling the air. The good witch was so sure it was all her imagination that she was almost asleep by the time the low growl emanated from beneath the bed.

"Oh, God!"

Clarinda sprang awake far too late for action. She cried out, bolting upright, frozen by an admixture of astonishment and fear to watch the long black tendril sliding out from beneath her bedspread. Only when its hypnotic gyrations punctuate in its attempt to wrap around her bare foot did she realize she needed to escape. When she turned to scramble up, a multitude of the hideous black tentacles had risen up on all sides of her bed.

Clarinda was trapped.

"What on Earth is this—Sabine? Where are you? I know this is your doing—agh! Let *go* of me—"

The growl turned into a noise like a low chuckle—the kind of chuckle an animal would make, if animals could laugh. All the while the tentacle that gripped her ankle slithered farther up her leg, winding steadily around the pale limb and easing its tip beneath the hem of her nightie.

You're right, said a hateful voice in her head, a voice like the sound of a coffin lid creaking open to let a hand reach out in the darkness. *Sabine did ask that I pay you this visit…but, after she showed me your photograph, I confess I grew inclined to meet you for the sheer pleasure of it.*

"Well you can just get out of here—hey! No!"

As the tendril advanced up her thigh, she pushed away the

blanket and gave it a sharp slap—hissing as she slapped her own leg in the process. Worse, she yielded no response from the thing that assailed her.

Well…maybe not no response. That hateful tentacle was now joined by others. The ones that blocked her in sprang across the bed and caught her wrists, coiling tight around her forearms and yanking them wide to leave her helpless.

"Oh, you brute! I thought consent was important to Satan! But I *don't* consent, you hear me?"

Consent may be important to Satan…but for the Old Ones I serve, observation is consent enough.

Clarinda's lips trembled. This wasn't some servant of the Devil? At least then she might have had a little bit of leverage over it. Now, as the black tip of that slimy tentacle slithered closer and closer to the crotch of her panties, she realized that was utterly powerless. All the same, Clarinda struggled against the grips of the monster, trying unsuccessfully to pull her wrists free of its briny clutches.

"What are you, demon? Oh, let me go!"

When I've done what I've come here to do, I'll let you go…but by then you might even ask me back.

Another pair of tentacles was encroaching, these now slithering the lengths of her arms to draw down the straps of her nightie. She might have protested if she hadn't been so busy protesting the tickling tip of one tentacle trailing over the crotch of her panties. Clarinda gasped sharply, brow furrowing, infuriated and violated from even that grazing over cotton.

"Stop, damn you! No—oh, stop, stop it—who are you, you wicked thing? Oh—"

That exploratory tentacle edged beneath the cotton barrier, pushing it aside to expose her labia while the other two tendrils exposed her breasts. Moaning despite herself while those wicked tentacles teased her hardening nipples, Clarinda tried desperately to shut her legs by clamping her free thigh against the tentacle-bound one. Unfortunately, another long tendril came snaking out from beneath the bed to catch that ankle and yank her pale legs wide. She cried out, biting back another undesirable moan while the sopping wet tentacle tickling between her pussy lips coated her clitoris with its dripping slime.

Men call me 'Nyarlethotep,' the demonic voice informed her while she sank her teeth into her lip to avoid showing any pleasure, *but that, of course, is the only name men can pronounce.*

"That's—oh, that's ridiculous, that's just—oh, um—a character, a character from H.P. Lovecraft, not a real demon at all—oh!"

Thanks to that initiating tentacle teasing back and forth over her clit, the flow of her arousal had started whether she wanted it or not. She could feel clearly how soaked she was, and not just from the demon's slime. Another tentacle, thicker than the others gripping her legs, slid insidiously between her widespread limbs. This one teased the exposed entrance to her body's most sacred temple, the thick tip edging barely into the dripping hole—just enough to stretch her, to stimulate the nerves. Not enough to fill her.

Howard got his ideas from somewhere, Clarinda…I'm not fictional just because he described me. It only means he understood what most humans were never meant to understand.

Clarinda might have liked to argue, but she was too busy struggling to close her thighs against the tentacle that seemed to be releasing some kind of viscous ooze into her pussy. Heat built in her abdomen and heart and head just to feel it drip back down out of her, and the nipples caressed by the higher tendrils grew more sensitive by the second.

So did her clit—soon, with that evil tendril gliding so teasingly, so lightly back and forth across its surface, the moaning good witch could only beg.

"Please, please! Stop—oh, no, I don't want this! Don't make

me cum, please…I don't want to, I don't even know you—"

Just a bit of harmless fun between strangers…it's good for the soul to let loose now and then, good witch.

The moan in her chest grew to a scream of pleasure as, at last, the torturous tentacle advanced into her slime- and arousal-soaked pussy. Clarinda's eyes widened as her cunt was filled by the slithery tendril, especially at such an aching pace. She threw back her head, curlers falling free from a few locks while she thrashed back and forth.

"Oh, no! No, oh…oh…oh, it feels *so good, but—*"

Then let it feel good, the demon urged her, *yet another tentacle caressing her flushed face. Savor the bliss of being used by an entity as esteemed as myself.*

Oh…she would have liked to argue, but it *was* bliss. Or very quickly became bliss, anyway. Once it had filled her completely the tentacle between her spread legs fell into a rhythm, sometimes removing itself all the way just to give her the pleasure of a complete plunge back in. Her eyelids fluttered in ecstasy while, amid this steady fucking, the other tentacle between her legs toyed leisurely with her clit.

Everything between her thighs was soaking wet and the frictionless. The effortless nature of its touches only made the pleasure more abysmally irresistible. Her heart drummed in her throat: the same throat a tentacle caressed like a lover's hand while its comrades trailed around her nipples.

There, see? Noting her protests had receded, the entity chuckled again. In the corner of Clarinda's fluttering eye another tentacle slid up the bedside, down beneath the bedspread. Soon the ones around her legs lifted her up a bit to present her ass. *Nothing to be afraid of…let me show you ecstasy, Clarinda, true ecstasy…*

"Oh…I've never—never taken it there before—" She whimpered, red-faced and embarrassed as a wet tendril slithered around her puckered little asshole. It felt like a tongue that soon began poking just inside. "Please—I'm so embarrassed—"

That just makes it all the better, the eldritch abomination assured her, provoking another gasp and a low, shuddering moan while it pushed within her rectum.

Now, with two of her holes filled by the slithering beast, her clit and nipples teased relentlessly by its slimy, dripping tentacles, Clarinda stood on the brink of an orgasm sure to be more powerful than any she'd had—yes, even the ones with Satan paled in comparison to the liberating helplessness of being bound, spread, totally used by some hellish entity with which she had no prior acquaintance. Moaning, panting, tongue lolling from her mouth with the sluttish intensity of her pleasure, Clarinda begged without control, "Oh! Please, please—oh, yes, yes, fuck me—oh, please, I'm so close to cumming, you make me feel so good—you do, you do—"

That's a good girl…if there's one thing I have in common with Satan, it's that we both love a pretty woman with an open mind. Here…let me give you a kiss.

Clarinda whimpered as the tendril near her face slithered into her gasping mouth, but she did not protest as its wet, oddly sweet slime mingled with her saliva and somehow only increased the heights of her pleasure. Even when it plunged down into her esophagus she hardly could have minded. Throat as full as her ass and pussy, she moaned, eyelids fluttering, and yielded utterly to the feeling of having every hole pumped hard and fast by the evil beast.

It was mere seconds before the rapid sliding in-and-out and tweaking of her aching clit drove her to an orgasm that rolled her eyes into the back of her head and had her screaming around the thick tentacle jammed in her mouth. Oh! The burst of pleasure of was outstanding—a long, drawn-out climax whose steady fluttering seemed timed to the pace of the tentacles' fucking, or vice versa. The entity kept her held spread-eagle, working her in every hole even while she came…and after, too. Though she was terribly sensitive after she orgasmed, as Sabine loved to exploit, and she whined around the tendril filling up her mouth, it wasn't long before its pumping in and out of her ass and pussy inspired a second, even harder orgasm.

A second…a third…a fourth.

Clarinda screamed in bliss, totally helpless, her eager cunt pouring with fluid of its own and from the beast. That dexterous tentacle soon commenced to push up against her g-spot, working the space again and again, and it wasn't long before its coordinated efforts had her rapidly squeezing pussy squirting wildly around its mighty black girth. The wave of pleasure, once started, seemed never to finish, and while other tentacles rose to lap at the bottoms of her feet like worshipful dogs, her orgasms increased in frequency. She lost count— she lost all conception of counting. Her eyesight failed and she saw behind her fluttering lids an explosion of stars, and the growth and death of vast, distant nebulas, and a beautiful, swarthy man who laughed in a way that was too wicked to be called gentle, but still seemed as such in the way of even a cruel lover's laugh.

By the time its pumping in and out of her every orifice had finally slowed, she had almost lost consciousness. Almost, but not quite. She was still aware enough to gasp for air when at last the tentacle down her throat slowly receded from her mouth; she was still aware enough to whine in protest as the one in her cunt drew away. As though to compensate, the initial aggressor continued teasing and working on her clit, yielding yet another orgasm even though the one sodomizing her also made its exit. While she moaned and shuddered through this final orgasm, the ones at her breasts slid away. That one dedicated to pleasing her clitoris finally disappeared beneath the bed. Only then did the others around her limbs let her down, keeping her held for just a moment as though in a cosmic embrace.

There, said the entity. *Not so bad, is it?*

"No," said Clarinda between gasps, "no, I guess—I guess it's not."

Good. Sweet dreams, Clarinda—

"Wait!"

The tendrils had released her arms and legs but now paused at the edges of her bed. She thought reflexively of submarine periscopes but couldn't muster the strength to smile, still awash with anesthetizing bliss as she was.

"You should—you should come back again sometime," Clarinda managed, staring blearily at the ceiling.

Chuckling with low pleasure, the entity resumed drawing its tentacles back beneath the bedframe. *As you wish, mortal... and you know, I had such a good time...I don't think I'll demand much of you at all.*

While the tendrils disappeared into the darkness beneath her bed, perhaps waiting until she was asleep to exit through the same window by which it entered, Clarinda scoffed a little.

'Much at all...'

Typical evil being from beyond spacetime.

Whatever.

It knew how to get down, anyway.

Sabine awoke the next morning with a splitting headache, vague memories of some bat-winged and tentacle-covered abomination, and a child's rotting corpse at the bottom of the attic ladder.

"Fuck!"

Scowling, the bad witch put her hands on her hips and glowered at her reflection in the dusty glass of the stored portrait. "You should have woken me up—did I really miss the whole thing?"

Before she could further complain to the inter-dimensional voyeurs with whom she spent most of her free time, Sabine realized what had awoken her. The doorbell rang again, now with a sharpness that seemed to indicate it was perhaps the fourth or fifth time. When Sabine had made it downstairs, Clarinda was almost leaving—and taking her tray of cinnamon rolls with her. Emergency! Gotta get her to stay.

"Hey"—Sabine, out of breath, threw open the door and grinned luridly at her friend—"hey, sorry, I fell asleep in the middle of a ceremony last night. Wow! Did you bake those for me?"

"I *should* tie you up and make you watch while Cable Dog and I enjoy them in front of you…but, yes. They're for you."

"You shouldn't have!"

"No," agreed Clarinda, "I probably shouldn't have."

With an expectant grin, Sabine asked, "Say, you're in a mood! Did something happen last night?"

The good witch maintained her dry expression. "Don't act like you don't know why I'm miffed at you."

"Come on—it wasn't even a little fun?"

Uh-huh. There was that blushing reaction she'd been expecting before opening the door. "Well! Well—why don't you let me in and I'll tell you about it."

Beaming all the wider, Sabine stepped aside. "Oh, please do! Then we can finish the first season of *Tentacle Girl Ami-Chan*…hey! Don't give me that look."

"I'll give you more than a *look*, you bad witch…"

Sabine cackled as she accepted the tray of cinnamon rolls from her friend's hands. "Baby, flattery will get you every-where."

The Witch's Alpha Pledge

TO SAY SABINE hated Halloween was too strong of a word. She *disliked* Halloween. It rubbed her the wrong way. Why should she be expected to answer the door and pass out candy all night to other people's kids? On the one hand, adults were supposed to drink and have fun, but on the other hand it was a holiday that came with all kinds of social expectation. As she had told her newest doll, Alma, the bad witch preferred to spend trick-or-treat inside, eating dollar store candy and re-watching old horror movies.

For the most part, this worked out great. But the year she met Jimmy Zevron, well, it was a little different. She should have known it was going to be a funny trick-or-treat when, a few days before, the grocery delivery arrived not just with the bags of candy she'd requested, but several cartons of unrequested eggs.

"Hey," she said with displeasure, having noticed the discrepancy only as the delivery person drove away, "I didn't order these! Although, all the baking I'm doing, maybe I should have…"

Nah. Even by the standards of her baking rate these days, Sabine couldn't help but think 72 eggs was just a little excessive.

"What's all this supposed to be for, Master?"

"I didn't order anything," insisted Satan from where he reclined for a post-coital cigarette that was triggering Sabine's rage-inducing nicotine cravings like woah. He was a tempter, all right. Struggling to remember that she'd quit for good, she turned away and studied the cartons of eggs.

"Yeah," she said, "but usually when something "accidental" happens, it's because you're up to something."

"Me? Up to something? Baby, Sabine, when have I ever been up to anything that didn't benefit you in the end?"

"Usually when you're trying to punish me."

"Have you done anything I need to punish you for lately?"

"Well…nothing meriting an *elaborate* punishment." She frowned down at the eggs again before deciding after a few seconds, "I suppose they do seem pretty harmless…unless a few of them are rotten."

No response. Sabine rolled her eyes and glanced over her shoulder just to check that Satan did, in fact, "pull a Batman" on her, as fellow coven member Hazel often put it. Yes, gone. He loved to disappear when nobody was looking…usually once he had gotten laid. Snorting slightly, shaking her head, Sabine tightened her robe around her waist and looked somewhat wryly into the mirror over her key hook. "You know, he's always doing this—teaching me lessons I never asked for but that he thinks I need. I suppose that's what Lords are for, whether Good or Dark, but what a drag! Sometimes I just want to get laid without learning a big karmic lesson, you know? Although…well. Not everything has to be about me, does it, reader?"

Tapping her chin, the bad witch said after a few seconds of fond sort of nostalgia, "You know, it just so happens that this reminds me of a story. What's that? You want it to be about *me?* You flatterer…well, I'm in the story, of course. But the world doesn't revolve around me all the time. Sometimes I like to think about what, say, Clarinda is doing. Only—no, she's so boring when I'm not around to rile her up."

Pushing up the sleeves of her robe, Sabine removed the half-smoked joint from the nearby ashtray and lit it while reclining in her couch. "So, why don't we tell a story about somebody different? Another friend of mine…you'll like this one, trust me. I like to call it, "Night of the Alphucc Boy Werewolf." Or, as the title page told you it was called…"

THE WITCH'S ALPHA PLEDGE

Jimmy Zevron had been, in no specific order, paddled, tased, woken up at 4 in the morning by the banging of pots and pans, and stripped of his clothes before being made to run across the quad while his alleged fraternity brothers laughed themselves until they nearly pissed. Why exactly Jimmy's mother had insisted he join such an organization, the young videogame developer wasn't really sure. Frankly, he wasn't even sure what he was doing at Fort University when the truth was that he would have more time to practice writing code and creating assets if he just kept up a fulltime job and worked on his passion in his off hours.

Network, his mother said. Expand your horizons. Get out of my house and let me live my life. Blah, blah, blah. Parents were so unreasonable! Jazzy Jeff and the Fresh Prince understood it, baby…they just didn't understand.

Although Jimmy did have to admit that his mother had a fair point about at least one aspect of the frat. Alpha Tau Pi did a lot of work around the community and so, when it came to things like spending forty hours working at the local soup kitchen, well…frankly he just appreciated he wasn't getting tased. Plus, the last weekend he was there, this total babe—some kind of yoga or dance instructor or something—had been there to help out, too. He couldn't remember her name, but two nights before Halloween he and his prospective frat brothers went door to door trick-or-treating for cans for the needy: lo and behold, who should open the door of a big white house but the same hot blonde. She smiled and then, somehow improbably, recognized him.

"Oh, you! I know you, don't I?"

The two active members of Jimmy's chapter turned to look at him in a combination of disgusted jealousy and true intrigue. While they gawked, Jimmy cleared his throat and tried to keep the awkwardness out of his smile. "Y-yes." His voice cracked—oh, man, time to die.

Clearing his throat *again*, willing his nervous larynx into good behavior, the youngest Zevron son and newest pledge of the Alpha Tau Pi fraternity *("Akolouthíste to Pnévma"*—'Follow the Spirit," a pun referring to the university's dual proclivities of theology and binge-drinking) smoothed his button-up shirt and repeated himself. "Yes, uh—yes ma'am, we met at the soup kitchen."

"Oh, 'ma'am.'" She blushed and rolled her eyes while waving a hand. "Please, I'm not old enough for *that*...'Clarinda,' 'Clarinda' is fine."

"Clarinda," repeated the young man, pleased with the sound of it, briefly floating away into thirsty fantasies at the woman's expectant, polite smile. She was looking at him. Waiting for something. A marriage proposal? Oh! No, no, haha. "Uh! Uh—ah, ma'am, Clarinda, we're with the Alpha Tau Pi fraternity, and we're just here hoping to collect some canned foods for the homeless. If you would have any to spare, we would sure appreciate it."

"Aren't you boys just *sweet*. Of course I do! Come in, you three wait right here."

While the young men edged into the brightly lit foyer, the two chucklefucks—uh, that was, frat brothers—who had come in with Jimmy leered after Clarinda on her way to the kitchen. "Just imagine running a train on that hot little ass," said the one, a football player whose voice was not nearly quiet enough for Jimmy's liking.

"Yeah—too bad we brought nerd-boy here. Chad would have had her gagging for it for sure."

"Can I get you boys some water while you're here?"

"No, ma'am," called Jimmy, glancing sidelong at his fraternity brothers.

"We won't be long. Say, uh"—Clarinda returned much to Jimmy's relief, and he opened the bag in his hands to receive the armful of canned corn and green beans she dumped into the waiting vinyl liner—"it seems like a lot of the houses on this street have their porch lights off. Are your neighbors mostly at home, do you think?"

"Sure they are! Go ahead and try everybody—it's worth a shot at least. Oh, but—"

Now it was Clarinda's turn to sound a little nervous. Her laughter had a strained note and seemed to trail off before it had even begun; as she spoke, her eyes trailed westward and she said, "Except, well, the big blue Victorian down the way, you might just want to skip that one…I don't think Sabine is very, uh, forthcoming with visitors."

One of the frat brothers did a double-take on the name, having spent most of the conversation pretending like he was inspecting the contents of the bag when really he was staring down Clarinda's a-line dress. "Sabine," said the frat boy. "Wait, is this where the witch lives?"

Jimmy laughed, shutting the bag and relieving his so-called brother of his excuse to ogle the nice lady who had just given them more cans than anybody else who'd bothered to answer the door.

"A *witch*," mocked Jimmy, arching a blond brow toward a hairline that had become somewhat disarrayed after a day of marching all over town. "And you call *me* a nerd!"

"Because you are," muttered the other frat member, a business major named Tom. Clarinda scoffed lightly.

"Oh, now, you boys shouldn't *tease*. Jimmy here is very sweet. He was awfully enthusiastic about helping at the soup kitchen."

"I'm sure he was," said the first frat member, the football player named Mike, eyeing Clarinda a little bit more openly than he probably should have.

As she turned and caught his stare, he said with a light cough, "Jimmy is one of the most enthusiastic new pledges we've had in a long time...we're only teasing him. But anyway—"

The jock leaned forward a few degrees, eyebrows working with intrigue. "This is really the neighborhood? Sabine the Bad Witch, the lady who turns people into dolls and lures kids into her basement to be made into pies?"

Jimmy absolutely couldn't believe what he was hearing. Sure, maybe he didn't get out much, but the idea that these very down-to-earth frat brothers—the sort of guys who had no business going to a college that was practically a starter seminary—had any belief in witchcraft was lunacy to him.

The pledge looked at Tom to try to laugh with him about the absurdity of it all, but the business major looked grimly serious. Then, looking back at Clarinda, he found no trace of humor in her face, and, well...he started to get a little nervous.

But—people fucked with pledges all the time. No way was he going to buy into this and look like a total ass, even if Clarinda nodded solemnly and related to the boys, "I keep trying to tell her that she has no business playing judge, jury and executioner for kids who don't go to bed on-time, but she doesn't listen to me. She just keeps insisting that it's okay because she sends a copy home to—well, you don't want to listen to me ramble about witchcraft, boys."

"My grandmother," said Tom abruptly, his blue eyes flashing toward Clarinda, "told me once that her sister was taken away by a witch for talking back and was never the same again."

While Clarinda made a sympathetic noise (about as lame sounding as somebody who had just told her their grandmother was a polio survivor, to be honest—the kind of meaningless sympathy that people showed just to get out of conversation), Mike said, "Far out," and Jimmy tried not to make his eyeroll too obvious. "You boys just be careful out there," Clarinda told them. Then, in a motion that all but stopped his heart and made him forget all about this witch nonsense, Clarinda reached out and touched Jimmy's hand. "Thank you for doing something so kind like this. Oh, it makes such a *difference* when young people care about their community."

Bolstered by this, standing up a little straighter, Jimmy considered that joining a frat maybe wasn't the worst thing his mother had suggested in the history of the world. "It's our pleasure, Clarinda," said the pledge, all the more pleased because he had remembered to call her by name this time. "Have a nice night."

"You, too! Happy Halloween!"

Soon the door shut and the young men found themselves on the porch again. Jimmy had made it down the stairs and was in fact halfway up the sidewalk when he realized his brothers weren't following and were instead whispering busily on the porch. "What's the matter," called Jimmy through the growing darkness of dusk, that ultra-stillness that seemed to crisp the very sounds of the world around. "You guys afraid, or something?"

Sharing a look of silent derision for the pledge who was suddenly just a little too confident, the frat brothers made their way down from the porch and caught up with him while he shifted the now really rather heavy bag from hand to hand. When they were near enough to speak at a far lower volume than normal, Mike asked, "Didn't your mother ever teach you about witches?"

All right. It was sort of funny at first, but now they must have thought Jimmy was stupid. And bringing his mother into it? "Of course nobody taught me about *witches*. Why would they teach me anything about characters from fantasy books? Fairy tales? I mean—I guess I know superstitions about witches. Like, my mother does say that if you don't clean up your trimmings once you've clipped your nails, a witch will use them to do magic on you."

"Fuck yeah they will," Tom insisted, obviously unable to hold it in anymore. "And all kinds of other crazy shit, too."

"You guys are nuts," insisted Jimmy. "No way are witches real—stop spending so much time going through the conspiracy theory videos people put up on Youtube. You know, while we're on the subject of things my mother told me, she also used to tell me that if I was bad she'd sell me to the gypsies."

Mike lifted his eyebrows meaningfully. "Where do you think that kind of thing comes from? Witches, bro."

Damn. If these two kept it up much longer, Jimmy might start thinking they actually believed it. Unwilling to fall for their ruse and look like the laughing-stock of the frat, the pledge shook his head and tried to turn away. "Quit messing around and let's finish with this neighborhood."

He got all of a step away before Tom, a note of something close to eagerness in his voice, said, "All right, tough guy— since you know better than us, why don't you prove how brave you really are?"

"Oh, God. I didn't say I was *brave,* I just said—"

Ah, too late. Tom snatched the bag of cans from Jimmy's hand and left him standing annoyed and interrupted while

Mike said, "Yeah, smart guy, if you know better than us, why don't you just go up to the witch's house by yourself?"

"That's not enough," said Tom quickly, looking back up at Clarinda's bright and cheery home. "You have to get in, and, uh…take something."

"What! I'm not going to take something, that's stealing."

The frat brothers rolled their eyes and Mike said, "Then bring it back tomorrow, dipshit. Whatever. We just want to see that you got into her house and came back out in one piece."

"I didn't realize you guys were so superstitious." Or jealous. Obviously Tom and Mike were just seething with jealousy that Clarinda had recognized him and invited them all inside because of it. "I assume cans don't count," Jimmy rightly asked.

"Nah, it's got to be something else. You could get cans from anybody on the block. Bring back, I don't know—like, a flower, or a weird book."

"Or a kid's skull," suggested Mike while Tom laughed darkly.

"Yeah, or that. Go on, pledge, quit delaying." Tom slapped Jimmy on the ass and the pledge scoffed, rubbing the point of contact with an annoyed look over his shoulder. "Get up there, let's see how brave you are."

Why were Jimmy's palms sweating? He glanced up toward the looming house, the blue Victorian Jimmy described. Honestly, it didn't look too evil or anything. The blue was a nice color that softened the façade and made it look a little less dramatic. He couldn't help but feel if she were really a bad witch, it would be, say, rotting and unkempt, or painted black, or something.

Instead the lawn was very neatly maintained, the paint was fresh, and Jimmy couldn't help but notice even the mailbox had been recently replaced. Maybe people thought this lady was a witch because she was so into Halloween. In addition to the pumpkin, carved but not yet lit since it wasn't Halloween yet, an extremely realistic skeleton sat on the porch swing. The decoration, dressed rather hilariously in a ragged old brown delivery driver uniform, was slumped back in the corner of the bench with its skull hanging back as though it were asleep. He thought about straightening it up but then was distracted by a double-take toward the jack-o'-lantern.

"Is that Tentacle Girl Ami-Chan," he was just saying to himself when the door flew open and he leapt out of his skin. Maybe that was what happened to the delivery driver…or maybe it was just a heart attack.

Holy fuck. Clarinda, who? For some reason, maybe because of all the talk of kidnapping bad children, Jimmy had been braced for some weird old lady with twenty cats and plastic on all her furniture. Instead he got an erection. He had always had a little bit of a thing for goth chicks, especially ones with big titties. But of all the big-tittied goth chicks in the world, Sabine was by far and away the hottest one he'd seen with his own two eyes. He was so taken aback, not just by her surprising opening of the door but by her appearance. To quote a classic horror comedy, "What knockers!" And what thick, slightly scowling red lips. And what impatient green eyes darting up and down his body before hovering impatiently around his face.

"Yes?"

Ah! Shit! Yes, talking. He had to talk his way in. Boy, you know—he'd been a lot of talk before about his confidence, and about not believing in witches and whatever, but now that he knew she was a *hot* witch he had the overwhelming urge to turn around and run. "Uh—uh—uh—hello!"

Somewhat taken aback by his obvious nervousness for the first second, then narrowing her eyes slightly in assessment of him, Sabine said, "Hello," with a light chuckle that made his heart race. Fuck! Ah! He made her laugh. Yeah, please laugh! Cackle, actually. Didn't witches cackle? Shit, he wanted to believe this woman was a witch so badly! If he admitted he'd been staying up past his bedtime, would she promise to lock him in the basement? Oh, man, all the blood had whizzed right out of his brain.

"I, uh—I'm—uh, Fort—"

"Hello, Fort."

Ah! Yeah, he definitely wanted to kill himself. Squeezing shut his eyes and trying to center himself, Jimmy stuttered out, "Uh—n—no, I'm actually Jimmy, uh, Zevron. I man to say I go to Fort University? I'm pledging to the Alpha Tau Pi and—and—I'm here to collect"—don't look don't look don't look don't look—"cans."

Fuck! He looked. His eyes bounced down to the gigantic, insanely perky tits practically spilling out of her black robe. Were those real? They couldn't be, right? Damn, he didn't even care. Anxiously smoothing his hand over his shirt and struggling to maintain eye contact, which, in truth, was difficult for poor socially awkward Jimmy on even the best of days, our dubious hero took a breath and said, "It's trick-or-treat for the needy, and the last thing I need to do before I'm initiated. I have to collect a hundred cans and—"

"Are you *really* going to join that obnoxious frat?"

Jimmy was so startled by her question that he stood, mouth open and muscles frozen.

Most bona fide adults, (that was to say, adults who were out of college and now part of The World, whatever that really meant), upon hearing he was joining a frat, swallowed their own opinions on the matter and patted him on the back. That was the way adults, American adults especially, were supposed to be: willing to say whatever it took to get them out of a conversation without controversy.

Instead here was Sabine, refusing to follow the conversational script. Jimmy felt like he'd been shocked out of a hypnotic trance somehow and blinked rapidly.

"Well," he said, "I think when people picture frats they think about *Animal House,* uh, but I can assure you that Alpha Tau Pi is, uh, an upstanding contributor to society."

"Mm. Are those boys over there your frat brothers?" Sabine nodded past Jimmy, who, grimacing even before he turned, followed her gaze to see Tom and Mike across the street. The two were openly staring through the dark and waiting to see if Jimmy would manage to get into the busty witch's house.

Trying to keep the annoyance out of his voice, Jimmy looked back at Sabine. "Yeah, that's them."

"They look like real assholes."

Unable to help his laugh, Jimmy looked over his shoulder once more and, seeing the two whispered to each other, he looked back at Sabine and lowered his voice to confess, "They sort of are."

"You look too nice to be joining a frat, Jimmy…maybe I'm stereotyping, but I can't help but wonder about any organization that requires you to bend over and take ten cracks over the ass to join up."

"It was twenty, actually," he answered before he could stop himself, instantly humiliated by his own tendency toward honesty. While he averted her eyes from Sabine's grin, found himself staring at her rack again and soon thereafter committed himself to studying the black polish of her toes, she threw back her head and let out a laugh.

No—a peal of thunderous cackling, high and unbridled. His skin crawled for reasons he couldn't explain and he told himself he was being ridiculous. "So, uh—would you happen to have any cans around, ma'am?"

"Oh, a couple…but bad witches never give to charity, Jimmy. We're too busy thinking about ourselves."

"Aha." Damn, it was one thing when other people were telling him this chick was a witch, but it was another thing entirely when the woman herself claimed that she was one.

And not just a witch…a *bad* witch. Torn between the anxiety that urged him as far off the porch as he could get and sudden interest in testing the theory that crazy girls were more fun than the usual ones he could barely make himself talk to, Jimmy ended up standing there helplessly and saying "My friends told me you were a witch, too. Guess everybody knows it but me."

"You don't believe me! Oh, nobody believes me unless they're a witch themselves…or they've had an encounter with one."

"No offense, ma'am, but I don't really, uh, go in for stuff like that."

"That's what they all say. I like it when you call me 'ma'am,' though." Still grinning when he looked up at her—a grin that was pure predatory menace, truly foxy in its inclinations in every sense of the word—Sabine tilted her head against the door frame where she leaned. One fastidiously manicured hand alighted upon her chest, sliding into her robe and over her heart as though absently. "I could prove it to you, if you wanted."

"Like show me some magic, or something?"

"Uh-huh…watch how fast I can make your virginity disappear."

Fuck, did it count if she made him cum in his pants? He was poised to explode, but not so poised that he wasn't totally humiliated by her callout. Literally feeling his face go red, Jimmy stuttered, "How—how did you know?"

"Lucky guess…come on, Jimmy. Just think how much it would piss off your friends."

"They're—not really my friends."

"Good. Then you won't feel bad about making them wait in the cold." Smiling, Sabine crooked a darkly glittering fingertip and backed into the gloom of the Victorian, the door hanging upon in invitation. Jimmy's nostrils flared and he looked around, half expected some prank. This chick hadn't been hired by those assholes, right?

Then again—Clarinda would have had to be in on it, too. And she didn't seem the type to lie, Clarinda…no more than she seemed the type to be in on some elaborate prank with Tom and Mike, who stared in mutual astonishment as Jimmy looked at them, saluted ironically, then followed Sabine into the house and shut the door behind him.

All right: the interior was a little closer to what he'd imagined when everybody started talking about witches. It was significantly more solemn in the foyer where he slipped off his shoes, the vintage anatomical illustrations arranged in frames up and down the striped wallpaper of the hall lending an unnerving effect to the antiquity of the place. Most every door he could see was shut and the stairs to the next floor were poorly illuminated, meaning he had to step forward and squint to make out the painting of the suicidal clown framed on the landing. He had just laughed at it a little when something to the left caught his eye. Jimmy hadn't even fully turned to look before his breath was stolen.

G-cups? H-cups? Did bras get that high? Fuck, oh, mama, Jimmy didn't know a damn thing about women's lingerie but suddenly he wanted to learn. Sabine had divested herself of her robe and stood in the middle of a salon that might have been cloaked in some kind of smog for all Jimmy saw of it. He reeled, quite literally had to brace himself against the frame of the room's entrance, a hand on the heart that drummed out of his chest and screamed as high as his brain and his cock.

"Poor little boy! You look so dizzy. Maybe it would help you if you crawled…don't be embarrassed, people crawl in front of me all the time. Go on…get down to your knees."

Mouth hanging open, stunned and excited, Jimmy did as he'd been bade and hesitated on the threshold even while on his knees. After a brief pause he did manage to kick himself into motion, his hands providing very necessary balance that his legs just couldn't manage on their own.

Holy shit, she was the most beautiful woman he had ever seen, ever. Not that he'd seen many outside of the Internet and, back in the early days, vintage nudie mags stuffed under his uncle's bathroom sink—but how could a woman be more beautiful than this?

While Jimmy was on his knees before her she towered above him, the thick flesh of her thighs extending for miles and decorated at their peak by a soft tuft of black hair that drew his eye even more eagerly than had those incredible tits spilling out of her robe.

Said incredible tits, now free, seemed somehow immune to gravity but if they were fake, they were fakes that looked totally natural. You could tell an implant in porn by the way the flesh strained—Sabine's were perfect, touchable, soft as the waist against which he gingerly placed his hands with an astonished gasp.

"Oh…what a gentle young man…" Sabine moaned softly to humor him as his lips applied themselves to the task of kissing her navel, her tight hourglass waist, her beautiful ribs. Soon he swayed upon his feet before her, his hands clumsily trailing over her breasts while she sighed in appreciation—and, no doubt, patience. Jimmy wasn't very good at touching women because of course he just hadn't. He'd kissed a girl in high school and been dumped after a month of hanging out and watching movies with no move made between either. Everything he knew about sex, he knew from porn, and therefore he yielded to Sabine utterly as her hands landed on his to foster a more daring caress of her breasts.

"You don't have to be so nervous, Jimmy…I love virgins. Not as much as my master does, but oh, a cute young man with no experience showing up at my door? I'm being rewarded for something, for sure. Do you know how to eat pussy, Jimmy?"

"I can learn," he said, trying not to shriek the words too eagerly, chills rolling down his neck as her dark nails trailed over his chest and to the top button of his shirt.

"I bet you're a fast learner, aren't you, baby…how cute you are!" With a laugh to flick open a few more buttons, Sabine trailed her fingers into his shirt and over the light dusting of his chest hair. "Come on…it's very easy. You watch porn, don't you?"

"Well—yes."

"So you must know the basics already." Taking Jimmy by the hand, Sabine arranged her nude body in the nearest chair, an overstuffed velvet armchair beside the crackling fireplace. He gasped aloud while she reclined in the furniture's embrace and spread her thighs, the lips of her pussy opening like the petals of a flower with the motion. The terrible, insatiable agony of desire brought him back down to his knees and, though he slid his hands up her thighs, he hesitated and looked up at her.

"Are you—um, are you really sure about this, ma'am?"

"Oh, fuck, you're *adorable*. Yes, I'm really sure…it's you who should be having second thoughts, but I'm sure it's hard for you to have any kind of thought at all right now…first or second or third…"

That was for sure! Oh, man. The pink flesh of Sabine's pussy glistened in the low lamplight of the room. With great reverence for this, the first vagina he had been permitted to touch, he inched his fingers up the path of her leg and dared tease along the patch of dark curls. "Don't be skittish, sweetheart, you won't hurt me…anyway, I'd like it if you did."

Holy shit—oh, man. It was incredible he hadn't had a mishap yet. Were all women secretly this forward? His mind reeled and he dared to follow her command, his fingers trailing down between her warm labia and caressing just within the silky path. He gasped, and as his fingertip trailed over the soft fleshy nub crowning her cunt, she gasped, too. "Oh—oh,"

Sabine writhed sweetly while he cautiously teased his fingertip back and forth over her clit, her low moans of pleasure drawing his attention away from his work and up to her flushed face. "Oh, that's very nice…Satan bless pornography, oh, all these virgins are just off to a flying start these days—oh, honey! That's right, be bold…"

His finger had found more deliberate, direct pressure. Now he worked the slick bead of her pleasure back and forth while she moaned in wanton bliss. Fuck, oh, it was just incredible! How could he, Jimmy Zevron, make a woman feel this way? And not just a woman, but a *beautiful* woman. Sabine could have been a model in a fetish video, though she lacked the usual array of tattoos and piercings such girls had.

Really, forget models in fetish videos—she could have been a queen, a goddess! Helen of Troy! She was so incredibly hot that he almost came while just daring to trail a finger down and slide it uncertainly into her cunt…praying, you may imagine, that he had picked the right hole, though it was hard to miss when it oozed her arousal so eagerly. That anxiety was probably the only thing that kept him from having an embarrassing accident and spoiling the mood: in truth, oh, just having a finger up to the knuckle in that glorious, dripping pussy of hers made him want to weep, to scream with ecstasy.

At last, his resistance breaking and his mind too eager to experience a taste of that rich feminine odor that suffused his senses with lust, Jimmy leaned in and applied his tongue to her clitoris.

Wow! Wow. He had thought somehow—well, he wasn't sure what he thought, how he had thought a woman would taste. Every woman was probably different but Sabine's pussy in particular had a taste that was…ah, *fleshy,* somehow. Moist. Those weren't really flavor descriptors but they were the only ones that sprang to his mind while he kissed and lapped her clitoris, his uncertainty fading more by the second as he heard how much she approved of what he did. "Oh! Jimmy…oh, fuck, you know, you're actually really good…oh, ah—ah, my girlfriend isn't half as good as you, oh, my, you're a natural, baby, that's right, keep going, oh, oh, come by sometime and give her lessons with me—fuck! Shit, oh, sweet Satan, you're making me so wet—"

Nice to hear it out loud but boy, she didn't need to tell him that. The cunt that gripped his finger grew wetter by the second and, legs splayed and hips pumping steadily into that crooking digit, Sabine very soon all but howled with lust. It was truly amazing, but somehow Jimmy found the rhythm of his finger was almost instinctively guided by the tension of her body—not just her clenching puss but also the legs that, once splayed, soon furled around him. His tongue tried to keep pace with his finger and this strategy seemed to excel. Soon, incredibly, the tension of those luscious thighs seemed to burst like water from a dam, and Sabine gasped, clutching his head with both hands to keep his face pressed down against her pussy while the orgasm rocked her body.

"Fuck, fuck! Oh, yeah! Oh—Jimmy, you naughty boy, oh, you dirty boy, you must watch a lot of porn to do a thing like that on your first try! Bad thing…oh, fuck, forget your frat brothers, let Auntie Sabine paddle you sometime, I'll give you what you need, oh—"

Jesus Christ! You know, Jimmy had imagined his first time fairly frequently, but somehow it had never occurred to him to dream of winding up with a woman who was just so…kinky. Or experienced. He had always expected somehow to wind up with, oh, Erin Innsmouth, who was cute and funny and perfectly innocent and sat a row down from him in psychology and wouldn't know he existed if they hadn't had to meet up in the library a couple of times for a project. Who was he kidding? He was never going to end up with Erin Innsmouth. She was too out of his league.

Although—Sabine, if you asked him, was even further out of his league than that, and her eyes burned with savage lust as she pulled him upright by the arm and leaned forward to hastily unbutton his jeans. "As cute as your ass looks in these," she told him, cementing these trousers' status as his favorite and ensuring he'd now be wearing them basically whenever he could, "I just have to see it—oh! And your *friend*. Hello."

With a wicked laugh, perhaps even witchier somehow than her cackle, Sabine grinned crookedly at the throbbing instrument ready to stab its way out of his boxers. Her eyes lifted toward his and he was amazed he was able to maintain eye contact, but the truth was probably just that he was so stunned he could never have dreamed of looking away. And, anyway…talk about once-in-a-lifetime experiences. He didn't want to miss a second of any of this, no way. Slowly, savoring the experience rather than fearful of it as he was, Sabine smiled up at him and slid his boxers away from his hips.

"Oh! Honey…you must be *suffering*, poor boy…not so little, though, are you, oh—"

With a moan of appreciation, Sabine lifted a fingertip and touched the glans of his cock—

And you know what happened, reader.

"Agh! Hnngagh oh—fuck! Ah—fuck, sorry—"

He was just too overwhelmed! Oh, man, it was a super intense first time to be touched by a woman. And to be touched by a woman so hot? So Siouxsie Sioux meets Elvira with a sprinkle of Morticia Addams banging, smoking, insanity-inducing hot? Fuck, man! Jimmy never stood a chance. He watched in horror as his cock twitched against the touch and the cumulative burden of desire came rushing out of him in a thick jet of cum that splattered across Sabine's face and provoked a soft laugh from her—not the mean, belittling laugh he'd fear, though, but a soft, almost tender noise like a coo.

"Why, you *like* me! That's so nice...I like you, too. Oh!" Moaning, the bad witch trailed a dark nail down her cheek and slid a strand of semen beyond her plush red lips. "Oh... and I like how you taste. Here, you angel...lie down, don't worry, I have the feeling you'll bounce right back."

While wiping the rest of the excretion from her cheekbone, Sabine stood and, barefoot before her, he realized she was just a little taller than he was. Damn, she was right, his cock was going to be right back in action in about two seconds. Well— twenty, maybe. There was a little work to be done but, after guiding him into the chair where she had just been sitting, Sabine made light of that work. Once having cleaned of her face with a catlike hand and elegant tongue, this same elegant tongue lowered to the tip of Jimmy's rattled cock. The pledge exhaled sharply at the contact against his sensitive member, her touch feeling as though it were almost literally electric so soon after his orgasm.

"Sh...just relax, sweetheart. Oh, how cute you are. Your virgin prick is just so sensitive, isn't it! Poor thing." Her lips pursed and he gasped again, wincing slightly while they slowly pressed to the shaft. Soon he was holding his breath; soon Sabine's soft lips parted and she took him into her mouth, warm and inviting and indicative of the hole that had been penetrated by his finger before. It took him a few seconds to realize he was having his dick sucked for the first time ever, but oh, when that realization kicked in—

"There it is," said Sabine with delight, lifting her head away from the cock that hurried upright to please her. "I knew you had it in you, baby...oh, isn't that nice..." The bad witch trailed her hand up and down his quickly pulsing member, the tips of her nails trailing down his shaft to the tightening balls that seemed to scream "At last!"

"Fuck, uh—uh, you're really good at this, Sabine—"

"Oh, why thank you...I'd be humble and say something

like "I try," but you and I both know this is more than a mere attempt at anything. Aah…" Her lips parted and her pink tongue lolled past them, her 'Aah' perversely reminiscent of the kind of response a doctor might yield from a patient while proffering a tongue depresser. Fuck, imagine being Sabine's doctor!

Damn, ah—for that matter, imagine being her chair! He would have done fucking anything to have her sit on his face. What was that joke? About being smothered to death by the thighs of a big-tittied goth girl? Oh, man, it really wasn't a joke. He would have loved it almost as much as he loved the feeling of her warm, moist mouth, ultra-soft but oh so vacuum-tight around the head and shaft of his cock. While her green eyes lifted to his above her hollowing cheeks, she lowered down farther and took him effortlessly into her throat. He gasped sharply, and the impossibly erotic sensation of her nose pressing up against his pubic hair wracked his balls with another fast-moving orgasm. Jimmy cried out, one hand caressing her head while the other braced against the arm of the chair; Sabine laughed with giddy delight, lifting her head away once she'd let his twitching prick spend its load down her throat.

"Oh, Jimmy…you're so flattering."

"Fuck—ah—sorry, sorry—"

"That's all right. I like feeling so irresistibly attractive… don't be embarrassed."

"I thought—I thought, ugh, uh, women were supposed to like guys who—last forever—"

"Oh, sure, I like a good marathon fuck as much as any slutty little bad witch…but I love a hot, young stud who can get it up at least three or four times before he passes out from exhaustion even more. The only man I've met who can do both is Master…and I think for human men, I prefer the latter to the former."

Master? Human men? Damn, she was wild. He didn't really know how to respond but, luckily, Sabine didn't leave him hanging. The bad witch simply applied a passionate kiss to his mouth, the tongue that swirled in against his tasting of sour, salty semen. Fuck, ah, she was so hot he couldn't stand it and soon lowered his head to bury his face in her breasts, his lips curling around a nipple that he teased for a few seconds while her hand reached down between them to steadily pump his cock back to life.

"I have to say, Jimmy, I don't usually open my door for trick-or-treaters anymore...I only answered tonight because we're not having our little candy beggars coming by until Halloween, but now I'm awfully glad I didn't just ignore the creaking floorboards of my porch or Cable Dog's whine."

"Oh...uh—me, too, I'm glad, too."

"I bet you are. Here, cutie, you just relax back in your seat." Pushing him lightly in the chest, Sabine slithered into the chair with him and straddled his hips with those glorious thighs. After a second's consideration, she stopped to remove his glasses and set them aside with a little grin. "You look adorable with them, but I don't want to knock them around when I get too vigorous...I want you to come back because you're ready to, not because I owe you money for new frames." Ah! Fuck, he was going to get to come back? Baby, Jimmy Zevron had never felt so charitable in all his life! Yeah, yeah, he was going to collect cans once a year for the rest of his life now...though he couldn't imagine finding anything better in exchange for that than Sabine. The bad witch hummed, pouting while her hand tugged steadily on his increasingly hard prick. "Mm...it gets stiff again so fast, oh, I love it, Jimmy. You've really never fucked a girl?"

He shook his head, mute with fearful anticipation. Sabine's nail delicately teased around the head of his dick and yanked a sharp exhalation from his lungs, but as her guiding hand gently grazed it back and forth along her dripping pussy, he found he could breathe no more. Not breathe or think or move. He just stayed there, still, watching, absorbed totally in her as the bad witch teased the sensitive crown of his nerves against her own aching clit.

"Oh…well, if I'm going to fuck you, you're going to have to do me one small little favor…"

"Anything—anything, Sabine! Fuck, oh, you're so hot—"

Laughing low, the bad witch made him gasp by just barely lowering her dripping cunt upon the tip of his dick, then lifting away again. "When this big, hard cock of yours is nice and deep inside me, I want you to scream "Hail Satan," okay? Just the way people cry out for God when they fuck in your dirty movies…we're going to scream for my master."

"Okay—sure—okay, of course, whatever you want—"

Her grin widening, Sabine said, "That's right, baby… whatever I want."

Then, with a prolonged moan of pleasure, the bad witch impaled herself upon his aching dick.

Jimmy all but screamed with ecstasy and only belatedly remembered to gasp, "Hail Satan," at his first feeling of warm, wet pussy pulsing around him. A second gasp rose from him while she twitched, tightened, slowly began the slick motion up and down his quivering shaft.

"Oh! Fuck! Oh, Jimmy…oh, that's right, baby." Sabine's hands moved over those great breasts and, hypnotized by pleasure, Jimmy became too absorbed in this wonderful woman bouncing up and down his cock to even question the lascivious vigor with which she, too, uttered the words, "Hail Satan!"

That sound you heard was the sound of Jimmy's sweet, gentle great-grandmother rolling over in her grave to know that the boy to whom she gifted his first Bible had now lost his virginity to a Satanic witch…but rest assured, what his family would think about all this was the last thing on his mind. After having already cum twice and now finding himself amazed to possess any vigor for a third round, he allowed himself to be, well, enchanted. One hesitated to use the term 'expert' or 'professional' in sexual matters simply due to the connotations, but rest assured, Sabine was an incredibly experienced woman.

Her body writhed like a great pale serpent as she bounced up and down upon his cock, her powerful thighs glistening with sweat as they worked her hips over the lap of the young man she straddled. The clench of her body left Jimmy so speechless he couldn't even blaspheme for her pleasure, but she did it enough for the both of them. After catching the pledge's face in her hands, then pushing his jaw away and shift her grip to her shoulder, Sabine looked him in the eyes that were glued not to her gaze but the bouncing of her incredible, perfect, massive tits. "Hail Satan," she gasped, "Hail Satan, oh, fuck, ah—oh, what a cutie you are, I thought I was supposed to *give* candy away on Halloween, not receive it...fuck, fuck, oh, Jimmy, you like the way my pussy feels, don't you? Can you tell how wet you've made me?"

Somehow he had the sneaking suspicion that her dripping cunt had less to do with Jimmy and more to do with the scandalous act of taking a boy in off the street to scream for Satan while she fucked his brains out, but this wasn't really the time to argue. Her words did, however, manage to snap him somewhat out of his hypnotic state, and Jimmy remembered he had hands he could put to use—could fill with the soft, warm flesh of those incredible breasts, or could trail down her stomach, her hips, her hard-working thighs. Sabine moaned wherever he touched her and very soon the shuddering of her body yielded to an extra degree of tension through every molecule.

She braced herself against his shoulder, gasping, staring into his face and encouraging him, "Are you going to cum in me, Jimmy? Going to shoot your cute little virgin load right into naughty, naked pussy? Yeah, you are, oh, I know you want to…"

"Fuck uh—are you—uh—on, on birth control?"

"Don't worry, baby…witches can't get pregnant unless we will it. Or unless our Dark Lord wills it, but, well, my Master would send me a few signs, first. Go on…" The pace of her hips increased and she gasped, a high moan trailing up from her lips and toward the ceiling. "Go on, little boy, oh—give me all that cum, the last virgin load you'll ever blow—"

No need to ask again! Her language was so depraved to him that it was more than enough to send him careening over the edge, and as his hips bucked and his hands pushed down upon her luscious thighs, Sabine moaned, slammed down at his behest, and buried her tongue in his mouth while screaming first for Satan, then for him. Her body clenching tight around his dick was intent on tugging every last drop of semen from his body, and with it went a rush of pleasure better than any orgasm Jimmy had known. The rough, wet kiss she delivered only increased the stimulus, a current from his mouth to his stomach and his emptied balls; throughout their orgasms, her fast slamming receded to a slower bounce, then a rock, and then, as the dust settled, Jimmy came to with this strange older woman panting in his lap, grinning down at him in a crooked way that, well, could only have been called 'wicked.'

"Ta-da," said Sabine when she saw he was more or less back down into his body. "What did I tell you? All gone."

It took him a few seconds to remember what the fuck she was talking about, but soon, weakly, he laughed. "Oh…wow. Guess you are a witch, huh?"

"Told you. Try not to drop any houses on me, now."

Laughing, Sabine kissed him on the tip of his nose and slid out of his lap. Jimmy's cock slid out and he looked at it, wishing for a few seconds that he cold give it a high-five. At last! At last, they'd finally done it. They'd been in a woman. He was weirdly proud of himself despite, you know, not really having done anything…but he guessed he had eaten her out, and even been praised for it. That was something to be proud of, he couldn't help thinking.

"Thanks for stopping by," said Sabine, bending for her abandoned robe and giving him a view of her ass that was so phenomenal he wished he could have taken a picture of it. "Don't worry about the front door, I'll lock it after you're gone."

"Uh—okay. Thanks, uh…Sabine—"

"You don't have to ask, cutie…you can come over again sometime if you've got that terrible itch that you just can't scratch."

Blowing a kiss, then winking his way, Sabine glided from the room and in the direction of those stairs Jimmy had seen before. "I'll bake some cookies next time…I love stuffing bad boys and girls full of sweets."

He wanted to ask her how she was going to bake him cookies when he didn't have her number and couldn't ask her if it was cool to come over, but she was already out of sight, and Jimmy was now naked and alone in the middle of a stranger's house. Uh…hoped she lived alone! Hoped this wasn't some kind of weird prank, after all. Paranoid for a few seconds about the possibilities of, say, cameras, Jimmy pushed himself unsteadily out of his seat and began to get dressed. The whole time, his grin stayed bigger than the downright priapic erection she'd given him from practically the start of their interaction.

Damn! Were his frat brothers even going to believe him? He couldn't believe himself. Maybe he wouldn't tell anyone…it was a pretty crazy story, after all, and he couldn't help but think Erin Innsmouth wouldn't have taken very kindly to hearing rumors that Jimmy had lost his virginity to a hot (crazy?) older goth woman who lived across town from campus. Too bad! He wished he had somebody to brag to, but that was just the way these things went. Some experiences were just so individual you couldn't hope to share them with another person...not in a way that the other person could appreciate, anyway.

Magick was a lot like that, too, Jimmy would soon find out. He had just finished dressing when his eye was drawn by a glint of red upon the coffee table in the middle of the living room. Was that a joint next to it? A pot-smoker, too! Maybe she could hook him up. Chuffed as he was about that, it didn't occur to him for another second or two that he was supposed to present his frat brothers with proof he'd been in her house. Glancing around quickly, Jimmy slid the lighter into his pocket, then made his way back through the house.

The young man had no sooner set foot in the hallway than the growling started at the other end.

Pale, Jimmy turned. Head low, teeth bared, the fur across its back bristling in warning, a German shepherd made its slow and intimidating approach. Jimmy's palm sprang with sweat at once. He liked dogs, of course, but this...this was a *big* dog. A big, unfriendly dog. And its owner was nowhere to be found.

"Uh...Sabine?"

No such luck. The dog snarled and Jimmy backed toward the door, looking around for the animal's mistress. "Sabine," he tried again, "I think your dog—"

As if inspired by his reference to it, the German shepherd sprang at once into fast action. Teeth still bared, it barked, then began to gallop down the hall right for him. Blood running cold, Jimmy turned on his heel and dashed to the door—and saw, with a curse, his shoes waiting there for him. Damn his polite family's values! One hand on the knob, he delayed to bend and snatch the sneakers up, and was just standing upright while turning the knob of the door when the shepherd's sharp white teeth sank straight through his jeans and into the flesh of his ass.

"YEE-OW!"

Considering that he had just been feeling like an actual man for the first time in his life, the scream he produced was perhaps the least manly noise that had ever come out of him. The mongrel held on, furiously attached to the pledge's right cheek, and Jimmy cried out a second time before turning and swatting his assailant over the muzzle with the shoes. In response, the dog released Jimmy's ass and instead snatched the shoes from his hand. Swearing, Jimmy watched the animal go to town on his Nikes for only a few seconds before deciding it was a worthy trade. Wondering if his ass was literally bleeding, the young man threw open the door to freedom and soon had the pleasure of slamming it shut in the angry animal's face.

Fuck! Well that was one way to ruin a mood, for sure. Jimmy rubbed his ass and, though he was grateful no blood was left on his hand, he had the sneaking suspicion that he was going to be in for a real sight when he got his pants off and looked in the mirror in his dorm room. Thank God, a clerical error and kept him from having a roommate to be witness to his suffering.

He had felt very left out of having another student to get to know off the bat, but since he was soon to move into the frat house (assuming they finally accepted him into their ranks), he wasn't too worried about it. That night he was especially relieved. Afterglow interrupted, shoes lost, all Jimmy wanted to do was get home, take a shower and go the fuck to bed.

Of course…getting there was the trick. He realized while standing on the sidewalk that his good-for-nothing frat brothers had left him to the wolves, as it were, probably figuring they were getting him good by ditching him while he got cans from the bad witch. Well…he got his fucking cans, all right, at the cost of his shoes. With no roommate to call and emotionally obligate into picking him up, no car of his own and no real friends to lean on in this situation, Jimmy sighed down at his socks, up in exasperation at the God who was no doubt punishing him for all of his entirely too casual blasphemy, and then, step by step, began to make the long walk back to campus.

The last thing he remembered of that night was looking up and around for the moon.

Knocking filled Jimmy's ears, then the repeated annoying buzz of—something. What? Alarm. Alarm clock. Oh, he had to get up. Groaning, the pledge rolled over and slapped a hand down on the snooze, only remembering after a second to slide the switch to 'off' to keep it from going off in his absence. "Finally," said the neighbor on the other side of the door, adding a passive aggressive, "Thank you," before wandering away with a mutter Jimmy didn't hear.

Ah—fuck. With a headache like this it was amazing the alarm clock hadn't woken him up sooner. Groaning, the young man eased himself up in his twin bed pressed against the painted bricks of the white wall and tried to remember…well, anything. Why was he so out of it? Why did his brain hurt? Had he been drinking? Partying at all? Partying—sort of.

Sabine!

After much delay, Jimmy remembered. Excitement, a pulse of pride, the natural emotions of a young man waking up after his first true sexual encounter filled him in the instant… followed by, after he glanced down at his cock, confusion.

Had he fallen asleep in his pants? Apparently…he frowned and groped around on the nightstand where his glasses always were, then frowned all the deeper. Fuck! Not there? Really, not there? Did he knock them off in his sleep? He slapped a hand across the surface of the nightstand a few desperate times, then very soon was on his knees, looking around the floor as best he could through his nearsighted squint. After about two or three minutes of panicked swearing, he decided they were truly not there. Well…hell. Where were those prescription sunglasses Jimmy had?

In his toiletry bag, barely ever used in their relatively dreary Midwestern town. After frowning at the poor condition of their lenses and buffing them clean as he could on a nearby tissue, Jimmy put them on, tried not to be too annoyed with the midnight blue tint the world now had, and began to get on his knees for one last look around the floor.

That was when he realized what terrible condition his pants were in…and the rest of him. Mud caked his stomach, his chest, his pants and, he soon found when looking in the mirror, even his face. Agog, he ran a hand over the substance and watched it fleck off in confusion. What was going on? Had that hot witch slipped him a roofie?

Now that he thought of it…well, he had no memory at all of getting home. Had he hitched a ride from someone? Though his head hurt, his feet weren't as sore as he would have expected after spending so long avoiding physical activity as much as possible and then being forced to walk something like three miles back to campus. Then, too, the fabric of his jeans was absolutely tattered around his calves, as he discovered when he slid them off. The back, too. Now he remembered the German shepherd's bite and grimaced even before he had turned around before the mirror to see the damage done to his ass.

His grimace relaxed into an expression of wonder—not a scratch!

Incredulous, confused, now wondering if perhaps all of that with Sabine had been all a strange dream, Jimmy poked and prodded at the pale cheek of his backside. No—unless those glasses were really fucking with his perception of color, and they might have been, Jimmy didn't see even a bruise from the shepherd's assault. Unable to make sense of any of this, he dropped back down upon the edge of his bed with his jeans over his lap and then noticed they contained something apart from his wallet and cell phone. After reaching in, Jimmy identified the object right away, but still had to remove it to verify that it was, in fact, the red lighter he had filched from the bad witch's coffee table.

So it *was* real, then. That night really had happened… Jimmy really had lost his virginity to a big-tittied goth chick.

Suddenly, in light of that revelation, the anomalous missing time was a secondary concern at best.

Fuck yeah, buddy! Jimmy Zevron, newest pledge of Alpha Tau Pi, was no longer a virgin. He gripped the lighter in his fist with a huge grin and might have leapt up to do some kind of stupid dance if his head wasn't screaming with agony already. Maybe later, when he'd had some water and was feeling better. And, speaking of water, he needed to shower…and to figure out just what the fuck had happened.

Luckily for his undignified appearance, Jimmy had become something of an expert at avoiding other students on his way to the bathroom first thing in the morning. Nobody saw him covered in the dark brown mud and so nobody was able to distract him by giving him a hard time, but that didn't seem to help him much when it came to figuring out what the fuck had happened. No matter how many times he tried to sort out the events in his memory, he kept coming up with nothing. Going out with Mike and Tom, collecting cans, meeting Clarinda, then Sabine…then Sabine's dog, ugh.

And then—

Then, a big black hole.

No matter what he did, no matter how he mentally retraced his steps, there was just no filling it in. Had he hitched a ride from someone? That would have accounted for his feet not being sore, but it definitely wouldn't have explained the mud, the condition of his pants, or his missing glasses. And forget the glasses—what about his shirt? Undershirt, overshirt and coat—all gone! Oh, man, that *coat*...shit. He was going to have to write to his mother. New coat, new shoes, and new glasses? He was going to be lucky if she gave him the finger for Christmas in two months.

Feeling marginally better after his shower, Jimmy changed into a clean set of clothes, dug his dress shoes out of the bottom of his closet, was grateful his mother had forced him to bring them along, then made his way to the student café and its sweet, sweet waffle iron. Waffle iron! You understood him.

Maybe you could tell him why he wasn't hungry. That was almost the weirdest thing of all. After his vigorous activities the night before he would have expected to wake up totally famished, but instead, once he sat down with his usual hand-pressed waffle smothered in bacon and syrup, he found he could really only stand to eat the meat. The rest of it was about as appealing as ash. Man, was he getting sick? Dissociative episodes, confusion, loss of appetite...what was this? Early-onset dementia?

He slid his phone from his pocket and bent over it, terrifying himself by Googling his symptoms for awhile before the uncharacteristic disgust of Erin Innsmouth caught his ear through the noise of the crowded dining hall. Her boyfriend, another member of the same fraternity that Jimmy was doing backflips to join, was showing her something on his phone.

"Oh, ew! That's awful, I don't want to see *that*, Chad!"

"Come on, baby, it's just the news—I thought you'd think it was cool, aren't you supposed to be a bio major or something?"

"Yeah, but I don't want to see eviscerated *animals*. Come on, get that away from me—those poor cows!"

Jimmy glanced up in the direction of the kerfuffle, glad at once that he'd been forced by strange circumstance to wear his sunglasses. Nobody, least of all Erin, could see him watching as she shoved her asshole boyfriend's phone away, then her plate of food. "I don't even want to eat now, ugh, I'm nauseous."

"Yeah, well it looks like something thought these cows were delicious. What do you think, Mindy?" He addressed Erin's best friend now, waving the phone in her direction. "Do we have a Chupacabra up here, or something?" "Maybe it's aliens," agreed Mindy while Erin rolled her eyes and shrugged her purse up her shoulder. "Whatever—you guys are so lame. I'm going to class."

"Ah, we're just kidding around! Christ…vegetarians." Sighing with displeasure, Chad slumped back in his seat and waved his free hand dismissively in the direction to the girl who stormed off. While he turned to pick up conversation with Mindy and her lab partner, Jimmy discreetly googled the news story on his own phone, morbidly curious. It was only a minute before he found the article—only a minute before his stomach twisted and, like remembering a fact he'd been forgetting all morning, Jimmy remembered his mouth filling with blood, and dirty bovine flesh catching on his teeth, and the hunger, and the power, and the screams—

A few seconds later the pledge was stumbling out of the dining hall to puke in the bushes. That was an awful lot of vomit for somebody who had no memory of eating dinner. Glad nobody was around to see him, looking about all the same, Jimmy wiped his hand over the back of his mouth and stumbled of in the direction of the dorms to brush his teeth and try to rationalize.

He must have had some kind of crazy dream, or something. Yes, that was all it was. In fact, his mother frequently claimed to have psychic dreams, which was always like, "Okay, Mom, that's great, leave my dinner on the dresser and close the door on your way out so I can finish this raid in peace." But maybe… maybe he'd had something like that. Maybe he had, or maybe he had walked past the site of the massacre and, though he hadn't noticed it, he had subconsciously absorbed the details and replayed it in some fucked up dream.

Yes. That was what it had to be. Because…otherwise…

Otherwise. Otherwise! Please. There was no 'otherwise' here. There was a logical, rational, material explanation for everything in life. Jimmy was just tired, rattled from his strange experience with Sabine, distracted for having lost his shirt and shoes. Yet the possibility plagued him, and during that day's psych lecture he ended up pulling the article up on his phone again to try to read the details. The victimized farm was, it happened, along the highway Jimmy would have taken home had he ended up walking back from the neighborhood where Sabine lived.

But, obviously, he didn't walk home. Obviously! Yes, somebody must have picked him up—and Jimmy, in a fugue state from the surreal experience of having lost his virginity in a practically anonymous encounter with a looney goth, must have fallen asleep on the way, or something. His shirt and other lost items? Maybe he just left them at Sabine's house. Surely that was all it was.

His head hurt harder every time he thought of it. Finally, by the lecture's end, he bolted up from his seat and made his way out of the lecture hall, this second spell of nausea tampered down by the fresh air outside. What class was it next? German? You know, fuck German. He wasn't really in the mood that day.

In fact, he was exhausted. If he didn't know better he would have thought he hadn't slept all night. Barely noticing (but still definitely noticing) how Erin looked at him for the first time since their library study group while he passed her on the way back to his dorm, Jimmy hurried back to his quiet room, shut the blinds, turned out the lights, and fell asleep nearly as soon as his head hit the pillow.

When Jimmy was ten he had gone to Lake Tahoe with his parents, and he was there now, in the same hotel casino where he'd wandered in astonishment as a boy. Amid all the bright-colored, clanging, mostly digital slot machines, people of all ages and genders were stupefied by the devices whose buttons they hit over and over. Few modern slot machines had the classic 'arm' of the mechanical models; most were now the equivalent of a videogame designed for, say, somebody with disabilities. One single button to be hit over and over with the promise that maybe the lucky might get a little bit of money. Almost as much as they came in with, sometimes.

Even as a ten-year-old, Jimmy had found the machines confusing and depressing. Why would anybody lose money this way when they could just play videogames at home? He didn't understand gambling addictions, didn't understand the appeal of slots that weren't cool mechanical pieces of art.

But one machine, bright red, caught his eye at the far end of the casino. Nearer to it, and he could make out the bright orange words plastered over the flames of the unit's case: *THE DEVIL YOU KNOW*. The game's name. Jimmy stood in front of it, somehow knowing that if he played, he would win big— not in the way that a gambler knew this time would be the time before striking out as usual, but rather the way a tightrope walker knew after years of practice on the same routine that they would get to the other side safe and sound.

Jimmy patted his pockets. His wallet was upstairs in the hotel room. Fuck! Just as he knew he would win, he knew that if he dared go upstairs to retrieve the lost wallet somebody else would take his place at the machine and, with it, the winnings that could have, should have been his. He had just been jamming his hands into his pockets only to find a red disposable lighter when a figure slid into his periphery.

"Need a quarter?"

The young man glanced over and found a slick-looking guy in a dark blue suit stood to his left. Pinched between the stranger's thumb and forefinger gleamed a shiny twenty-five cent piece. Jimmy took one look at the man's sharp features, his strong nose and dark brows and combed back hair, and knew just as he knew that he would win big at this machine that this guy was the Devil himself.

"Sure I do," answered Jimmy, a little frightened but nonetheless able to maintain a steady tone of voice. "But—not from you."

"Ah, come on. Don't be like that, kiddo. I'm not all bad as they say…everybody wants to talk about the people who tried to screw me over and got hell for it, for lack of a less on-the-nose phrase. What about all the people I've helped? What about Sabine?"

"You know Sabine, really?"

"Sure, I know Sabine. I know everybody, no matter whether or not they know me. Here, take it." With a quick free hand, the Devil caught Jimmy's unready left one and forced his palm upright. He pressed the token into the young man's palm and released him before Jimmy could even think of trying to escape. "It's on the house," the Devil said. "No obligation to do anything at all for me. You're welcome."

With a reluctant sidelong glance, Jimmy fed the quarter into the machine and bent to hit the button. The screen representing what in mechanical slots were once reels of cartoon images now flickered through a poorly randomized series of the same, and one at a time, Jimmy watched the reels slow, then snap to stops. First a cheeky red cartoon devil, horns and goatee and nothing like the man to his left, disappeared beneath the appearance of a golden oval—a halo, Jimmy guessed. In the second column, a pile of fruit also yielded to a halo, and in the third, a little icon representing fire looked like it was doomed to stay until it also disappeared to make room for that symbol of angels and divinity.

The machine lit up and began to chime wildly. Money poured out of its mouth, ceaseless quarters vomited across Jimmy's feet and the poorly colored carpet that reminded him of the kind they put in movie theater lobbies. So taken aback that he didn't even remember most modern slot machines tended to operate on a ticket system, Jimmy looked up to find the man to his left receding through the crowd that had gathered to enjoy a bit of secondhand success.

Forgetting all about the money in an instant, Jimmy called, "Wait," and shoved through the crowd to dash after the man. He caught up with the Devil by the casino's central bar, where he'd perched upon a stool and now leaned back with a drink in his hand.

"Don't tell me you want more already," said the Dark Lord with a playful wink.

"Why are you here? Why did you give me that quarter?"

"I just hate how everybody thinks I'm such a bad guy. Really, I'm not...I'm a problem-solver. A life coach, in the modern parlance. It's just that I'm a very strict life coach—and very unconventional. Not everybody's willing to do what it takes to get ahead, after all, Jimmy. Sometimes they think they know what they want—know what's good for them—and they cling to it no matter what I try to tell them." The Devil spread his free hand and lifted his brows. "Can't help somebody who doesn't want to be helped, Jimmy."

"That doesn't mean you have to punish them, either."

"People punish themselves. Look at you, for instance. You don't have any business seducing a woman home alone and taking her property." While Jimmy's face burned like the telltale lighter in his pocket, Satan smiled behind the glass he nursed. "You made your choice. What happened, happens, and the consequences will sort themselves out."

"What consequences?"

"Nothing I couldn't help you with, if you'll let me. It happens, in fact, that I could help you with a lot of things, Jimmy. Say—"The Devil waved a hand and a cute girl dressed as a bunny appeared from the other end of the bar, an old-fashioned cigarette girl whom he only recognized as Erin when she turned away with a sway of her hips and a fragrant flow of highlighted hair. While the Devil lit his newly acquired smoke, he followed the young man's gaze and said, as if he didn't know, "Oh! You like her, do you?"

Jimmy said nothing, too busy staring helplessly after her, the cotton tail attached to her ass luring his gaze like a magnet.

"I could give her to you, too."

"In exchange for?"

"Americans are so suspicious…everything's got to be worth something in your country. I'll tell you what"—Satan leaned back against the bar again, lifting the cigarette from his mouth with a ringed finger and tipping back his head to blow a smoke ring away from Jimmy's face—"why don't I prove I'm not such a bad guy? I'll give you a tip about how to get Erin. And since you won't be comfortable if I don't give you something in exchange, you have to promise to give me a bit of open-minded consideration. Promise to think of other things I might be able to help you with."

Jimmy wanted to refuse. He did. This whole thing frightened him terribly—but, ugh. There was Erin giving cigarettes to Chad, who was so busy drooling in front of his slot machine that he barely even saw how gorgeous, how lively, how cool and smart and funny she was. "All right," said Jimmy at last, tearing his eyes from Erin's ass and forcing himself to stare the Devil down. "All right. Tell me how to get Erin—and if I do, I'll listen to what you have to say."

"That's all I ask." With a smile, Satan gestured the way of the bunny girl and told Jimmy, "The next time you get a chance to be alone with her, you take it, and you tell her, "Sorry to hear about Chad.""

It was sort of hard not to snort at that. As if Jimmy would ever find a chance to be alone with Erin! She was always surrounded by her friends and, even during that group project, well—it had been a *group* project. There had been other people at the library with them every night they worked together. The truth was that, as much as he liked her, Jimmy hadn't spent any time at all alone with his attractive classmate.

"Do you really think that's going to work? And what's the matter with Chad?"

"Only one way to find out."

Annoyed, Jimmy looked back at Satan, close to voicing a complaint about the ambiguous statements of paranormal entities. Instead he found the suited man had disappeared along with his drink and his cigarettes, and at this, Jimmy knew he was dreaming. He snapped awake in his dorm room bed to find four hours had passed—he had slept not just through German but through Creative Writing, too. Fuck...ah, well. At least it was dinner time, and this time, he was hungry.

What a weird dream! He rubbed his face as he sat up and frowned at the dark sunglasses he was forced to wear until he found his old pair, or until his mother could send him money for a new one. All of that was clearly guilt-induced, not just for taking the lighter from Sabine's house but for the whole, uh, generally blasphemous motif of their encounter. It wasn't so much that Jimmy personally minded, but he couldn't help cringing to wonder what his family would have thought of all the Hail Satan, bad witch stuff. Ugh...he had been such an innocent, bright-eyed kid once!

Now, the dark-glassed man pulled on his hand-me-down leather jacket, put on his slightly uncomfortable dress oxfords, and made his way down to the dining hall to grab a bite to eat. Maybe after, if the buses were still running for the evening, he'd swing by Sabine's and give her the lighter, apologize. Maybe he'd even get laid.

Or maybe he wouldn't have to go across town to do that, after all.

He was about halfway to the dining hall when he saw her, his mouth opening in his astonished recognition. One hand hiding her tearful eyes, Erin sat on a bench by the edge of the quad with a tissue wadded in her other hand and the leafless fingers of a tree offering her poor shelter from the wind. Her white-blonde hair rippled in the breeze and Jimmy stopped in place, almost frightened. Surely this was just a coincidence.

Only one way to find out.

The voice rang crystal clear—alarmingly, not with the tone of a remembered dream but with the sharpness of an inner monologue. A voice of intuition. His stomach tightened and he was at once far more aware of the lighter in his pocket; the urge to flee rose up in him, but that same voice of intuition delivered the simple message, *Blow it now and there's no second chance.*

With a deep breath, Jimmy dried his sweaty palms off on his jeans, then made his way to Erin's side. "Hey," he said from a few feet away, announcing his approach so as not to startle her but all the same eliciting a sharp gasp of surprise from the girl who lowered her hand to see him. As her tear-reddened eyes focused on him, he swore a hint of faint red interest bloomed across her face. Maybe he was just imagining things. Maybe it was just because her face was blotchy from crying. Trying not to stare even behind the safety of his sunglasses, Jimmy asked, "Are you okay?"

"Yeah," lied the girl, "I'm fine."

Just say it. Get it out of your system and see what happens.

That voice again. Certainly not his. Not a literal voice, of course…Jimmy wasn't schizophrenic, even if he was starting to feel like it. But it was a thought, a vivid, sharp thought that seemed to come from somewhere beyond him and that had instantly supplanted his usual nervous inner soundtrack of total indecision.

Yes—the voice commanded, and he knew if he followed it, he would get what he wanted. He knew it just like he knew he'd win at that dream slot machine.

So, what could he do?

He obeyed the voice.

"I—uh—I'm sorry to hear about Chad."

The girl's eyes widened and at last her tears looked like they were prepared to at least momentarily abate amid the shock. "Did he *tell* you? Has he been telling everybody at that stupid fucking frat house—oh, my God, I'm so embarrassed."

"What? No, don't be—I'm not in the frat yet, you know. Not really. They could still reject me if they felt like it…for all I know they will, the assholes." Erin laughed a little at that, wetly, and Jimmy said again, "You sure you're okay?"

"I mean, I'm *alive*," was the girl's response, wiping her cheeks with the same tissue she then briefly examined before looking back up at Jimmy. "You want to sit down?"

Holy shit. What was going on? Ignoring his urge to turn around and literally run in the other direction in response to the invitation, Jimmy sidled up and took a seat on Erin's bench. The girl inhaled shakily, her shoulders rising as she said, "I guess half of campus must have heard our fight…I shouldn't be surprised you already know we broke up."

Just be interested in her, said the voice, that voice of intuition that sounded like the Devil's.

"What was that all about, though?"

"Oh, it was stupid…break-ups are always stupid, but this one—you heard that news story about the Bensons' cows over by Highway 37?"

"Sure." Trying as hard as he could not to evoke the tinny taste of blood that flooded his mouth when he so much as thought about the article he read that morning, Jimmy had no need to ape looking disturbed and saddened. "It's awful."

"*Yes!* See, thank you. Chad, he showed me the article and all these terrible pictures, and it was just, like—fuck you, man, I don't want to look at this! But he kept insisting it was no big deal, talking about how cows are already burgers anyway and—I don't want to repeat it, it was awful. Anyway…he's a real jerk."

"Sure sounds like it. Honestly…I think most people in Alpha Tau are."

Laughing, wiping her fluttering eyes one by one, Erin agreed, "You said it! But you've never seemed like a jerk, Jimmy. Why are you trying to get into that stupid house, is it just because you don't like living in the dorms?"

"Well, it does sort of feel lonely not having a roommate, but—"

"Oh, shit!" Her amazement drawing her out of her sorrow just a little, Erin lowered the tissue and gawked at him. "You don't have a *roommate?* Lucky! Why not?"

"I don't know, some administrative problem…I was supposed to have a foreign roommate or something, but they never showed up."

"Wow, geez, that's crazy—I sure wish I didn't have a roommate. Ugh! I hate my roommate. I hate this school."

"Sounds to me like you really hate Chad," said Jimmy at the behest of that prodding inner voice, that voice putting words in his ear and his mouth.

Softly, darkly, Erin laughed at that supposition. "Yeah, well…I don't know, you could be right about that. I used to think he was hot but now I just think I've bene stupid. Who cares what people look like? I like your glasses, by the way."

"Oh, thanks." He almost told her about his lost pair but the intuitive sense in his head made him stop. "I like your sweater," he said instead, earning another little laugh from her.

"Thank you…you know, Jimmy, you seem different today somehow."

"Probably just the glasses," he said, glancing down at his feet and adding, "or the shoes."

"Maybe," she said with an agreeable laugh, more genuine than the others. "Maybe that's what it is, but, I don't know—you've never talked to me before right now. I always thought you didn't like me."

"What?" Unable to help his shock or the briefly sharp pitch of his voice, Jimmy cleared his throat and corrected his tone before going on, "Why would you ever think that?"

"I don't know, you never talk to me—or anybody, really. I kind of thought you were the sort of guy who just felt like he was too smart to talk to anyone…but maybe you're just shy?"

Yikes! Jimmy had never stopped to consider how he came off to other people. Now he wanted to crawl in a hole and die. Did everybody on campus think he was just some know-it-all asshole with no respect for other people? Sure, he was smart, but other people were smart, too. Everybody had something to teach him in one way or another. Smiling slightly, Jimmy admitted, "Yeah, well, I guess I really am shy…" Then, on the Devilish strain of advice running through his head: "Especially around pretty girls."

"Oh—oh! Shut up." Erin laughed again and slapped his arm, and the contact seemed to make his heart skip a beat. Truly blushing, now, Erin said, "Who even *are* you? I didn't know you were, like, a player or something."

"No, no, I'm not! Really—I just, uh—you're really beautiful, Erin. And cool, and—I don't know. Sorry, I don't mean to be weird, I just—"

"No," she said quickly, "it's all right."

Then, while she pondered his face, Erin's lower lip vanished into her succulent mouth. "You know…you're pretty cute, too, Jim."

Five minutes later the door of Jimmy's dorm room flew open beneath his barely contained touch; he hurried to stuff away a gaming magazine while Erin followed him in, smiling a little at the Italian zombie movie poster on his wall. "You totally seem like the type of person to like horror movies," she said. "What's your favorite?"

"I don't know…I used to really like *Night of the Living Dead*, but I've been meaning to re-watch Suspiria, and—"

When Jimmy turned back, Erin stood right behind him. The words flowed from him still, but slower—especially as, with a careful hand, she reached up to remove his sunglasses from his eyes and thereafter appreciated his exposed face with a crooked little smile. "—and that one's uh…definitely high up there."

"Is it?"

"Uh-huh."

"What's it about?"

"It's, uh…about a girl who goes to this, uh…this ballet academy, and—" It was so hard to talk with Erin unbuttoning her shirt and making this kind of eye contact, holy shit, was he still dreaming? How had this even worked? "And it, ah, turns out that maybe the academy is run by a, uh, a coven of—witches."

Speaking of witches…Erin's breasts beneath the black lace of her bra were not as big as those of magickally-assisted Sabine, but they were just as enchanting. Maybe it was her delay in taking her bra off; she pushed away his hand, begging, "Fuck me in the window—do you have a condom? Fuck me in the window, let's make a lot of noise and see if Chad walks by anytime soon."

"Sure," said Jimmy's penis through his mouth, one of many ill-advised decisions that Jimmy would be later forced to admit were not Satan's fault by any means. While the grinning girl led him by the shirt collar to the weird protrusion from the wall that served as a window bench and AC unit and extension of the awkward 70s-style desks, Jimmy stumbled forward and obligingly opened the blinds.

Up-close he discovered he could tell the very powder of her makeup from the hue of her face, his eyes were so sensitive to light and color. It must have been the migraine: at least it was pretty dark outside now. He kissed her while she pushed away his overshirt with a moan and tugged his dark t-shirt over his stomach.

Don't let her push you around, said the voice in his head. *If you want to have her more than once you're going to have to surprise her enough that she'll want to come crawling back.*

Thanks, Satan. Jimmy caught Erin's delicate wrists and repressed his urge to smile around the explorations of his tongue. How eagerly she moaned when he showed a little control! He pushed her back upon that window bench and bent his head to kiss the column of her fragrant neck, some fruity perfume with notes of orange and lavender. He barely noticed how well he smelled, being focused as he was on the scent of woman far more than the scent of any department store *eau d'asthma.* Oh, woman! The taste and texture of Erin's body made his cock rigid in his jeans, but the scent was somehow what did it for him. That humid, human musk, it pervaded the sinuses above his brow and trailed circles around his brain, and down, down, down!

"Oh, Jimmy! I didn't expect you to be so *forceful.*"

Ask her if she's ever been tied up before.

"Have you ever been tied up before?"

"Fuck, and you're kinky? Who even *are* you?"

"I don't really know," said Jimmy, removing his belt in response to this diabolical inspiration. "But at least I know that I'm the next guy who's going to fuck you."

"Fuck, oh—Jimmy—"

This time when his hands trailed around her slim ribs to the hook of her bra she permitted him to open it, and he held his breath to see her rosy nipples. After dropping the bra aside she bit her lip and permitted him to tie the belt around her wrists in front of her soft stomach. With her hands out of the picture, he worked on getting her jeans open while his lips brushed over hers. "I've wanted to do this to you for a long time now, Erin."

"I thought so…I just thought you'd be so much more—*shy, I guess—oh!*"

Erin gasped again as he turned her over and bent her upon that same protrusion of the old in-built air conditioner. While he ran his hands over her hindquarters she moaned, then lifted upon her toes to assist him in pulling down her panties. Her dark bush glistened with very real lust and Jimmy got on his knees to apply the same skill he had with Sabine, his nose buried in Erin's ass with this new position. Ah, fuck, even the dark scent of her ass was phenomenal, but he loved most of all the taste of that hot, dripping pussy his tongue lashed and his fingers spread.

"Fuck, oh, Jimmy! You're so good at that. Why did I think you were a virgin? Ah, ah! Fuck, oh, yeah, yeah, oh, Jimmy—"

Make her call her boyfriend, said the Satanic voice of his new intuition.

"You should call Chad and let him hear me fuck you… make damn sure he or somebody he knows comes by."

"Oh, Jimmy! What an idea. My phone is in my purse over there, hand it to me, here—"

After obeying her and enjoying a few seconds of her struggle to get it open between her bound hands, Jimmy resumed running his free ones over that beautiful, tight body and fingering her gleaming cunt.

As a finger slipped easily into her tense pussy, Erin moaned over her shoulder and begged to know, "How does a quiet guy get so fucking good, Jimmy?"

He had no answer—he couldn't explain it even if he wanted to. It was more than intuition, the things he did and wanted to do to Erin. It was instinctive: yes, wildly and inexplicably instinctive. Primed by her scent and taste, his body ached for her, hurt for her, cried out for the relief of her embrace. While he looked around for one of the condoms he had received in some stupid safe sex gift bag the college passed out at the beginning of the term, the phone rang.

"Hello? Erin?"

"Hey Chad," she said, her voice husky as she switched the device to speakerphone. While Jimmy let his throbbing length out of his pants and rolled the rubber down its shaft, Erin grinned in approval over her shoulder and said to the phone, "I just wanted to talk to you about earlier."

"You finally come to your senses, baby?"

"Something like that...I just felt so bad about the way things ended between us. You don't want it to be awkward every time we see each other on campus, do you?"

"I mean, I guess if you're worried about it..."

Chad sounded distracted and if Jimmy didn't know better those were the sound effects of the latest *Call of Duty* videogame going off in the background. He almost laughed, but then he pushed the tip of his dick against Erin's shimmering labia and instead found himself gasping. Shit! Thank God for the condom...he thought of how quickly he had cum as a result of Sabine's expertise and the intense pleasure of her touch, her body's hot embrace. Without the rubber he might have embarrassed himself in front of Erin—frankly, just having her naked and tied up in his room was enough to make him feel like he was going to explode.

That might also have been his head, though. The bluish tinge of moonlight pouring through the window seemed like too much light the longer he was near it. Ugh, this migraine was unreal! Good thing he had a distraction. As he eased his sheltered dick into Erin's cunt, she gasped and was barely able to respond while Chad asked, "So what do you want to talk about?"

"Oh—oh uh—fuck—what a fucking asshole you are, mostly—oh! Jimmy—"

"Jimmy? What the fuck are you talking about, Erin?"

Erin's moan became a high scream of pleasure as, hands on her hips, Jimmy buried himself to the hilt and steadily drew back out for the next thrust. While he fell into a comfortable pattern, each plunge into her tight hole sparking another throb of pleasure in his brain, Erin lifted her hips back against him and whined, "Oh, fuck, Jim, Jimmy, fuck me like an animal—fuck, oh, Chad, Jimmy fucks me way better than you ever did!"

"What the fuck? Jimmy Zevron? Are you letting that nerd fuck you right now?" "Sounded like you weren't interested anymore," Jimmy grunted, tugging playfully at Erin's cute bob haircut to make her moan with appreciation. While he braced against her hip with his other had and savored the sensation of being buried to the balls in the co-ed, he assured the frat brother through clenched teeth, "I figured I'd just take an opportunity to show her how a real man can fuck."

"You're dead, you fucking nerd. You hear me?"

"Loud and clear, you cuck piece of shit."

While Erin laughed in delight, her head lifting into the fingers that curled against her scalp, Chad sputtered in bafflement and outrage. "Cuck! What the fuck—where are you right now?"

"About to blow a load in your ex-girlfriend, asshole, where are you?"

"About to get Mike and Tom to come with me to kick your fucking teeth in. Aren't you a pledge or something? That's right, I watched Randy break a paddle over your ass two weeks ago. Well good fucking luck getting accepted into Alpha Tau now, asshole—"

"Oh, yeah! Yeah, oh, fuck, fuck, you fuck me so deep, Jimmy—oh!"

Erin's voice grew higher by the second, her tone reaching the pitch of a nearly pained whine as she begged, "Harder, harder, fuck, fill me with that big dick, oh! Oh, you're so hard, yeah, yeah—"

"That's it." Chad hung up on them with a noise of displeasure and Jimmy laughed, bending over to kiss Erin's ear and cheek.

"Guess I should probably make you cum before he shows up to kick my teeth in, huh?"

"Oh, oh—Jimmy, yeah, oh, fuck, sorry, I hope I didn't ruin your chances of getting into that frat, but—"

"Fuck Alpha Tau," said Jimmy, fucking Erin as fast and as hard as he could and feeling a thrill of satisfaction as her voice rose all the higher. Ah, man! Her ass was cute and pert—not as big and grabbable as Sabine's had been but still soft and nice to push against. He landed a couple of sharp swats before settling in to grip her flesh and sink his fingers deep into that soft, yielding skin. "Fuck Alpha Tau and fuck Chad. I've wanted to do this to you for too long, Erin."

"Oh, oh, Jimmy! Oh, fuck, I wish I'd known it would be like this—oh, yes, yes! Jimmy!"

He gasped to feel her flutter tight around him—to realize he'd made Erin Innsmouth cum around his dick. While her body contorted beneath his, he kissed the ridge of her ear, her neck, her shoulder. Her flesh was so soft it made his mouth water: he kissed the same few spots over again and soon was scraping his teeth along her flesh, his tongue lashing against the spots that made her shiver and moan. Fuck, ah! That wonderful woman-scent, it made him want to bite her, bruise her, crush her!

"Oh, Jimmy…Jimmy Zevron…Chad never fucked me like that…"

"Probably too busy thinking about sports," grunted Jimmy to the sound of her laugh. His head swam and when he looked up from Erin to glance toward the window a spell of vertigo overcame him. While he braced himself against the A/C vent, Erin smiled over at him.

"You're funny, Jimmy…you want a blowjob? I'll bet you'd love to blow a big load in my mouth, huh."

Fuck yeah he would. Just the thought of watching his cum drench Erin's face and ooze out of her pink lips had him sliding free as fast as he could and whipping off that condom. The co-ed grinned and turned her glowing eyes toward his while lowering upon her knees. After a sensual dart of her tongue across her lips, she applied that shining organ to the tip of his cock. Jimmy exhaled, braced himself and watched every second of the action as she opened her mouth a little wider, took the glans into her lips, and commenced to gingerly suck him off.

By no means was Erin as skilled as Sabine, but that just made it better somehow. He believed it when she enthused that Chad hadn't fucked her the way he did and had no qualms enjoying an ego-boost from cuckolding some asshole meathead in exchange for failing to get into the frat that had already hazed the living hell out of him.

Fuck it! Too bad! He hadn't wanted to join anyway. Sabine was right, he didn't belong around those cockbites. Anyway, there was something pretty gay about joining a frat, willfully being surrounded by those guys, getting your ass publicly paddled to earn the privilege to commit the same offense against somebody else next year. If only there were some way for him to be surrounded by women! If only.

His forehead broke out into a sweat as his skull throbbed like the dick Erin eagerly worked. While her hand stroked the shaft and her tongue and mouth suckled the tip, he braced himself now against the window frame. Fuck, ah, he was dizzy suddenly!

Maybe that was the pleasure, or the light sensitivity. His heart raced in his chest and his breathing became ragged under the force of finally having a chance to achieve what he'd always wanted to achieve with the Innsmouth girl—and oh, his dick was sensitive! Impossibly, wildly sensitive. It reminded him of jerking off when he had the cold. For some reason when he was unwell his prick got stiffer than ever. Maybe he was coming down with some kind of cold? He hoped he didn't give it to Erin…then she'd never want to fuck him again.

"I love the way you taste," she commented, removing her mouth from his schlong while, down the hall, a burst of noise drew his distracted attention. "What a hot, manly taste—Jimmy? Are you all right? You look like you're sweating."

"I—uh—you're just—so hot—"

"Aw," said the admittedly fairly oblivious girl, winking up at him. "You're not half bad yourself! Maybe we should talk about making this a regular thing."

"Uh-huh—sure, oh, of course—"

"Once you're finished and can talk again, I mean," said Erin with a giggle, going back to work and now putting in the practice of taking as much of him into her mouth as she could. Though he gasped with pleasure, Jimmy slowly had to admit within the privacy of his own head that something was seriously wrong. It was much more than having his dick between Erin's lips that was making him lose his capacity for speech—or for concern as the door to his dorm room began to slam and rattle with the force of the three Alpha Tau brothers outside trying to barge their way in.

"Come on out, Jimmy, you piece of shit!"

Laughing at Chad's voice, Erin wiggled her eyebrows up at him. "Guess I'd better finish you off as fast as I can, huh?"

Jimmy could only pant and moan and gasp for air—the truth was that his brain almost seemed to be stuck mid-thought. He'd only tried acid twice, only because a friend in high school had gotten a few tabs from an older brother and generously shared it with him, but this reminded him somehow of that. There was a moment right at the beginning of an acid trip where language became hard to process—speech was almost impossible. At his feet, Erin moaned and removed his dick with a salacious sounding *pop*. "It's like it's getting bigger," she enthused loud enough for the frat brothers outside to hear it, sliding her free hand down between her legs to touch herself while plunging back to work again.

As much as Jimmy normally would have enjoyed the sight of Erin touching herself while fondling his dick, he could barely see anything at all—and not just because of his nearsightedness. He looked down and the one blurred Erin became two blurred Erins. Double vision? Was he having a stroke of some kind? And his lungs—fuck, he could barely breathe! His ribs ached and in a gambit to get some air he cranked the window open while the door creaked with its desperate attempt to stay shut against the onslaught it endured. "Let us in now, Jimmy," Chad continued, "and we'll leave it at an ass-kicking—maybe we'll still let you join if you beg us enough!"

Jimmy, who had a mouth that had gotten him into trouble more than once in life, couldn't produce any of the smart-assed responses that he normally might have in such a situation. Instead, pouring sweat, he pressed his head against the cool metal of the window frame and took gasping breaths of the outside air that blew in. Through the opening in the glass he could now see clearly outside—not just his own reflection, yellow with the light of the room and tinted with the glare of moonlight from the darkness outside, but the darkness itself. The stars.

The moon.

His eyes lifted to it and his heart seized in his torso. Jimmy cried out and clutched at his chest, gasping, trying desperately to get his breathing in order and his heart to calm. Was this some kind of an asthma attack? Was he dying? On top of all his fears of organ failure a terrible itch began beneath his hand and spread up over his neck. While he sank his short nails in to scratch, Erin stopped her motion and looked up at him.

"Jimmy," she said, her voice sounding as if it were on the other side of a tunnel, "are you okay?"

His legs gave out from under him and, falling back against the de facto window bench, he pushed her away and instinctively drew his pants up a little. The heaving breaths rising from his lungs soon grew to a strange noise of desperate, a kind of crying gasp as he worked to scratch the itch down his throat and his pecs. While he pulled away the t-shirt Erin hadn't full removed from him, the girl stumbled up and asked, "Are you okay? Jimmy? Are you epileptic or something?"

"Let us in, nerd, or we'll break this fucking door all the way down—"

"Shut up," he at last managed to snarl, his fingers catching in his own flesh as the itch only grew. "Shut up, shut up and let—let me think—"

Something peeled off in his hand. Erin's eyes widened, but she didn't scream until he finished tearing the flesh of his neck away from the fur springing beneath. While he looked, uncomprehending, at the big tatter of bloody flesh in his palm, Erin's voice rose in a shrill cry that seemed even in that moment straight out of a horror movie. She stumbled back and Jimmy screamed, too, or tried to. He only realized once the sound left his mouth that it was a howl—yes, a wolf's howl that rose from the base of his throat, from the depths of his lungs. He gasped in horrified astonishment but, feeling how pulling away his skin had relieved him of the terrible itch along his neck, he began digging his fingers into the meat of his chest and tearing away more strips. His skin fell away like tatters of garment and while Erin hurried to throw on her panties with her bound wrists, screaming, "What's wrong with you, holy shit, what's wrong with you," the door began to give way beneath the frat brothers' onslaught.

"What's he doing to you, Erin? I'll fucking kill him if he's hurting you."

The itch had grown to his gums. Human teeth fell one by one out of his mouth, open with the pain and drooling blood along with saliva and bone fragments. Forced to accept that this was as dressed as she was going to be able to get when her hands were still caught in a bind, Erin dashed to the door and threw it open before her ex-boyfriend and his asshole friends could completely bust it off its hinges. Chad barely even looked at her despite her undressed state, his eyes as full of rage and bloodlust as they were—but when Jimmy lifted his own yellowed eyes toward the encroaching frat brother, the burly young man was taken aback.

"What the fuck," said Chad while the werewolf tore its human host's face from its muzzle like a cheap Halloween mask and threw it with a *splat* upon the floor. As the half-animal monster snarled at him, Chad wisely backed toward the door again, forced to shove his frat brothers out to give him room. Erin had already run screaming, mostly naked and still half-bound down the dormitory's hallway: the sight of her dashing out of the room provoked the urge to chase in the territorial wolf, but that instinct was not near as powerful as the urge it had to stop its itching.

Ah, all this constricting human flesh! While it scratched pieces off with a matted hand of great, black claws, the center of its animal mind stirred with strange memory.

You don't have to ask, cutie…you can come over again sometime if you've got that terrible itch that you just can't scratch.

Yes, yes—the witch, the witch would help him! The witch

would free him from these rotting human remains. The witch would help him feel suited to his own skeleton. She would relieve him, yes! And keep him away from these humans who went scrambling out of the room where he stood amid a pile of bloody flesh and abandoned clothes. The jeans he still wore tearing with the contortions of his legs, the wolf-man shoved open the glass window with effortless strength and ignored its whine as the metal of its frame bent beneath his great hand. Without a second thought for the two stories it needed drop, the half-man, half-animal demon vaulted out the window, landed with well-balanced ease upon its four paws, and galloped off into the night in pursuit of his instincts' persistent call. Each step it took the earth was more pleasing beneath its pads, the creations of man more hateful and confusing to it. The natural world was none of these straight lines and hard brick and towering buildings! When at last it was free of the wretched campus its host called home, it took a great breath of cool night air and lifted its head to the freeing moon in a howl that seemed to echo across all the town.

It was that town it crossed to reach the witch, the claws of its feet sinking into the dirt and launching him into the next stride every step of the way. Its heart hammered in its breast while it followed the manmade highway, navigated through confusing suburban neighborhoods and finally, finally, found itself before the towering Victorian where lived the bad witch, Sabine. Several of the metal vehicles humans favored had been parked outside. Ill at ease beneath a moon not quite full, the wolf stumbled up the steps and slammed its hands against the front door.

Something rattled beside it. With a snarl of surprise, the wolf turned to see the skeleton upon the porch swing had stumbled up and was now looking around with its empty eye sockets as though for a place to escape. While the animal bared its terrible teeth, the animate collection of bones chose to leap over the porch and flee around the back of the house. Now unobserved, the wolf turned back and tried the knob.

Unlocked! It might have laughed if it was a human but now it had no sense of humor—only victory as it barged into the dark house, nostrils flaring at the familiar scent of a dog that was nowhere to be seen. More than that scent, though, the scent of woman—women—settled deep in its sinuses and lured him into the sitting room where candles burned upon every surface and Satan, the bad witch in his arm, watched a trio of other witches hold hands and chant something that made no sense to his animal ears.

The only words that made sense to him were the ones that came from the Devil, who released Sabine to beckon the wolf over.

Obedient at once to its dark master, the wolf approached and knelt before the Lord of the Flies.

"You shouldn't take what doesn't belong to you," Satan remonstrated. "Keep it as a token of our bargain."

While the busty bad witch who had gotten him into this mess slid from the armchair where she perched and trailed over to run her hands through the great half-animal's fur, the Devil watched approvingly and went on, "This is going to happen to you every month now, Jimmy. Do you understand that? Every month in the belly of a wolf. You've been cursed, and there are no powers among mankind who can lift the spell. It takes infernal panache to save you from it now."

Sabine peeled a scrap of flesh from the back of the wolf's hear and ruffled its fur. Her slim fingers were bliss as they gently scratched along the true skin beneath its matted hair. The wolf wagged its tail and turned its head, deferentially lapping at her beautiful fingers to encourage more kindness.

Soon other hands were upon it and it turned to find the rest of the witch's coven were working at the same: stripping off the remaining pieces of flesh and working away the human's jeans to leave the animal exposed, especially once they eased it down upon its back in the center of the floor.

"Look," commented the redhead witch with a chuckle of delight, "why, one part of him still looks like a man, doesn't it…"

As this outspoken witch lowered her head over the massive organ throbbing amid the thick gray fur, the growling beast's muzzle fell open to pant with the rhythm of her tongue. Sabine stroked its face, gazing earnestly, fondly into its eyes.

"Master will help you, Jimmy. He'll help you if you let him…but if he's going to help you, you'll have to dedicate yourself to his service."

"I don't ask for much," the Devil assured the young man trapped inside the body of the wolf that reached out to touch the witch with beaded hair, who ran a hand over his chest and sent a line of fire trailing down to the cock the redhead worked.

"I don't even ask for your soul, really…all I ask is that you do the works I tell you to do upon the Earth. I want you to change your major to theology. And from now on, when something good happens to you, whenever you accomplish something, I want you to tell anyone who asks that I made you do it."

The wolf growled, its yellow eyes seeking for focus upon the Devil before darting down toward the redheaded witch who lifted her head from its lap. Sabine pushed away the black fabric of her robe and smiled at the member that lay twitching against the beast's furred stomach. While the wolf looked back up at the Devil, that same suited man from Jimmy's dream said, "In exchange for all that, I'll let you wake up in the wolf, Jimmy. You'll still have your illness, of course…you stole from my girl, there's no real cure for it once you've done a thing like that. But, well, you'll be able to control it. A diabolical treatment, if you'd like."

A low whine rose from the animal's throat as Sabine,

straddling its great hips, trailed her hands through the fur of its chest and down over the pulsing hard flesh of its cock. As she guided the organ near her hot, wet opening, the bimbofied blonde witch of the coven bent her head to plant kisses along its grunting muzzle; the wolf's long tongue slithered out and into her mouth, yielding a moan from her that in turn made its cock twitch in Sabine's hand.

"Raise your fist if you agree to join my service, wolf," said the Dark Lord at last. "Raise your fist and the man in you will awaken."

The beast's breath hitched, its tongue sliding out of the blonde's mouth while Sabine impaled herself with a high shriek of ecstasy down the length of the wolf-man's oversized member. While the bad witch's eyes rolled back in her head and she looked at once on the verge of tears for the intensity of her pleasure, the sisters of her coven lifted their left hands and screamed with delight those two frightening words: "Hail Satan!" "Hail Satan," answered the Dark Lord, waiting for the wolf's response.

"Hail Satan," cried Sabine, her hips working her body up and down the shaft that spread her so wide it surely must have hurt, however good it felt to fuck herself on the giant demon's prick.

"Hail Satan," the Devil answered her, watching the wolf-man expectantly.

Gasping with pleasure as the tight little human gripped his organ with hers, the wolf caught up one of her beautiful hands and marveled at the contrast of her small, pale fingers against his great furred claw. This claw, he lifted in a fist while all the witches keened in pleasure, in delight, in blasphemy. While they kissed one another, Jimmy snapped awake in the body of the wolf and howled through its muzzle, "Hail Satan!"

The Dark Lord, having made his pact, had already vanished. Jimmy groaned, a noise like a growl, and caught the bad witch by the hips. "You bitch," he said, guiding her motions, fucking her up and down on the gigantic rod that made her eyelids twitch. "You did this to me—you ruined my life—"

The wolf-man sat upright, then pushed the bad witch back against the armchair and commenced to fuck her savagely. Sabine's tongue lolled out while all around the other witches cackled, moaned with envy, kissed and fondled one another with desire.

"Oh, Sabine, let him fuck me next," all of them begged at one point or another. "Sabine, Sabine, give us a turn."

"Ugh—ugh—fuck, fuck, oh, fuck, never, you bitches, he's mine, oh, fuck, get your own wolf-man—mm, it pisses you off that I like this huh, Jimmy?"

Fangs bared, Jimmy fucked her like his life depended on it, dreaming he might rupture her internal organs with his new, gigantic one. Instead she only screamed with greater delight, biting her lip, moaning to run her hands over the same wolf all her sisters eagerly petted and kissed and caressed while he plowed away. The wolf-man snarled in her face and all the same Sabine moaned, thrilled, her hips arching up to him in offering.

"Fuck, yeah, oh, yeah, that's a good wolf, what a good, big animal you are—give it to me, give it to me, wolfboy—fuck, oh, fill me up with cum, I've never had a wolf's cum in me before—"

"You're lucky I don't kill you," Jimmy said with a snarl.

"But she's done you such a favor," pointed out the redhead witch.

"That's right," agreed the witch with beaded hair. "You've joined our coven…we've needed a man for so long."

"And *what* a man," enthused the bimbo, biting her lip, then reaching between the beast's legs to pet its furry balls. While Jimmy released a howl he simply couldn't help, the blonde giggled lightly and gave them a gentle squeeze.

"Mm…he's perfect. Think he'll have it in him for another turn when you're done, Sabine?"

"Fuck, fuck, oh, he came three times when he was just a human yesterday—I'm sure by the end of the night we'll all be dripping with his dirty wolf-man spunk, oh, fuck, yeah, just the way I like it—yeah, yeah, make me feel like a fucking whore, degrade me, you big dog!"

Baring his fangs, Jimmy sank his bite into her flesh, hoping to hurt her, hoping maybe even to make her like him—but witches, of course, cannot be afflicted with such a thing as a werewolf's curse. Instead Sabine only moaned, her pussy clenching tight enough around him that his cock, already on the edge from fucking the co-ed, buried itself as deep in the witch as it would fit and, with an explosion of animal bliss, spilled its seed in the depths of her body. Jimmy lifted his wolf's head and gave into his urge to howl, a strange and bizarre sensation not unlike the natural inclination of the human to scream for God during sex. But oh, it was not the Good Lord for whom the animal had praise in that moment.

"Hail Satan," screamed Sabine, her brow furrowed and her teeth bared as she looked down at the point where her body conjoined with the wolf, whose human cock slid from her to release a depraved flow of cum that dribbled down upon the surface of the armchair.

"Hail Satan," cried the other witches in tandem, the redheaded one wasting no time before tugging on Jimmy's furred arm. He whipped his head in her direction, fangs still bared even amid the fog of pleasure. The bad witches all laughed at that, but none so much as the redhead, who eased him down upon his back once again.

"What a foul mood you're in…well, don't worry. I'm sure once you've finished with all three of us you'll be as happy as a pup."

Early he next morning, after awakening amid a pile of beautiful women to find himself in his human body, Jimmy felt, oddly, not a pang of blasphemous guilt but rather a twist of frustration in his gut. What was his mother going to say when she heard he'd ruined his own chances of getting into that fucking frat? He sat up a little and, snoring in her sleep, the bimbo witch named Gina flopped away from him. After looking around himself and noticing Sabine was nowhere to be found, he extricated himself from the sleeping bodies, pulled on the tattered remains of his pants, and followed the scent of coffee.

"Hey," whispered the foremost bad witch from where she sat at her dining room table. "You want some?"

"I don't really drink coffee," admitted the young man, sliding into the empty seat beside her. The dog that had done this to him—no, the dog that had enacted the fate Jimmy had himself set into motion—lifted his head, wagged his tail in vague recognition, then lowered his muzzle upon his paws again. With a sidelong glance at the animal, Jimmy sighed, ran his hand over his face and said, "I don't know what I'm going to do, Sabine."

"About the human flesh left in your dorm room? Oh, that's disappeared by now."

"Well—that's good to know, but I just meant…in general. Ugh." He let his head drop so that his forehead came to rest upon Sabine's kitchen table. While she cooed and carded her fingers through his hair, Jimmy sighed heftily again. "I worked so hard to get in that fucking frat. Now what am I supposed to do? What am I going to tell my mother? Not to mention— what am I supposed to do next time that happens to me?"

"Well, next time that happens, you'll still be yourself… you'll be more in-control than you were at first last night. Next time that happens, come here and party with us. We always meet on the full moon…and even if for some reason the other girls aren't around, well, I'm here to help you out."

"But what about Erin? What about the people who saw me?"

"Oh, people see horrible things all the time…if you act like they're crazy and like nothing is wrong, they'll never bring it up again."

"I don't know…I don't know."

"You rely on other people for your self-esteem way too much, babe." With a playful tweak of Jimmy's ear that got him upright to grouse and rub the place where her fingers pinched, she said, "Women like a self-assured, confident man. You're a wolf once a month? Well, good thing for you werewolves are 'in.' Most ladies love a big, hairy man who can fuck them senseless. I know I and my friends do. And if Erin isn't into that, well…" Sabine spread her hands and shrugged. "You'll find a girl who will appreciate it."

"Yeah."

Frowning into the distance, Jimmy said nothing more. Sabine watched him with a slight frown of her own before, looking inspired, she nudged him in the arm. "Hey! You know what might make you feel better?"

She indicated three oversized cartons of eggs sitting out on her kitchen counter for want of room in her fridge. About an hour later, still before the sun had risen, a pair of those eggs shattered to release a splash of yolk across yet another frat house window and finally a light went on. "Go, go, go," enthused Sabine, laughing wildly as she pushed Jimmy in the direction of her car.

While they drove away, pausing only at the end of the block to watch the bewildered frat members stumble out to find their house and its lawn absolutely covered in raw eggs, Jimmy couldn't help but think that maybe these witches really did know how to live.

377

The Witch's Monster Mash

REJECTION FROM ALPHA Tau Pi was one thing; but being evicted from the dorms practically ruined Jimmy Zevron's relationship with his parents. As the RA said with a few disappointed shakes of his head, "We have to replace the whole window *and* its frame, dude. Even some of the bricks are damaged. Don't know what you did, but whatever it is, you need to cool it with the partying."

Partying! Please. Jimmy wanted to flip out on the guy and say, "Look, asshole, you ever heard of the ADA? The Americans with Disabilities Act? You ever stop to think maybe I had—I don't know a seizure and fell out the window or something?"

They said Julius Caesar was a lycanthrope; really, he just had epilepsy, or so the young man had always been taught. It seemed like Jimmy was going to be using that as a cover for the rest of his life but for now, in this instance, instead of defending himself or faking a more conventional ailment, the recently transformed werewolf went storming down the stairs by his room and out to the path curving around the building. He paced a little while his cellphone rung in his hand.

"Hello?"

"Hey, Sabine"—Jimmy glanced up at his taped-over window, one hand running through his short blond hair—"so, uh, this is going to sound like an imposition—"

"Are they evicting you?"

"How did you know!"

"I saw that window when I dropped you off this morning… you really did a number, wolf-boy."

Rolling his eyes, Jimmy said, "Anyway, uh—I don't think I should go home with my, uh, my problem, and—you've got a pretty big house—"

"Six hundred a month for room and board."

"Six *hundred!* I don't have a job!"

"Then you should get one…that, or you can be my cute little fuckboy gofer. I might even let you put it in me sometime. Oh! Big, tough wolf-man, you make me howl."

Ah, fuck. His dick sprang to life in his pants and he cursed his nature, hand slapping over his own eyes as though the busty goth witch stood before him all over. Damn! First she took his virginity, then her dog's bite took his humanity—now she was taking his dignity. But Jimmy really did have to find a place to stay, and no way could he go home and risk have an episode in front of his parents. They were already going to be pissed about Alpha Tau Pi.

"Fine—please, just don't ask me to do unreasonable stuff for you. I want to live my own life sometimes."

"Oh, don't worry, I won't be too unkind. I just need someone to do all the things that I don't want to do! And Bonesy's been working so hard…I think he deserves a break now and then."

"Bonesy?" Vaguely, he remembered the skeleton leaping up and high-tailing it around the house. The wolf had still been in control in that moment and as such memories were bleary. "Is that your—"

"Gardener, uh-huh. Anyway, go on, get your stuff together… Auntie will pick you up."

And all that was how recent werewolf Jimmy Zevron ended up living with Sabine the Bad Witch...but he wasn't fully committed to her master, Satan, until he had no other choice.

The first day Jimmy lived with her honestly wasn't so bad. She was very consoling and gave him some weed and then gave him a mind-blowing blowjob while they listened to King Crimson. *In The Court of the Crimson King* would give him a Pavlovian erection for the rest of his life, it was so good. Then, the almost-full moon came out with the downing of night, and she helped him scratch off his skin until the fur came out and Cable Dog went whimpering from the living room.

"What a big bad wolf you are," she gasped theatrically, her hand sliding down his chest and over the fur of his groin. While he growled softly at the contact, the bad witch moaned and worked him over. "I bet you wish you could eat me, huh? Oh, what big teeth you have..."

"You shouldn't say things like that, Sabine," he gasped through the animal's snarling mouth while she climbed into his lap. They both moaned as she impaled herself upon his transfigured member and soon she rocked above him, her fingers plunging through the fur of his chest and her mouth dropping over his fanged muzzle.

"Oh, don't worry...if you ever lost your mind I'd give you what you deserved. But it's fun to talk about, and anyway, I have faith in your ability to control yourself now that Master has helped correct your mind. Now your consciousness will always be in control, Jimmy...even in the eye of the hurricane, during the fullest of full moons, you'll still be yourself inside of this big, great beast...able to experience every second of what you do with your second body. See? It's not such a curse...not when you remember it, anyway."

Was that a fact? Jimmy wasn't so sure...in fact, it seemed like remembering was a much greater curse. Remembering, for instance, landed him in the strange situation of becoming the boarder of a crazy witch who kicked him out of bed at four in the morning, saying, "What are we, married? Go on, quit lying around and get to work...Bonesy does the outside, so you don't have to worry about that, but there are a lot of rooms in here for you to work on, so you'd better get going."

"I have class in three hours."

"That's two hours you can use to take care of my house and an hour to get ready and get where you need to go."

"But I don't have a car!"

"So, take the bicycle in my garage! It just needs a little dusting, it's perfect for you. I won't even charge you to use it."

Gee, that was sure swell. After fending off a small army of black widows in his attempts to vanquish their webs, Jimmy did in fact manage to extricate the bike from the bad witch's garage. At least it was a unisex bike and not, say, one that was pink with streamers on the handlebars...but it wasn't a mountain bike, meaning peddling around their somewhat hilly town left Jimmy out of breath.

This on top of his first dive into cleaning...well, basically anything other than his own room...and a long night with Sabine meant that he'd might as well have skipped the lecture. He slept right through it and, whether the German professor had heard rumors of his evictions and wild night or just didn't want to deal with it, nobody bothered to wake him up. He jerked awake from a thick, dreamless slumber while all the rest of the class around him got up to grab a bite to eat or go to their next lecture.

It was just as well. He needed to look fresh for that day's Psych class, where Erin Innsmouth sat trying not to stare at him from her seat down the row. He supposed it was just too much to hope that she didn't remember anything from the other day; her stare said it all, and Jimmy found himself plotting out the fastest possible route to the exit to avoid conversation.

Alas, it was not to be. She called out to him from the other side of the hall as he hurried past the many rooms of the Psych building, and her voice had been to audible to ignore. Trying not to visibly cringe, Jimmy stopped and turned to watch the girl of his dreams hurry up to him.

Erin stopped about four feet away, unable to approach further, perhaps frightened. He couldn't blame her…though he wasn't expecting the sensual bite she gave her plump lower lip, or the somehow shy scrape of her shoe along the floor.

"Hey," she said while she came to a stop, shifting her books under her arm. "How are you?"

"Fine. Tired."

"I'll bet." Then, laughing awkwardly, perhaps wondering if it wasn't something she should have said, Erin looked around and asked, "Want to walk with me? I have Greek Tragedies next."

"Sure you want to walk with me, Erin?"

Was it his imagination, or was she blushing? Erin glanced around and then, overcoming her bashfulness enough to nod, now stepped a little closer. "You don't have to worry about— the other night. I won't tell anyone…and anyway, if I did, who would believe me?"

Holy shit. Maybe Sabine really had something when she said chicks were into werewolves. Jimmy tried to look cool and aloof as much as he could, even if inside he was suddenly freaking out as much as he was when he picked Erin up in the wake of her break-up with Chad. Talking, he turned to lead the way from the building and through the campus whose dying lawns looked more like November every day.

"I guess that's true…thanks for keeping it quiet, all the same. I don't exactly know what to do with this new information about myself. Sort of feel like I should donate myself to medical science…at least then I'll for sure never hurt anybody on accident."

But her eyes blazed with that. She slapped him in the bicep, saying, "Don't kid around, Jim!"

With a nervous laugh, Jimmy told her, "Sorry," and by the time his anxiety has faded he realized her expression had changed. Erin looked at him sidelong as they strode along. Before long, her sank her teeth into the luscious flesh of her lower lip.

"So…uh…" Her head tilted in a somehow coy way that drove him—and the wolf inside him—absolutely wild. Both their ears perked as, shifting her books to her right arm and letting her body edge nearer to Jimmy's, Erin lowered her voice to a murmur.

"Can you, like…do that *any* time?"

Sheesh! Oh, brother. Jim willed his voice not to crack, willed himself to stay cool. Surely, if Satan's intervention meant James could live within the wolf when it took over on a full moon, then the wolf must have lived in him with just as much awareness during the rest of the month. He searched for it within himself and felt the warmth of its power trickling through his limbs.

"I don't know," he admitted to Erin, his voice low enough to intensify the fire of her eyes. "I haven't experimented with it too much yet. I just started to experience it the other night."

The tip of her tongue appeared to flicker across her lips. His mouth ached to kiss her while, glancing up at him in that girlishly shy way that drove him wild, Erin glanced furtively toward her dorm across the quad.

"My roommates aren't usually around until, like, three…"

About five minutes later Erin fell into her room's door beneath Jimmy's embrace, his mouth working furiously against hers and inspiring a moan even before they were safely shut inside. He couldn't even take a second to glance around the room; he wasn't interested. All he was interested in was Erin, who had driven him crazy from the first time he saw her and who now threw down her books, pushed him away and stripped off her t-shirt and yoga pants quick as a flash. She started to get down on her knees again but Jimmy grabbed her around the smooth, tight waist and threw her into the bed, where she bounced with a giddy laugh and a hot little groan of desire.

"Oh, Jimmy—oh!"

After drawing her to the edge of the bed, Jimmy dispensed with her underwear and got down on his knees in between her legs. Glancing down at him with a gasp to see his lips apply themselves to her lower ones, Erin covered her mouth with the back of her hand and moaned almost sweetly. "Fuck, oh, Jimmy! I can't believe I ever thought you were a virgin—"

He stifled his impulse to grin. Until just a few days ago, he had been. Now, however, he was banging a big-tittied goth witch with an absolutely rocking body, the skill set of a pornstar and the assertive inclination of a dominatrix. She had been very quick to educate Jimmy on the finer points of eating pussy, and what she hadn't yet taught, he made up for in rabid enthusiasm.

Especially for Erin's pussy. She smelled so delicious, hot and eager and feminine, that his mouth watered. The wolf inside him stirred well and truly, pounding at his chest and filling up his mind with images of more, more, more. He wanted to fuck her right then and there—to mark her as his territory, hold her down, assume total control of her body and mind with his cock alone. Erin panted at a faster pace by the second, her toes curling and, soon enough, her slim thighs tightened around his head while he lapped against her clit and the oozing cunt that wanted him so badly he could taste it. Gel manicured nails curling through his hair, gripping, pulling, Erin whined and thrashed. Her stomach tightened above his head, her back arching as she screamed loud enough for the dorm to hear.

"Oh, fuck! Jimmy, Jimmy! Nobody eats pussy like you do!"

His cock leapt in his pants while Erin came for him, her orgasm rattling through her without the need of his least penetration. Thrilled to at last stand on the cusp of completing a fantastical dream, Jimmy stood to undress. Erin sat up to hurriedly help him, pushing back his black overshirt and tearing away his graphic tee. Soon, to his astonishment, he lay in Erin's pink twin bed crammed against the dorm room wall, her dainty body naked and hot against his.

Sure, yes, he'd had the whole witch orgy experience, and he'd definitely had more than a couple rolls in the hay with Sabine in about half a week of knowing her. But it was so different to hold Erin in his arms. To see her after so long of fantasizing about her; every soft, subtle curve of her demure body, from the delicate but grabbable hillock of her ass to the peaked nipples of her goosebumped breasts. Not being a psychopathic bad witch who got off on the risks and/or used abortions for body wash, Erin insisted on the use of a condom, but Jimmy couldn't have cared less. Those first few seconds of sliding into her made him go nearly blind, she was so tight, so hot, so fine.

"Fuck! Fuck! Jimmy, Jimmy Zevron, oh, fuck—oh, uh, so I guess—uh, I guess it's not on-demand…that's okay…" As Jimmy fell into a rhythm of thrusting into Erin's tight little hole, she moaned and thrashed beneath him, then twined her arms around his neck to gaze longingly into his face. "We'll just have to do it again…again, some full moon…oh, fuck, Jimmy, you can take me out of town and ravish me—go wild on me—fuck, fuck, Jimmy, Jimmy!"

Ah, damn, these women today sure knew how to dirty-talk! Must have been porn…or Amazon erotica. Whatever! He wasn't complaining. Breathless as he pounded into the girl of his dreams, his whole body guided by instincts that were perhaps more the wolf's than his own, Jimmy caught her face in his hands and kissed her. Erin moaned with delight, completely submitting to his tongue, his cock, his burning desire for her. His balls slapped against the flash of her beautiful ass while he pushed her thighs up higher to give himself deeper access, amazed to perceive himself disappearing into her all the way up to the base. Arching, grasping more tightly at him and scratching at his back, Erin screamed with delight and quickly came again.

Now…Jimmy had always heard that condoms were supposed to make you last a little longer, and that was true. But something about seeing Erin cum around him for the first time—not only that, but *feeling* it, that fast gush-flutter through the thin layer of latex—man, he just couldn't resist. Her body, squeezing and begging around him, it did the job it was designed to do and pushed him right over into a climax of his own. Jimmy gasped, instantly humiliated to have cum so early, but the sight of his orgasm and the feeling of his increasing rigidity inside of her seemed only to inspire another moan of pleasure from Erin.

"Oh, yeah, Jimmy! Fuck, yes, oh…mark me, make me your *mate*, Daddy—"

Wow-ee! Hot damn! Jimmy gasped in astonishment, his pleasure sharpened by the howling delight of the wolf within him. Soon he collapsed atop her, spent and panting, his face and chest glistening with sweat while Erin caught her breath beneath him and sometimes kissed his ear.

"Fuck," he gasped, "ah—"

"That was really fucking hot," she whispered to him while he collected himself. While, laughing weakly, Jimmy drew himself out of her and removed the condom, Erin remained dreamily upon her back and gazed up at the ceiling. "So fucking hot…you're such a fucking stud, Jimmy Zevron…"

"Keep talking to me like that and I'll be able to do it again in no time."

Erin produced a sleepy little laugh at that and, smiling a bit,

Jimmy rose unsteadily from the bed. With a bit of searching he located a trash can beneath one of the desks along the wall. After limping over and depositing the condom, he looked up with a laugh.

"Jeez, Erin, looks like we left the blinds open."

She didn't reply. Jimmy glanced over his shoulder.

And he thought men were supposed to fall asleep quickly! Erin was zonked. He worried at the time it had something to do with being fucked by a werewolf, but someday he'd learn that was just how Erin was. He touched her shoulder to make sure she was okay and, already dozing, she frowned a little and rolled over into his caress as though to give him a bit of room to wiggle in. With a laugh, he obliged…and regretted it.

Oh, sure, it was nice to hold Erin's sleeping body, and he needed to catch some sleep of his own. But when he woke up after a very solid nap of two or so hours that meant they had both missed their next lectures, he found himself pinned tightly between the dorm room wall and Erin's deceptively small body. The amount of force was truly astonishing and in fact made him feel like his bones were cracking. Nudging Erin yielded nothing; she snored a little harder and shifted so little it was truly negligible. Gritting his teeth, Jimmy pushed himself out of the bed and tripped over the footboard with the force that this required. As Erin quickly filled his warm space, Jimmy sat upright in the pile of his clothes.

The phone in the back pocket of his abandoned jeans blinked with a green light indicating a text message. Somehow, he knew even before he saw it that it would be from Sabine.

LOOK LIVELY, DOGBREATH.
House meeting at 4!!
Be there or be evicted.

PS Here's my grocery list.

That Jimmy was expected to pick up all twenty of the listed items was implicit...and somewhat bizarre. Especially because it was all booze. Sure, the bad witch seemed like she enjoyed her share of drugs and alcohol, but Jimmy couldn't help thinking five jugs of Kraken rum was a little much even for her.

A little much, and a little expensive. Jimmy dressed silently in Erin's room, all the while trying to decide how exactly he would ask Sabine for money. He didn't even have enough for the deposit on a keg—funding her liquor cabinet was out of the question. He might be able to swing some beers, though. After writing Erin a little note with his phone number and an apologetic explanation that his unreasonable landlady needed him to run some errands, Jimmy paused by the door to check the contents of his wallet and see how much cash he had to work with.

He faltered.

A little red credit card he had never seen before winked at him from the leather of the wallet.

With a glance over at sleeping, snoring Erin, Jimmy eased the card from his wallet to find it embossed by his name, an expiration date of 06/66, a security code of 420, and a phone number preceded by the word, *Questions?*

Oh...maybe one or two.

When outside of the dorm and on the way to retrieve his bike, Jimmy called the number on his cell phone (a 1-900 number, infuriatingly). It rang once, then again before an automated voice picked up.

"Hello," said the robot woman politely, "and thank you for calling the Daddy-O corporation service line. To order a Daddy-O product catalogue, please press 1. To inquire about a refund for a defective or incorrect product, please press 2. If you believe the Daddy-O identity has co-opted your identity for purposes of advertising, framing and/or replacing you and your family members one person at a time, please press 3. To learn who's watching you right now, please press 4."

Jimmy looked sharply around, a chill rolling down his spine while the voice continued without pause.

"If you're calling in response to a help wanted ad, please press 5. If you're calling because you've just eaten a Daddy-O branded treat and you've begun to break out in a cold sweat, please hang up and dial 911. Want to report a malfunctioning toy? Press 6 to talk to our quality control department. If—"

Gritting his teeth, Jimmy said, "Operator."

"—you feel low on iron this week, press—"

"Help," Jimmy said into the phone, clearly and crisply anounciating over the voice of the robot. "Operator, operator, help, let me talk to a person."

The voice cut off mid-sentence as though impatiently listening to his demands.

The silence on the line was pregnant for a few seconds.

"Hello," the robot voice began all over again, "and thank you for calling the—"

Jimmy almost smashed the phone into his own forehead.

Sixty-eight options were presented to Jimmy before he finally came to the one he wanted.

After listening to the voice rattle off her options all the way to Gus Glugs, the one spot in town where Jimmy knew for sure they wouldn't card him, it finally came to a crucial juncture just as Gus finished packing up the freshman's elaborate liquor order.

"Can I have it delivered," Jimmy whispered over the edge of the phone while, on the call, the robot voice finally obliged him.

"…If you've just opened your wallet to discover a Daddy-O

corporate card, press the pound sign followed by the numbers six, nine…if—"

"Should have just guessed," muttered Jimmy under his breath, hitting the buttons prescribed while the clerk asked him the address. Realizing he didn't have it, Jimmy described the neighborhood, the street and the look of the house in question. Before he could do better, an actual (theoretically actual, anyway) human being picked up on the other end of the call.

"Thank you for calling the Daddy-O Corporate Hotline," said the somewhat nasally operator on the other end. "For verification of your identity, please recite the first four digits of your childhood house number."

Sputtering somewhat, Jimmy looked into the phone, ducked out of the store and said, "Uh, uh—shit, hold on, I know I know this…"

"Happens to everybody, sir."

"52—no, no. 5324?"

"Very good, thank you Mr. Zevron." Trying not to be too freaked out to hear the woman say his name so smoothly, Jimmy got on the bike and drifted through Gus's parking lot with his mouth nonetheless somewhat agape. "How can I help you today, sir?"

"Uh, well, it's just—I found this card and—you mean you don't know why I called? After I went through that whole phone tree system for twenty minutes?"

"I'm sorry, sir, this is Hell. Our machines are always running slow. It's much faster if you just tell me. You mean to say you just got your corporate card?"

"That's exactly it," he said, trying to remind himself that Hell employees probably made minimum wage. "I don't remember signing up for anything, but—"

"Of course you did, sir."

"Excuse me?"

"When you made your agreement with the Dark Lord," explained the Daddy-O rep boredly, "an essential element of the agreement is your use of a company card."

"Did I—did I sign a contract?"

"Saying 'Hail Satan' during sex has been an accepted form of contractual agreement since the landmark 1982 case of *Satan v. Bowie.*"

"David Bowie? Really?"

"Yes, sir."

"Crazy. Anyway—so I don't have to worry about paying for this or anything, do I?"

"Not with cash, sir, no."

Rolling his eyes, Jimmy peddled down the street and thought to himself he ought to have paid Gus some extra to give him and his bike a ride in the back of the delivery truck. "Then what?"

"Eternal servitude to our Dark Lord and Master, Satan. Hail Satan," she said boredly, while a few reps in the background responded to her with a few low-energy "Hail Satan"s of their own.

"Gee, that's great." Keeping his tone modulated to avoid taking out his annoyance on the rep, Jimmy shifted his phone from one ear to the other and watched traffic carefully. Didn't he recognize that blue car coming the opposite way? "So, I just want to be clear—I'm not going to get a bill or anything, am I?"

"No, sir."

"Okay, good. What's your name?"

"Regina, sir."

"Well, 'Regina'—do you have an extension?"

"Sorry, sir. Internal use only."

"Fine," groused Jimmy while the car flew past him and the men inside hooted over something they'd seen, all producing noises loud enough to be heard through the shut windows of the vehicle. "If I call in and get somebody else, can they transfer me to you?"

"It's theoretically possible if I'm not on another call at the time, but—"

"All right," he said with a sigh, "I get it, I get it. Well, thanks for your help."

"Thank you for calling the Daddy-O Corporate Hotline," said Regina agreeably. "Did I answer your questions today?"

"I guess."

"Glad to hear it. Have a great day, Mr. Zevron. And watch out"—he'd just been about to hang up but froze with his thumb hovering over the red *END CALL* button—"Chad's car back there is pulling a u-turn."

Blood draining from his face, Jimmy hurriedly hung up and looked over his shoulder to find the call center rep was correct. The car of men he now recognized as Alpha Tau Pi frat members had reached the end of the street and was now careening around the way it had come. Swearing, Jimmy peddled faster, urging the fixed gear bike up the hill for which it simply was not made. His muscles burned and he wheezed with the exertion, glancing a few rapid, panicked times over his shoulder as the car rumbled up behind him.

He was just about to throw himself and the bike off the road altogether when, honking and cursing him, Erin's ex and all his frat brothers swerved in front of him to cut him off on their way into a gas station at the top of the hill. The car whipped through a mud and oil-soaked puddle on the way, and Jimmy grimaced, crying out in slow-motion as a filthy tidal wave rose up and splashed across him to leave him looking as badly off as a penguin after a BP spill. Sputtering, grimacing, Jimmy braced his foot against the ground to stop the bike and perched upon it while removing the glasses that had, thankfully, acted as goggles. He tore them off and wiped his face vigorously while the frat brothers laughed from their car and once more peeled off the way they'd intended to go.

Gritting his teeth, Jimmy reminded himself he never had to see those fucking toolboxes again and resumed his journey to his new home. What an idiot he had been for trying to join a frat in the first place! And why? All because his parents wanted him to? Come on…he was an adult. There was no reason for him to live his life the way Mr. and Mrs. Zevron wanted him to. He was too old to care so much about their opinions! So, his life wasn't as perfect as they'd envisioned it. So what? It was his life, not theirs. It seemed to Jimmy that it was about time for him to stand up to his parents! To present himself, mud and oily water and all, and say, "Here I am, Mom, Dad! This is me."

And who was he, exactly? Well…a werewolf, he guessed. A werewolf, and a nerd…and maybe the future boyfriend of Erin Innsmouth.

Wasn't all bad, he guessed.

To Jimmy's surprise upon returning to the house, he wasn't the only one called to the aforementioned 'house meeting.' He walked into the foyer and slid off his shoes, calling, "I'm home," with his backpack still over his shoulder as though he were back in high school. Laughing gently to himself, he carried on through the hall and into the sitting room, where he stopped at the entrance to absorb somewhat all the new faces.

"Excuse me," he said, looking carefully at the Latina woman who sat next to the skeleton. A guy in a cable company work uniform sat on the floor with his back against the sofa were the first two relaxed. The tableau was strange, but stranger still was the way Jimmy's eye kept being drawn in by the woman.

"Do I know you from somewhere?"

Rolling her eyes, the woman folded her arms over the hooded sweatshirt emblazoned with the logo of Fort U. "Maybe it would jog your memory if I were in high heels and a cocktail dress."

Hesitating, Jimmy looked closer at her and said after a moment of hesitation, "The *doll?*"

"What's up, homie," she said with a sullen jerk of her chin and an aggrieved sinking back into the arm of the couch. "My name's Alma."

Dropping his backpack and hurrying over to offer his hand, Jimmy said, "Nice to meet you. I'm—"

"Jimmy fucking Zevron, yes, I know, I had to hear that shit all last night, bro. 'Oh, Jimmy! Oh, oh! Harder and I'll give you a bedroom with an adjoined bathroom!' Did she, by the way?"

"No," sputtered the boy, red to the tips of his ears at Alma's dead-on Sabine impression. "So, um—damn, did she make you real, or—"

"I've *been* real, *ese!* This *pinche bruja* turned me into a fucking doll for no good reason at all!"

The skeleton in the delivery driver uniform and the cable guy both looked at her. She looked back between the two of them, her face contorting into a scowl and her brow furrowing as she said, "Oh, shut up. Don't even fucking start with me, you dipshits."

"Obviously I know you"—Jimmy exchanged a nod with Bonesy, who rattled with the slight jerk of his skull, before looking over at the cable guy—"but who are you?"

"Sup," said the cable guy, lifting a hand. "Sorry about the whole werewolf thing. I'm—"

"That's Cable Dog," answered Alma with a jerk of her thumb.

Jimmy's face turned an even deeper scarlet. He balked in amazement, looking twice at the guy sitting on the floor while said guy said, "Man! Don't call me that. It's not Cable Dog, Cable *Guy*. I mean, it's—"

"You're Sabine's dog?" Jimmy's mind whirled to remember when exactly it was that Cable Dog had left the room the night before.

Skin crawling, the college freshman said with a crack of his voice, "Oh! Uh—ah-huh, well, uh…sorry, I didn't—"

"Trust me," said Cable Guy, lifting his hand. "I've seen worse in this house."

The ceiling sure was beautiful in this room. Hands on his hips, Jimmy admired it and prayed to leave his body while Alma agreed, "Yeah, man, way fucking worse. Just wait until you're around for a Child Sacrifice Saturday, that'll really—"

"Well don't *spoil* it for him," protested Sabine, slinking into the sitting room and draping an arm around Jimmy's shoulders. While the teenager fought an instant boner, Sabine grinned at him, pinched his cheek, and went on with one hand propped on the hip of her Morticia-esque black wobble dress, "Let him have the adventure that is living in my house without your intervention…it's more fun that way. Did you have a good day at school, baby?"

With a scathing roll of his eyes, Jimmy said, "I got the stuff you wanted, the liquor store owner should deliver it in an hour or two. What's this about a house meeting?"

"Oh," she said, "I don't know yet! Master called it…I just called *you.*"

"Okay, well, you picked a bad time for it. Or he did. Either way—"

"You mean you don't love spending time with Sabine?"

Where was Satan's voice coming from? Jimmy and all the other tenants of Sabine's house looked around So did their landlady. Eventually, Jimmy caught his own reflection in the mirror over the mantle and gasped in sharp terror the Devil reflected there did not mimic. Elegant as ever, Satan simply smiled.

"Hey, kids! Sorry I can't be there in person just yet, but I've got a lot of preparation to do. Anyway, I've got so much stock in Zoom…might as well use it, huh?" Laughing to himself, rubbing his hands together, Satan looked around from face to face and winked particularly at Sabine. "There's my babe. Looking good."

"Can't wait to see you, Daddy."

"The feeling is mutual. I love a good Halloween celebration with my Sabine." While the witch practically purred with pleasure at the praise, Satan smiled in a, well, devilish way while continuing. "All these years of staying in, keeping cozy, watching some horror movies and heating budget candy. I love it! But you know…we've done it so many years in a row, and after seeing you learn how to make friends this year, well—I'm just so proud. I thought, how better to celebrate than with a Halloween party?"

Sabine's jaw dropped, her entire expression falling to grim disappointment. Alma and Cable Dog, however, exchanged glances of pleasant surprise, Alma in particular lifting her eyebrows. Satan continued on the screen while blind Bonesy looked over along with them.

"It 's such a special day, only comes once a year…with all the new people you know—"

"You know I hate parties, Master! Unless the coven and I are ruining them!"

"Well, then relax, because the coven is invited, obviously."

Scoffing, withdrawing her hand from around Jimmy's shoulder to fold both arms beneath her sumptuous breasts, Sabine tapped her foot and said sourly to Satan, "You mean you've already invited everybody?"

"Uh, hello! Today's the 31st—Halloween? I had to invite most people weeks ago to get them to agree! A lot of time under false pretenses…it's all right"—while Sabine sputtered, the Devil pursed his lips, shook his head and waved his hand in the way of an ignorant boss—"don't worry about a thing, baby, you just roll with it."

"How many people are coming."

"Oh," said Satan, reaching outside of the boundaries of the

mirror and acting as though he was handed something by an invisible entity. While Jimmy glanced around on their side of the reflection and found no demons that he could discern, the Devil smacked his lips thoughtfully and lowered his eyes to the long scroll he drew back with him into frame. "Let's just see…you, me, Alma, Bonesy, Cable Guy…oh, Jimmy, of course, hah…the coven, said them already, Gina, Bernice, Hazel all said they'd come…"

While Sabine looked witheringly over at Jimmy, as though he had ought to be doing something to prevent this, Jimmy spread his hands helplessly. Satan continued through it all, taking his sweet time while reading off, "Clarinda Lovegood, oh! You'll like this. Her whole Bible study group thinks they're coming to a Christian thing. Chick Tract reading or something, who knows what I told 'em. I sure don't! Speaking of, Sister Ignatia and Father Tristan are both invited…super excited to see them…

"Hm…Nyarlethotep, one out of every ten members of the town between the ages of twenty-one and thirty-five, Erin Innsmouth"—Jimmy perked in astonishment, listening with careful attention and roiling with conflict as the Devil went on—"and the entire Alpha Pi Tau fraternity. Oh! And Mr. and Mrs. Zevron."

Jimmy's jaw nearly hit the floor. "What!"

"Yeah! Your parents were sure a sweet couple of people, Jimmy. Oh, your mom was just thrilled to hear about it! A little surprised the Alpha Tau Pi frathouse was so far from campus, but…"

"You told them I made the frat?"

"*I* didn't tell them! They just assumed. That's your mess to deal with, I just called to invite them to a Halloween party you were hosting."

"Wh—but how—" Quickly realizing it was fruitless to ask how such a thing was possible for the Devil to have foreseen,

Jimmy dropped the whole thing and focused on the sheer horror of it. Rubbing his brows, groaning in frustration, Jimmy said, "Ugh! Why would you do this? My parents don't know I'm a freaking *werewolf!* They can't see me hanging around with a—a bad witch, and a werewolf, and a—Satan!"

"What the fuck, Jimmy, are you going to ask them to wear a blindfold for the rest of their lives?" Tossing the scroll off-screen, Satan arched his dark brows and said while they waggled theatrically, "You're working for me now. When you're successful in life and thanking me, you don't want it to be a surprise, do you?"

"Look, I guess it's one thing if they just think I'm a Satanist. It's all the other stuff that I'm worried about!"

"Tosh." Waving his hand, Satan said, "It'll be fine. Won't it, Sabine?"

The bad witch cackled, her voice rising and falling like the crashing of waves. Jimmy felt like he was going to be sick, his attention caught only by the knock at the door. "That'll be the booze," said Satan. "Well, kids, I'll leave you to set up the party. Don't forget to have fun! And try to make sure everybody's having a good time before I get there. I like a lively shindig!"

Jimmy, busy going to answer the door, didn't see how it was that Satan's reflection left the mirror. His mind rushed with terrible thoughts and urgent questions. What was he going to do? Maybe if he rode fast enough he could bike over to their house and slash their tires before they got in their car. Fuck, oh, but Satan just told him to help Sabine set up for the party—

Clarinda Lovegood, the nice lady from down the street, stood on the other side of the door and smiled prettily as Jimmy greeted her. Her eyes flickered with recognition after a belated second and that smile grew. "Jimmy! What a surprise—"

As if remembering whose house she stood before, Clarinda's smile faltered a little. At the very least, it no longer reached her eyes quite as easily while she continued, "Uh…to find you here at Sabine's!"

Ugh. Clarinda was such a nice lady. He knew her from volunteering at the soup kitchen while he was still trying to get into the frat (Seemed like so long ago! Was it really only the day before?) and she was the kind of sweet, pretty older woman whose respect Jimmy desperately wanted. Almost like he was projecting his parents' expectations onto her. Ugh, ugh, ugh!

If it was this embarrassing for Clarinda to see him consorting with the bad witch, it was going to be fucking awful for Jimmy's parents to see him there.

Folding her arms over her chest against the chill, Clarinda smiled sweetly at him and said with a glance down the street, "Um, I think I got a delivery meant for Sabine. The man said he was told to take it to a blue house and just wouldn't take no for an answer…I guess he didn't see that this house is blue, too! Do you think you can help me bring it over? And…do you have a wagon? It's kind of…big."

Clarinda peered over and Jimmy, stepping out upon the porch, leaned around to gaze down the lane at Clarinda's driveway some houses off. His stomach sank to see a pallet of alcohol waiting to be moved, and soon he was back in the house, looking hopefully at the couch of his fellow tenants.

All three exchanged variations of the same glance. Alma in particular looked sharply between Bonesy and Cable Dog before saying, "Well! Don't look at me."

Sabine waved her hand in agreement. "Really, don't look at her…she's got to help me move the furniture."

In a matter of minutes, Jimmy, Clarinda, Bonesy and Cable Guy were all busy hauling alcohol down the street—or, in the case of Jimmy and Clarinda, loading it into the back of Clarinda's car so she could drive it down. When Jimmy and Clarinda were alone huffing and puffing back and forth between the pallet and the car, Clarinda smiled at him.

"So," she said gaily, "are you excited for the Halloween party tonight?"

Jimmy laughed a little. "I guess."

"What do you mean?"

"I don't know…" Not sure how much Clarinda knew about witches, exactly, but thinking about to the conversation had in her foyer when he and the frat brothers were doing trick-or-treat for cans, Jimmy glanced furtively up the street to Sabine's house. "I was kind of surprised to hear you were invited. You don't really seem like the type to hang around Sabine."

With a light laugh, Clarinda pointed out, "Well, neither do you."

"I guess that's true. Still…I mean, Sabine seems kind of dangerous to me. When you said she was a witch, I didn't mean you meant, like, a *real* witch." At the sympathetic furrow of Clarinda's brow, Jimmy went on to ask, "How did you know that?"

"Oh, well—I don't know, I'm a witch, too, and—"

"Really!"

"Uh-huh, a good witch anyway. And I guess you just sort of get to know the other witches in the neighborhood over time! It's hard to miss Sabine's magic, anyway…she's—quite a card!"

That was putting it politely, for sure. "Do good witches and bad witches usually hang out?"

"Not *really,* but, I don't know. It's the 21st century, we've got a lot in common outside of witchcraft…" Shrugging lightly, Clarinda surveyed the empty pallet, dragged it to the side of the driveway, and strolled over to open the door of her car. "Who cares who's friends with whom anymore?"

While, inside the house, Sabine barked orders to Alma and Cable Dog, Bonesy hurried over to the car to help relieve it of its burden. Jimmy, arms full of beer cubes, was in such a hurry up the stairs of the porch that he nearly tripped over the

Tentacle Girl Ami-Chan jack-o-lantern, hissing and cursing himself as he did it.

Was it his imagination, or did that pumpkin make a noise that sounded like "Ow?"

Whatever…no time to question life with Sabine too deeply. More mindful of his steps, Jimmy hurried back and forth with Bonesy once Clarinda was pulled aside, given a drink and told under no circumstances was she to do anything to help set up. Soon enough the task was complete, Clarinda's car was empty and Alma was setting up the bar in a cheesy French maid outfit that Sabine had evidently magicked her into.

"Well!" The part-time doll scowled to see him admiring her, her eyes blazing with fury. "What are you staring at?" Shaking her head with a mutter for the work she resumed, Alma said mostly to herself, "This fucking witch…you'd think if she can magic me into this get-up, she could magic all this stuff into place."

"Don't just stand there," called Sabine, briskly clapping her hands as she hurried down the stairs in her nun costume. "There's been enough delay! Let's get this furniture moved and get the speaker system set up. Clarinda! What did I tell you about helping—"

Guests started arriving at a quarter to eight, about fifteen minutes before Satan had promised they would. Jimmy shouldn't have been surprised the Devil would lie about a thing like that, and really wasn't that taken aback by the early knock, but Sabine still groused all the way across the floor until she threw open the door to discover her coven on the other side.

"He-ey," cried Sabine in harmony with them, extending her arms to the trio dressed like the witches from *Hocus Pocus*. Huh! Now that Jimmy thought about their color scheme…

"There are my bad witches. Oh! Gina, you look so cute." Spontaneously reaching out to grab her blonde bimbo friend and draw her in for a deep kiss that Jimmy and Alma watched with similar interest, Sabine drew her aside and permitted the other two to pass. As Hazel and Bernice spied Jimmy, both grinned.

"Hey, Wolf-boy," said Bernice with a wiggle of her eyebrow and a sly smile of her brilliant white teeth. "And look! The dolly's come to play."

Sniffing, Alma nodded in a cold way at the witches—but, upon a scathing glance from Sabine, she cleared her throat. An unnerving transformation overtook her and, suddenly perky, Alma pranced over with a tray of drinks on the offer in her hand. "Happy Halloween, Mistresses," said Alma in a breathy voice, mincing about and showing off her cleavage while handing each witch a glass of hard liquor and fruit juice.

Jimmy cleared his throat and looked away, grateful when the doorbell rang and Sabine was too busy making out to get it. Clarinda, in the middle of chatting up Cable Guy while he bartended, (which, Jimmy supposed, made him Bartender Guy for the remainder of the night), glanced briefly up as one of the only other normal people in the room left her line of sight.

Not without good cause, though. To his surprise, he opened the door to find Erin.

Erin, dressed up as Tentacle Girl Ami-Chan.

It wasn't hard to make a fetishized Japanese schoolgirl uniform decked out with fancy ornamentation and a magical broach look good, but Erin took it to a whole new level. Especially with that cute pink wig! While Jimmy braced himself against the door frame, Erin looked briefly up and then gasped in shock at the sight of him.

"Wh— Jimmy!"

While her face turned red, Jimmy said with a meek smile,

"Hey, Erin."

"I didn't realize you'd *be* here tonight! You didn't tell me you were coming."

"Well, I didn't realize my new landlady was having a party. I love your costume! I didn't realize you liked anime."

Blushing all the deeper, she said, "I feel like such a nerd… but, whatever, it's Halloween, right? You're supposed to have fun. Take chances. And anyway"—grinning, she pointed down at the pumpkin glowing on the stoop—"it seems like I'm at the right house!"

"Who's this?" Sabine had slithered up behind Jimmy like a shadow, her smiling face appearing over his shoulder. Those eyes glinted with a predatory like that immediately had Jimmy on edge, and the wolf in him, itchy with the coming of night, growled through Jimmy's mouth. The bad witch laughed in surprise and batted her eyes at him, saying, "Oh, now…don't be *jealous, Jimmy. It's share and share alike in our coven.*"

"This is Erin," he said with a wave toward the co-ed, locking eyes with Sabine as he introduced them both. "Erin, this is Sabine, my new landlady. She's been kind enough to take me in."

"Happy Halloween, baby, come on in." While Sabine departed with a swat of Jimmy's ass that was thankfully left invisible behind the door, the laughing witch wandered off to the rest of the room. "Better keep an eye on her."

No fucking kidding. The running gag of Tentacle Girl Ami-Chan was essentially that the eponymous character was constantly ravished by tentacles with varying degrees of consent. The costume was designed to facilitate this, with a short skirt that revealed the nates of her ass as soon as she so much as bent forward to adjust the strap at the back of her shoe.

Jimmy's body howled to fuck instantly, his dick leaping in his trousers, and he had to count backwards from twenty-five while she straightened up again and said with a tone of intrigue, "A *coven?* A coven of what?"

"Witches," said Jimmy weakly, not seeing the point in hiding anything from Erin what with her wanting to fuck him as a werewolf and everything.

Oh, man…maybe this party wouldn't be so bad after all, now that he thought about it. Glancing toward the stairs, Jimmy slid his arm boldly around Erin's waist and guided her in the direction of the sitting room as she enthused, "What? No *way,* shut up."

"Yeah way," said blonde Gina, laughing as she fixed her hair from the effects of Sabine making out with her in the same mirror that had, a few hours before, hosted Satan's reflection. Adjusting also the bust of her outfit until her tits were ready to burst from their too tight containers, the bimbo witch went on, "We're all witches, sweetie. You want in?"

"Even Jimmy?"

"Uh-huh," said Hazel, who was far hotter than the character she'd chosen to dress as that Halloween night. Patting her crown of red curls, she reclined in the sofa that had been pushed over to block off the kitchen for all but the bartender at the bar arranged adjacent. "I guess *you* would probably prefer to be called a 'warlock,' Jimmy."

"That's what Satan called me."

"Satan!" Scoffing, looking somewhat scandalized but largely intrigued, Erin looked at Jimmy with new interest while the doorbell rang yet again. While Sabine waved her hand imperiously, Jimmy turned to get it, but Clarinda stuffed her phone away and said, "I'll get it! It's one of my friends."

Slowly but surely, one doorbell ring at a time, the party began to find its footing. Perhaps because the witches were so gregarious, it seemed to have a smoother start than most of the parties Jimmy had endured. After letting in a guy who looked nervous to be there—Father Tristan, he ascertained as Sabine slithered up to greet him—Jimmy returned to the sitting room to find Erin being grilled by Hazel and Bernice about her college studies. It occurred to him with an odd jolt that the witches may have gone to school, too, and had fairly mundane lives before becoming witches. Hell knew, Sabine's was pretty mundane now…in a way.

Not really, though. The smell of pot smoke gradually thickened in the air and Jimmy began to get nervous. What were his parents going to say? He pushed open a few windows to fruitlessly ventilate while, with a joint in one hand and a drink in the other, Erin threw herself against his back.

"This is some party," she shouted in his ear, a conversational method already rendered necessary by the size of the chatting crowd. More cars parked outside, but Jimmy found with her body against his that he wasn't in any hurry to make sure the new guests got inside. He turned to face her, his arms fitting around her waist while Erin ground gently against him and slid the joint between his lips.

While he puffed at her behest, Erin gave a sexy little pout and said, "You're not going to lose interest in me, hanging out with all these sexy bitches, are you?"

Bitches, or witches? Hard to hear over the din. "No way," he told her, letting himself run his hands down her back since she was already grinding against his body. Her lips parted in a soft moan of desire while his hand slid under her skirt, an action unnoticed in the party by all but perhaps Sabine. "They're fun and all, but you drive me crazy, Erin."

With a glance across the sitting room and over toward the stairs on the other side of the hall, Erin pressed her pert breasts to Jimmy's chest. "Which room is yours?"

Dying inside, Jimmy looked around for his landlady and said with his lips pressed to Erin's ear, "I have to watch the door for just a little while."

"It's okay…I'll wait for you. Hold down the fort to make

sure nobody else comes in and uses your bed before you're ready to."

Groaning, Jimmy said, "Okay," and wheezed out directions to his room. "Lock the door and I'll knock shave and a haircut to be let in."

Winking, Erin took the joint from his fingers and traded him the beer. Somewhat dizzy, Jimmy watched her slide past a pale guy in a black cloak and a cute Bible thumper who, like most of the Sunday brunch bunch, seemed to be desperately looking for Clarinda. There certainly was quite a dichotomy being presented at this party. Amazing the two groups got along.

The doorbell rang again and Jimmy thought to himself that they were just going to have to leave the damn thing open at this rate. Squeezing through the crowd, he yanked open the front door with the red solo cup openly held in his free hand.

His mother smiled broadly at him from the porch.

"Jimmy," she said with pleasure, "Happy Halloween! What a beautiful house this is!"

So staggered by the sight of his parents that his brain seemed to require a kind of reboot, Jimmy froze while his father leaned around his mother and said with an adjustment of the cap upon his bald head. "Happy Halloween, son," he said with pride. "Congratulations on getting into the frat."

"Uh," said Jimmy, stepping back and looking over his shoulder as he did, "I'm not—this isn't the frat house. Please… come in…"

"Where's your costume!" Disappointed, his mother trotted in to pinch and kiss his cheeks. Over her shoulder, Jimmy nearly gagged to see Bonesy rattling past with a tray of hors d'oeuvres, and he kept her held in place with his embrace and a pat on her shoulder.

"Well, you know! It's been such a busy first year at school, I just didn't have time to put one together."

"You should have called me! I would have bought you one. I always loved buying your little Halloween costumes when you were a kid."

"This is a pretty swell place," commented Jimmy's father, who looked around with a slight adjustment of his cap and, thankfully, only did so once Bonesy had slipped back into the crowd. "If it's not the frat house, then what is it?"

"It's uh—an off-campus—uh"—his father's roving eye tracked Alma sweeping past in her sexy maid outfit, a wry little twinkle in the old man's eye until Jimmy stepped in front of him—"housing for, you know, upperclassmen and…art students."

Realizing he had the solo cup still in his hand, Jimmy leaned around his father and set it on the phone stand. "What would you two say to a drink? Come on."

"So how's school been?" His mother smiled as he shepherded them into the sitting room and guided them along the wall to the bar, keeping himself between them and the bulk of the crowd as he did. "You don't call me enough! At least write me a few e-mails now and again."

"Sorry, I will."

"Woah," said several people from the crowd, applauding as Bernice turned herself into a beautiful Bengal cat right in front of the fireplace. While his parents' heads turned at the reaction, Jimmy dodged between them and the vision and said with another shattering of his voice, "Uh! Uh, uh, so, so who are you two dressed as tonight?"

"You mean you don't know! Kids today." Jimmy's old man shook his head and then, thinking better, shook a playful hand at his wife, saying, "One of these days, Alice…"

"Oh," said Jimmy with a weak laugh, glancing over his shoulder and relaxing a bit to see Bernice had turned herself back to normal. "*The Honeymooners*, right?"

"Your grandmother just loved that show," said Mrs. Zevron

with nostalgic pleasure while they at last reached the bar. As he leaned against the glossy top, already mentally and physically exhausted, his mother went on, "They just don't make comedy *wholesome* like that anymore."

"Oh, yeah, threatening to beat your wife is hilarious…a gimlet for my mother, please, and, uh—"

"Just give me a beer," said Mr. Zevron, eyeing the co-eds who chatted happily around. While Jimmy wondered if he was quite so obvious in his own admiration of the fairer sex, a certain shadow loomed up behind him and set a hefty hand upon his shoulder.

"Now, Jimmy," crooned Satan while the pale boy turned to face him, "you know you're not old enough to drink yet."

Feeling a little faint, palms sweating immediately, Jimmy extended his hand. The Dark Lord appeared that night in his preferred form: that of a dark-haired, blue eyed, handsome-in-a-serial-killer-sort of way white man. The red smoking jacket was one thing, as was the crimson silk ascot…but the fake horns on his head were a little much.

As he and Satan shook hands, Jimmy managed a pitiful, "Hi, uh—"

"Dr. Samuel Faust…Dean of Classical Studies here at Fort University. How do you do, Mr. and Mrs. Zevron?"

"Oh!" With a pat of her wig and a delighted extension of her hand, Mrs. Zevron enthused, "How *do* you do, Dr. Faust! Such a pleasure to make your acquaintance at last, we're still so honored you personally called our home."

"Well, now, the honor's all mine. I'm little more than an overseer…Jimmy here is one of our shining young stars." With a shining smile of his own, Satan patted her hand, then shook that of Jimmy's father. "It's such a pleasure to see the brilliant minds of the future develop into tip-top shape. You enjoying the party?"

"Oh, yes! It's an absolutely wonderful time."

"Good, good. Perfect night for Halloween." Satan smiled as Cable Guy handed over the drinks. The Devil's eyes locked on Jimmy while his parents were momentarily occupied. "Crisp, clear, the moon practically still full…certainly puts me in the mood for a celebration. Have fun, everyone."

While Satan slithered up to the bar to place his order, Mrs. Zevron sipped her gimlet, beamed, and said, "Now, where to next? Where's someplace we can talk? I want to catch up with my baby boy for a few minutes at least."

Blanching in humiliation, Jimmy looked around and thought about the parlor in the back of the house with its view overlooking the back yard. That might be a safe place…maybe, except for the fact that by now the whole downstairs floor had grown packed with guests of all types. It took them a solid three minutes of transit to make it to the room in question, which, Jimmy discovered, was host to a pair of magicians apparently practicing some kind of sex magick in a ritual circle in front of the sofa. Sharply turning his mother and father around before they could get so much as a hint of boob, Jimmy said, "Well, uh! Uh, how about, uh, someplace upstairs—"

Which reminded him of Erin. Shit! Piss! Fuck! God damn, Jimmy was blowing his chance with the hottest babe at Fort U! Praying for a miracle, Jimmy scanned the hall and then, to his relief, saw Clarinda Lovegood engaged in conversation with a tall, swarthy man who had to bow slightly to speak to her amid all the noise.

"Clarinda," called Jimmy, interrupting their conversation with the look of a truly desperate man. "Hey, good to see you! Have you met my parents?"

Looking effortlessly delighted, Clarinda turned and shook hands with them. Jimmy explained to them both, "Clarinda and I were at the soup kitchen together."

"You've raised a very good son," said Clarinda to beaming Mrs. Zevron. For her part, Clarinda smiled and placed a hand on the arm of the man beside her, asking Jimmy, "Have *you* met Mr. Nyarlethotep?"

"Wow," said Jimmy, who would have been much more impressed if it wasn't for having to protect his parents from the awful truth of everything going on with him, his life, and his education, "so great to meet you, I've heard so much about you."

He also would have been much more impressed if, in that second, he hadn't locked eyes with Chad from over the brim of the fraternity brother's solo cup. His stomach twisting with a mixture of anxiety and gratitude for the presence of his parents, Jimmy released his grip on the immortal being's hand and said to Clarinda, "Sorry to interrupt! Just wanted to let you know that we're going to step outside for some air, so if Sabine comes looking for us, that's where we are!"

"All right," said Clarinda merrily after him before resuming a surprisingly flirtatious posture toward her conversational partner, leaning her elbow against the wall and smiling suggestively as chatter recommenced. Not having time to think about all this too hard, Jimmy ushered his parents out through the door and away from the frat brother who probably would have kicked his ass in front of his parents if that was what was required.

The part was big enough that people milled about on the porch smoking cigarettes and making out on the porch swing. That might have been almost acceptable were it not for the fact that his mother glanced in the direction of those people and said with a noise of shock, "Father Tristan?"

Cursing to himself, Jimmy hurried them along down the stairs and around to the side of the house, saying, "Ah, probably not, probably somebody who just looks like him. Somebody dressed up in a costume, who knows."

They were just around the corner and right by a cluster of pot smokers when the front door slammed open. Thank God!

Normalish people doing a normal thing. As Jimmy decided to let them babysit his parents for a few minutes, Chad emerged on the front lawn and whipped his head around with a look like he was out for blood. Trying not to sweat, Jimmy scooted his parents over in the direction of the smokers, a group which he noticed included Gina and Hazel.

"Mom, Dad, meet Gina and Hazel. Gina, Hazel, Mom and Dad. Be right back!"

Darting back through the side gate of the house, Jimmy emerged in a yard populated with its own music and busy atmosphere. The boy doubled over for a few seconds, glancing up toward the moon with a reluctant grimace.

Satan wasn't kidding! That puppy was big. Sweating with more than just anxiety, Jimmy looked down at himself and tried to decide if the hair on his arm was thicker than usual, or if it was just his imagination. His skin was certainly crawling with the urge to be scratched off: to transform and free himself from his surly human bonds. He shook it off when his eyes landed on Erin's face peering out the window of his bedroom, her features pressed to the glass as she searched for him beyond her own reflection.

Comfortable with the idea that his parents were occupied for at least the moment, Jimmy rushed into the house to try for a quickie with Erin.

He made it to the bottom of the stairs before Sabine caught him by the arm. "Hey, slacker! There you are. I need you to go switch out the keg—oh, and there's a clogged toilet in the downstairs bathroom."

Cursing, Jimmy diverted course to do as she bade him: first switching out the tap of the keg, something Sabine easily could have done herself, and then…then, fixing the toilet.

The light flickered ominously on and Jimmy stared with horror at the bowl. No water filled it. Had it been that way before? He was tempted just to put a sign on it and call it good, but that was how people ended up pissing in sinks and puking in hallways. Sighing heftily, Jimmy bent under the sink, removed a plunger, and tried to work the clog out of the plumbing.

The suction noises were horrible, but not as horrible as the spiders that came flooding out in an enormous wave. While they scuttled in all directions, Jimmy sprang on top of the sink and cursed his landlady.

What a clusterfuck! By the time the spiders had dissipated, the toilet was working again and Jimmy's hands had been washed, enough time had passed that he was forced to make a snap decision. Erin, or his parents?

Easy. The nagging of his lust hounded him relentlessly while he worked, and the immensity of his desire for her couldn't be denied. Slipping back out of the bathroom, Jimmy slipped through the crowd and hurried up the stairs before Sabine could find him again. Just the thought of Erin waiting for him made his cock hard; sighing, Jimmy knocked upon the door of his room as agreed.

A few seconds passed. Had she changed her mind?

The door opened and Jimmy slipped in to find himself at once assailed by kisses. Moaning, he clutched the co-ed to his body and buried his tongue in her thirst little mouth. "Finally," she whispered, "I'm so horny, so fucking horny, Jimmy…"

"Oh, sure…this time you closed the window," he observed, pushing her back down on the bed. He undressed in an eye blink, then, naked, stepped away from the bed altogether. While, gasping, Erin arranged herself to watch, Jimmy strode over to pull up the blinds. His lust was so great he didn't think about his parents, didn't think about the party and the insanity of it all. He thought only of Erin, whose eyes glowed as moonlight shone in across Jimmy's body.

Sure enough, after a few seconds, the itch renewed. This time, Jimmy gave into it at once. He scratched, the muscle of his wolf's arm quivering beneath his human skin and soon revealed by the peeling away of morality. The panting of the animal filled the room and Erin moaned at the sight, one hand upon her breast, her legs spreading as Jimmy shed his human clothes and body to become fully animal.

"Oh, fuck," moaned Erin with desire, gasping and looking almost liable to spring away as the great beast closed the distance. Fighting against her instincts, she succumbed at once, offering her body as a plaything to the appetites of the wolf. It tore her panties from her while she screamed, and, much as Jimmy had earlier, the hound lowered between her legs to pleasure her with its growling mouth.

Now, though, that tongue was far more dexterous, and its nearly prehensile flexibility meant it could probe into every crevice the girl had to offer. Its fangs scraping her clit, its hot breath making her pussy wet with fear, the wolf tongue-fucked Erin while she screamed on the bed in a state of absolute rapture. The co-ed offered her pussy to the monster while thrashing back and forth, screaming Jimmy's name and dripping the fluid of her lust all over his muzzle. All the while the wolf inhaled with blissful desire the essence of that femininity, its great red cock pulsing to life against the muscles of its furred stomach while her body readied itself to be mated.

Too hungry for her to wait, the wolf pushed Erin over onto her hands and knees. The girl moaned and offered her dripping pussy to the animal that snipped and licked her labia and anus before rising up on its knees behind her to mark her with its dripping cock. That precum oozing red muscle lined its pointed tip to the lips of Erin's cunt and, once the position was right, spared no time in ramming home.

Erin screamed in a noise that was half shock, half pain, all pleasure. "Oh, fuck! Oh, yes! Jimmy, Jimmy, yes!"

The wolf had no name. The wolf had only desires, impulses as it gripped Erin's hips to keep her still as a fucktoy. Snarling, the wolf pounded into her cute little cunt while she went absolutely limp, moaning, reaching down only to touch her clit or tickle the knot that rammed itself into her.

"Oh my God, oh my God, oh my fucking *God! It*'s so fucking big, Jimmy, oh, fuck yeah!" Erin moaned like a porn star, her voice whiny and high, and the wolf howled with pleasure to work its throbbing shaft in and out of her. "Fuck, fuck—oh my God, your big wolf cock is stretching my tiny pussy, Jimmy! Fuck, fuck, Jimmy, fuck—"

The wolf tilted her head forcefully back and plunged its tongue into her throat, fucking her in both ends while she teased her clitoris. Gagging with a noise like moan behind it all, Erin stared up into the face of the wolf that pounded her for as long as she could. Soon, though, her vision seemed unfocused, and the moans that hiccupped from her reached a tone of hypnosis. The wolf lifted its head while her eyes crossed, her cunt dripping with pleasure all over his twitching red shaft.

"Yes, Jimmy!" Erin's whimpers were soft, but eager, desperately high notes that leapt with the rhythm of his pounds into her. "Yes, oh, fuck, yeah, fill me up with all your wolf-cum—oh, fuck, fuck, uh-huh, mark me with your semen, fuck, I want to be your mate! Fuck me with that big, bare animal cock, oh, fuck, what a big dick you have! Yeah, yeah, oh, fuck! Fill me with your cum, Jimmy, oh, fuck, breed me like your little alpha bitch! Oh, yeah, I want to have your puppies, fuck, fuck, oh, yes, I want to feel your cum dripping out of me!"

As Erin's voice rose in her high orgasm, the wolf howled with one of its own. A climax like none Jimmy had ever felt swept over him, his consciousness collapsing beneath its weight.

Satan had told him he would always be in control, but in that second, the wolf took over, and its fangs clamped down around the pillow beside Erin's head. While the panting girl gasped in shock, the wolf shook the pillow in a flurry of feathers and poured its semen into the vessel of her cunt.

Then, all was silent. While Erin moaned, the beast's swollen cock held fast in her puss. Jimmy's wolf turned its head to nuzzle tenderly against Erin's ear, kissing her and sniffling the factory scent of her lavender shampoo.

"Oh," she moaned softly, "oh…Jimmy…Jimmy Zevron…"

The wolf was only about to inform her that it had no name when its sensitive ears picked up a curious sound across the far scope of the party. Its animal senses were so overstimulated as to be nearly agonized by the music and laughter and conversation and drinking and fucking and smoking of the party. Aware of everything all at once by virtue of its nose and ears, it was forced to tune out certain sensory experiences and hone tightly in on others.

Beyond the din of the party, audible through the window glass of the house, men talking. A group of men. Couldn't make out the words but the tone set the wolf's fangs on edge and pinned its ears to the back of its skull. Beneath the pounds of fur and flesh, Erin moaned with pleasure, twisting against her beastly lover to whisper something that went unheard.

With a savage tug that left Erin yelping in pain (and maybe, just maybe, a little hint of pleasure after), the wolf freed its engorged member from Erin's cunt and rose to its hind legs at a baleful eight feet tall. Unable to fit through the window and disinterested in trying, the wolf shattered the glass, wrenched the frame out of the opening and clambered up along the façade of Sabine's house.

A few people in the back yard noticed, and everybody outside heard the noise, but with a party that grew wilder by the second, a few broken bottles were par for the course. Only those in the back garden—like Bonesy, for instance, whose jaw fell off of his face and dropped upon the ground at his feet—who saw the massive man-wolf maneuver through the new hole and up to the roof understood that something was very amiss…and most of those people stood around gossiping about it, instead of doing something sensible like leaving the party.

Not Bonesy, though.

Bonesy ran inside while, atop the roof, the wolf crawled to the front of the building and crouched in the shadows to listen to the conversation of the Alpha Tau Pi fraternity brothers.

"…fucking stupid, man, I told you to bring eggs!"

"They wouldn't sell them to me," protested one of the frat's lowliest members, a role in which Jimmy easily could have found himself upon gaining admission to the not-so-very prestigious order of assholes.

"They don't do that on Halloween, they said. They wouldn't sell me toilet paper, either."

"You're so fucking useless. Old ladies are always baking things—why didn't you just call your mom and have her do it? Oh, right, I forgot, she spent all afternoon with my dick in her mouth."

The lower ranking member took a swing at Chad, who laughed and shook his head upon an effortless dodge. "You fucking chump…all right, guess we'll just have to find Zevron and beat his fucking ass."

"We could smash their pumpkin while we're at it," suggested Tom, one of the frat brothers who had showed up with Jimmy to Clarinda's house that fateful night he first met Sabine. Mike, the other one who was there, smacked his fist into his hand.

"Good idea, bro. You bring your bat?"

Baseball bat? Jesus! Astonished back to his conscious senses to peer through the wolf at the scheming fraternity brothers below, Jimmy couldn't help but wonder at exactly how brutal of a beating was merited by all that had happened.

He guessed, though, that they'd seen his wolf form just as

well as Erin had. They had probably known to come prepared…
and hopefully not intended to kill him.

"Ex-cuse me," said Chad, shoving past somebody sitting
on the stairs of the porch for a cigarette break. While some
woman's voice said "Hey!" Chad picked up the poor Tentacle
Girl Ami-Chan pumpkin.

Before he could smash it on the front lawn, the wolf
leapt down upon the grass with a snarl so terrible all the frat
brothers and onlookers screamed in unison. A few people fled,
and those members of Alpha Tau Pi who had not been there
to see Erin flee a compromising situation with a wolf-man
seemed downright traumatized by the sight. The wolf smelled
somebody's piss, and the piss smelled like acrid terror. The
wolf charged just as Tom managed frame of mind enough to
lift the baseball bat and take a swing.

The animal's jaws clamped down around the wood of the
bat and snapped it in two.

"Holy shit," screamed the lower-ranking member, the piss-
smelling one who then turned off and ran into the night.

"You're out of the fucking frat, coward," shouted Chad after
him, dodging the onlookers who were scrambling into the
house to collect (read: evacuate) their friends before things got
even worse. Pumpkin still in-hand, Chad stormed down the
stairs and pointed at the wolf.

"Hey, fleabag! Heads-up!"

With the posture of a shot put thrower, Chad braced himself
and hurled the jack-o-lantern right into the wolf's back. The
beast snarled as orange gourd smashed into pieces upon him
and whirled around to see the aggressor, still spitting splinters
from the ruined bat.

"Free," screamed Kilnor the Impregnable with delight. "I'm
free! Sabine, you bitch, turn *me* into a pumpkin, will you? I'll
show you—"

While one of the frat brothers said "What the fuck" and

Kilnor disappeared in a puff of orange smoke, the wolf bared its teeth.

It lunged straight at Chad.

Boy! Sabine sure hadn't had a lot to say in this story yet, huh? Well, you can only do the Elvira introducing a movie-style bit so many times in a short story sequence before it's old hat. And, anyway, that Zevron boy was such a good kid! Why not give him a little space to tell his story?

Sabine was occupied with things you would find boring, anyway, until the moment Kilnor zapped into the middle of the party screaming for Sabine to come out and fight him. Before that, it was all networking. Casual conversation, light gossip, making sure everybody was getting good and plastered, dancing with Satan, grinding on Satan, giving Satan a blowjob in the downstairs bathroom and flushing all his cum-spiders down the toilet when there were too many to swallow...you know. The ushe.

In fact, Satan had just grabbed her and drawn her upon his knee while he talked business with Clifton Moss, a necromancer who lived under the town's cemetery. Clifton, a pale, bald-headed man with the dark eyes of a vole and a small, shifty little nose, turned his gaze on Bonesy while the skeleton hurried over.

"Very rudimentary skeleton," observed the necromancer in his usual sinister tone. "But quite mobile...seems rather personable, too."

As Bonesy dodged through the crowd, nodding apologetically and waving his hands for Sabine's attention, the bad witch felt the fun part of the party evaporating and felt the real reason why she hated parties settling in. It was because whenever parties happened, bullshit inevitably followed. At minimum, the cops would be called for a noise complaint and would have to be bribed away.

Then there were times cops were called and couldn't be bribed away because, oh, somebody had been killed, or there were hard drugs, or they were assholes. And Sabine was not interested in having those experiences during her Halloween house party, so, with a kiss on Satan's cheek, Sabine slid from his knee and went to speak to Bonesy.

"What is it," she said, arms folded and eyes appropriately piercing beneath her nun's veil.

Bonesy's jaw rattled silently while his tongueless mouth struggled to articulate the noises his hands demonstrated. Pointing outside, Bonesy then pointed upstairs and mimed jumping out a window.

"Somebody fell down a well?"

The skeleton's hands dropped and it stared witheringly at her with those eyeless sockets.

"I'm kidding," she said, patting Bonesy's hand. "Somebody jumped out a window?"

Nodding, Bonesy resumed and held one hand straight up and down. With his other, he walked his fingers along as though to demonstrate climbing. Gesture by frantic gesture, Sabine pieced together the story—that Zevron had wolfed out and was about to maul some frat brothers on the front lawn—just as Kilnor appeared in a bright fireworks blaze of orange light.

"Sabine," he screamed above the din, "you bitch!"

"That's not short for 'bad witch,' you know," responded Sabine, green light at once emanating from her eyes. Those partygoers who had noticed the developing magician fight had begun to back away, with the exception of Satan and Clifton, of course. Bernice and Bonesy both hopped to the task of shepherding away all those oblivious guests while Kilnor threw a thunderbolt at the party's host.

Sabine raised a hand to absorb the bolt with her own magic, grimacing as the power of the incel's rage knocked the veil from her head. Her dark hair blowing free, Sabine drew on her pact with Satan and knocked Kilnor ass over tea kettle with a great glob of green energy.

"Hell no," she said, only vaguely aware of the screams also coming from outside the house as well as from partygoers watching the conflict within. "Not during *my* Halloween party, shit-for-brains."

"It's so nice to see you taking ownership," said Satan, smiling with approval while the bad witch strode over to the sorcerer and pressed a very un-nunly high heel into Kilnor's chest.

"You were the one who turned your*self* into a pumpkin, remember," she chided the incel, her arms crossed as she scowled down at him. Kilnor sputtered in response, waving his hands in displeasure. "Where do you get off blaming me for your bad decision?"

"You—you tricked me!"

"Did I? It seems to me like I just showed you what you want."

The bad witch cried out as a shove of invisible force slammed her up into the ceiling, narrowly avoiding the chandelier in the middle of the sitting room. Hissing, Sabine clutched the ceiling and stayed as effortlessly poised upon it as might have one of Satan's cum-spiders.

"You just wanted to humiliate me for fairly reviewing your work," Kilnor accused, raising his hand to toss another orb of bright light at the bad witch.

Fists glowing, Sabine launched herself down and forced Kilnor to expend his magickal energy as a shield, instead. "Modern review culture is a toxic artifact of the 90s Internet and should be completely re-evaluated!"

"How dare you!" His shield reshaped into an abstract blade of golden light that was soon met, sparking, by the dark green blade of Sabine's energy. By now the crowd around was hooting and cheering, but the magic-users were oblivious, busy parrying one another's blows and speaking through dramatically gritted teeth over the crossings of their swords.

"The Internet has given the consumer the power to choose," Kilnor hissed, his eyes glowing as he attempted to force Sabine's blade down out of her hands. "It's removed the gatekeepers and tastemakers of old—talk show hosts, magazine critics, Oprah!—and given consumers an opportunity to perceive a more honest opinion!"

"At what cost?" Standing strong, the air around her crackling with energy each time their blades met, Sabine held off his blows and shouted, "New gatekeepers have been established, Kilnor, don't you see? Gatekeepers who know nothing of taste, who are untrained in the formal structures of reviews! Rudeness and snark has replaced honest dialogue! The need to be politically correct to avoid controversial review sections prevents artists from expressing true thoughts!"

The golden blade shattered in Kilnor's hands and he cried out, falling back and raising his hands. Sabine drew her blade, which some might have called some sort of saber made out of light, back at once. With an empathetic twitch of her lips and a softening of her glowing eyes, she extended her free hand to the sorcerer helpless upon his back.

"Look at yourself, Kilnor. Look at your reviews." Her brow furrowed. "Are you really reviewing to inform your fellow readers, moviegoers, recipe users? Or are you just giving things one to four stars to make yourself feel better—to make the creator feel bad—to gain back-pats from strangers in the form of imaginary Internet points, whether it's 'karma' on Reddit or 'helpful' votes on Amazon?"

Kilnor's eyes bugged from his head. "My God," he whispered hoarsely, looking off to the side, then up into Sabine's face. "You're right."

Nodding earnestly, her hand still extended, Sabine dismissed her sword.

"I'm always right," she told him with the utmost sincerity.

Lips pursed, Kilnor looked into her face, then down at her hand.

Slowly, cautiously, he accepted her hand up to his feet.

"Happy Hallowen, Kilnor," she told him with a pat of his shoulder. "I'm glad you made it!"

"Wh—it's Halloween?" Looking all around himself as if only just now realizing he'd interrupted a Halloween party, the incel looked with some delight. He snapped his fingers and, with another blitz of golden sorcerer light, he soon stood dressed in a cheap mummy costume that had space enough for his mouth to move unobstructed.

"Then let's party," cried Kilnor while the rest of the partygoers hooted and cheered with approval.

The music turned up, and Sabine smiled in approval as Kilnor began to mingle. While the crowd once more subsumed the sitting room, the bad witch looked around. "Anybody seen Clarinda, by the way?"

Bonesy caught her eye, instead. The skeleton bent over the coffee table that Kilnor had crashed into when thrown by Sabine's spell. While her magical slave picked dutifully up without having to be asked, Sabine bent over Bonesy.

"Good work, buddy," she said approvingly, patting him on the shoulder blade. Bonesy looked briskly up at her, then continued with his work until Sabine said, "How about I give you a little Halloween bonus?"

With a hopeful glance of his empty eye sockets up at her, Bonesy waited for the other shoe to drop.

Instead, Sabine blew him a kiss. Eyeballs blossomed in both his black eye sockets, expanding like little balloons.

Well! That was pretty fucking unnerving. Now, instead of a regular skeleton, she was staring down a skeleton who stared back. Endlessly. Not having muscles or flesh or tissue of any kind other than bone, Bonesy didn't really have a way to move his eyeballs around. He certainly didn't have the capacity to blink. How was he seeing with them? Sabine didn't know, but he seemed to. His jaw fell open in shock, awe. The skeleton, eyes wide, touched her hand in gratitude.

Forcing a smile, Sabine patted his hand and said, "You're welcome…look at those beautiful baby blues, I didn't even remember…anyway, I'm going to—go. Thanks again."

Adding this, Sabine patted Bonesy's hand once more and quickly dodged him. Emerging from the sitting room with a gasp of relief for a few seconds of space from the thickest part of the party, Sabine leaned against the entryway of the room to fan herself with a sigh.

Outside, Mrs. Zevron screamed.

New to all this as he was, Jimmy hadn't really had a chance to see firsthand how much ass his wolf could kick. Chad, his pupils dilating in terror as soon as the wolf turned its fangs toward him, vaulted over the hand rail of the porch stairs and picked up a rock from the garden. Ready for a projectile this time, the wolf dodged it nimbly and lunged upon the frat brother.

Chad screamed in terror that leapt up only higher as the wolf pinned him down, jaws dripping foam. With one paw, the wolf reached down into the back of Chad's trousers and yanked out his drawers in a testicle-crushing wedgie. The frat brother screamed like a girl while the drooling wolf snarled in his face.

"I was just upstairs fucking Erin Innsmouth bareback," said the beast, the words poorly articulated with its lupine muzzle but nonetheless clear enough to the horrified frat brothers.

"And she loved it, the little slut—begged me to cum in her, too. Did she ever do that for you?"

Chad whimpered. The wolf pulled harder. "Tell me."

"N—no," gasped the frat brother.

"Didn't think so."

Stepping aside, the wolf drew Chad to his feet with another, more violent yank of his underwear. The foremost member of Alpha Tau Pi limped down the lawn to Mike and Tom, who held each other in terror and seemed to have only waited around because Chad was their ride.

"Stay away from this house," snarled the wolf while Mike and Tom guided their brother away from the scene.

They were just on the street when the fireworks started inside the house.

The wolf's sensitive ears and eyes were impacted, but not near so much as Jimmy within its body. The boy was frantic at once. Shit! What was going on inside? Was that the wizard who had popped out of the pumpkin? Oh, man! What were his parents going to think? He had to keep them from going into the house to see what was going on.

Jimmy began to make his way back to the smokers who had wisely stayed out of sight from the chaos at the front of the house, but he paused and looked down at himself.

Still a wolf.

Gritting his fangs, Jimmy shut the wolf's eyes and sighed. Come on, Satan. Come on, Master. If Jimmy really had control, then he had the ability to turn back whenever he needed to. If he really had control, the wolf's form would begin to fade.

It occurred to Jimmy that he had never before been conscious for his transformation back to human as the wolf ripped off its own head like a man removing a mascot costume. Jesus! No wonder he was unconscious. Jimmy screamed in agony, the wolf's blood running down his face at the wrench-pop of the animal's head coming off of his shoulders. Gasping, Jimmy dropped the head and let it fall at his feet while pushing the furred body off of his own. Jimmy, who had removed his clothes before his transformation, peeled the animal flesh off to find his own body naked and perfect beneath...albeit bloody. Each tearing of skin from his caused him terrible, eye-watering pain, but he fought through it and soon stood on Sabine's largely evacuated lawn, dripping blood, panting for air, waiting for the endorphins to come and relieve him of his suffering.

"Jimmy *Franklin* Zevron!"

His mother's voice rose in a shrill cry while she and his father came careening around the corner. Hazel and Gina appeared seconds after, grimacing. Mrs. Zevron stared, appalled at her naked son.

"Where are your *clothes*, young man!"

Barely able to catch his breath, Jimmy looked down at himself, wondered if she even noticed the blood all over him, then looked back up at his mother while she at last approached with a wagging finger.

"Just what kind of frat *is* this?"

"Yeah," echoed his father, "what do you think this is? *Animal House?*"

"But—"

"Here I thought this would be a decent sort of organization, since the dean went out of his way to call us personally." Patting her wig with a glower at the son who was clearly out of her control, Mrs. Zevron sniffed and said, "Well, maybe I'll have a personal word with Dean Fasut, and—"

"No," cried Jimmy, "don't do that!"

Far from listening to the urgency of her son's cry, Mrs. Zevron looked smug. "And ruin your fun? I think maybe I'd better if you're going to use your time at college wisely instead of—I don't know, *streaking* while covered in Kool-Aid or whatever this is." Her lip curled. "Come on, Franklin," she said with a jerk of her husband's arm. "We're leaving. And you'd better cool your jets, mister," she added, pointing at her son in warning. "Another incident like this and I'll write to every professor in Fort University and tell them to keep an eye out for my trouble-making son."

Jimmy stood there, shocked, while his mother and father tromped off to find their car. Slowly, he grew aware of peals of absolutely howling laughter rising from the front door of Sabine's house. He turned to see the bad witch doubled over, slapping her knee and sometimes wiping a tear from her eye.

"Jimmy! Oh, poor dude…come on inside." She waved to him with a not unkind smile, stepping aside. "Let's get you some pants…and maybe a drink, too."

Sabine looked around the emptying party with a satisfied sigh. All in all, not a bad time! A few road bumps here and there, but once the Zevrons left and Jimmy could cut loose, things got pleasant again. Soon, with most of the guests trickling out and even the coven starting to head for the door, the sitting room consisted largely of Satan and Sabine, who canoodled while chit-chatting with Jimmy and Erin or anybody else who came by. As Bonesy began to pick up, eyes boggling from his skull every time Alma walked past with another bag of trash, Satan nudged Sabine.

"That wasn't so bad, was it?"

The wicked witch rolled her eyes. "Not *terrible*," she admitted from behind a little smirk. As the Dark Lord pinched her waist, she laughed merrily and wiggled upon his knee. "No, no, it was pretty fun."

"See? You've just got to live a little, Sabine. You're always so serious, trying to get things done and teach karmic lessons or whatever. Sometimes you just have to live in the moment, baby! Let yourself lose track every once in awhile. Shake that hair down!"

"I guess it wouldn't be so bad for me to take more time off," she admitted in an absent tone, momentarily distracted again by his choice of words. "Say—has anybody seen Clarinda?"

All those present in the sitting room exchanged looks. Jimmy and Erin shook their heads; Satan looked at Sabine, then looked at the ceiling.

Slowly, Sabine looked up at the swaying chandelier.

A minute later, all four were crowded in the upstairs hallway while Jermy tried to peer through the keyhole of a spare bedroom.

Sabine pushed his shoulder, her voice an eager whisper. "Come on, who's she with?"

"I can't—I can't tell, I can't seem to make out what's going on—"

Rolling her eyes, Sabine shoved her tenant aside and used magick to blast open the room. Barely hanging onto its hinges, the door knocked a chunk out of the frame and revealed a quite literally insane mass of throbbing black tentacles that, tangled around Clarinda, pumped in and out of her every hole while she moaned in orgiastic ecstasy. Sabine gasped in delight, her previous missed opportunity at once forgotten beside this chance to observe firsthand Nyarlethotep locked with Clarinda in a slimy carnal embrace.

"Woah brother," said Satan with a laugh, his hands sliding into the pockets of his smoking jacket as he stepped aside for the other two to see. "Sure does take me back...you know what I'm talking about, Sabine, baby."

Giggling at the Devil's wink, Sabine stepped back while Jimmy and Erin nosily leaned around the doorway. While Jimmy's eyes bulged out of his skull, Erin's did, too—though her bright red face and high scream of shock was something special.

It was normal for the average mortal co-ed to react to the sight of a good witch being tentacle-fucked with a scream like that, of course…but Sabine was hardly expecting the real reason behind it.

Hand slapping over her eyes, Erin screamed, "Dad? What the fuck!"

Jimmy and Sabine looked sharply at Erin, then at each other, each saying in unison, "*Dad?*"

With a brisk clap of his hands, the Devil grinned at the hall mirror behind all four of them.

"Happy Halloween, kids," he exclaimed to the reader, waving at you and throwing in a wink. "Be sure to come back for Season Two!"

While "Do Ya" by Electric Light Orchestra played downstairs, the credits rolled.

SEDUCED BY SABINE
SEASON ONE OF THE WITCH'S WICKED SHORTS

SABINE .... HERSELF
CLARINDA .... HERSELF
SATAN .... HIMSELF
CABLE DOG .... CABLE GUY
THE DOLL .... ALMA
BONESY .... SOME POOR SCHMUCK
THE WOLF-MAN .... JIMMY ZEVRON
THE INCEL .... KILNOR THE IMPREGNABLE
THE CHUMPS .... FATHER TRISTAN
SISTER IGNATIA
THE VICTIMS .... CLARINDA'S BIBLE GROUP
THE COVEN .... GINA ROCHESTER
BERNICE CORPENING
HAZEL DREAM
NEXT VILLAIN .... CLIFTON MOSS
REGINA WATTS .... M.F. SULLIVAN

WITH A SPECIAL THANKS
TO MR AND MRS ZEVRON
AND THE MEMBERS OF
ALPHA TAU PI FRATERNITY

NO ASSHOLES WERE HURT
IN THE MAKING OF THIS STORY

EXCEPT FOR CHAD

HIS NUTS WILL NEVER BE THE SAME

BE SURE TO CHECK OUT SEASON 2!

ABOUT THE AUTHOR

Regina Watts is the penname of M. F. Sullivan, founder and flagship author of Painted Blind Publishing. From her cozy home a few universes away from this one, Watts transmits stories to Sullivan that are then transcribed and published. Her available titles range from transgressive erotica to psychedelic fiction to horror to romance. Be sure to sign up for her mailing list at hrhdegenetrix.com!

ABOUT THE PUBLISHER

Painted Blind Publishing and its erotic imprint, Painted Blue Publishing, are the brainchild of author and devoted editor to Regina Watts, M. F. Sullivan. Founded in 2015 while Sullivan resided in Tucson, PBP is a house dedicated to bringing readers the finest in consciousness-expanding fiction. Be sure to check out the wide variety of essays available for free at paintedblindpublishing.com to learn more about the company, Watts, and Sullivan.

OTHER PAPERBACK WORKS
FROM PAINTED BLIND PUBLISHING

REGINA WATTS

INDUSTRIAL DIVINITY (2020)

WILD GIRL RUNNING (2020)

DOTTIE FOR YOU SEASON 1 (2021)

THE BURNINGSOUL SAGA (2021)

BE MY BULLY (2021)

I WAS AN OP DEMON LORD (2021)

M. F. SULLIVAN

DELILAH, MY WOMAN (2015)

THE LIGHTNING STENOGRAPHY DEVICE (2017)

THE DISGRACED MARTYR TRILOGY (2019-2020)